I0692920

Major Arcana:
Thrice Weird Tales from the Opheliaverse

Chris Ebert and Adam Nebel

ISBN: 0988019027
ISBN-13: 978-0988019027

DEDICATION

Chris says:
"For Boo, Mom, and Dave"

Adam says:
"For Ashlee, Tiaus, and a thanks to Chris for letting
me play in your sandbox "

Ophelia says:
"For everyone reading this"

THE SPIDER SPREAD
(Table of Contents)

ACKNOWLEDGMENTS AND PREFACE
TO THE FIRST EDITION

The authors have already given their personal dedications elsewhere, but Ophelia Myth Media needs to acknowledge a few people who have truly helped the book series and the whole franchise since the last release.

Though not storytellers in this work, this book would never have seen the light of day without the support of a few people. Our wonderful illustrators who were the forerunners of an art department at OMM who have gone on to new projects of their own, thank you.

Ashlee Kuschner, who has worn every hat and played every part imaginable during OMM's growing pains, a thousand thank yous.

Chiara Fariello, our brand purity and new media director, thank you for helping us start to spread our little wings beyond the printed page and keeping us from looking like a bunch of amateurs while we do it.

Without Ashlee and Chiara, we would not be reaching into languages beyond English and expressions of the mythos beyond books.

To everyone who helped make the leap to becoming our own publishing house, thank you, and our own CVO and CEO do need to get recognition here.

And finally to all the fans, especially those abroad who have spread our little reputation via the web and word of mouth, our heartfelt gratitude.

In place of a traditional preface, we have chosen to use an internet chat transcript between the two principal authors.

A MESSAGE FROM THE BOYS IN THE BAND

A Message from the Boys in the Band

Chris: So, we finally got the third book done.

Adam: Finally, is definitely the right word.

Chris: I think I was surprised how much that characters have become so much more self-directed now. They seem to almost possess their own wills. There are just things they will and will not do.

Adam: There were definitely some moments I tried to write that just wouldn't work with some characters, like trying to split up David and Lindsay.

Chris: Well, David and Lindsay each get separate stories. Lindsay finally has an adventure on her own.

Adam: So I guess we should talk about how this book got started.

 Chris: Well the first story written was the Testament of David, although it's not the first story in the book. It's your first full-fledged effort as a writer in the mythos and not just my continuity guy. Andi it definitely has the most 'direct sequel' feel to where we left off at the end of *Hades Ascendant*.

Adam: Yes, That was intentional. I was so inspired by Hades Ascendant and *Chocolate, Incorruptible!* that I had to know what was next, so I wrote it.

Chris: Do you wanna tell what you wrote the first draft on?

Adam: Oh yes, you mean on a PDA with a stylus while in between runs driving taxi.

Chris: With barely a moment to breathe.

Adam: It was funny really having people come up to me for a ride or directions just thinking I was texting or surfing the net.

A MESSAGE FROM THE BOYS IN THE BAND

Chris: Did anything from one of those people make it into the story?

Adam: Well the only things directly taken from taxi driving were the two ONLA agents based on some other drivers, and some of Na'da's personality is based on the hundreds of ESU college students I drove to bars and parties. I also think at least in my head there is a real location that is the basis of Jesse's old folks home. I even had a customer from there that might be old enough to be Jesse.

Chris: We see a lot more Dug in this story. I think people will like more Dug.

Adam: I know I like more Dug, that's why I wrote more.

Chris: We meet a new villain in *Testament* who will be around for a while I think.

Adam: Ah yes, funny thing about this new villain is he started as a throw away background character I was originally focusing on other characters. The same can be said for a new hero from this story.

Chris: Yes, overall in the book we get four guys who were in the ONLA together. David Maier and Martin Belles, also a new current ONLA agent, and a new former ONLA agent. Though that's where these characters similarity to David or Martin ends. The book actually starts with *An Open Gambit* though. We learn a ton more about Braxus, we see a huge 'transitional' chapter in the lives of both Jesse and Ethan, especially Jesse. This is Jesse Perfect between *Folktale* and the *Horror That Came to Bethlehem*. We learn a lot more about the Illuminati.

Adam: I think you're right, with this book it was more appropriate to start in the past and see how some of the people that inhabit this universe get where they are including a few historical figures. We also get our first introduction to Nathanial Orin for those who read the E book story *Vae Victus*.

Chris: Then for the second story we go way into the past. Back to Hasat Aten again. You see the next chapter in his life, but, it turns out that's the precursor to a lot of other things. The pieces start coming together. This is cliché but for every question we answer more are posed. You mention *Vae Victus* which kind of takes place about the time *Major Arcana* is ending. It would have fit in this book, or in the fourth.

Adam: Don't forget that in these stories we also get a deeper, albeit cryptic look at Ilitu's city of Is.

Chris: There is a lot more major mythos stuff in here. The stand out that doesn't fit is *Unwrecked*. It's a throwback to book 1 in tone. I had originally planned for *Vae Victus* to sit where *Unwrecked* is, but, who knows what the plot elements of *Unwrecked* will lead to.
There were a lot of stories that didn't make it into the book, even though we sort of decided they happened. *Pivot* had a 'sister piece' called *Green River Mystery Lights*. *Pivot* is Thurston Waite, one of our new guys, and Martin Belles, as ONLA field agents in the 1990s. *Green River* was going to involve all our major human characters, the city of Seattle, a flash back to 1991, Bigfoot, and a lot of flannel. It was also going to be our main Asmodeus vehicle in this book.
That we must say, while Asmodeus is in this book, and is reaaaaallly important, he does not get much, 'screen time.'... or 'page time' I guess. And I guess that's okay after seeing him as one of the most central pieces in the last book. But someone, somewhere, will be rubbed the wrong way by pretty much every major character having a side story except him.

Adam: *Green River* does seem like a project or at least concept we will have revisit. We should definitely get a glimpse of the boys past as ONLA agents. Fear not readers I'm sure Asmodeus will be back as a protagonist, to be honest all his experimenting with parallel realities is some very fertile story telling ground. There may even be some fan fictions in there.

Chris: Are we supposed to encourage fan fiction? Somebody will write some slash, no doubt. Yeah, *Green River* can come back.

Adam: If not *Green River* then at least we have to give the fans something of their past exploits and maybe even some expansion of the ONLA. Maybe some of the peripheral agents will pop up again like Agent Knusch.

Chris: We can clue the audience into the fact that Maitland County,

Texas, where the good guys seem to win, does have a corresponding counter pole called Narromysing, NJ. There were a trilogy of stories set there which were more horror and tragedy. They never made it past draft. But somehow I think Narromysing does exist and plays into the Mythos. And Ophelia is back, she gets some screen time. There I go again... We're writers, so, we should use writer lingo. Though the whole book has a theme running through it meant to be a tribute to both concept albums and to the idea of tarot cards. We mentioned Lindsay has her own story - *Clade, Wheat, and Chaff.* I was happy with that one.

Adam: I love that one. I always felt other weres besides werewolves don't get enough love, and it really expands Lindsay as her own character, not just as she relates to David - not to mention Ilitu's new hair style.

Chris: And unless I am forgetting the rest are short and surreal, though *Demontia* is actually very mythos heavy and filled with hints and clues, despite being so short and bizarre. For *Major Arcana* itself – it's like a story and a movie and a comic book. We tried to put action, adventure, along with weird literary concepts to melt your brain. It's almost like several stories at once. The last thing I'll say is if we had stopped after the last book, the characters were in a good place. We can't stop where we leave this one. And let's not forget there is a story entitled *Arbor Day Love Story*, arguably the greatest title ever for anything in the history of titled stuff being given titles. I told Adam in one of my strange moments, 'imagine if the readership audience opened the book and it had a story called *Arbor Day Love Story*, prompting the reader to react with 'What the hell is that?', and poor Adam wrote a story around the title at my behest. Creative writing course teachers everywhere are screaming at us right now.

Adam: I still think you like that story more than I do.

Chris: Well, people bought these books to read stories, not listen to us prattle.

Adam: I hate to keep referencing *Testament* , but I did want to mention that I was originally writing it for you, and that I wanted to keep it a secret until it was finished, which proved impossible. I just wanted to thank you for years of awesome storytelling (most of which no one else will ever get to hear) and for letting me play in your sand box.

Chris: Thank you for giving me continuity - reminding me that if the proverbial gun that goes off in Act III has be on the table in Act I. And thank you for letting me get my fix of writing one short piece in antinovel out of my system without too much eye rolling. And we're celebrating our first time out as our own publishing house. Well ladies and gentlemen, enjoy *Major Arcana: Thrice Weird Tales from the Opheliaverse.*

AN OPEN GAMBIT

The first card drawn is Paige of Entropy. This card reminds the Operator that it is the secondary Pleroma system which creates the illusory differences in the various exertions of will toward extropy and against entropy, whether by that exertion arises from the magickal system, the machine, or the consciousness quanta. If the Operator can bypass the other secondary eruptions, it will become obvious such differences, such as the need of intent in the one versus the reliable mechanical flow of the equation balance in the other, vanish once an open gambit has been established whereby all sentients in a given cosm all have free access pathways.

Unfortunately for humanity Abraham Braxus, in the entire history of his being, only ever once made a mistake. It would have been better for every sentient being on the face of the Earth if he had made more. In nearly every case, when one of Braxus's strategies bore fruit, it spelled a further darkening of the light of the world; an additional contribution to the inhumanity of the human condition. And in a twist of the sickest of ironies, the single time that Braxus made a miscalculation is the one time that humanity would have fared better if he had succeeded.

The itch stated in the autumn of 1906. Braxus was able to push it aside for much of 1907, as he had spent the bulk of that year deep in the study of new technology and how that might aid him in bending the ebb and flow of history toward his ends. But by January of 1908, he could no longer ignore it. Although he tried to calm himself in the Italian villa he had rented on Lago Maggiore, built ironically on a site he had once thrown lavish parties at two millennia prior, he knew the real reason he made the sojourn to Europe. It was so he could be closer to the start his journey. And as he would need to save all his strength for the difficult task ahead of him, he began to wean himself off sorcery slowly, balling all the magicks inside himself up for release at that critical moment.

He would need to travel like a man. The beginning of the journey was not too terrible, from Rome to Helsinki by rail, stopping in beautiful hotels on the way, and then from Helsinki to Moscow. He was even able to take more primitive rail part of the way east of Moscow surprisingly enough. But in late June, he set out by horse drawn carriage, across the Siberian steppe, then by horseback, to the place he went every two or three hundred years to satiate the one mortal appetite he still had. The normally powerful looking gray haired man of Mediterranean countenance, commanding somehow both the best parts of age and youth in his towering person, looking like the incarnation of civilization, now carried the aura of rabid viscera that had been finely draped over bone then dressed in an expensive suit. The darkly reasoned mage was completely eclipsed by the hunger by the time he reached the remote village of Khrustal'nny.

He had already slaughtered his horse with his bare hands and eaten it, and had been on foot for miles. He burst into the small trading post in the village, and luckily for the man at the payment desk, he was more interested in the dried meats in the smoke house in the back. He consumed pounds of food, then a few dogs who made their home near the rear of the trading post, and had the man at the payment counter not fled, Braxus would have consumed him as well.

But now Braxus was close enough to his real hunger, that he was driven into the swamps. He was driven back to the place he had trapped her in all these years ago. Deep into the wetlands, where men rarely came, he finally began to release the energies he had all this time contained since he began storing the magick up those many months ago.

It took him a full day to invoke the doorway to the cell he had made for her. He kept her out of step with linear time just enough that she would not find her way back. Had he been a bit wiser, he would have sealed away the barrier to her realm forever, but he had a hunger for her, an addiction. He had led her to this spot two thousand years ago, claiming there was an ancient form of shamanism in these remote lands they needed to learn in order to add it to their ever growing repertoire of magicks, so that the ancient order they founded might be forever at dominance's apex.

She trusted him then, so getting her through the doorway the first time was easy. Each time thereafter he needed to be increasingly careful, but it was necessary if he was to have his way with her. That was the itch he could not ignore.

This time the doorway seemed as if did not want to yield her back to this plane of existence. Braxus had never encountered this before. While Phitonissa dreaded being pulled back to this world, just to be had by Braxus, she usually burst forth from her prison eagerly at first, just to escape her exile. It was only upon stepping into these swamps that she remembered Braxus had brought her back just to be his plaything for a few hours, only to be returned thereafter to her torment in limbo.

The vortex would not release her. He pulled.

His transformed mind itself already primordially rapine in nature, he pulled harder, pushed harder, poured harder, and pulsed harder, using perhaps too much energy in the process, but his judgment was all but gone.

Seldom did anything still resist him once he increased power to deal with it. He never had to raise his level of power a second time. But here he did. He pulled again at the vortex, all reason gone now, and to his delight, she stepped forward.

The Witch of Endor's historical basis. The Morrigan's antecedent.

Phitonissa.

He had no words for her, only lust. He dropped his energy levels to almost nothing, and his thinking to less than nothing, as he prepared to take her like a Roman on a Sabine. And for the only time in his long existence he ever would, Abraham Braxus made a mistake.

Phitonissa spoke only one word before it started.

"Abraxes", she said, calling him by his Minoan name.

She stepped slowly, her tattered Phoenician purple gown of antiquity muddy as her bare feet, as she advanced toward him, juxtaposing his Edwardian suit and coiffed white hair and beard, her Levantine features and long dark hair unrecognizable beneath the mud and dirt she was caked with. Her tiny frame seemed all the more reduced by his towering presence.

He reached for her, and she swatted him away. He had consumed too much power in releasing her from the vortex.

He reached harder, and she spat a great curse at him. He tried at first to direct the energies to combat her from his hands, but they flowed only from his mouth, as the ancient ways came out of him. He spat back. The energies built up more and more between them. Each move he had, she countered, and seemed to have just an iota more energy than him.

They jumped, hopped, and crawled after one another, destroying the barren landscape as they went deeper into the swamps.

Finally, he noticed she failed to counter one of his blasts. That was his last rational thought. He unloaded blast after blast of spells and psychic force on her. Each pushed her back further, but she did not fall.

He needed a rest. She lifted the Phoenician gown slowly, in a seeming acquiescence to him. Her short but muscled legs were bruised and unshaven, but as the gown reached her knees, Braxus was overcome with desire for her, the one human weakness he still possessed and only manifest in relation to her.

He began to walk forward as the gown reached her thighs, no less bruised and lacerated than the rest of her. He wanted the hem of her garment to rise past the thing he desired to behold. She displayed an increasing look of submissive fear on her face.

Braxus began to breathe deeply as he smelled her scent from his position. And it was through the channel of his nostrils, a weak spot in the shield of his chakras, that the wave came.

She dropped the hem of the dress, and the pretense to fear. She focused all her energy on him at once, and that energy traveled through his olfactory pathways to what remained of his human animal self within the sorcerer.

Braxus was raised into the air, high above the swamp. He realized what she had done. This would not kill him, but it would severely injure him. He decided to enjoy it.
He only had the sensation of nudity and the feel of the chilly Siberian stratosphere against his skin for a second, until his skin, like his clothing, peeled away. His heart pumped harder as his muscles and organs burst one by one, and his blood froze. His human, then his mammalian, and finally reptilian brains gave way to the rapture of explosive destruction and his mind vibrated deep down in his brain stem, his heart beating faster, and faster, until it exploded in a blinding white light over the Tunguska River. Braxus's fossilized bones fell to the Earth with the greatest of fury, bringing with them a blast wave that leveled everything around them for miles.

Phitonissa admired her handiwork. Abraxes, as she knew him, could heal even from this, but it would take him years. That would allow her time to re-establish her place in the halls of the Luminitae Order she had helped to found, and cement her place in the mastery of the world.

For now, she began to march through the swamps. She scanned the collective mind of this age, and learned many things. She needed a city to start to build power from. She sniffed the air, and the trees pointed to a city for her, and they taught her its name.

"Moscow", she said, "It will do".

A graceful smile crossed her tiny lips, as she made her way to the city.

"I thought you said you spoke Spanish", Jesse smirked.

"I picked up how to ask for a shoe shiner", said Michael, "That's all. Give a man a hand, Dr. Perfect, and tell him I'm not going to eat that".

The man who had brought their lunch looked at the Irishman with disdain, not understanding what Michael Calloway disliked about what he deemed to be the perfectly fine meal he'd served.

"What kind of animal was that even from?", Michael asked, looking at the food on his plate.

"Something, related to a sloth, maybe?", Jesse Perfect laughed.

The waiter at the small coastal restaurant glared at Michael who forced himself to wolf down a portion of the smoked meat now sitting on his plate.

"Well?", asked Jesse.

"I don't think that I like sloth, or anything related to it, Dr. Perfect", said Michael between mouthfuls of food.

Enoch Mahatmas regarded the two men from afar. The thing which was of interest to him sat in a simple brown burlap satchel the black man had brought into the restaurant with him. The Iron Fey had trailed these two men incorporeally while reporting back to Enoch on a regular basis. Enoch had some trouble believing that what the Illuminati Order had been unable to do an Irishman and a Negro, who appeared to be nothing more than a pair of wanderers, had succeeded in doing.

Enoch retraced the steps that brought him here to this despicable place. A few years ago during the summer of 1908 Abraham Braxus had made a solo and mysterious pilgrimage deep into Siberia. No one had heard from him for nearly nine months, though certain protocols he had placed into effect among the Illuminati Order let everyone know that he was still alive. Indeed there was some doubt if a man like Braxus could even die.

A fairly major portion of the High Council had been in conclave in Vienna when a gorgeously exotic woman simply walked through all the security spells which normally kept the Council chamber hidden, and would have for that matter killed even among the most powerful mages, as if the enchantments were nothing. Enoch himself would have perished had he tried this, and he was among those who witnessed the event.

The woman claimed she was Braxus. It was certainly within the realm of Abraham Braxus's power to transmute his physical form. In his growing ennui with existence itself it was even believable he would do such a thing.

The woman was at first challenged, but she knew more about the Council members assembled than they did about themselves. In addition to that, after a few sorcery battles she demonstrated herself to be the clear alpha among them. Most of them believed there was only one being walking the earth who could have accomplished these feats, and that she must be Braxus as she claimed.

The most stunning evidence of this of course was that it seemed impossible an imposter could for a period of several years now, claim to be Braxus, without the genuine article himself rising to quickly squash the rumors unless the claim was true. She did not like being addressed as Braxus. She preferred not having a name at all and simply asked even the highest ranking Illuminati to refer to her as 'Mistress'.

The Illuminati, Enoch included, went along with their new Mistress's plans. Even over the last two years or so when that agenda had become influencing the reigning crowns and heads of state of Europe to start the Great War.

Enoch had survived for centuries due to several things. The first was his skill as an alchemist which had given him physical immortality even prior to his joining the Illuminati, and his transmutation of the Iron Fey from its original natural state. The Fey itself was considered a valuable member of the Lower Council circles and a reliable operative.

In addition to his skills and nascent charm, Enoch also learned not to anger the wrong people, and that especially applied to Braxus, or something in a pretty dress they could get away with calling itself Braxus. But Enoch had appetites. He liked food, drink, and most of all sex. He had somehow accidentally become a bit of a diplomatic bridge between different branches of the Council's political factions. The Mistress must have felt that although Enoch was already loyal some additional reason to adore her was in order.

Braxus or the Mistress or whatever she was called him on one occasion into her bedchamber. Though accomplished as an alchemist, Enoch had to admit he had, by certain other sorcerers and powerful entities, been fooled over the years. And he had been fooled by the Mistress up until this point. However, there was one thing Enoch Mahatmas knew in and out. And that was sex.

He had managed even during the throes of passion to keep his thoughts suppressed from the Mistress. After centuries of honing his skills he was quite good at what he did in the boudoir, both physically and metaphysically.

But in 1912 Enoch fled Europe in fear because of what he had taken away from his dalliance with the woman who now headed of the Illuminati order. Her body had told him what she had kept secret away from anyone else.

She was perhaps as dangerous if not more so than Braxus. She had to be nearly as powerful as him. Her plans, though calculated, were potentially even more chaotic than his. And it was sure the most important thing Enoch had learned when he was, in the literal sense, inside her was that she was not Braxus.

Enoch languished in a plantation house he had rented in South America for months.

Then the Iron Fey finally found him. The Fey was a hateful thing, forever separated from its own kind due to the transformations Enoch had put it through, but it was loyal to the Illuminati order and to Braxus. It too suspected that the Mistress was not what she seemed or claimed to be. The Iron Fey considered Enoch the closest thing it had to a friend.

They were both in agreement that whatever magicks the Mistress held could not be overcome by any of their resources. They considered the possibility of advanced science, but no new recent Atlantean technologies had been found. Betting on a long shot, the Fey investigated local legends of a cave in which time did not flow correctly. It gave off no vibrations of a magickal nature, and must therefore be technological.

The demon Asmodeus had also shown up out of curiosity about the thing. He seemed to be interested in its properties to dissolve the fabric of time, and therefore the boundaries of reality. This was not normal behavior for Asmodeus. Since the turn of the century Asmodeus had been displaying increasingly out of character patterns of action. The Fey noted this for later, but for now the woman heading the Illuminati order and the Great War she'd started among the mortal nations of man was more of a threat than whatever Asmodeus might be planning in the long run.

Asmodeus possessed a local man and made contact with two travelers who had also come to investigate the stories of this cave. The strange energy readings which came off of it had prevented the Fey from entering. So it watched.

For days the Fey remained outside the cave. And then the strange time energy signatures ceased. An Irishman, a black American, and the demon in his host body emerged. Whatever had given off the signals was neither Atlantean nor magickal. These three beings had managed to, for lack of a better term, turn it off. The Fey had to move quickly away when Asmodeus left his host for fear of detection.

After enough time passed he began following the two mortal men, and it was from this he learned that it was neither the Irishman nor the demon who had figured out how to deactivate and remove the device which caused the strange anomalies in the fabric of time itself. Credit was due to this man named Jesse Perfect. And with no other source of power available that could possibly combat the Mistress, the Fey found Enoch and haunted him until Enoch agreed to help it try to acquire this device and the aid of the only man on Earth who seemed to know anything about it, whatever it may be, to subdue the Mistress and locate the true Braxus.

That is what led Enoch Mahatmas to his current position.

Michael and Jesse had both relaxed now, and had begun to eat the food which was available to them, whatever exotic creature it might have been in life.

"So what do you reckon the damned thing was supposed to do?", asked Michael.

"Somehow Eyah intended that cave to either be a place where time didn't pass for those who went into it, or a place where a lifetime could be lived out in the blink of an eye. I don't know which, but most likely it was some kind of beacon for those who discovered his true nature", said Jesse.

"I have to tell you Dr. Perfect, I'm getting used to these presents your Martian friend left for us, but this demon we met has me a little bothered. If we're going to be dealing with will-o'-the-wisps, as well as little green men, you're going to owe me better pay", said Michael.

"I don't think Eyah was a Martian. I suspect his world was much farther from Earth than that. All I know is like all of his technology, the damn thing was so old that it was poking holes in time like a nail on cloth", said Jesse as he patted the device contained in his burlap satchel with his hand.

"What do we do with it now?", asked Michael.

"Damned if I know, Michael", said Jesse.

Enoch realized he needed a way to make contact with these two men. The Fey had deduced there was something truly special about this Jesse Perfect, and perhaps more so about the unearthly device he held. However powerful this woman posing as Braxus was, an arcane technology was the only idea Enoch and the Fey had for anything that could dethrone her. Loathe as he was to admit it, Enoch did not have the knowledge Perfect somehow possessed innately in how to use such a thing.

"Are you ready?", Enoch asked the Fey, "This is going to need to look convincing".

"Yes", it answered.

The Iron Fey had been holding up any reason to physically manifest, but now it was called for. It went off into the shrubbery near the small patio where the guests of the restaurant sat eating, and crafted matter around itself. Lacking imagination, it hoped the form of a giant scorpion would be enough to frighten the humans.

It crawled into view, and on cue, went straight for Enoch.

Michael was the first to see it, as Jesse was seated in such a way that his back was to it.

"Well, Dr. Perfect, I see something that makes my unidentifiable dinner look downright appealing", Michael said.

Jesse turned around.

"Good Lord", Jesse said, "I know animals grow larger in tropical climates, but I don't think I've ever read anything like that is supposed to exist".

The Scorpion formed Fey made its way to Enoch, and put two of its legs up upon him.

"Look like you're attacking me, not begging me for scraps", Enoch said to it.

It drove into Enoch's upper thigh with its tail.

" *You bastard*", Enoch said to it telepathically, " *You didn't need to actually wound me!*"

" *You'll heal fast enough*", said the Fey.

Michael had grabbed a large stick from nearby brush, and found a second one which he handed to Jesse.

Most of the other guests had departed in terror, including the villagers who ran the establishment.

Michael came around from the rear and hit the scorpion hard.

"Ouch!", said the Fey.

"A talking scorpion?", asked Jesse.

The Fey froze. Normally something born of Tyr Afal had no trouble mimicking another creature or playing the part of trickster, but separated from its true nature for so long the Iron Fey lacked creativity of any kind.

"Insolent mortal", it said unconvincingly, "Prepare to face..... the... uh... Devil Scorpion".

This time Jesse hit it from the side, poking one of its compound eyes.

"Ouch", it said again, and losing concentration but not its physical cohesion, shifted into the metallic humanoid form Enoch knew it to be normally.

"What is this?", Michael asked as he knew a trick when he saw one.

Enoch took the lead this time.

"My leg", he said, "Please, good men, help me away from this thing and to somewhere I can get medical attention".

With no fear and a look of anger in his eyes at someone trying to dupe him, Jesse walked over and ripped Enoch's lower pant leg farther open where the stinger had gone in, and he could now clearly see the wound had all but healed.

"The tropical air must agree with you, sir", Jesse said indignantly. By this point in his life, having dealt with aliens and now demons, he was calm enough around things which would confound and frighten most men of his time.

"Wait", said Enoch, "Yes, we tried to deceive you. We need your help. The world does".

"Then ya shoulda just asked", said Michael.

Jesse began to make his way for his satchel as they were not interested in whatever it was these two beings had to peddle.

"Wind of Life to me", said the Fey as it waved its hand.

Jesse turned to notice Michael was having trouble breathing.

"I have taken his breath", the Fey said.

"Undo it", Jesse demanded.

The Fey complied.

Enoch waved his hand over his trouser leg, repairing both the injured flesh and the clothing damage.

"My friend can take your friend's breath at any time", said Enoch.

Something within Jesse's blood let him know what this man was saying was true.

"Hear me out", said Enoch.

Jesse and Michael took seats, assuming they had little choice but to do so.

"For ages", Enoch said, "There is a certain group of men, women, and beings, who have shaped the destiny of the world, outside the influence of even Gods and spirits".

"The Rich", chuckled Michael.

"Oh no, my friend", said Enoch, "Our power does lie in money and politics, but also in magick and secrets. We survive the fall of empires and kingdoms. We are the power behind the power behind the power. Even the God of your Bible allows certain pathways to us without interference, in exchange for certain services".

"The Illuminati", said Jesse, "I've read of you. Spenser Lewis believes in you. I didn't think you were real".

"Quite real", said the Fey.

"If you have all this power", said Jesse, "Then how could you let Europe erupt in war the way it has?".

"That is why I have come here", said Enoch, "We have not. It is true that all Illuminati hold equal rank, in theory, but in practice there is one who is our leader. The greatest of us all. In these times he is called Abraham Braxus. Some years ago, he disappeared. Never, in the centuries that I have known him, and yes gentlemen it is centuries, has this happened".

The Fey began, "A woman appeared to us sometime thereafter, claiming she was Braxus. Strange as this may sound to your ears, we have known for some time that

Abraham is, shall we say, becoming tedious of the human condition and its limits. So the idea that he might try a variation upon it, as you might try a new fabric in an overcoat choice, is not impossible. She had knowledge and power that even by our standards, both in magnitude and style, made it plausible that she was who she claimed to be. In addition, her power made even us fear to challenge her".

"It is she who started this war", said Enoch, "manipulating the crowns and governments of Europe. Even now she has moved to the east to further shape this bloody conflict, but the ends of where her scheme goes even we cannot see. Nor can we discern what has become of our righteous brother Abraham".

"What does this have to do with us?", Michael asked.

"No power in this world can stop this woman", said Jesse, "All their connections and hocus pocus are useless against her so they're hoping we can use the machines we've picked up from Eyah to take her by surprise", said Jesse.

"Very good, Jesse Perfect", said the Fey impressed and now convinced that it had made the right choice.

"You don't know this will work though", said Jesse, "You admitted you know nothing about this... woman".

"We don't intend to send you into battle without intelligence on your foe", said Enoch, "I have in my possession tickets on a ship bound for Paris. There is a woman there who is the descendent of a long line of mystics. It is said her forefathers invented the tarot. We dare not make contact with this woman ourselves or else the Mistress, for this is what the one claiming to be Brother Abraham demands to be called, would know immediately that we had sought this seer's aide. But if there is anyone walking the Earth in living form who can penetrate this mystery, it is she".

"She is not expecting you, nor can we tell you how to find her precisely, but we can get you passage there", said the Fey.

"Kill me if you like", said Michael, "But we'll not help you".

Jesse sensed that although these beings were looking out for their own interests, this Mistress they spoke of was a danger to the whole of humankind.

"Michael", he said, "I think we need to do this, not for them".

Michael nodded.

"This is the part where you say something that makes me want to be noble, right Dr. Perfect?", Michael responded.

Michael found himself in a few hours aboard a finer class cabin on an ocean liner than he thought he would ever see. Jesse wondered how their en suite bathroom had a freshwater shower, and found himself tracing the pipes, his tinkerer's mind never fully shutting down.

He retired to his bed, and propped up on a few pillows, studied the Pendulum the Iron Fey had given him. He still wondered how the whole affair had gone down in a semipublic place and yet gone so unnoticed.

He did know that shortly after agreeing to undertake his reluctant assignment, he found Enoch making arrangements like a traveler's agent for them, and thereafter heading into hiding. He had thought Enoch would at least accompany them to Paris.

The Fey said the Pendulum would lead them to its target, and that the Fey had targeted it to *What were in these strange days the clearest eyes in the world!*

Their voyage was mostly uneventful and filled with moments where humble men found themselves admitting there was some pleasure in the finer things of the world, with oscillating measures of comfort and discomfort therewith.

Two days before arriving in Paris though, Jesse and Michael ended up taking their evening meal at a slightly later hour than had been their habit for most of the voyage. They noticed a tall, unkempt Russian man who despite his dishevelment held an air of the regal about him. He seemed to notice them at moments, but the two diners could easily chalk this up to paranoia as the Russian was entertaining a pair of well-to-do English ladies that were clearly the focus of his attention.

When they arrived in Paris, Jesse lamented that they would be thrust into almost immediate work as the city was beautiful and they would have no time for sightseeing. Their task would begin sooner than they would hope, as they were headed to drop their belongings off at the hotel Enoch had arranged for them to stay in, when the Pendulum began to vibrate inside Jesse's satchel. Michael awkwardly stood in front of Jesse to try to draw away the attention of passersby while Jesse fished the object out of his bag. No sooner was it in Jesse's hand than he noticed a glowing pathway as if someone had painted a line on the sidewalk in luminous paint.

"I guess that's the way we're supposed to go", Jesse said.

"What way?", asked Michael.

It did not take them long to deduce after passing the pendulum back and forth that the glowing pathway was only visible to the person holding it, which was perhaps beneficial

in a crowded metropolitan city. They ignored its urgent
vibrations for a few minutes while they checked in at the
hotel, yet were back on their course within half an hour. The
sun was setting, and they followed the guiding glow to a small
wooden door.

Jesse was about to knock, when the door opened. A small
man with dark rimmed spectacles stared at them.

"Uh... hello", Jesse said.

The man realized Jesse spoke English and he smiled instantly.

"Monsieur Tanner!", he said, "Yes, yes... here to see our
girls... and then maybe paint them?".

"Um... yes", attempted Jesse Perfect, the chosen of Eyah, the
hope of mankind, and the most pathetic of liars.

The man showed them to a table, and they sat. Within
minutes they and the other patrons of the small candlelit
establishment were watching can-can girls do a dance.

"I'd like to ask you to not drink", Jesse said to Michael.

"You're going to ask an Irishman, about to risk his life, again,
to help you save the world, sitting in a bar, in Paris, watching
dancing girls, to not have a drink?", Michael asked.

"I said I'd like to ask you to not drink, not that I am going to
ask you to not drink", Jesse said.

"I would suggest a glass of the house's red", said a woman's
voice in a French accent but with perfect English, "But I
believe Etienne keeps a few bottles of English and Irish spirits
of a harder nature in stock as well".

Michael turned around to behold a woman dressed in a men's suit, yet with her makeup done immaculately. Despite the strangeness of the scene, he found himself drawn to her. Her hair was blonde with tinges of color, done tightly under a hat. Her features were slight, perhaps a Franco-Roman profile. Her figure was trim, and she was of some height but her form not discernable under the outfit, nor her eye color in the candlelight. Her voice was feminine but carried a sternness in timbre only found alluring in women of the continent.

"And you are?", Michael asked.

"A corpse soon", she answered, "Or maybe your wife soon", she said sitting down with them.

Jesse, holding the pendulum saw her illuminated.

"Yes, I am the one you are here to meet", she replied.

"Marie-Pierre Vivienne Aliette", she said tipping her hat, "But you may call me Ettelia, like my ancestor".

The music stopped, and an Englishman in uniform approached them. This interrupted yet another enigmatic statement from Ettelia, which Michael and Jesse just seemed to accept. The whole conversation felt like the speech one hears in a dream and accepts while asleep, but strikes the dreamer as being of the oddest nature if recalled upon waking. There was however no doubt they were fully awake.

"Pardon me, but I believe I heard English. I am afraid my French is not perfect. May I join you?".

Jesse did not have time for a soldier on leave looking for the company of a lady to interrupt his mission.

"Yes", said Ettelia.

"There was a French nobleman by the name of Aliette who went by Ettelia. He is credited with adapting Tarot cards from an Italian card game to a means of divination and introducing it to the French court. Are you a relation? I'm sorry, I am ahead of myself", said the Englishman, "Forgive me, I am Captain Ethan Rhys-Davies II".

Now Jesse spoke.

"If your father was Professor Rhys-Davies, it would explain why you know so much about occult lore. I am quite familiar with his work", Jesse said, "But, Captain, begging all pardons, Ms... Ettelia is here to discuss business with my friend and I".

"Seems odd", Michael said, "That the Captain here knows of the lady's family, and Dr. Perfect here knows of the Captain's. I feel naked without my pedigree".

"Let us drop pretense", said Ettelia, "I have come to this wretched place for a fortnight hoping to run in to Mssr. de le May who, I have certain knowledge, acquired the skull of the English occultist John Dee on the black market some months ago. You see gentlemen, I receive visions".

"And I have seen you", she said to Jesse then smiling to Michael, "And you in them. Not you, however, my good Captain. I do however know by my ancestor's gift that to move events forward as they must I should waste no time in speaking openly to all three of you".

"I have been in Paris for some time", said the Captain, "Trying to recover the skull for the Crown. Since the time of Dr. Dee himself, His Majesty's government has in a very subtle manner recognized the existence of the occult, and recognized its value in warfare and intelligence".

"I am normally, gentlemen, an artist's model and an artist myself, preferring to put my visions on canvas. Yet this war is all swirling around a solid point, a single point, and it should not be. An event of this nature should be either directed by multiple human, or inhuman wills, and not a single human one", said Ettelia.

"There is a single will directing it", said Jesse, "She is called the Mistress".

Jesse was drawn into Captain Rhys-Davies's and Ettelia's openness for a moment and then wondered exactly how much he should say. Suddenly he was alarmed he had blown any cover by even acknowledging and admitting what he did.

The proprietor then seemed to indicate trouble to the patrons, and seemed to be motioning them to a second exit. Ettelia explained it was just the local authorities come to enforce someone's morality arbitrarily. Jesse noticed as he clutched the Pendulum that Ettelia still glowed, but he saw a second glow coming from the Captain's rucksack.

The quartet rushed with the other patrons down a flight of steps and into a corridor that lead to another corridor. Some other patrons ran off into the darkness and continued singing, and drinking.

Michael knew where they were. The catacombs. It didn't take long for Jesse's electric torch to illuminate a mountain of carefully arrayed bones to show that. He looked down and saw Ettelia had grabbed hold of his hand in the commotion.

"Guess you thought I needed a guide", Michael said in a charming voice.

"No", said Ettelia, "As I said... I am your wife to be assuming we live. I do not mind fate taking away the surprises in life as I once did, as long as it shows me at least a few doors to choose from. Fortunately I was left in my youth not knowing my gift. I did not even know I was nobility. I was certainly not raised that way."

"If you ask me, there is no way you could be mistaken for anything but nobility", Michael complemented.

Jesse scratched his head. He wondered, when he barely understood the situation he was in, and did not know these people why he felt such an urge to discuss the matter with such openness.

"It's the skull, Jesse Perfect", said Ettelia picking up a few of Jesse's thoughts, "He is urging you to speak. It is not this representative of the Illuminati who sent you here bewitching you. It is him".

"The skull?", asked Michael, "Which one?".

"John Dee", replied Ethan.

"I will start", said Ettelia, "When I was a girl, as I said, I did not know I had noble blood. Nor did I know I had my ancestor's gift for prophecy, mediumship, and the psychic. I am, in these days of my life, content with expressing my art, reading books, dancing, and drinking. The world seems to be falling apart, so I am content to live well. My skills to live in this city, filled with its thieves and thugs who number as many as its poets and painters, are sharp. I left my mother's home when I was 16, and have managed my own affairs since then. I have no doubt when the world calms I can find myself a new path, but I digress. Several months ago I heard that Mssr. Antoine de le May, a man who has the means to purchase occult objects but not the skill to use them, had acquired the skull of John Dee, the sixteenth century English mystic and spy on the black market for a tidy sum, to add to a rather macabre collection he already had. He decided to resell it, for considerably less, after he claimed it haunted him with awful visions. He spoke of it boldly in the very tavern we just left. I too, was urged by visions, to come to that tavern. Dr. Dee appeared to me in my sleep. He said that this war was being directed by a single intelligence, and that I needed to help him stop it. He said I must recover his skull and I would meet four men, two living, one neither alive or dead, and the last an immortal. The first three would be allies, the last an enemy. Only when I held his skull could he speak through me and reveal a forgotten piece of the world's history".

"I came here as well", said Ethan, "Hoping to recover the skull for the Crown. I discovered that a man named Rasputin, who had of late ingratiated himself to the Czar of Russia, had also made inquiries into it but that was some months ago. Intelligence I received from a reliable but unconventional source informed me Rasputin was in the temporary employ of someone other than the Czar, and this new master sent him to South America".

Jesse was not ready to speak yet, but Michael it seemed, who already felt a deep bond to Ettelia, needed no further coaxing to open the floodgates.

"That's where we just came from and on our ship over here there was a queer looking Russian monk fella. I swore he was following us. Dr. Perfect and I here... uh... Jesse... we go on adventures around the world. We just finished one up and recovered this machine, when this dandy of a wizard and some kind of nasty boggle attack us to get our attention, and tell us this woman called the Mistress has taken over this secret group that runs the world. See normally, they're lead by this bloke named Braxus but nobody's heard from him for a spell. And this woman shows up, and takes charge of things right after he disappears. She uses this bunch... they're called the Illuminati... to start this war. So two of them, this man and this creature run in terror and find Doctor Perfect here. He knows how to find these machines that were left here years ago by this creature from another planet called Eyah. Most of them don't work right anymore, and if you knew what they're made to do, you'd probably agree it's all the better they don't work anymore. But this machine he just got his hands on, they figure they need Jesse here to help them defeat this Mistress... or better said to defeat her for them cause they tried bombs and knives and magick geegaws and nothing can stop her. Most of these Illuminati is afraid to even try, but a piece of machinery from another world... maybe she doesn't know how ta' defend herself from it. So they send me and Dr. Perfect over here... and they gave us this little trinket that guided us to that tavern".

Jesse glared at Michael, but pretense was lost. All possible cats were out of all possible bags.

"It is the skull that makes us speak so openly, Jesse Perfect", Ettelia said looking into Jesse's eyes, "It must be near".

"And here it will be buried", said a voice from down the corridor.

It was the Russian, "Hello, Abomination", he said with a smile to Ethan.

"Your Queen is more of an abomination than I, Rasputin", said Ethan.

"You know him?", asked Jesse.

"Our paths crossed", Ethan said.

"You managed", said Rasputin drawing a pistol, "to change your clothes, Professor. A gypsy glamour, to make you appear as if you are in a modern soldier's uniform, no doubt. Tied perhaps to a bauble worn about the neck?".

Rasputin fired one shot after another now at Ethan's throat until one of the bullets sounded as if it hit ceramic or clay. Ethan now appeared dressed in an idiosyncratic mash of clothes, but clearly civilian and from the last century. Ethan himself however stood unphased.

Ettelia drew a revolver from beneath the men's coat she wore, and fired back at Rasputin. He stepped back with each shot. Jesse shined his light at the man. Still smiling, Rasputin lifted his frock. Bullets ejected themselves from his chest even as his wounds healed.

"A gift from my Mistress", Rasputin said, "As for you let your bones, and Dr. Dee's skull, rest among these piles. The good professor can remain held forever in silent agony and the rest of you will simply repose with the dead interred here, but before you join them let them wake for a moment to welcome you".

Rasputin produced a glass vial with some kind of glowing ichor within it. He threw it on a wall and it cracked. He laughed wildly as he ran into the blackness...

Michael noticed that the bones in the side chambers were moving. They gave off a flickering light like they were being hit with the rays of a film projector. They were assembling themselves into figures. Within seconds, the chamber to the left and right of Jesse and his companions were filled each with a half dozen animate skeletons made to look all the worse by bones from disparate individuals being joined together as they never would have been in life. They advanced on the group in a slow fashion, their walk being a stop, followed by motion, another stop, and another jerking motion.

Ettelia fired three of her remaining shots at one of them. The third, her final bullet, cracked its skull, but there were eleven more left.

Jesse grabbed one of the closest, and started slamming it into the brick wall to their left. Not quite able to match his strength, Michael tried to grab one, but was thrown down.

"Michael!", called Ettelia in horror.

Ethan stood motionless. Two of the creatures were on him, but he was only concerned with something in his bag. He seemed to be talking to someone.

"You're sure of that last verb conjugation?", he asked, "Oh... vulgate Latin... of course... that's why it sounds so awful and lowbrow... very well... *Omnes hic qui sunt mortuus et gallico nunc ad somno. Quid iam, si placet".*

No sooner had Ethan intoned the last syllable of the Gaulish Pseudo-Latin then the bones fell like the dry and inanimate things they were meant to be.

"Our friends seem, for the time, finished", he said.

"Do you mind telling me exactly how it is that you survived being shot?", asked Michael.

"Because", said Ettelia, "He's already dead".

"Dead... undead... immutable... the vocabulary changes up but that's the gist of it, yes", said Ethan.

"You aren't Captain Ethan Rhys-Davies II. You're Professor Ethan Rhys-Davies", Jesse said, "The original".

"Correct", Ethan replied, "The original and only".

"How do we know you don't work for this Mistress?", Jesse asked.

"Rasputin is immortal. I am undead... or what elsewise you would like to call it, though not like a vampire. To make a long story short and also somewhat inaccurate, I sold my soul, shall we say, but managed to remortgage the contract to a higher bidder, leaving me in an immutable state. I am impervious to all changes, natural, scientific, or magickal. I took the skull of John Dee because I hoped to communicate with him. Just because no magicks have yet affected me, that does not mean there are none that might... and so I hoped to perhaps find a way to alter my current state; but, alas, no luck", Ethan said.

With that Ethan produced the skull from his rucksack.

"So why were you at that tavern?", asked Jesse.

"I took the skull from Mssr. de le May during his attempt to sell it, which is where I first encountered Rasputin. I quickly realized though the skull was of no help to me it might perhaps gain an advantage for His Majesty's forces in this damnable war. I did manage to use a necromantic technique or two here or there to communicate with Dr. Dee, but he had no knowledge which was of any personal use to me. He was, however, as you will remember from your history courses, a great patriot of the Crown and even involved in some espionage in his time, so he and I have been working to gain information for the benefit of British forces. He sensed you were going to be at the tavern looking for de le May in order to track him down, and, thusly became curious. He insisted we go to the tavern to learn more".

"He's telling the truth", said Ettelia.

Jesse looked at her as if to say, " *Why should I trust you?*".

Michael responded with a nod to him.

Ettelia trusted Ethan. Michael trusted Ettelia. Jesse trusted Michael. Jesse Perfect would be willing to work with Ethan Rhys-Davies for at least the duration of this voyage, and for the curious it may be revealed that John Dee vouched for Jesse Perfect in his silent communications to Ethan.

It was Jesse's turn to tell a tale now as they walked out of the catacombs and into the streets of Paris, though much of it Michael had already covered. Jesse told how he learned of aliens, particularly one named Eyah who had left his technology all around the globe. How in South America he had just made the acquaintance of the demon Asmodeus, to which Ethan simply rolled his eyes.

When he got to Enoch, he was surprised to learn Ethan already knew about the Illuminati and Abraham Braxus.

"So the Illuminati think this woman who says she is Braxus, is indeed Braxus?", asked Ethan.

"Except for this Enoch Mahatmas. He says it is not. And he says this woman is responsible for the war", Jesse replied.

"And why do they want your help, Mr. Perfect?", Ethan asked.

"All the magick in the world won't stop her apparently", said Jesse.

"And you can forget about bullets", added Michael.

"So they are hoping Eyah's technology might gain some advantage", Jesse finished.

"How does the skull come in?", Michael asked.

"Ettelia is descended from a long line of sages... her ancestor..." Jesse said.

"Invented the tarot card system... We covered that", said Ethan, "And Dr. Dee was a great seer himself. He was also an Illuminatus. There are a few honorable ones. His essence remains bound to the relic of his skull".

"If I can reach out to John Dee, together he and I might have the ability to learn who this woman is, and perhaps, then we can see how the machine could stop her", Ettelia said.

Ethan regarded the skull for a moment, and nodded to indicate that the late Dr. Dee was agreeable to lending his aid. He passed the skull to Ettelia, who gazed into its eyes.

In a moment, she faded into a trance and spoke words in a voice that was not her own...

" *He was born... so long ago... so very long ago... and he grew powerful in magick and politics and riches and war. By the time he was 20 death meant nothing to him...*

Abraxes was his name... but he was not rare... this was a time when the world was young... so he was not the first to achieve the things he did. But he was the first to not be satisfied with them. He realized that some gods draw their power from worship... most gods... but some cull a spark from something beyond divinity itself. Try as he might, he could not tap this power beyond even the cosmos himself... but he could perceive it... he learned of a time the Earth was home to a great race of reptile men... yes... reptiles... and they too had gods. The hidden power told him that this race abandoned magick for science... and then the race were destroyed by cataclysm... but a few among them had hidden magick... the last spark of their magick... and it survived the days of their destruction.

One among the reptiles lived to the days of the first men... and he gave magick to men... yet there were men... not like the others... who were present at the moment the one magick passed to the other... and in that passing, for a brief second, the power beyond cosmic had to manifest itself on Earth... The last reptile gave it to a hidden race, but also the men who saw it from afar hiding as they watched the moment of passing were of an ancient tribe, and took this spark of the cosmic into their rituals. Never understanding it... and passed it down... this Abraxes learned happened long before his time. This is not to be mistaken for the beginning of things or the explanation of all things, but, this is to be understood as the moment Abraxes became more than others.

Then he found her. The last of that tribe who had watched in hiding at the moment of passing and stole for themselves a piece of that which was beyond. He had to live with her in the desert, and he destroyed his kingdom for her, to show he could turn his back on this world. Atlantis, called also Minoa, with its great technologies built from relics of the past races and those beyond the stars, and its great and intricate magicks was of his devisement, but as a failsafe it could not survive without him. And so he abandoned it and let it fall.

For Phitonissa, the last member of the tribe who, alone among waking men, held the cosmic spark he did this. A woman who lived in the desert. He left Minoa, which he already ruled and had for ages, to find her. He seduced her in mind, body, and soul. But also in ways subtler. She taught him the cosmic power... they drew their magick from the void... not from gods or from the cosmos... but they were still a man and woman... they were not as gods... The gods left them alone... they left the gods alone...   For once in the Green Hilled Island they challenged the gods, and one red haired goddess among them who now is a lady of bones, taught them the cosmic power may manifest as it wishes, and she pushed them back. And thus conquest of the divine was no longer their desire.

By the time of Rome, Phitonissa, as she is called, known to us as the Sybil and as the Witch of Endor, and Abraxes were concerned with men and nations and these games. For eternal life was a goal they had long ago attained... They did not found the Shining Ones... but they took over their control from a small cabal of men in Rome, and of cutters of stone, and shining ones, and thinkers and circles all over the world of the ancients from Chin to Popo Vul. They made them cohesive, and ruled together.

The few among us Shining Ones, also called the Luminitae, and in your day Illuminati, who are old enough to remember Phitonissa used to say that Abraxes, or the one you call Abraham Braxus, did away with Phitonissa because she was the only one who could challenge him. This is true. But this is not why he rid himself of her. He actually liked that.

It was that he could control everything about himself, except his carnal desire for Phitonissa. She had no charm or spell on him. It was her scent. Her scent on him. It simply was what it was, the one mortal hold that held on in Braxus was this desire for her, for he had shed all other limits that he wished to shed.

But he could not bear to never know her again, so, he took her one day during the reign of Tiberius to an empty place far beyond Europe. Some say this was the day Christ died and

Braxus made a deal with God for this to happen on that day and not on another simply to distract the world from what he meant to do in the wilderness beyond the civilized world.

He battled and raped her for days, for this was the first time she denied herself to him. He forced himself upon her and tore open a gate to a prison which was a universe in itself. Once an age, he would free her, and re-enact that day. Have no pity for her. She is cut from the same cloth as him.

But this most recent time, she was ready for him. She bested him, returned to civilization. To the Illuminati. She began this war... If you can somehow... make the ancient machine you carry work... modify it so it can re-open the doorway... I cannot guide you in doing this to the space traveler's relic... but I will cast one last spell... which I can empower with the energy of my soul leaving this world and force her back through the doorway if you can get the doorway open... This will place me in the judgment of a tyrant god in the afterlife, but it must be done. Enoch Mahatmas and his Fey do not know this. They only knew the Pendulum would guide you to me. I have Brethren, two, among the living Illuminati who will aide you... they are the ones who manipulated the fool Mahatmas into contacting you. You must go to the place of the doorway... where Braxus rests and where he first exiled her... she will come... I will shield you from her eyes until then... I now return this young woman's body to her, and I will retune the Pendulum to now seek the place of the doorway".

The four lodged that night at Ettelia's home, daring not to return to the hotel Michael and Jesse had checked into. Jesse worked through the night on Eyah's relic with nothing but his hands, being guided by something in his blood. Ettelia and Michael looked at maps and took turns holding the Pendulum.

Jesse knew his work was done, and at some point, realizing
Ettelia and Michael had gone out, seeing Ethan sitting on the
floor, motionless staring at Dee's skull, and seeing the sun
rising, Jesse fell into a few hours of sleep.

When Ettelia and Michael returned, they revealed they had
been pickpocketing. No one scolded them. The Pendulum
and the map showed them the first part of their journey would
be by rail, and they needed money for train tickets.

Ease, on that train ride, settled in for the first time as they
sped through cities and made their transfers. The four
spoke, Ethan the least. He engaged evenly enough on the
intellectual topics, but withdrew and detached from Jesse,
Ettelia, and Michael, who were getting to know each other
better.

Jesse was sure more incidents would have occurred like the
one in the catacombs if John Dee was not protecting them
somehow. But he felt something else, besides just Dee was
masking their movements.

In the final leg toward Krasnoyarsk, now on the Czar's
railroad, the closest they could get to the remote spot the
Pendulum was guiding them to by train, Jesse was up and
about for a constitutional when a small man in a fine suit,
balding, older, chubby, with spectacles, and his hair in a
ponytail bumped into him.

Jesse instinctively clutched the bag with Eyah's device closer to
himself, which he had not once let out of his immediate
person since leaving South America. This time Jesse was the
one who found himself hit by a sudden sense of ease which
relieved his tension. He was beginning to be able to discern
psychic impressions, and realized Dee was communicating
with him subconsciously, telling him this was one of the men,
Dee's allies, whom they would meet on the way.

"May I see it?", the man asked.

Jesse turned the bag over to the man, who opened it and examined Eyah's machine.

"I'd say you adjusted it perfectly... if only Jefferson were still alive. He had a flair for machines from other worlds... though you won't find that in the history books", the old man smiled.

"Benjamin", said a second man, this man tall, younger, muscular and looking uncomfortable in a suit, his long hair hanging freely, "Introduce yourself for Odin's sake".

"Being corrected on my manners by a Viking", the old man scoffed, "Franklin... Benjamin Franklin...".

He shook Jesse's hand, "My friend here... well... now he goes by Nathaniel Orin. You won't find him in the history books though".

Orin raised his eyebrows at Franklin.

"You... you're?", Jesse asked.

"Still alive... Yes... I must admit I chose the unoriginal gift of longevity when I joined the Illuminati. Not immortality as did my friend here", said Franklin.

"May we see the other item also?", asked Franklin.

"Him", corrected Nathaniel, "Him... John was my friend, Benjamin".

Jesse brought the two men to the car his friends were waiting in. Ettelia verified their story, as did Dee. Dee had reached out psychically to Orin so he and Franklin would rendezvous with Jesse and his companions. The group assembled at a house Franklin had ready in town, to circle the wagons, but they found there was little they could do in the way of planning and within hours, found themselves in a steam tank of Franklin's devising, on their way to the site of the doorway

Dee channeled through Ettelia that the Mistress would indeed be there.

Rasputin brought Enoch into the Illuminati Council chamber. Phitonissa sat in Braxus's spot on the dais.

The Mistress was speaking into the whirling vortex that was the Abscended...

"You are an Illuminatus... and our liaison to HIM... He cannot refuse to answer me", Phitonissa screamed.

"YOU MUST LEAVE ENOUGH OF MAN BEHIND IN YOUR WAR SO HIS PLANS MAY NOT BE UNDONE. HE HAS TOLERATED YOU THUS FAR... BUT YOU MAY NOT USE THE SEVENTH SEAL FOR YOUR PURPOSE. IT IS GOD'S ALONE", the Abscended stated.

"Tell Yahweh if he does not want the strands of the silk moved such that the last shard of the old ways falls into the hands of those who would unmake him, then he will allow me to...", Phitonissa continued.

"Mistress", interrupted Rasputin.

"Be gone", she said to the Abscended.

"Enoch", she smiled, "I am so sorry you heard all that unpleasantness".

"Abraham, your new form is so lovely I forgot it already", Enoch said, "And besides... of all the Ethereal Illuminati, the Abscended is the most unpleasant to deal with. You handled him well. But why did you have your man here handle me so roughly?".

"I know you know I am not Braxus... and single minded as the Abscended may be I find the Iron Fey worse as far as ethereals go... traitorous as he is. And I find you even worse still. I know you have been to South America. Your pet covered your tracks well, but not well enough."

Enoch knew any attempts at feigning ignorance would not increase his chances for survival.

"I can help you break the veil that Franklin, Dee, and Orin have cast over themselves...", said Enoch.

"And the veil over the three humans and the anomaly you found in South America? I know you have been working with them, Enoch", she replied.

"I already broke the veil. Have you forgotten who I am", she said, "I am the first witch", Phitonissa intoned.

"Then, I have been your chess piece all along", Enoch said.

"What I will do here today", she said, "Will scramble the Illuminati. Killing three Illuminati all at once will require that I have some of the old guard for a short time. Serve me, and while I am unlikely to let you live, it is possible your afterlife will be a bit less unpleasant. Remain here, like a good dog, while mother goes to chores...".

"Of course", said Enoch, "But Dee is already dead. How do you count three?", Enoch asked, already knowing the answer.

"There are bits of Abraxes around. I think now, I can clean up the last of that mess. And with the assistance of your little friend Perfect, I can open a gateway to my own former prison. One ability among the few that Abraxes has that I do not. Your attempt to defeat me will give me the very tool I need to complete my last bit of business with my former partner".

Enoch watched as she took flight through the Council Chamber ceiling.

——

They found the site of Braxus and Phitonissa's battle of a few years ago blasted and barren. Jesse was trying to get the machine to deploy as Michael and Nathaniel dug.

"I've found it", said Nathaniel, and with that he pulled from the mud and soil a skull and spinal column that looked more like a sandstone sculpture than human remains. In the left socket, one healthy eye that had regenerated looked out, and up at Nathaniel.

"This is an excellent look for you Braxus... down in the mud with other unclean things", said Nathaniel, "Why did we even dig him up?".

"How else do you propose we get Phitonissa here?", asked Franklin.

"He is... still alive", said Ethan.

"Yes", said Nathaniel, "To call Braxus immortal is a bit like calling the ocean a puddle... despite appearances this dog is very much still with us".

"And he is angry", said Ettelia.

"Even an immortal", said Franklin, "Can take quite a while to recover from a severe enough trauma".

Michael stood looking at the steam tank. It was a piece of engineering. Then he looked at Jesse.

"Is it ready?", Michael asked in reference to the Eyah artifact.

"It's set up right", said Jesse, "I just don't know how to turn it on".

Franklin then touched a series of buttons on the side of the stream tank.

A series of gears and valves opened a door, and a huge Gatling gun emerged. Franklin begin firing it in Nathaniel's direction. Rasputin had emerged directly behind Nathaniel, and this was clearly the focus of Franklin's bullets. The bullets seemed to all carry a minor electrical charge, like miniature bursts of lightning.

Nathaniel turned around to see Rasputin reduced to a pile of bloody pulp and blackened goo.

"Benjamin, that's disgusting," said Nathaniel.

Phitonissa walked slowly into the area.

"Benjamin... Nathaniel", she said pleasantly.

"My poor Rasputin. You will survive. I am afraid that will use up a good portion of the immortality I have given you though to heal", she said.

"And you", she continued pointing to one person after another, "Jesse... Michael... Ettelia...".

Jesse hit something on Eyah's machine and a gateway to what had been Phitonissa's prison opened.

Nathaniel drew his broad-axe and clutched Braxus's skull and spine in his other hand.

Phitonissa did not become any more aggressive, or seem alarmed that the gateway was open. She simply walked into the mud and picked up another part of Braxus's remains.

"I am not any worse than what is in my arms, Jesse Perfect", she said, "By me disposing of this, we would rid the world of as much of what you would call evil as if you had rid the world of me. As far as I am concerned, after my little chore... you can all go home".

"She is not lying to us", said Ettelia, "She will let us all live".

Franklin began firing a hail of bullets at her with his turreted Gatling gun. She did not react.

Ethan held the skull of John Dee up.

"Dr. Dee", he said, "Depart this world now, and release your final spell".

Dee's skull glowed with an ethereal light and for a moment, a spectral outline of the man he once was stood there...

"Fascinating", said the wraith, "A hole in space, made by a machine... not magick. But no time to wonder... Winds beyond winds... push this abomination within!".

Phitonissa begin to slip toward the portal, but slowly and still showed no change to her calm.

"John", said Nathaniel, "If you have a moment of magick in you before you go to the place of heroes, do to my broad-axe as you did when we faced Ibliss!".

Nathaniel threw his axe and hit Phitonissa hard, and she lost more ground to the portal. But still too much distance. He also tossed the piece of Braxus he had to Ettelia.

Michael, Jesse, and Ettelia had been watching all of this... Ettelia pulled Michael a few feet over to where Braxus's additional remains were...

"Help me pick the rest of these up", she said.

Phitonissa was still too far from the gateway, and Eyah's ancient machine was showing signs of giving out. The gateway was shrinking.

"You really think I am just another sorceress?", she laughed.

Dee was beginning to transmigrate and could not hold the spell.

Ettelia turned Braxus's head so the eye looked at Phitonissa. Her rage toward Braxus broke her concentration just enough. She slipped back one foot and into the aperture.

"The gateway...", she said, "I am still not on its horizon".

"Yes you are", said Jesse, "The machine also creates an illusion... that opening is closer than you've thought".

Dee looked to Nathaniel.

"Good bye, old friend", Dee said.

And with that Dee looked to Ethan, who brought a hard rock

down onto Dee's skull.

Dee glowed with heavenly light as he transmigrated and in a brilliant array of energy he boosted his final spell. Phitonissa was cast into the portal and looked toward where Dee had been, Ethan now standing in the space behind the manifestation.

Phitonissa from the other side of the portal tried to summon Braxus's body parts in toward her and he began to float but she saw it was pointless. The tiny bone of his she held was not something Braxus needed. She looked at Ethan.

"You'll be the last and the first to see him", she said as she looked directly in Ethan's eyes.

Nathaniel saw an opportunity. Phitonissa's attempt at telekinesis was failing to move Braxus, so he grabbed the skull, spine, and arms from Ettelia, as the rest of Braxus was floating in the air from Phitonissa's attempt at sucking him into the portal. Nathaniel heaved the bones toward the portal, to be rid of Braxus as well, but even as he tossed them the skeletal arm reached out and grabbed him and the floating bones fell into alignment. Flesh began to reform around them, and clothing from the raw materials of the Earth.

Healthy and whole, Braxus's gaze met Ethan's for a moment, and now that Braxus was in one piece again he prepared an energy blast and fired it at Eyah's machine.

"A minor adjustment dear, Phitonissa", said Braxus, "to ensure this is the last time our paths will cross. And in the tiny piece of me you carry, there I have placed the last of my human weakness for you".

Her final look at him was the rare combination of hatred and awe without fear or respect. The gateway to her prison sealed once and for all, and then Braxus finalized the blast and destroyed the machine.

"I heard everything you said, Nathaniel", Braxus said. Braxus then turned around and locked eyes with Jesse Perfect.

"We got rid of your enemy for you", Jesse said, "What now?".

Braxus turned again to Nathaniel, and made an energy ball appear in his fist. Nathaniel had by now retrieved his broad-axe. Enoch Mahatmas had been approaching the scene for a few moments. He arrived on a Pegasus, with several troops in black, unmarked uniforms who were on conventional, terrestrial horses.

Franklin ended the stand-off.

"I believe what we do now", said Franklin, "Is retire to the council chamber to sort things out".

_____

Most of the Illuminati were still scattered.

Council was held with Braxus, Enoch, Franklin , Orin, and the Abscended present. The Iron Fey was still in absentia.

Ethan had managed to disappear back into his borderland existence, while Ettelia, Jesse, and Michael sat in the council chamber.

Franklin spoke.

"We welcome Abraham Braxus back among us", said Franklin, "For good or ill".

Franklin continued, "Braxus has motioned, and Enoch Mahatmas has seconded, that Jesse Perfect, Michael Calloway, and Marie-Pierre Vivienne Aliette be executed for security purposes".

Ettelia grabbed Michael's hand.

"Nathaniel Orin and I", said Franklin, "Can offer an alternative. Michael and Ettelia may live and their memories remain intact, provided, they are in regular contact with an Illuminatus for the rest of their natural lives. That Illuminatus would be you, Jesse Perfect. Nathaniel cannot enter the motion unless you accept".

Jesse looked left and right, to Ettelia and Michael, and then said:

"I accept".

Nathaniel looked up...

"The remaining vote" , said Braxus with feigned patience, "Goes to the Abscended and I believe I can count...".

"NO", spoke the Abscended, "BRAXUS'S HUMAN LUST CREATED THIS SITUATION. A SITUATION IN WHICH THAT WOMAN WHO TRIED TO COMPROMISE MY MASTER, AND WHO INSULTED AND THREATENED THE LORD WAS FREED IN THE FIRST PLACE. THEREFORE... I VOTE TO MAKE JESSE PERFECT AN ILLUMINATUS".

Braxus smirked.

"Enoch and I are overruled then", he said, "Welcome, Illuminatus Perfect".

He walked over and shook Jesse's hand. As he did, a tattoo appeared on Jesse's wrist and he felt an energy entering him.

"As an Illuminatus", said Braxus, "You will choose a gift after the first year of membership. I have just given you a personal gift, one for a day you are old and tired. Welcome to our family... my boy".

"Thank you", said Jesse growing angry, "Thank you, my boy".

Braxus scowled with rage, then regained his composure.

"Is *boy* how we shall address each other?", asked Jesse not backing down from Braxus.

Braxus smiled and motioned for Enoch to follow him out of the council chamber and the Abscended's opening to the physical plane closed.

"So... where to now?", asked Micheal.

"Back to France?", asked Ettelia.

"You can't go wrong with France", Franklin said smiling, "Perhaps I shall come with you. Nathaniel is due for a little time outside of archives. I am not getting any younger, Mr. Perfect and Nathaniel and I have a little project I need a successor in".

"We have a lot to show you", said Nathaniel.

"And not all of it good, I assume", said Jesse.

"What I have to show you... is quite good", said Ettelia to Michael as she took his hand.

"France it is then...", said Jesse Perfect with uncharacteristic regret at the decision he had just made, though for the moment he looked forward to the immediate future.

Jesse Perfect did not carry many regrets. But fortunately for humanity, he was willing to carry one.

MAJOR ARCANA

BEL AND THE DRAGON

The next card drawn is the Princess of Resonance. Few cards drawn teach a lesson so deep and profound, but yet can be expressed so shortly. The liminal moment in time is defined not by what comes before, after, or around it, but by how any given moment reacts with its neighboring quanta.

The huge hooved behemoth lumbered slowly across the primal savanna. Not one member of this creature's species would live into an era when there was a biologist to classify it. The beast looked out across the windswept African plain, and toward a small area clearing of grass. Had it possessed the faculty to discern what it was seeing, it would have realized the small grass and wood huts were the sign of an intelligent species, and the other structures made of a sort of gleaming white metallic dome were evidence that the thread of a once advanced culture still permeated this Earth that was between Masters.

The animal's mind could not have processed this, of course, but if it had it would have been distracted from its task as soon as the two bipedal figures ran out of the clearing with spears.

The first, a Caucasian male but with feathery hair and slightly clawed digits took the lead, and a female with even more Reptilo-Avian features pursued.

"J'el", said the male, "Remember we must aim for its neck".

"We're supposed to be taking it by surprise, Taius", said the female.

The creature knew enough to flee as the male grew closer. The object that Taius held could do it harm if the animal was struck in the sensitive and thin skin near its jugular.

Gifted with slightly more Saurian lineage than her brother, J'el was able to overtake Taius in ground pursuit of the animal. She nearly had her spear in its main neck artery when a flapping sound was heard behind her.

The small bit of Ang DNA introduced into the genome of the tribe by the Sire and Siress for variation was pronounced enough in Taius's wings that he could actually fly.

"Mother's Egg", said J'el angrily, "You startled me to death. The thing is getting away".

Taius was nearly on the creature from above, when he realized the animal was heading for the tree line. He would never overtake it in time, and could not fly through the dense jungle.

The Grandsire would be very angry with him if he did not bring back this creature for meat.

Taius landed and J'el caught up with him. She ineffectively threw her spear, missing the thing by several feet. The beast had nearly escaped, when a blast of bright blue light struck it in the side, killing it instantly before it reached the safety of the jungle.

Hasat Aten placed the pulse gun back into its holster and walked slowly up to his descendants.

"I am getting far too old for this", he said with a smirk.

"Grandsire", said Taius, "We nearly had it!".

"Nearly, nothing", said Hasat still wryly, "You would have had it if the two of you had worked together instead of competing for glory".

"We are sorry, Grandsire", said J'el as she looked down.

"Don't be sorry", said Hasat, "Just hike back to Is and get a few others to help you carry the thing back to the village".

Hasat walked slowly on the main trail back to the small encampment, and passed three of the grass and wood dwellings until he came to one of the metal domed structures he and Lili had built nearly two centuries ago from parts they scrounged from Saurian bunkers. She was chopping vegetables up inside.

She had aged only a decade or so since he had met her, due to Hawah's tampering with her genome, and he had aged about 15 years. Already her senior, and not the same species, Hasat often wondered if she still found him attractive.

"We got meat", he said as he rested his forehead against hers.

"And we got vegetables", she said as she met his lips to his, a custom that he had grown accustomed to and was popular among many of the offspring.

"When will you stop trying to feed me that stuff?", he said with a snicker.

"You like the spices", she said, "And those only come when we forage".

He picked up one of the green leafy plants, "This is what food eats", he said.

"Oh, I'm food?", she asked.

"Depending on what kind of hunger I have", Hasat said as he playfully wrapped his tail around her.

"Hasat", she said, "I have something to tell you".

"What?", he asked.

"You know how we said no more scrounged Saurian tech?", she asked.

"Yes", he answered, "Our offspring are going to need to learn to rely on technology they can build themselves".

"I agree", she said, "But the AI found something very strange".

He smirked and remembered back to the time she thought the AI was magic, and now she could operate it better than he could.

"What?", he asked.

"A Saurian facility giving off an energy signature of 100% capacity", she responded.

He went over to the AI and spoke.

"Computer, identify source of newly found energy signature", he said.

"*Non-governmental Saurian facility*", it said, "*Operating on full fusion power*"

"Fusion power?", he said, "We used Void Energy Collectors at the time of the Impact. No one used fusion anymore... except...".

"Except who?", she asked.

"Ovis Pneuma", he said.

"Who was that?", she asked, still enjoying hearing her mate's tales of his vanished world.

"Not who. What", he said, "They were an organization devoted to spiritual practice."

"Among pure Saurians?", she asked, "I thought belief in anything other than the material was a strict taboo", she said.

"There's an exception to every rule", he said.

"Hasat", she said, "If we could get enough technology from a fully operating facility our offspring wouldn't need to live in simple huts. The fifth generation will be here in a decade. There is enough genetic variance and population that our children won't need any more manipulation to overcome inbreeding. There's enough of a gene pool for all the phenotypic variants to keep going. But we're going to need a bigger settlement".

"I know fully working technology could help", he said "Especially with the Hawah humans getting closer to us all the time. But I don't think we're going to get much from a facility built by Ovis Pneuma. They shunned technology. They were outcastes, perhaps unfairly so in my time, but they didn't use advanced science".

"No?", she asked.

"No", he answered.

"Then why is their little bunker outputting at 100% when nothing your government or military built can do anything but putter along?".

He realized she had a point. An excellent point. For a moment his mind fancifully said to him that perhaps Ovis Pneuma had the magick they claimed to have all along. He thought of trekking there to check it out, and glanced at his still functioning Enviroarmor which sat in a corner of the dome.

And he remembered his first contact with Ovis Pneuma many years ago. Millions of years ago, before his slumber at the time of the impact.

"Vagnos's ship blew up attempting to enter hyperspace", said Hasat as he put his cup of neuroblood down on the bar, "It was tragic, but, it was an accident".

General Thrace, with no food in front of him, since the good General had had heavy cybernetics implanted into himself after a few too many battlefield injuries and no longer needed organic sustenance, smiled a friendly grin at his inferior officer which he managed despite the titanium teeth.

"How do you explain the telemetry of a secondary energy signature?", asked Thrace, "The media admits there was a second energy signature just as old Nath's ship crossed the light barrier".

"But to say it was an alien race? That's a stretch. I know the conspiracy theory. Thirty years ago Planetary Command supposedly received a long range message from an alien race warning us a giant meteor was coming. And the second energy signature was that race abducting old Nath Vagnos as he went into interstellar space. I think it's preposterous", said Hasat.

"Maybe the government covered it up", said Thrace.

"We are the government, Sir", said Hasat, "And I think it makes light of Captain Vagnos's tragic death"

"Not so tragic if what the rumors of him doing to civilians during the Siege of Sharan'Ta'Kah are true", said the General", "But he was well connected... guaranteed him to be the first to be allowed to try faster than light travel... which we were not ready for anyway if you ask me"

"Sir, I think the odds of the conspiracy nuts being right about alien races are about as likely as Ovis Pneuma being right about Mother's Egg and He of the Long Tail literally existing. May as well believe in spirits if you're going to believe in extraterrestrials", Hasat said,

"Ovis Pneuma say Long Tail abducted Vagnos since Saurians were trying to leave Earth. Funny, you should mention the OP though...", said the General.

"Oh, no", said Hasat, already able to guess where his commanding officer was going with this.

"You know how I need to appoint someone to liaise with the Great Sitter of the OP? The Science Directorate wants to use the military to bridge the gap between themselves and the religious right", the General continued.

"Me?", asked Hasat, "I don't want an assignment with those mammal eating idiots".

The General grinned, "We might be friends, but I can still order you. Besides, you might find those mammal eating idiots as you call them aren't as crazy as you think..."

"Sir?", asked Hasat.

"Did you ever ask how I got these cybernetics soldier?", the General said.

"Battle of Strathus, Sir", Hasat answered, "I read military history".

"I took fire directly from a fusion cannon, soldier", Thrace answered, "You know, I was technically dead for a while".

"And? You saw Long Tail? The white light and all?", asked Hasat.

"No", said Thrace, "But I did see... an ancestral raptor. Like the kind you see in the evolution diagrams in textbooks. It was real... some kind of real. And it lead me back to this world. And when I woke up, the first face I saw was Des Druge.".

"The Great Sitter of the OP?", asked Hasat.

"Well, back then he hadn't 'found the egg' yet, as they say. He was a scientist. He developed the cybernetics that keep me alive. He was also the first one to prove consciousness is quantum based, and can exist outside the body. He was even working on the transference of consciousness into an AI core...", Thrace was interrupted.

"When he found religion", said Hasat.

"Yes", said Thrace, "It was science that ironically lead him back to faith".

"There's no way out of this assignment, is there sir?", asked Hasat.

"None", smiled Thrace.

Hasat Aten found himself in Enviroarmor headed for the energy signature by the next morning. It was ironic Lili was the one who told him to leave their small village of Is to go get technology. But she was right. It could be a game changer.

Hasat Aten had never made it to the assignment to be the military liaison for Des Druge and Ovis Pneuma. The news of the meteor went public before his reporting date, and the priorities for all of Saurian kind were re-ordered.

As he hiked to the location he gave an order to the AI.

"Computer", he said, "Display file of Civilian Des Druge".

The AI complied and images and text were displayed on the inside of his visor.

As his assignment had never gone through fully, he only ever once met Des. It was only a few days before the news of the meteor went public.

Des Druge was a fully organic, tall Raptorian male. Well dressed and mature, but strong looking. He had asked to meet Hasat at a small cafe.

"Lieutenant Aten", he said as Hasat turned around, "Don't bother standing up for me, I think I would rather sit down".

"Of course... Dr. Druge... Rev. Druge... I'm sorry... how would you prefer I address you?", Hasat asked.

"Des will be fine", Druge smiled disarmingly, "You know soldier, it's funny... in ancient times the military made wars. Now in our culture, they preserve not only order, but reason and ethics. The media, the aristocracy, the Science Directorate, all the more radical pieces of our society held in place and in balance, by soldiers. So I guess Ovis Pneuma is also considered a radical element, or we wouldn't be here, you and I?"

"The military doesn't make judgment values, sir", said Hasat, "but the public, while in intellectual alignment with the science directorate, overwhelmingly feel that Ovis Pneuma are marginalized unfairly by them".

"Because, secretly, deep down, every Saurian craves the spiritual", said Des.

"With all due respect, sir", said Hasat, "I do not".

"You do your best to do what you think is right while you are alive?", asked Des.

"Yes", said Hasat.

"You'll be perfect", said Des and with that he pulled some kind of heated branding device out and marked Hasat's skin.

Hasat flinched, then rose and pulled out his sidearm.   He didn't aim it at Des, thinking better of it.

"What on Earth was that for?", asked Hasat.

"Our custom", said Des, "I am sorry... so sorry".

"Lunatic", said Hasat as he began walking off.

"General Thrace assigned you to me", said Des.

"And I'll show for duty as scheduled", said Hasat, "If the General actually keeps me on this assignment after I report to him what you've done".

That conversation with Thrace never happened of course. Because Hasat, Thrace, and every other dinosaur on Earth were only talking about one thing within a few days.   The coming end of their world.

Hasat didn't see the entrance hatch to the Ovis Pneuma compound when he arrived.   But he did see several humans, not of his children's stock, gathered around.

"Computer", said Hasat, "Scan and confirm these are humans created by Yah Hahwah's evolution virus".

" *Sixty percent of the specimens are*", said the AI, "*Forty percent are naturally evolved humans*".

"There are no naturally evolved humans", said Hasat.

" *That information cannot be correct as direct observation shows it to not be so. Analysis of genome proves your statement incorrect*", said the AI.

Hasat drew his pulse gun, stood up and fired a warning shot in the air. Humans other than his children always ran in terror from any display of Saurian tech on previous occasions.

The humans did not react other than to look at him. Two came running toward him, one with a spear drawn.

"Than" said the taller of the two who held the spear, "Bless my spear with your magick".

"It is done, Bel", said the other.

Hasat was laughing as the primitive spear was thrown at him. He was not laughing as the intense pain violated his Enviroarmor and he looked down to see the spear thrusting through his armor, and out of his chest.

_____

He woke up on a beautiful fern covered plane. Wildlife from his own time was all around him. He looked up, and saw a huge metal spaceship floating overhead.

"That'll be old Eyah", said a voice, "He's scanning for sentient life".

Hasat looked up, and saw a primitive raptor, like the one his ancestors had evolved from, standing in front of him.

Speaking.

"You can talk?", said Hasat.

"Talkin' goes back a lot farther than you think", said the creature.

It spoke in the accent of a Saurian musician, and looked at him merrily.

"Is this the afterlife?", he asked.

"Nah", said the creature, "Well... yeah... but... nah... think of it as school".

_____

Hasat flashed from that place and found himself now in incredible pain, back in his body. The spear was still in him, pierced straight through his armor but he was lying on a table. He was inside what he could tell was the Ovis Pneuma compound. There were no Saurians present. Only humans, and pain and lots of questions.

They had placed him beside what he knew was the central AI core.

"*Hello Hasat*", said a voice.

"Druge?", Hasat managed.

" *Yes*", Druge responded, " *Wanna guess where I am?*".

"I'm gonna guess knowing what you know about quantum consciousness, you transferred your mind into an AI core".

"*I'd like to say smart boy*", Druge said, " *But that one had a lot of foreshadowing. Forgive me... I don't have much entertainment in here... just films... books... I am beginning to think the universe is governed by artists... Musicians rule the waves and particles... painters and architects make the structure... and writers conceive of it all, carry it out, and make sure it moves*".

"So the gods are artists", said Hasat.

"Oh no. Not the gods... gods rule planets or universes... I am talking about the big players that run the whole multiverse... the whole cosmos. Not that I am over concerned with them, just that I want them to be aware I know they are there... writing... scripting forever... Sorry. I've become obsessed with archetype. And I always know where I am", said Druge...
" We for instance are near the liminal point of exposition which carries us from Act II to Act III".

"I'm not much one for literary theory", said Hasat.

" Then let me explain... a story within a story", said Druge.

Hasat Aten wanted to fight back, but he couldn't even move. In fact, he would probably be dead within an hour from his wound. He figured he should listen to the story because at least it might give him some order to all these things that didn't make sense

---

Hasat was back in the meadow. The primitive raptor was still there, but the spaceship was gone.

So was his pain.

"He's telling you a story to waste your time", said the creature, "I'm telling you one to save your ass. But, you're gonna bounce between here and there a little, and he is actually gonna tell you the truth... so... think of it as one story".

"What?", said Hasat.

"Okay", said the creature, "You want something linear if that is going to keep your attention, then, you got it. Earth is one world in the Universe, and the Universe is one universe in the Cosmos... big things run the cosmos, but, little things run individual universes and worlds... think of them as system operators. Those little things are what your ancestors called gods... little being relative, I suppose... the Cosmos... well... some places... not all, but some, it creates this stuff called the Pleroma. The Pleroma flows from those big things... outer things... or the cosmos itself, whatever you want to call it, into the system operators or gods. It feeds them, gives them their power. Now 'cept for a few who cheat the system or break out of it or was aroun' afore it, most gods can't feed directly from the Pleroma as a sort of balancing mechanism to keep things all square and even... they've got to rule an aspect of nature or govern a group of creatures to have the Pleroma flow through them correctly... Well they don't have to govern or rule... they can co-exist... but most are lazy and figure it's easier to govern and rule... and one of the easiest ways to get a Pleroma system is to rule over mortal creatures, whether you created them, they just arose, or, someone else created them... You Saurians were lucky... you were created by some pretty decent gods... they loved you, and when your technology got so advanced you forgot them, they willingly started dying. Even the one you call Mother's Egg... faded sorta... became a floating remembrance rather than a being... Now, the god called Long Tail... He stuck around... kinda on divine battery saver mode, cause he thought you'd need 'im, and, he's a right. You was gonna need him. So while you were off getting ready to start your own evolution, he was feeding on a little spark of worship with those folks called Ovis Pneuma".

Hasat was back on the table now, and Druge was speaking though the AI speaker. In a twisted way, he seemed to be picking up where the creature had left off.

"*I was not interested in Ovis Pneuma when I first met them*", he said, "*I was not interested in religion. I was interested in magick. But I learned there were hidden circles among them who preserved it. I learned it, and became a master of it... but magick was growing weak. Our species was doomed and, thanks to my skills, I knew that the meteor was coming even before the scientists did. I also knew the cosmos would one day repopulate this world with life... humans... the divination showed me many things, even you and Dr. Yah Hawah and his attempt to create sentient life even though it was already evolving on other parts of the planet. After you went dormant, but before you awoke, new, young primal gods were born on this world... they birthed man and he birthed them, but, then they went to sleep... as he evolved. Hawah didn't believe in gods. And he didn't have the technology to detect the aliens who came after the gods went dormant. I hope this isn't all getting too confusing for you.*.

"I don't know that I believe it", said the dying Hasat, "But basically you're saying we had gods once, they died out when we forget them. Now man is coming and with him... new gods... waking?".

" *Close enough*", said the disembodied Druge dismissively, " *But after man and the gods woke, the gods went to sleep, so man could worship them. Then the extraterrestrial came. Like Saurians, his race forgot anything but high science long ago, so he assumed man's gods were just myths, but thought it would be wonderful if he posed as a god so he could study man... that...along with Hawah making his own batch of humans, accelerated everything. Soon the alien will leave, and the young gods will awake. They will have a moment where they can create magick on this world and give it to man, or not. They have decided not to, these sleeping gods, so I mean to use the last bits of Saurian magic... the last bits of Long Tail's magick, to make a new magick, neither human nor Saurian... not dependent on gods or creatures, and with it leave my computer form prison behind... pure cosmic magic... directly from the Cosmos...*".

Hasat was back in the meadow with the creature.

"Ol' Ghost in the Machine there figured magick weren't enough to save his butt from the meteor... so he used science and transferred his mind into the computer and waited. Used some tricks to gather a few humans around him poof... there you go", the animal said.

Hasat stared at the creature.

"I think I'm having a delusion", he said.

"OK", the creature said, "Play along though, okay. Pretend you understand it intellectually"

"I think I do, but, what's his plan?", Hasat asked.

"The moment is at hand when these new young gods of Earth will re-awaken. Small ones first... simple honest ones who perform a service for a service... that won't last long. The power hungry ones'll start chompin' soon enough. There will be a moment when they must choose to share magick with humanity or not. That moment will not come again. And they plan on not... but Druge tends to use that moment to recreate a magick that is neither Saurian nor human. Cosmic magick. With no body, he doesn't hold the last spark of Saurian magick anymore. He has passed it to a human called Than. He in turn enchants a warrior named Bel", the creature continued.

"Where do you fit in with all this?", Hasat asked.

"I was the first Saurian ancestor to be sentient... long ago. What you call Long Tail, the one you call Long Tail let me guide the cosmic essence, the Pleroma, or raw essence beyond the cosmos, into the whole species. Well, I'm partially that. I'm also the last piece of Long Tail that would qualify as a being. The rest of him's a big ol' fabric thingy now. Anyway, we were kinda hoping you defeat Bel in combat and Than and Druge, and release magick back into the world".

"But, I'm dying on a table", Hasat said.

"Yup, and Druge is planning on using you as a sacrifice of sorts... the last Saurian, to create the moment he needs to make his own pure Pleroma magick and get off this world... Hell, that's why he mystically marked you all those millions of years ago", the being said.

"What do you suggest I do?", asked Hasat.

"I dunno, bud", said the creature, "you're the protagonist here...".

Hasat was again in writhing pain.

"My lord", said Bel, "Shall the priest deliver the deathblow to the serpent?".

" *No*", said the disembodied Druge through the AI , " *You, first of warriors, drive your blade into him... but only on my command*".

Hasat now began to doubt everything he had seen in the meadow. He must have recycled parts of Druge's monologue to him into the more pleasant form of the creature.

Bel stood over him.

"Now", came a voice.

He thought it was Druge giving Bel the command to strike, but it was the creature, and somehow, he knew it meant he needed to get up. And get up he did. The pain was gone. He didn't understand it. He only understood he needed to run, and he did. Down a corridor, and another, until he was out under the starlit sky, and behind a structure where he collapsed.

"You used up a lot of the second spark on that one, kid", said the creature.

"What spark?", asked Hasat.

"You didn't think a feller like Druge does things by accident, did you?", asked the creature, "He is an ornery, but bright dinosaur. He has reasons for everything he does".

"You mean... the brand...?".

"The creature is nearly dead, Bel", came the voice of Than the human sorcerer, "But use not your hand to destroy it. It must die by the weapons I have blessed, your spear and club".

"This is the second time", Hasat thought, "That I have run for my life from humans manipulated by one of my kind who was posing as their creator. Now what did I do the last time? Oh yes, I showed them their mythology was a lie... only this creature has magic... real magic... and I have a gaping chest wound".

He reached his hands into his Enviroarmor and touched... skin... there was no wound. But if he didn't find better cover Bel would surely make another one.

"I shall split you in twain, creature", said Bel, "And then Druge has promised order will come".

"You healed yerself", said the ancestral raptor, "Good".

Hasat suddenly realized his pulse side arm was still with him. It has been discharged when he left home, but his Enviroarmor suit had been charging it. In the journey and the time spent unconscious had it charged enough for one blast?

There was of course only one way to find out.

He stood, drew it, and angled a shot that was in perfect line with both Bel and Than. If it was charged he would be able to take them both out with a single shot.

"Here's my magic", Hasat said and fired. A round did come.

Bel stood and the blast somehow got absorbed by his club. Its blue glow was encased in a yellow radiation. Bel did seem to struggle for a moment as if the weight of the club in his hand had increased slightly, but as the energetic glow faded, he regained his balance with a grunt.

Than was not so lucky. He fell to the ground. Somehow the luminous drama which had protected Bel still allowed some of the pulse fire to go behind him. Bel turned to check on his companion.

"Burn my flesh... scatter my ashes to the wind and half to the water... Bury my bones in the Earth... But the fifth... is mine..." said Than cryptically as he gazed into the nearby brush, as if he spoke to someone other than Bel.

His staff exploded in a bolt of lightning...

"Human magick... real human magick, has just been born whether the PTB's want it or not", said the creature, "Well... that's part of Act III. Sorry, Druge kinda got me goin' with that story telling thing".

Hasat threw his now useless weapon to the ground.

"What in the name of Mother's Egg is all this? What else am I supposed to do?", Hasat asked the creature.

"Yes, in the Name of Mother's Egg... and not die for one would be a good start", answered the creature.

"I got that part", said Hasat.

Bel seemed little grieved for his companion. He pursued Hasat.

If it had been a normal human with a normal club, Hasat would have simply taken him out in hand to hand combat, deleted Druge's consciousness from the AI core inside the compound, got what he came for and gone home.

Home. Is was home now. A good home. He was not however in the simple scenario he imagined. And something gave the club this human carried an edge; one he could not counter.

"If only you were more open minded", said the creature, "Like General Thrace. He was at least open minded".

"You mean if I believed in magick", said Hasat, "I could summon the spark of it in me from this brand, and fight this human?".

"Nothing so simple, partner", it said, "You really don't know what's going on here? The Cosmos, Pleroma, whatever you wanna call it... giving you all these clues too. Some of them in words. This thing is being spoon fed to you, and you ain't getting it".

"The story part...", said Hasat, "That this is a story. I get it. I'm the hero. The human is the secondary villain, stop him then stop Druge... the primary villain".

"Nope...", the creature said, "No... no... no...".

Hasat stood and removed the gloves of his Enviroarmor suit. He looked at his closed wound. And the brand Druge had placed on his arm long ago. It was an image of an ancestral raptor, like the ethereal one, chomping down on a small prey, and looking positively lustful as it did.

Despite being slightly influenced by humans genetics by Hawah, Hasat still had sharp claws. He charged at Bel and without speaking, drove his fingerclaws into the human's neck. Bel went to counter with the club, but it brought no magick.

Hasat clawed at Bel's back and Bel struck again. This time the blast of magick did come, but not enough to wound Hasat. Hasat now bit at Bel's neck brutally and savagely. Bel struck, but now a spark of magick came from Hasat's wrist. It moved within his form.

Hasat felt the energy build up in him... through the chakras of his body... like heat... he wanted to speak, like a word of power. Speak his name, and Druge, and Lili's, and Ada, and Yah Hawahs, all the stories of his people... even speak the name of Eyah the alien who orbited above... oblivious to all that went on below him, but the names floated away... to be copied as stolen names by the waking young gods of Earth... along with other names of Saurians, and primal humans, to ring in the ears of those young sleeping gods of men, who were born when Long Tail passed his age over to them, who cried as infants, then like all newborns slept, suckled Pleroma, and were only now waking.

But no words came; only fire from Hasat's throat that burned Bel to his bones.

Hasat calmed.

"Hello", he said aloud, to make sure he was still capable of rational speech.

He took Bel's club which had the only spark of magick in it which was not magick of men or their gods or their Earth. The pure Pleroma magick, painted in an homage to the ancient Saurian magic. Or had Druge culled a portion for himself?

Druge himself answered the question.

"*No*", said Druge's disembodied consciousness through the AI.

Hasat accessed the panel.

"Computer", Hast said.

Druge spoke.

" *You'll be the only Saurian left*", said Druge.

"I already am and have been for a long time, but I'm okay with that since I am far from alone", said Hasat, "Computer, delete file containing consciousness engrams of Des Druge.

Hasat managed to contact Lili through the equipment at the base.

"There's enough tech here to combine with our own... supplies... and something else".

"What else?", she asked.

"You'll see", he replied, "You believe in magick?".

"You tell me not to", she said.

"With everything here", he said, "We can make Is self-sustaining And hidden I think".

"How long?", she asked.

"Indefinitely", he replied.

"We should come there then?", she asked.

"A small party", he said, "To help transport items".

"Okay.", she replied, "I love you".

"Love you too", he said.

Hasat turned around to see the ancestral raptor one last time.

"Guess you're leaving?", asked Hasat.

"Yup", said the creature, "I'm going to have a long time to wait around before I have work again. Not steady work, mine, but I love the pay. These human gods, not sure they best be left without a little policin'"
.
Hasat held the club.   It has a design on it of two serpents coiled around each other. This design has not been present when Bel wielded it.

"Thank you", he said.

"No", said the creature, "Thank you but tell me, how did you finally figure it out?".

"That I was in the middle of a myth being born? That I was the strange threat from the ancient past so I needed to play the role of monster, and not hero?", Hasat asked.

"Yeah", said the creature.

"I didn't", Hasat replied, "I just got pissed off and it worked somehow. I figured it out later".

"I don't believe you", said the creature.

"Where are you going after you clean up here?", asked the creature as it vanished.

Hasat Aten gave a simple reply and smiled.

"Home", he said, "Home...".

MAJOR ARCANA

THE BALLAD OF JOHNNY
CRONEQUICK

The Viceroy of Fulcrum in its nonsense will seldom cause the Operator to do more than momentarily blink. Its secret lies in the fact that the Operator sees not his or her own inner mind in the moment of that blink, but the sheen of the strand's illumination through the mind's own eye. The external and internal cross in the mesoternal for a moment and perception is allowed for one instance without parallax, lens, or effect upon the object viewed.

The Bards! The Bards!
Go on and drone
Of times when dragons
Were flesh and bone

They sing of fair folk
And boggle lights
And maidens rescued
By virtuous knights

'*How dull! How dull!*

As I grow sick...
Til one asks if I heard
A' Johnny Cronequick?

'*Nay, Nay*,' says I
Ta' that bard alone
And he tells me tales a' he
Who quicked a crone!

Cronequick twas
The Second Son
Of laird who didn'a
Own a ton

Take priestly vows
His family said
But Cronequick woulda
Rather been dead

No wife, no wife
Would he a' had
For he liked to kiss
Many a lad

But most a' all
That little jerk
Hated, loathed
Detested work

He'd pick a pocket
Or sell a rock
As a saint's bones
To the peasant stock

One night so dark
At Satan's hour
Johnny crossed

THE BALLAD OF JOHNNY CRONEQUICK

Black Annis's bower

Black Annis, oh Annis
The beastly witch
Ya'd not wanna cross
That blue faced bitch

Three houses tall
And teeth like steel
Annis made children
Inta' meals.

She regarded Johnny
Said she'd kill 'im dead
And eat his flesh
But o... instead.

He questioned her
But he didna' plead...
'Is a crone immune
From a woman's needs?'

From the stories Johnny'd
Always been told
When Annis ate folks
She'd shite out gold.

Now Johnny liked men
When it was pleasure alone
But for the right fee
He'd quick the crone

Annis was pleased
And let him go
And she was a favorite trick
Ah those he known

And Cronequick travelled
Far and wide
With a dwarf named Dimshitz
By his side

Dimshitz'd keep
Johnny's schedule tight
For quickin' the hags
Day and Night

Jenny Greenteeth paid Johnny
With gold found in her Bog
While Dimshitz played pea knuckle
With a Frog

The Moor Hag stopped
Boiling infant lard
An' ask'd Cronequick
If he'd take Mastercard.

All went well
For Dimshitz and Johnny
Til the Pope decided
The crones weren't bonnie

The king o' England
Had a crone problem it seemed
And of a witch free England
He had dreamed.

He wrote to the pope
To seek his aid
N' the Pope came himself
With a paladin brigade

They gathered the crones
Took their books of power

THE BALLAD OF JOHNNY CRONEQUICK

And sealed 'em all up
In London's tower

Johnny was gonna leave 'em
That little Jerk
But Dimshitz asked
"What'll we do for work?".

So to London town
Young Cronequick rode
And into the tower
Straight he strode

The king he laughed
And the pope did bellow
But Cronequick showed no sign
Of a streak a' yella

In pillowtalk the Crones
Did speak and more
And told their secrets
To their beloved man-whore

These beastly maids
The brides a' hell
Had accidentally taught Johnny
A Score of Spells

He made the paladins
Into Nuns
And gave the king
A case a' the runs

He melted the bars
A' the crones' cage
And the pope he screamed
With cardinal rage

He charged at Johnny
With that pointy hat
But Cronequick weren't up
Fer havin' that

Johnny incanted
Like a maddened loon
An' sent the pope
Inside the moon

Out of London they fled
Cronequick and his crew
And what happened next
The bard did not knew

My rhyme scheme
On that last line
I lost it, I lost it
That rhyme scheme of mine

But 'tis alright
Tis just as well
Of Johnny this
Is all the Bard did tell.

Cheers for Cronequick
Though he be absurd
Tell his tale
To a fairy tale nerd

And on the night wind
As the Banshees groan
Maybe they long for Johnny
Who'd quick even a crone.

THE TESTAMENT OF DAVID: PART I
THE EPISTLE TO THE
PHILADELPHIANS

Now the Operator has drawn the Knight of Propensity; This card allows the tendency toward a possibility or outcome to be manipulated at the level of its quality prior to expression, for the most minute and accurate adjustments of a manifestation which will be entering existence among a sea of teaming variables.

Almost a year after the battle of Armageddon David Maier was checking his e-mail and just debating whether to read or delete the e-mail from Martin Belles, when from behind him he heard the familiar click of his own lighter. He looked over his shoulder to see the now semi-physical Dug lighting one of his clove cigarettes. How Dug kept getting both his lighter and cigarettes off his person without him noticing was something he tried not to think about.

"Help yourself", David said sarcastically to the goblin.

Dug smiled, "Dug likeses the crackly smokeys"

"I tell myself I don't like them", said David, "But I do and that's the problem.

David made a 'gimme' motion and Dug tossed the lighter and cigarettes to him. David lit one and inhaled deeply, sighing as he blew out the smoke.

"You were on the phone a long time this morning", said an animalistic yet somehow fatherly voice entering the room from behind him.

David looked over to see Quetzalcoatl, in dragon-man form, a sort of a hybridization between his human guise and his 'true' feathered serpent form. His smooth shimmering blue-gray scales, prismatic crown of feathers, and piercing yellow reptilian eyes were still a striking sight to David even after a year in his presence .

"Hims was talkin' to girly girl he went on chocolatey adventure wiph", informed Dug

"Ah... and...?", asked Quetzalcoatl.

David took another deep drag and let it out slowly, and brushed his long hair out of his face, as much to delay having to answer as to help with his stress.

"Well, as much as it pains me to admit it, Lindsay's right. Between the distance and the differences in our lifestyles, it's probably not going to work. I don't know, I guess things are kind of up in the air right now. We agreed to give it a try but we're keeping things 'open', her word. But I...", David trailed off remembering the look on Lindsay's face when he and Jesse showed up riding Quetzalcoatl. After the whole Mother Ava incident it was just too much for her.

"Let's face it, she's an amazing girl who deserves a normal life, and I'm, well, not normal", David added.

"Dug thinks Davey is normal", said Dug patting him on the head.

"I agree", commented Quetzalcoatl, "You're a reasonably rational and level headed person, considering what you've been through in the past few years.

"Gee thanks", quipped David, "Look, I know what you guys mean, and to you guys I'm normal..." '*for what that's worth*', he thought then continued aloud "but... ".

David was interrupted by a loud knock at his door.

Quetzalcoatl gave David a look that asked if he was expecting someone. David shook his head 'no' in response.
The reclusive and occasionally socially awkward writer and foe of the supernatural didn't often receive visitors; not good ones anyway, so this was a cause for some alarm. David crossed the room to the door, and Quetzalcoatl moved so that when the door was opened he would be standing behind it.

Dug decided he was more interested in what was on the History Channel than visitors, and remained invisible. David took a quick moment to pull his hair back into a ponytail and exchanged a nod indicating readiness with Quetzalcoatl and opened the door. On the other side were two men in the all too familiar cheap black suits of ONLA field agents.

"What can I do for you gentlemen?", David asked while reaching behind his back to feign grabbing a weapon. It was a bluff of course as he was completely unarmed, but his reputation paid off and it had the desired effect, the two agents took a step back and assumed a respectful posture.

"Former Agent David Maier?", the first agent asked

"You know damn well who I am, and why the hell do you guys keep calling me 'Former Agent' like it's my peerage title or something?", David asked.

David wasn't truly enraged but felt it necessary to adopt this air until he knew why they were here.

"Uh... yes, yes sir.", the agent stammered in response "I'm Agent Cook, and this is Agent Hill. We have a message from Director Belles", the young man managed to spit out.

"Ok, what is it?", David asked.

David had ignored about a years worth of calls and e-mails from his former partner, and was now a bit curious as to what was so important to warrant a visit from two agents.

Agent Cook held out a set of keys. David took them and looked at them curiously.

"It's out front sir", said Cook.

"What is?", David asked.

"The message sir", replied Cook.

"What are you playing at Martin?", David asked himself.

"What sir?"

"Nothing."

The agents stared at each other then at David with a look that said 'we want to ask a question we are not sure we should ask'.

David rolled his eyes, "Fine what is it?"

"Is it true sir?", Hill said speaking for the first time. David recognized his accent as being from Pennsylvania farm country and was a stark contrast to Cook's more urban lilt.

"Is what true?", David asked.

"Did you really beat an archangel?"

David felt the slightest twinge of mischief and remembered Ethan's 'I killed God' claims.

"Well boys let me put it to you like this. I did battle with the Archangel Gabriel at the battle of Armageddon, and I'm still alive...", David turned his back to the two young agents keeping his hand on the door and after a moment said "and he isn't", shutting the door in the faces of two very stunned and dejected agents.

This left David face to face with Quetzalcoatl, who was doing his best not to laugh. And as soon as they heard the agents leave the hall outside the apartment, they did laugh.

"Well, technically it's true", said David

David then turned his attention to the keys.

"What are they to?", asked Quetzalcoatl.

David shrugged, "They're car keys"

"Did Davey win a vroom vroom?", Dug asked finally tearing his attention away from TV and back to reality.

"It would appear so. We'll let's go see what we've won.", David said.

They decided to give the agents a minute to depart or to get into surveillance position, whichever they were going to do, then went outside to see David's "message". Quetzalcoatl did a quick scan and confirmed that the agents had indeed left, but had a vague feeling they were being watched.

Sitting in front of David's building was a black van, the kind he used to drive as an ONLA field agent, only this one didn't have any of the subtle and hidden ONLA or government markings, other than government issued plates, not specific to any state.

David pressed a button on the keychain, and the van's doors could be heard unlocking.

"I guess this is it", David said while slipping into the driver's seat, as Quetzalcoatl got in the passenger side.

The van was a full out ONLA tactical van, equipped for surveillance, combat, survival, search and rescue, and just about any other purpose an ONLA agent might need.

" *Welcome back, Agent Maier*", said a disembodied female voice.

"Phoenix?", asked David.

" *Yes, Agent Maier*", it replied.

"Holy shit, this is my van. From back when I was still an agent. Waite and I did so much customization to...", David said trailing off.

"Why do you think Belles sent it?", asked Quetzalcoatl.

"I have no idea", replied David.

"*Agent Maier, I have a video message from Director Belles that might explain.*", said the computer.

"Thank you Phoenix, but I'm not an ONLA agent anymore."

" *Yes, Agent Maier, I am aware that we are both civilians now*"

"Then why do you keep referring to me as agent?"

" *It is the designation for you I was programmed with, and out of habit.*"

"Alright Phoenix, play message", said David.

The small but high resolution monitor centered in the van's dashboard came to life with the image of Martin Belles.

"Hello David. I know you've been ignoring my attempts to contact you, and I can't say I blame you. But I knew you couldn't resist your old wheels, and you're going to want to hear what I have to say. David I apologize. You were right, about a lot of things. I made some horrible mistakes that a lot of other people have had to pay for. Look David, I've talked with the board and in light of recent events, and because a reassessment of your file concluded that the Spider Incident was beyond your control, or anyone's control for that matter, we're willing to reinstate you, at a higher rank and pay grade. Whether you decide to come back or not the van is yours. It's completely autonomous, it's not tied to the ONLA network. And there are no tracking devices, bugs, enchantments, or other surprises. I sent it to you just how you left it. I promise, but if I know you, you'll check anyway. It wasn't hard to get it released to you. It was about to be retired anyway, and I couldn't assign it to any other agent. I don't know what you did to it, but as far as that AI program is concerned you're God... Maybe not the best choice of words considering recent events, but you know what I mean. And David I really am sorry, I know this time of year... I mean I hope you don't blame the ONLA for... anyway good luck whatever you decide to do. I hope to hear from you soon. Belles out."

With that the screen shut off.

"Interesting" said Quetzalcoatl, "Do you think he was sincere?"

"I think so, but you're the deity, you tell me", David said.

"I believe he is, does this mean you'll be going back to the ONLA?"

"I don't think so. I trust Martin, but I don't believe in what the ONLA stands for anymore. We'll see what happens after you and the other gods start to come back into power... or... whatever you're going to do...", David said with a little uncertainty if that was really an idea he had complete comfort with.

"Is we goin' for a ride in your new, vroom vroom?", asked Dug excitedly.

"Well first we have to see if Martin really is true to his word and check the van for tampering".

It took the rest of the afternoon and part of the evening for them to check the van both physically and magically. And it seemed that even all of David's old enchantments and protection spells were in place and unaltered. They then checked the Phoenix AI itself for tampering, taking special care to check for hidden encryption or program files. When David was convinced it was clean he downloaded his current information and case files from his laptop including everything from the mother Ava incident and the battle of Armageddon and the manuscript for his latest book. At this point David was exhausted, and didn't feel up to driving. And Dug was very disappointed not to be going for a joyride.

All David wanted to do was relax and riff on History or Discovery with Quetzalcoatl and Dug. It was great for them making fun of the programs and pointing out everything they got wrong.

Quetzalcoatl was in rare form during a special about the Zapotec peoples, and David was just starting to feel relaxed when there was another knock at his door.

"What the... Dug did you order a pizza or something?", asked David.

Dug just shook his head no.

Tiredness and frustration made him forget to be cautious, and he crossed the room and opened the door. Behind it stood a young girl, in a black London fog style trench coat. She was just under five feet with incredibly long dark red hair that seemed to progress to an ambered bronze at the end, worn down in the back, the rest in a high cascading ponytail. She had sharp but youthful features and felid eyes. Her pointed ears suggested she might be older than she looked and gave a hint she was not a local girl from South Street.

"Oberon and Titania send their greetings David Maier", she said in a musical voice.

"Oh uh... Hi, I uh", David stammered trying to compose himself.

She glanced over his shoulder as Quetzalcoatl approached.

"Greetings Great Quetzalcoatl of the Aztecs", said Na'da.

"Greetings elf of Tyr Afal", said Quetzalcoatl.

"Elf?", she said looking and sounding quite annoyed "I'm not one of those stuck up stuffy elves. I'm a sylph".

She slipped the coat from her shoulders and let it drop to the floor. She turned around to reveal large pixie like wings, and spread them out for effect, but that wasn't all she revealed. Most of her body was sparsely wrapped in thin vines, with leaves in autumn colors covering the essential places. She had tall boots and gauntlets, also made of vines. She was very slender but still curved and ample in the places which modern human aesthetic encouraged women to be so.

"See?", she said.

Dug reacted first, and in his best impression of a washed up 1980's rapper turned reality television star said "Daaaamn!".

David thought two things at once; that Dug had been watching too much television and that he agreed with Dug's assessment. Despite having been in the presence of great supernatural beauties such as Ilitu and Titania in the past, his body reacted without his consent as it sometimes did, and he had to stand uncomfortably to hide it.

"My apologies, Sylph of Tyr Afal.", said Quetzalcoatl apparently the only one not affected by her.

"My name is Na'da.", she announced "and I know by what names you are known... Except for you goblin", she said looking over at Dug smiling.

"DUG!", he said pointing at himself and standing up as straight as he could while adjusting his 1920's style cappy hat, the only part of his outfit that wasn't medieval. Even doing that, and standing on the seat only his head and upper torso were visible over the back of the couch.

A look seemed to be exchanged between the two Sidhe on the revelation of his name, but then passed.

"Greetings Dug", she said.

Looking at Na'da, David couldn't help feeling the way men, and women for that matter, feel when they see an attractive young specimen whom society deems it inappropriate for them to fancy, even though he figured Na'da was probably older than him, perhaps by centuries.

"Oh, I almost forgot. I come also bearing a gift for you David Maier", the waif said.

She quickly slid her hand under David's shirt and placed her hand on his chest. He barely had time to react before he was overtaken by an electrical burning sensation over his entire body. He collapsed to the ground and twitched slightly.

He woke to Quetzalcoatl shaking him by the shoulders, "David? David, are you alright?"

David groaned. He felt like he'd been dragged around the city behind a taxi for a few hours.

"I think I'll be okay, in a minute, once my head stops ringing and every muscle in my body stops spasming", David said sarcastically.

David looked past Quetzalcoatl to see Dug riding Na'da's shoulders and beating the back of her head, and she was flailing her arms trying to get him off.

"What you done to Davey?", he was shouting over and over.

"Get off me, you mad little beast, I haven't harmed...", she started.

"Dug, Dug I'm fine, stop!", said David.

They both stopped and looked at him with their arms still in mid swing, then Na'da dumped Dug off her. He landed with a loud thud, and sprang quickly to his feet. The whole scene was so comical David and Quetzalcoatl couldn't help but laugh, which for David was short lived, as it caused his muscles to ache more severely.

"Uhgh", David said.

"Are you alright, David?", Quetzalcoatl asked.

"Yeah, just help me up." he said.

"What did she do to you?".

"She..."

"He has been given the gift of the mists of Tyr Afal", Na'da interrupted.

"Yeah that", David said rubbing the back of his head.

Dug let out a low whistle, "No humanses man or woman has ever been given da mists".

"Really?" asked David.

"Really", said Na'da and Dug in unison.

"At least not to the level you have been given it. You have its full use permanently", Na'da commented.

"I know", said David "Apparently I have not only the mists but knowledge of how to use them and a lot of other information my mind is slowly unlocking".

Na'da stared at David with a dreamy sort of stare.

"What?", he asked.

"Is it true?", she asked.

"Is what true?", he asked.

"Did you really best the Archangel Gabriel?"

"Oh that", David decided to answer more honestly this time. "Well as you probably know I had help from Oberon and Titania, and I was wielding the sword of the demon Asmodeus. And I really only immobilized him with some well-placed slices. It was Yahweh himself that actually destroyed him".

"Is that, them?", Na'da asked pointing to a pair of swords on David's wall.

"What? No, those are actually replicas I had made. Well close to replicas. They're a bit smaller to make them easier for me to wield, and I can still only use one at a time. And they lack some of the metaphysical appearance of the originals. Quetzalcoatl enchanted them for me, but I doubt they're as powerful...", David said, speaking with extra verbiage as men will do when they are nervous.

"Still, even as you say it's very impressive for a human, or even a fey", Na'da said.

"Thank you", David actually blushed a little.

Na'da then plopped herself down on the couch next to Dug, apparently having already forgotten their earlier altercation.

"So, I take it that wasn't the only reason Oberon and Titania sent you?" David said.

"I am to watch over you", she said very matter of factly. "And to learn from you".

"For how long, and to learn what?", David asked.

Na'da just shrugged, "Do you all dwell here?"

"Well Dug basically does and Quetzalcoatl is here a lot so I..."

"I thought I did live here", Quetzalcoatl stated.

"What? Well not that I mind, but well, you never eat here and you usually leave right before I go to sleep. I kind of assumed you were going home", David said.

"David, I'm a god. I don't eat or sleep. Or at least I don't need to. While you sleep I go and do things. I explore the modern age, I look after my people. And sometimes I just go somewhere and chill.", said Quetzalcoatl.

"Right. Sorry, we deal with each other on such equal footing on a day to day bases that I keep forgetting", said David.

"You know, for some odd reason that makes me feel good", said Quetzalcoatl.

"And now I live here too", Na'da interjected cheerfully.

"I'm going to need a bigger apartment", David mumbled to himself rubbing the bridge of his nose with thumb and forefinger.

Then he had a sudden realization, "I have to check and see if the last e-mail address I have for Ethan and Ilitu is still good".

"It isn't", informed Quetzalcoatl. "I tried it two days ago and it got bounced back. Why do you need to get a hold of them? Oh wait, the mists. You're thinking of using the mists to take them to Tyr Afal?"

"Right, so that Ilitu can gain the information she needs to find Is. The problem is finding them. Can you locate them?", David asked.

"Unfortunately no, Ethan can't be sensed and Ilitu is very good at masking her presence. Perhaps once I have attained more of my former power", Quetzalcoatl said.

"That could be awhile, right?", David asked.

"Yes, my reemergence is still a few years off. I have to cultivate a lot more awareness in the minds of men to be fully restored", Quetzalcoatl said.

David yawned loudly, "Maybe some sleep will help me come up with some ideas. I guess I could try to contact Asmodeus on the astral plane, but I imagine he's pretty busy these days".

"Alright my friend, I'm off. I've got some work to do. But I'll put out some feelers and see if I can't get some leads on them. I think I may be gone for a while this time", said Quetzalcoatl.

"I hope you don't think I don't want you here because of our earlier conversation. I do, I just didn't realize..."

Quetzalcoatl put up his hand to stop David, "It's not that. Fact is I had decided that fighting in the battle of Armageddon had earned me a vacation, but there are a lot of the old guard jockeying for position right now and I need to get some serious work done if I want to have a good standing in the new order of things".

"I understand. You know where to find me if you need my help, but I doubt you will", David said.

"You never know, and same here. It shouldn't be too much longer before you can actually beseech me", Quetzalcoatl said.

They both laughed, and shook hands. With that Quetzalcoatl took a step back assumed a smaller version of his iconic feathered serpent form and disappeared in a blaze of sunlight. David suspected the next time he saw Quetzalcoatl it wouldn't be quite so face to face.

"Alright you two, it's been a long day and I'm going to bed.", David said.

"Night Davey", Dug said waving over his shoulder without looking away from the TV.

"Good night, David Maier. Sleep well", said Na'da leaning over the back of the couch leering at him.

David stirred half-awake in the predawn early morning. The room was pitch black, which kept him from being any more than just barely awake. This was not unusual for him. Years of well-earned paranoia had made him a light and troubled sleeper. What was unusual was that this and his training had failed to alert him to the fact that someone had entered the room and that the someone was lying next to him. What made him aware of this is when this person rolled over and draped an arm over him. David quickly shot out of bed and assumed a defensive stance. He could just barely make out a silhouette on the bed in the darkness.

"Did I offend you David Maier?", said Na'da in a sad and apologetic voice.

David clicked on the lamp on his bed table and winced at the sudden change in light. He had been so tired he had only managed to remove his shirt before falling asleep and was still wearing his pants.

"No", he said rubbing his eyes, "No you just caught me off guard. I was pretty sure I was sleeping alone." he said.

"Would you rather be?", she asked coyly.

David knew how he wanted to answer, but he didn't want his desire to make that decision. It had been three months since had seen Lindsay, but he wasn't sure pursuing any sort of physical relationship with Na'da would be appropriate. However she had other ideas. Fey have no such compunctions. She did not wait for him to answer. She got out from under the covers and stood in front of him, and he saw now that she was completely undressed. A quick glance across the room revealed that her 'outfit' was now coiled around his desk chair and part of his desk.

"David Maier, it is entirely possible that I will be in your company for the remainder of your relatively short lifespan. I do not wish to go all that time without physical contact", she smiled and took a step forward so that their bodies were lightly touching.

"Well when you put it like that.", David smiled and ran his hands down her sides. She softly moaned at the touch of his hands, and her wings reflexively fluttered.

"Besides," she said laying her head on him, "I believe nineteen is of age among your people."

"NINETEEN!?!", David jumped back as if he had just been informed she was toxic.

"What?", he stammered.

"Jesus, I'm old enough to be your father. Well barely, but still...", he said.

"My father is 470 years old. And the Nazarene is on the etheric spheres now, I believe", she said annoyed, "Would it make you more comfortable if I were the hundreds of years old you suspected I might be and you were as a child to me?"

"I... I...", he stammered unable to come up with a good argument.

"Dug thinkses Davey should accept girly cuddles", Dug said becoming visible, sitting on David's desk with a movie style bag of popcorn.

"What the... Dug what are you... Would you go so Na'da and I can talk about this?", David asked.

"You no fun Davey", Dug said while hopping off the desk and leaving the room

"Ok where were we", asked David.

"I believe we were right here", she said stepping forward and pressing herself against him.

David backed up quickly with his hands up, causing him to hit into the wall.

"Look Na'da, you're very attractive, but I'm not sure how I feel about this", he said.

"I am not completely familiar with the customs of your people, but I believe you know how you feel", she said annoyed.

With that she began to leave the room. As she passed David's desk the vines grappled her and coiled about her reforming her outfit. It vaguely reminded David of something he had seen in a horror movie. It probably should have disturbed him, but he found it strangely intriguing.

"Do not take too long to decide David Maier, my need is great and my patience is not", she looked back at him, "And I sense yours is as well."

David found himself alone in the half light of his room wondering if he wasn't being very stupid.

The next morning David decided he needed to think a lot of things out, and some advice from a trusted source might help. And since he did some of his best thinking on long drives a visit to his old friend Jesse Perfect was in order. He now knew that Jesse lived only about two hours away in Stroudsburg. Perfect amount of drive time and the Perfect person to get advice from. With no cases at the moment or book deadlines, there was no reason not to go.

David showered and got dressed. Then found Dug and Na'da watching TV, though it was more Dug explaining TV than actually watching. She was absentmindedly playing with one of Dug's long pointy ears, while Dug grinned with a look of smug satisfaction, making David wonder just what happened after he went back to sleep. Apparently, Na'da was an impatient creature indeed.

"So then most of it is fiction and the rest is inaccurate truth?", asked Na'da.

"Yup", replied Dug.

"But what is its purpose?", asked Na'da.

"Good question", David chimed in, "Ok guys road trip."

"Yay, finally new vroom vroom. Where we takin' to?", asked Dug.

"To see an old friend.", David said.

"Who?", Dug and Na'da asked in unison.

"Jesse Perfect." David informed.

"Goody, Dug likeses nice old man", Dug said.

" *The* Jesse Perfect, who also fought in the battle of Armageddon?", asked Na'da.

"That's the one", said David.

They went down to the street and David moved a few things he thought he might need from his old car to the Phoenix. And on gut instinct decided to sheathe and pack his swords.

Having replicated demonic blades enchanted by an Aztec god nearby made him feel better.

"Shotgun!", shouted Dug.

"Shotgun?", asked Na'da.

"Yeah, it's like a game. Sitting in the passenger seat is sometimes called riding shotgun. The first person to call shotgun once you're in view of the vehicle gets to ride up front", informed David

"That's unfair no one told me the rules", Na'da pouted.

"Just let him have it this time, he has been jonesing to go for a ride", said David.

Na'da looked at him sideways, "I believe it will take me some time to learn all of your dialect."

" *Good morning, Agent Maier*".

Na'da looked shocked, "Vehicles can speak?".

"Most can't, this is an exception. This van has an AI computer built in. It's called Phoenix. Phoenix this is Na'da.".

" *Identifying authorized passengers Na'da and Dug*", Phoenix responded.

The trip down was quiet and uneventful. David was deep in thought both about his current situation and what might lay ahead. He had a very foreboding feeling.

Dug spent the entire trip just enjoying the ride. Na'da on the inverse sat in the back quietly sulking. The route from

Philadelphia to Stroudsburg would take him through the Lehigh Valley. He vaguely remembered Jesse telling him about an adventure he had there many years ago at Christmas, but couldn't remember what it was. It was a mission to Bethlehem, which David was now passing, which was the last one his colleagues Thurston Waite and Martin Belles went on together. David had been in Europe at the time. A driver not properly in his own lane snapped David back to the present, but after that minor crisis was averted, David drifted once more into a waking dream.

All of central and northeastern Pennsylvania always had a haunted feeling to David, which strangely proved to be pleasantly distracting at the moment. When they arrived in Stroudsburg, David thought that for all its small town feel there were sections that were desperately trying to mimic Brooklyn. The entire Pocono region was odd. Recent rapid growth in the area made it an uneasy mixture of rural and urban. It seemed to be at war with itself.

When they arrived at the assisted living facility that Jesse lived in, David wondered why Jesse stayed there. He was quite fit for a human into his triple digits, and wasn't in need of any special nursing care. He supposed it was possible that Jesse was there to keep up appearances, but that didn't seem likely.

"Na'da can you become invisible like Dug?", David asked.

"Yes, but why? With my long coat and my ears covered I can pass for human", she asked.

"I just thought it might be simpler, but you're right there's no need", he said.

David decided that perhaps he had better be more careful. He was inadvertently insulting Na'da quite a bit.

The three of them walked up to the front desk. Though Dug was unseen by any but David and Na'da. David waited patiently while the woman behind the desk finished her phone call that obviously had nothing to do with her job.

"Can I help you?", she asked sounding a bit annoyed.

"Yes", David said smiling pleasantly "We're here to see Jesse Perfect".

The woman slid a sign-in book across the counter at them. David began signing in and Na'da leaned over and whispered in his ear.

"I cannot write in your language", she whispered.

"You can't?", he whispered back.

"I suppose you can write Tuada'an glyphs?", she asked annoyed.

"Actually... I can", he said trying not to annoy her any further.

The woman was growing impatient. David groaned slightly and signed them in as David and Na'da Maier. The woman looked at the book and then at them and raised an eyebrow and shook her head. She then wrote out guest badges for them, and gave quick directions to Jesse's room.

"Popular guy today", she mumbled.

"What's that?", David asked.

"You and your daughter aren't the first visitors he's had today. In fact I think the other guy is still here".

David didn't even have time to notice Na'da's slightly smug amusement at the woman's faux pas.

"Thank you", David said as he began to move down the hall as close to running as he could without looking suspicious, which he did anyway. Dug was already ahead of him hitting the elevator button. When he got to Jesse's room the door was shut and he silently cursed himself for not coming armed. He turned the door handle silently, took a deep breath and quickly opened the door and burst into the room.

He immediately saw Jesse and a man in a what appeared to be the black suit and trench coat ensemble of an ONLA operative, or rather a designer version thereof, sitting and talking calmly. Jesse was in his pajamas and an expensive and comfortable looking robe and slippers.

"Hello David, the front desk called up and told me you were here. You made good time", Jesse said.

"Yeah, when she told me someone else was here I guess I overreacted", David said.

"You know David I do actually get plain ol' social visitors from time to time", Jesse said.

"Hey handsome", the man in the black ONLA suit said to David, as he stood up and took off his mirrored sunglasses.

"Abe? Abraham Sieurd", David said startled

David and Abe shook hands and pulled each other into a quick one-armed hug. Before he released him, Abe bear hugged David and lifted him off the ground by only the slightest inch. All the fond memories of his fellow agent from his ONLA days were suddenly accompanied by memories of those few traits of Abe's of which David was less than fond.

"So he is a friend also?", asked Na'da.

Abe looked past David at Na'da.

"David, who's your friend?", asked Abe.

"She's...", David started.

"Na'da", she interjected, hugging David's arm and leaning her head against him.

"Uh right, Na'da this is Abraham Sieurd an old friend of mine from the ONLA", David said.

Abe had boyish features, all American but with a tiny drop of an ethnicity one could not quite place in him, perhaps Hispanic or Native American, and left parted short black hair. His face showed some of the hard living he had done as an ONLA field agent, but conversely that same life had kept him in great shape. David used to joke that never growing up had kept him young.

"Howdy, Senior Agent Abraham Sieurd, at your service", Abe said and extended his hand while giving his best James Bond smile to Na'da, which she shook cautiously. She had heard many stories of the ONLA and most of them not good.

"And this is Jesse Perfect", David said.

This time Na'da extended her hand first. Na'da had also heard many stories of Jesse Perfect, all of them good. Jesse stood took Na'da's hand and kissed it lightly.

"It is a pleasure to meet you", Jesse said.

"And I you, I have heard many tales of you Jesse Perfect, and your heroic adventures", Na'da said.

"Well I don't know if I would call them heroic. But who am I to argue with a beautiful lady. Where are from?", Jesse said.

"From Avalon", she said, "Though we ourselves call it Tyr Afal"

"Ah, I thought you might be", Jesse said.

"Same old Jesse, you don't miss anything", said David.

"Is Dug not going to be introduced?", asked Na'da.

"I was getting to that", said David.

"Who you talking about?", asked Abe.

"Dug", said David.

"Dug is still around?", asked Jesse.

"Who's Dug? Your imaginary friend?", Abe asked jokingly.

"No, Dug is a goblin. He can only be seen and heard by whom he wants to be, and I assure you Agent Sieurd he is quite real", informed Jesse.

"Yes sir", said Abe.

"To answer your question Jesse, yes, Dug stuck around after the battle. So did Quetzalcoatl for a while but he had to get back to the business of being a deity", David replied.

"Jesus, David, I heard you were keeping interesting company these days", commented Abe.

"Yeah, I know him too", said David.

"What?", asked Abe.

"Never mind, Abe. David, Agent Sieurd here was just informing me of the ONLA's latest problems. And I was informing him that I am retired", said Jesse.

"And I was begging him to reconsider. You see David it seems that Yahweh and Tipeshiel are up to something in Texas", Abe added.

"And I am still retired. I accomplished what I set out to. It took me a lifetime and a half, but finally the afterlife is as it should be. I am too old and tired for any more adventures", Jesse said with the first tone of severity he had introduced since those gathered had been in his presence.

"You've earned it, Jesse. You have done more, seen more, and accomplished more than any of us. The world has no right to ask any more of you", commented David.

"That's exactly why we need him. He knows more about this kind of thing than anyone", implored Abe.

"Forget it, I'm sorry but at my age I just don't have this journey in me", Jesse said.

David had never heard Jesse talk like this. Last he had seen him he was as fit as a man half his age. David suspected Jesse's completion of his life's work must have let things catch up with him.

"I know I'm going to regret asking, but what is Yahweh up to?" asked David.

"Well we're not sure actually. We are not even entirely sure where he is. He has been incredibly effective at evading our seers. In fact the one who got us the little information we have was... damaged", Abe said.

"Is that how you talk about people these days, Abe, damaged?", asked David.

"Hey, I don't know any other way to put it. She wasn't physically injured, and she wasn't killed. She is recovering from some sort of psychic... damage", said Abe.

"Why does the ONLA want to stop this anyway? I thought they wanted Yahweh in power", said David.

"Well two reasons. One: We didn't really know what he was up to at the time. And two: Since his fall and the destruction of the Abscended the Yahwist aspects of both the ONLA and the Illuminati have lost a lot of power and influence. Now what's with all the hostility all the sudden?", Abe said.

"Abe, I have good reason to distrust the ONLA these days", said David.

"I get that, but trust me not as much reason as you used to. Besides I am not the ONLA. I got into this for the same reasons you did. An interest in the unseen parts of the world and to help people", Abe said with an offense that was genuine.

"I know Abe, I'm sorry", said David.

"*And that's why Martin got in at first too*", thought David.

"Actually David, you were my next stop after Jesse. Martin wanted me to try to recruit you again", said Abe.

"So this Yahweh thing is why he has been trying so hard lately", said David.

"'Fraid so", said Abe with a southern drawl effected for humor in attempt to defuse some of the tension in the conversation.

David realized that fate and probably a half dozen other forces he could name personally were pushing him toward this.

"So is this you asking or the ONLA asking?", David inquired.

"Both actually. I need you on this one, bro", said Abe.

"Two conditions", said David.

"Ok, shoot", said Abe.

"One: I'm not rejoining the ONLA. You can consider me and my team subcontractors. Which means I do expect to be paid for this", David said.

"And two?", asked Abe.

"Don't tell Martin", replied David.

"Now how the hell do you expect me to not tell Director Belles and get money allocated for a subcontractor?", asked Abe.

"I don't know, but I'm sure a resourceful guy like you will come up with something", said David.

"You know David, you can be a real ass sometimes", said Abe smiling, "But I guess I'd be a little cocky too if I took down an Archangel".

"I held him off, Abe. And I don't think taking on a god, even a fallen one, is quite the same thing. So Jesse sure you don't have one more in you?", asked David.

"Positive. I'll leave this one to you youngsters", Jesse replied.

"I didn't think so, but I had to ask. Alright Abe, so we have no idea what we're up against, and no idea where to find them", David continued.

"Yup, just like the good old days", Abe said.

"Ok, since the ONLA seers have been ineffective, you have any other ideas?", asked David.

"Nope, can you think of anyone?", asked David.

"Several, but the problem is I don't know how to get in contact with any of them at the moment", David said.

"Well I'm sure a resourceful guy like you will come up with something", Abe quipped.

"You know Abe...", said David.

"I can do it", interrupted Na'da.

"What? No way forget it, it's too dangerous", David protested.

"I am touched by your concern David Maier but I assure you I am more competent at divination than any human", said Na'da.

"That's a little specist, my dear, and while I am sure you are a competent diviner, this is seriously dangerous. If Yahweh senses you snooping around there's no telling what he could do to you", Jesse interjected.

"I have an idea for that as well. David Maier can project the mists of Tyr Afal into the astral plane to conceal me from Yahweh's divine sight", she said.

"Will that work?", asked David.

"It should, in theory. The mists have concealed Tyr Afal itself from him for ages, and that was when he was the one God", confirmed Na'da.

"Mists of Tyr Afal?", asked Abe as if he thought the term sounded passe.

"Long story, Abe. I'll fill you in later. Ok. I'm still not comfortable with this but it doesn't seem we have any other option", David conceded.

"That is becoming a running theme with us David Maier", Na'da retorted.

"I think you're going to need to explain that one too buddy", Abe said.

David just shot Abe an evil look.

"Anyway, we can't do this here. I don't want to risk calling unwanted attention to Jesse", David replied.

"I appreciate that David. I don't know if there's any place local I can recommend though", Jesse replied.

"I sense a place nearby", said Na'da.

"Dug feels it too, big rocks and good dirt", Dug said.

"Yes, that's it Dug. Celtic standing stones. It's not too far away. I think I can follow the energy to get us there", Na'da said.

"I have heard of a place like that nearby, but I don't know where it is or what it's called", said Jesse.

"Well it sounds good to me, let's go", said Abe.

"I agree it definitely sounds like it will suit our needs. Jesse, our visit will have to wait", said David.

"Don't worry about it David, you go save the world. We'll catch up when you're done", Jesse said.

"Wow, you make that sound so ordinary", commented Abe.

"For us it almost is", Jesse said winking.

They said their good-byes and made their way to the street.

"Shotgun!", Na'da yelled as soon as she could see the van.

"Awww", Dug said sulking.

"Oh, let her have it you were up front the whole way down." said David, "So Abe, you riding with us or following?".

"I don't think they would appreciate me abandoning my car here", said Abe.

"You could always call a local office and have it picked up.", said David.

"There is no local office out here. Besides I would still rather have my own car for now", Abe said.

"Ok ,let's go", said David.

Following Na'da and Dug's impressions they proceeded out of town. Once out of town the roads got rural very quickly. As they traveled the roads got increasingly mountainous, winding and wooded. The scenery was actually quite beautiful but David could barely enjoy it as he had to react quickly to the sporadic directions Na'da and Dug gave with little warning as they drove. After several turns they came upon a small parking area, which was really just a small dirt clearing alongside the road with a wood sign that read "Dolmencella".

"This is it", Na'da and Dug said in unison.

"You guys are starting to make a habit of that", David said.

"What?", again in unison.

"That, speaking in unison.", David said.

They both looked at each other, then at David and shrugged.

The park itself was beautiful with rolling hills, huge standing stones, and small stone structures. One could forget these were the Poconos and think it was a genuine Celtic landscape. The vibe of the place was the same.

"Yup", said Abe looking around with well-trained senses, "This is definitely the place".

After wandering around for a bit, Na'da finally settled on a spot she felt comfortable. The spot she picked was next to a particularly monolithic stone on top of a hill. David and Abe thought the large circle of stones would have been her choice but they were wrong. For some reason this particular spot resonated with her more. Dug perched himself on a smaller boulder nearby. Abe took up a defensive position out of habit, and covered them from a distance. David and Na'da sat on the ground opposite each other, and began to enter a meditative state. David projected his mind into the astral plane and summoned the mists of Tyr Afal and centered them around Na'da. She, meanwhile, sought out their enemy. She found his trail all the way back to the battle of Armageddon. He first went to the Midwest, to the Bible belt, where he formed a new cult. In his new cult Christ was an outcast, cast out of heaven. He had taken a new name. Yaldabaoth. The men in his thrall no longer had to pretend allegiance to Christ while rejecting his teachings. They could now do so purely and nakedly. Yaldabaoth had a strange power over these people but Na'da couldn't tell what exactly. Then he absorbed a militia group. They were the start of his new army of crusaders. From there he moved south to somewhere familiar to what little remained of his host body. There again he took over another militia group. He was somewhere called... Genesis Land.

It was a park of some kind but it was slowly being converted into a religious compound. It would be the seat of his new empire where he would begin anew his quest to be the one god. Then Yaldabaoth saw her, not her exactly but the mists. He hit it with a broad energy blast and her visions were no more.

The blast was strong enough to have physical effects and knocked David and Na'da back several feet in opposite directions. Na'da was knocked back into the monolithic stone and lost consciousness for a moment. David was quick to his feet and rushed to her.

"Na'da!? Na'da are you all right?", David asked panicked.

"I'm... Ugh I..", she said rubbing the back of her head where it struck the rock.

David examined her and found that she was bleeding quite badly, and appeared to have a slight concussion, as well as a few smaller cuts and bruises.

"Come on, Na'da, talk to me", he said.

She only groaned in response. Then her "clothing" did something strange. The vines burrowed into her flesh and the ground beneath her. David set her down and backed away. He had some idea what was happening.

Abe and Dug came rushing up to them
.
"What happened?", asked Abe.

"He spotted us. W ell ,he spotted the mist anyway.", David replied.

"Are we compromised?", asked Abe.

"I don't think so. The blast he used was pretty broad. He just saw something. He had no idea what it was. The blast itself didn't do any damage. That bastard just got lucky and knocked her into a rock. I think it was only through the mists that he was even able to project himself. His power seems pretty limited", David said.

"Is she ok?", asked Abe.

"No. But she's healing herself... I think. She should be ok, as long as we aren't disturbed", said David.

"God, I hope so", said Abe with genuine concern.

"Wrong god", commented Dug.

After almost an hour Na'da began to stir awake, and the vines retracted to normal. David slid over to her and spoke softly.

"Na'da, are you all right?", David asked.

"I am feeling much better David Maier. Did we get the information we require?", she asked faintly.

"Yes, I think so. You scared the hell out of us", David said.

She gave a huge smile, "Once again David Maier I am touched by your concern, but I was in no real danger, as long as I was connected to the earth, especially in a place like this".

She did however take the opportunity to cuddle up to David. This time he didn't shy away but lightly stroked her hair, albeit in a paternal, but completely genuine way.

Abe put his hand briefly on Na'da's shoulder to say 'good work' and retracted it quickly.

"What did we learn?", Abe asked.

"Well I saw everything she did. Apparently Yahweh... or Yaldabaoth as he calls himself now, is building an army and has started quite a large cult that's very Old Testament based. He condemns Christ for siding against him", David said.

"So where is he now?"

"Apparently Genesis Land. Pastor Wally's creationist theme park. Though I couldn't tell you why", David said.

"I could. I'm not supposed to it's classified, but...", Abe said.

"Out with it Abraham".

THE TESTAMENT OF DAVID PART I

"Well technically Pastor Wally still owns it", said Abe.

"Yeah, and technically he's also dead", David pointed out.

"Define technically", said Abe.

"I'm not going to like this am I, Abe?", asked David.

"No. You see because of the ONLA's, shall we say messy involvement, in Pastor Wally's escape from prison it was covered up as an early release. We had no idea until just now that Yahw... I mean, Yaldabaoth would actually try to use Wally's assets as a stepping stone to power. We didn't even think he knew that on the paper Wally was listed as still alive", Abe said.

David spent the whole of Abe's explanation just trying not to have a stroke or embolism.

"So, what you're telling me is that all this managed to escape one of the most powerful organizations in the world, but the mystery was unraveled by me and a teenage fey?", asked David.

"That's what I'm telling you", Abe said.

David rubbed his nose between thumb and forefinger, "Of course it escaped you. The ONLA thought there was nothing weird about the Mother Ava cult even after their creepy slogans were on TV for years. What should I expect? So now what?".

"Now I report in, they'll feel like morons for not putting it together on their own, pass the blame around, and most likely order me and my team to investigate further", said Abe.

"And just who do you plan on telling them your team is?",
asked David.

"The truth, an anonymous freelance subcontractor and his
team", said Abe.

"You know he'll know", said David.

"He'll suspect, but it's the best I can do. Guess I'm not as
resourceful as you thought. Or I wouldn't have needed you in
the first place", Abe said.

David grumbled under his breath then said, "Fine you do
your thing. Looks like I have to start getting ready for a very
long trip".

"Hold on! You aren't planning on driving all the way to
Texas?", asked Abe.

"Yes, we're not calling for ONLA transport. You're the only
agent who gets to know of my involvement in this", said
David.

"David this could be time sensitive", said Abe.

"You're right Abe. So we'll just pull out some fake ID's and
fly commercial then I guess, and since my credit cards are
maxed, and you can't charge it to the ONLA... I guess this
one's on you...", David smiled.

"On the other hand a road trip will let us catch up", said Abe,
"Ok, we'll drive back into town, to the nearest market to stock
up, and I'll call to have my car retrieved. The Philly office is
not going to be happy about that one".

Abe transferred his gear to the Phoenix. Abe and David
drove in shifts, and Dug drove overnight. Abe knew David

would never hit the manual switch all ONLA AI endowed
vehicles had allowing the operator the choice of whether the
AI could actually self-direct the motion and weapons systems
or not, as a few too many sci-fi movies rendered David
paranoid of machine take over. Because of this, when the
Phoenix appeared to be driving itself, Abe finally accepted
Dug as a reality, even though he had yet to personally witness
the Goblin manifest.

Na'da began to warm up to Abe's charm, and the stories he
told of his adventures and conquests raptured her. David felt
a little discomfort with their forming bond, and wasn't sure if
it was because he was harboring a genuine interest in Na'da
and wanted to protect his own interests, or harboring a slight
annoyance with Abe who still felt the need to turn on the
charm despite all the women, and men for that matter, he had
had as paramours over the years.

Na'da watched both men with genuine intellectual fascination
as they told stories of their early days with Martin Belles and a
man named Thurston Waite who neither had seen for years,
as well as tales of friends and allies who, for Na'da, were
beings she had grown up hearing of in what were, for her, the
equivalent of fairy tales. When David and Abe explained
how common it was for ONLA agents to have died and come
back to life multiple times and in so many bizarre and unique
ways that it warped the average agent's sense of what mortality
was, she sat riveted. She was moved when both her friends
displayed sadness when recalling a shocking time when
despite the frequency of death and resurrection, the Illuminati
brass had, for undisclosed reasons, chosen not to resurrect a
decorated agent who died in a simple car accident during his
off time. Death could become permanent at any time. A
new type of tragedy could always prove to be beyond the
ONLA's scope of control, and sometimes service to the
organization did not end with the heartbeat. Na'da could tell
that part of David did miss it.

It was not Na'da sleeping to the left of him in his borrowed Vilanova t-shirt, or Abe to the right of him in those ridiculous European briefs, cramped in a bed worthy of a flophouse in the motor lodge hotel room the group were able to afford on their pocket cash which kept David Maier awake. No arrangement of the sleepers would have done better or worse, but, he was not even able to notice any discomfort or awkwardness inherent in the situation because his mind was preeminently occupied by something else. The slumber that somehow easily found his companions would have eluded him even if he was alone in the big bed in the guest room in his mother's house on the Massachusetts coast she had lived in after his father died.

He tried to summon that house. Not for thoughts of home, nor of Tai Chi practice with his mother on the beach, but for the sound of the sea. The North Atlantic. The sound of the North Atlantic was what he craved. He has been all over the world, and New England or Europe, it didn't matter. The North Atlantic's white noise in the distance calmed the mind chatter that never settled in him. The other incarnations of the Ocean never did it.

He was going to win. Ethan hadn't shown up. He didn't need to worry about failing, or worry about the Battle of Armageddon turning out to be a stumble Yaldabaoth recovered from. He could handle this on his own, because any time he was in over his head, Ethan showed up. Or Jesse. Just like his mother always showed up when he thought his latest manuscript wasn't up to snuff or he thought he was a failure with women. Since Jesse hadn't come along, David didn't need to worry even though this was the biggest thing he had ever faced where he was the one with whom the buck stopped.

But what if this situation didn't follow the rules? What if the pressure he felt was real? It really was up to him to save, not part of, but all of the world. Not from a monster, or a chocolate saint. But from a being who was once God. David managed to shove fear into corners of his mind for the most part. Even the most objective of cynics would describe him as insanely courageous. He had trepidation at trying new foods, an aversion to people with headcolds, a sensitive stomach or headaches when he thought too long about his finances or something too... human. But on things like this, he was a rock.

But as he lay wide awake, staring myopically into the unlit room without his glasses and itching a little in the uncomfortable ONLA sweats he had borrowed from Abe since he didn't pack for a long trip, he tried to summon the sound of the North Atlantic. It would give his already great courage critical mass to overcome the doubts plaguing him, and then he would find sleep, then morning, then the mission and the leadership role, and once there, doubt would have no purchase.

Dug appeared between blinks of his eyes, sitting on David's chest like a classic nightmare. The look of seriousness in Dug's eyes that only came when Dug actually had something relevant to say kept David from strangling him.

"Dug!", David whispered.

Dug pulled some kind of flute-like instrument out. It was the bone flute Dug usually sat playing with on the couch, playing sitcom theme songs on.

"She don't jus plays music. She's plays elementes", he said, "Dug'll plays water for you".

David looked at Dug with a perturbed inquisitiveness, "How can you know...".

"Dug don't hears your head words", Dug interrupted, "Thems is Davey's and only Davey's. Just that Davey wants to hear waters is all Dug knows".

The Goblin cannot be described to have played the instrument, but he did operate it somehow. And soon the sound of the North Atlantic... and sleep found David Maier.

THE TESTAMENT OF DAVID PART I

CLADE, WHEAT, AND CHAFF

The π of Wands allows the Operator to carefully measure how close the asymptote and the immutable are to the pyramid threshold in a given temporal position on a given silk strand. It does more than establish the metric. It allows the Operator existential position establishment of the Operator's own will and choice.

Brandon Lassiter manually wiped the windshield one more time, finding the defroster to be completely ineffective. He cracked the driver's side window hoping that reducing the atmospheric differential between the interior of the car and the outside environment would reduce the moisture which kept building up on the windshield and obscuring his vision.

Lassiter didn't have to endure the cold blast of air for very long, for within ten minutes time he would arrive at the cabin of one of his best paying customers, Andre Miacis. Lassiter had secured many black-market items for Miacis over the years, and usually shipping and payment didn't need to be done in person with the advent of the internet, but the item that Lassiter was transporting this evening warranted personal delivery. Lassiter knew that anything was worth what someone was willing to pay for it, but really was baffled at the price tag that Miacis was willing to pay for the item in question.

Lassiter didn't bother locking the car, both because he carried on his person the only item he had taken with him on the drive which was of any value, and because he suspected there were little more than woodland creatures in the surrounding environs.

Lassiter knocked loudly on the front door of Miacis's cabin. The tall lanky man who answered the door wearing a Wal-Mart knock off of something which looked like it came out of the Land's End catalog was not Miacis himself. The man's angular features put Lassiter off.

"Are you Lassiter?", the man asked a gruff voice.

"Yes", said Lassiter.

"Come right in. Mr. Miacis is in his study. You know the way I presume?", asked Angle face.

"I do", said Lassiter "it's not my first time here".

The man only nodded in response and stepped aside so that Lassiter could pass. Lassiter made his way to the rear of the cabin and found the oak door to Miacis's study already open.

It was only as he entered the room that he realized that the angle faced man had followed him and closed the doors as they both walked through.

Lassiter was cold and tired and didn't feel like wasting time on pleasantries.

"You won't be able to display this item as you have most of the other things in your collection", said Lassiter, "if it became public knowledge that I have sold this to you, we're both looking at some very serious jail time".

"Mr. Lassiter, the piece you brought me today is not really objet d'art, it is something for which I have a functional purpose", said Miacis.

"I don't care if you use it to wipe your ass with as long as nobody finds out that you have it. If you don't mind Miacis, I'll take the cash and get the hell out of here. I've got about an hour to make it back to the main highway before this ice storm sets in", Lassiter said.

"Of course", said Miacis, "you'll find the agreed upon fee in the briefcase, and a copy of my latest book as well. Oh, I know that wasn't in the original deal, but I've thrown it in for you as little bonus".

Miacis was a well-known corporate motivational speaker who made his money through books, DVDs, CDs, and the hosting of corporate functions and executive retreat weekends. It was through the connections he made in business that he was able to collect the various pieces of anthropological and paleontological interest which sat on the shelves of his study. Those pieces which he could not acquire legitimately through these business contacts, Lassiter had always been able to get for him.

The angular faced man made Lassiter uncomfortable. Lassiter was sure the man was armed. He took the briefcase and placed the hard backed and dust jacketed book under his elbow. Had it just been him and Miacis, he probably would've made a quick quip about how useless the book was to him, and what a fraud he knew Miacis to be, but all things being equal he thought it best to make a quick and polite exit.

Miacis had already begun unpacking the item, when his attention was drawn to the large picture window behind him. A large white blur moved closer and closer to the window, and finally smashed through it. Whatever the shape was jumped on Miacis's back and knocked him, his chair, and his desk to the ground.

Lassiter turned around at the sound of the commotion, and when the initial shock of it wore off he realized the thing which had pinned Andre Miacis to the ground was a huge man sized rabbit.

Miacis growled an inhuman growl.

A feral voice replaced his usually smooth and calm pentameter as he spoke, "Angela! You're really still trying to stop me?"

"Of course I am, you Fascist son of a bitch", came a female human voice from the rabbit.

Miacis began to struggle with the thing which outweighed him by at least 100 pounds. Lassiter watched the scene in disbelief and his attention was drawn away from the wondrous creature for an instant allowing him to notice that Miacis's features had changed. His hands were curled in claw like arrangements and an abnormal amount of hair grew on them. Similarly, the millionaire's face in its lower portions was beginning to jut out in a muzzle like protrusion.

This change in mouth structure did not prevent Miacis from speaking to the angular faced man.

"Get your damned gun out", said the Miacis-thing.

Lassiter looked at the angular faced man who was undergoing

a mirror of the transformation which Miacis was.

"I only have gold bullets", said Angle-face, "you said if we got any interference tonight that it would be from the avians".

"Then shoot Lassiter! We don't need any witnesses to this", said Miacis who had now nearly completed his transformation into a wolf twice the size of any specimen which one would find in nature.

Before Lassiter could react Angle-face shot him in the chest with two slugs which though meant for a very particular kind of target could be used to dispatch a regular human just as effectively.

Angela had managed to use her forepaws to get the object into her mouth. She knew Miacis would be complete in transformation in short order and so as soon as she had secured her cargo hopped with her swiftest speed back out the broken picture window.

It only took Miacis another ten seconds to complete his transformation, but it bought Angela a lead. Normally a Lepus could outrun a Lycanthrope with ease, but Miacis was a clade alpha and swifter and stronger than even most other lycanthropes. She knew her best advantage was to try to stick to the ground on her way to the sanctuary.

Raging determination filled Miacis as he pursued Angela, for the artifact which the girl had taken from him was the last one need to complete his master work.

"Angela, you wretched little impure thing, I could've made your death quick, but now my pack and I are going to feast on your bones. You little rabbit bitch, I'm not sure if I'll eat you as you are, or beat you until you're back in human form so we can have some real fun", said Miacis.

Miacis grew closer to Angela with every second. He was now directly behind her and she had to plan each jump so that her hind paws didn't end up in his powerful jaw.

As the level of the ground evened out she could see on the perimeter a second wolf, and a human figure.

"To the left, Angie, move to the left", said the second wolf.

Angela did as she was told, but Miacis had heard the instruction as well. He was able to get the upper portion of one of her legs into his mouth, but before he could do anything other than damage flesh the second wolf was on top of him, forcing him to release Angela's leg.

The two wolves rolled slowly downhill in combat, each trying to get a grip on the other's throat.

"Jude, you sickening traitor, still helping these aberrations instead of your own kind", said Miacis as he concentrated and shifted his hip structure slightly back into a primate configuration so he could stand over the second lycanthrope bipedally.

Jude bit at the alpha wolf's leg since he could not match Miacis's skill of the mingling of wolf and human anatomical features at will which elder lycanthropes mastered over the centuries.

"The other wolves may not have an idea what you really intend to do, Miacis, but I do. Without the last artifact you can't hope to succeed", Jude said.

Miacis had now managed to reform opposable thumbs on his front paws and grabbed around Jude's neck, bringing the younger wolf's jugular closer to his own jaw. Angle-face had finally caught up with Miacis and paused for a moment as he arrived on the scene, momentarily unsure what to do.

Even as he struggled with Jude, Miacis addressed his inferior, "The relic, shit for brains, go after it. I can handle this pup".

The wolf form Angle-face approached the bleeding naked white haired girl, who was applying pressure to the wound on her thigh after having resumed human form. She clutched the relic in her right hand.

"Hello bunny, you look much prettier this way", said Angle-Wolf.

The second human figure who had stood on the top of the ridge with Jude aimed point-blank and hit Angle-face in the chest. The man then walked over to Angela.

"Daniel", she said, "take this thing. Get to the sanctuary".

"I'm not leaving the two of you", said Daniel.

"Yes you are", said Angela "but you're leaving me your gun".

Daniel complied. They exchanged the relic for the firearm, and Daniel clenched the small stony object in his teeth as he ran to the top of the ridge.

Miacis noticed this, and gave up on the already wounded Jude to chase Daniel.

Daniel would have to be fully transformed in order to take flight. He had already begun to shift but this cost him ground speed against Miacis who had a clear advantage over the avian, at least on land.

In order to reach maximum speed Miacis assumed full wolf

form, and was nearly on Daniel when the Eagle-man had changed enough to his other form to risk a jump. Miacis coiled himself as much as possible to try to get a burst into the air.

Angela couldn't get a clear shot at his heart, so she aimed into the area below Miacis's shoulder blades. Just as Daniel took to a true flight, a shot hit Miacis in the spine, and he fell over the edge of the ridge. Anything short of a hard shot would not prove lethal to a lycanthrope of Miacis power, but it would allow Jude and Angela to get home.

The girl limped over to Jude who had not changed fully back to human form. She managed to wake him, and help him to his feet. He then caught her, as the wound on her upper leg limited her ability to walk.

"We better get the hell out of here", said Jude, "even a shot and a fall like that might not hold him til morning".

"I know", said Angela, "he won't try and attack for the next few days. It's the new moon tomorrow night. Between that and his wounds he won't be able to heal easily. I saw that he had lights set up on the road leading to the main house".

"That means he'll be getting guests Angie", said Jude.

"Guests? What do you mean?", the girl asked.

"Humans", said Jude, "without trying to sound too Gothic horror here he's going to need a good old-fashioned human sacrifice to accomplish what he means to".

"We need to stop him", said Angela.

"For now we better get home", said Jude "Miacis will be up and around by morning, which means we have a little time to sleep before we run interference on his plan".

Jude re-dressed in the clothing he had removed before shape-shifting while Angela took Daniel's trench coat to cover up her modesty. They made their way slowly back to the sanctuary, and the protection of Rowena Shema's shamanic workings which kept its location hidden from Miacis and his men.

Lindsay was proud that she managed to get all her luggage for the weekend down to two bags. She had opened and re-closed both pieces multiple times to make sure everything she might need was in there. Each time she told herself she would not reopen either bag, and then ritually rechecked everything an additional time.

Now there was one more OCD habit she would engage in.

She reset her cell phone so that the caller ID would be restricted, and tried dialing David again. She'd been the one who said they needed time apart, but when she tried calling him the day before someone with a young sounding and sickeningly melodious female voice answered his phone with the words ' *This is the residence of David Maier. Who beckons for him please?*',

She suddenly missed her geeky and goofy but sweet and loving knight in shining armor who had literally shown up at her home on the back of a Dragon. When she contrasted the fantastic world David lived in that she had sometimes witnessed and participated in first-hand, with the mandatory corporate retreat she was about to go on, she suddenly wondered if the world of the fantastical wasn't more appealing than the world of nonprofit fundraising.

The same voicemail which David had when she met him picked up. A piece of music which David had recorded by holding his cell phone up to a speaker played followed by David's voice.

"You reached the voicemail of David Maier. I'm not available. Obviously, or you'd be speaking to me and not a recording. Leave me a voicemail then hang up when you're done. Okay. Thank you", said the voicemail message.

Lindsay hung up before the recording portion of the call session began. David's voicemail message was so awkwardly functional, yet so sweet in a way.

She checked her watch again, and realized it was at least 45 minutes until Ruth would be picking her up. She wished she could be on the road now. At least the forced conversation with her co-workers would stop her relationship, or the lack thereof, with David from playing over and over again in her head.

An incomplete and hollow digital rendition of Funky Town began to play and Lindsay realized her cell phone was ringing. She picked it up.

The area code was northeastern Pennsylvania, not Philadelphia. It wasn't David but she knew who it was, and he might mention something about the good Mr. Maier. She couldn't asked directly though.

"Hello? , said Lindsay.

"Hello, my dear", said the voice of Jesse Perfect. Jesse's voice with its wise and paternal tone, yet loving and gentle rhythm could calm anyone. That was why despite the fact that Lindsay had first met Jesse when David brought him to her house along with a demigod, an incident which had been the first wedge between David and Lindsay, Jesse Perfect nonetheless quickly become a surrogate grandfather to Lindsay and they had remained in regular communication.

"Jesse!", she said with genuine excitement "How are you? Your voice sounds clearer. Is that bronchitis gone yet?"

"Oh, I'm feeling much better", he said, "For a man my age. How are you doing girl?"

"I'm going on vacation", she said, "but not with David".

"I'm afraid I know that my dear", he said "David is occupied with something at the moment".

"Something important no doubt", said Lindsay.

"Yes, my dear", he said "but things can be important without them involving saving the world. Speaking of which , where are you going on your trip?".

"My company is sending us up to British Columbia, on one of those Magical Menagerie retreats you see on TV. Personally all that weird trust exercise, finding your inner spirit animal stuff hits a little too close to... you know", said Lindsay.

"I hope you're not going to say David", said Jesse, "I know you two were taking a little breather, but I still think you make a damn fine couple".

"Thanks Jesse", said Lindsay "but I wasn't going to say too close to David. I was going to say the whole thing rings a little bit too much like Mother Ava. Speaking of which Dolly Leon, the girl that everybody thinks threw up on Tina Griggs because of that mind wipe dealy-o, was supposed going to be on this thing, but the poor girls been in therapy for a year because of it and hasn't come back to work. Still, it was nice of David get that buddy of his to throw in at least a few little tidbits to their spell so the world wouldn't remember me as the one who threw up on the GIA show".

"That was me actually", chuckled Jesse, "don't they hold those retreat things in the Caerleon Mountains?"

"Yeah, they do. Why?", asked Lindsay.

"I hear they're supposed to be haunted is all. And with David away what will you do if something that goes bump in the night comes your way?", asked Jesse.

"Why call you of course", said Lindsay.

"I'm retired", said Jesse.

Strange sensations took Lindsay over and her subconscious directly commanded her vocal cords.

"You won't be for long", said Lindsay.

"Why do you say that?", asked Jesse.

Lindsay shook it off.

"I don't know. I honestly don't. It just came out. Anyway, Jesse I'll be fine".

"You need to get going don't you?", asked Jesse.

"Yes", said Lindsay.

"Okay, two promises", said Jesse.

"Yes, Jesse, in the unlikely event on my calm relaxing corporate retreat that something supernatural or otherworldly does happen I will call you or David", said Lindsay.

"That's not what I was going to ask you to promise" said Jesse, "the first promise is that as far from a real vacation as this crazy thing you're going on in is, you will still try to relax and enjoy yourself. And the second promise is that you'll call David when you get back".

"I can't promise either of those things, Jesse", said Lindsay.

"Well, just try pretty girl. Alright let me let you go", said Jesse.

"Bye, Jesse", said Lindsay, "I'll talk to you soon".

"Not if I talk to you first", said Jesse and then he let out a loud belly laugh.

Lindsay hung up the phone and couldn't help but smile as the old man's aura seemed to radiate all the way from Pennsylvania to Georgia. More time seemed to pass than she thought and so she went on the front porch to wait for Ruth.

Ruth pulled up about 15 minutes later, and the old woman had her eternal blissfully ignorant smile on. She did not however get out of the car and offer to help Lindsay with her bags. Lindsay loaded her luggage into the back of the car and got in the passenger seat.

Even before Ruth spoke, Lindsay noticed that Ruth wore her ugly yellow ring with a hideously cloudy yellow diamond as its centerpiece stone. The ring always freaked Lindsay out. Just as Ruth had been one of the first people in the office on the Mother Ava bandwagon, and now the stupid Magical Menagerie thing, Ruth had similarly become entranced with the idea of something called a Life Diamond when her father passed away. This was a new fad in which the dear departed's ashes would be condensed into a synthetic carbon diamond after cremation, which could then be worn by the bereaved. Ruth proudly told the story of how the rest of her family had meant to block the idea after her father's long and protracted battle with prostate cancer. They had rushed his body quickly into a conventional embalming and burial before Ruth could make the arrangements with the life diamond people. Ruth however, always the determined woman, managed to convince the oncologists who had attended dear old dad to provide her with the carcinogenic prostate itself, which the folks at the life diamond place were all too happy to make into a stone so that Ruth would always have a piece of dad with her, albeit in a lower carat diamond that she might have wished.

Still, that damned yellow ring always creeped Lindsay out because she knew it used to be a cancerous written prostate, worn by the daughter of the man to whom the prostate had belonged.

"We have some time, girlfriend. Wanna stop for lunch?", asked Ruth.

"No", said Lindsay, "I already ate".

Lindsay thought to herself that Ruth drove what must've been the boxiest car ever. Somewhere a mathematician had found the formula which allowed a cube to have right angles that were more right angle-ish than 90°. This seemingly impossible exception to Euclidean geometry was allowed by the fates just so that Ruth would annoy Lindsay all the more. On one occasion when leaving work in the summer when the sun was still high enough in the sky to illuminate the parking lot, Lindsay made sure to purposely check the boxy Ruth-mobile for a manufacturing brand-name. All cars had them. Lindsay jokingly thought to herself that Ruth's would somehow not. The lime green backend of the car bore no markings, names, or branding

Ruth essentially served as nothing more than a communication node between Lindsay and the staff out on the floor. Traveling much as she did, and spending a great deal of time out of the office on client meetings to solicit donations from corporations for nonprofit entities, or to set up charity events at which the wealthy spent more on their own clothing and dinner plates for the evening than they did on whatever charity the event was intended to support, Lindsay had little time to communicate with the men and women at the office. Ruth's purpose was to serve as a relay. Somewhere, in the classified human resource files, Ruth was also the office gossip, and bringer and introducer of all things nifty. During a leave of absence for her knee surgery, Lindsay had Ruth to thank for sending her the Mother Ava chocolate in the first place.

Sharing a drive to the airport with Ruth was bad enough. Lindsay had a plan to ensure that she wasn't also seatmates with Ruth on the plane.

"I hear this Andre Miacis helps you find your inner spirit animal or something", said Ruth, "and I've seen him in magazine advertisements. He's pretty easy on the eyes".

"I'm just going on this thing because it's pretty much mandatory", said Lindsay.

Six persons from the office had been chosen to go on the Magical Menagerie retreat up to Canada. Lindsay and Ruth, along with Dana a hard-working secretary who could've run the place if senior management had been willing to look past her GED and her weight problem, Simon Von Peterson, CFO and head of accounting, Janet Heacock from human resources, and Shannon Robbins, the overweight and malodorous sister-in-law of the CEO, who no one ever saw in the office and never seemed to do anything, yet still got a salary and full benefits.

Lindsay's only hope for any fun this weekend was to be able to sneak away with Dana here and there for no other purpose than to be able to make fun of their coworkers, make fun of this stupid New Age corporate retreat bullshit, and to make fun of their coworkers for falling for this stupid New Age corporate retreat bullshit.

"You should have some fun while you can, Lindsay", said Ruth, "It's only going to be us, Andre Miacis, and his immediate staff. And you know sweetie, you're the only one of us who looks at all decent in a cocktail dress. Maybe you can get laid. You're not still dating that writer or UFO hunter guy are you?"

"His name is David, Ruth, and no, we're on a hiatus", said Lindsay, "and he's not a UFO hunter, he's an expert on cults".

"He wasn't nice to me at the company picnic, Lindsay. I'm an extremely forgiving woman, but I only give people one chance", said Ruth.

Lindsay internally wanted to strangle Ruth for the stupid contradictory statement she had just made, but instead chose to focus on defending David who had been rather aloof to Ruth at the company picnic, due to Ruth's initial statement to David upon meeting him and shaking his hand.

"Your very first words to the man were 'are you a vampire?'. I mean, did you really think he was a vampire? Do you think that would be something funny to say to someone who for all you knew was the significant other of your immediate supervisor?", asked Lindsay.

Ruth squirmed slightly in the driver's seat. Lindsay rarely confronted Ruth, and the other woman seemed thrown off by it, if not downright offended.

"I feel as if you were just talking down to me there. I'm sorry Lindsay but I'm not going to sit with you on the plane".

Lindsay reacted calmly to the statement, but inside was jumping up and down for joy.

"Well, we're here", said Ruth as they arrived at the airport, "do you think it will be alright to leave my Roper parked here the whole time we're gone?"

"Your what?", asked Lindsay.

"My Roper. My car.", said Ruth, "I call my car Roper after Mr. Roper from *Three's Company*".

Lindsay preferred not to think about why Ruth felt the need to name her box shaped car after Norman Fell's character from *Three's Company.*

She sat with Dana on the plane. Lindsay was blessed with being one of those people who could actually sleep on a flight. She woke up somewhere over the Great Lakes and found Dana too had fallen into sleep. An old copy of People Magazine was available in the seat pocket in front of her, but as Tina Griggs was on the cover, she opted to read the only other material available to her. She picked up a brochure for Magical Menagerie. It featured Andre Miacis on the cover.

She hated to admit it, but he was attractive. He was obviously a man in his early fifties, but with a nearly perfect physique and face that were the result of good genes, clean living, and rigid care with diet and exercise. She could tell as she studied him Miacis was a man who had earned his good looks, and had not been given them by a surgeon.

She rubbed her eyes slightly, and began to get a feeling she had had once before in her life, one year ago in her kitchen. She checked the front pocket beneath the seatback tray in front of her.

No evil chocolate.

She ignored the feeling, a feeling of information from an exterior and unknowable source entering into her mind, and fell into sleep.

Dream images seeped through her cortex. Understandable ones came first. David. Jesse. Ruth. The office. Andre Miacis.

A wolf was walking alone in the forest. He lead a pack, but as the procession of animals followed him, it was clear he was not followed only by wolves. Bears, hawks, snakes, and a veritable menagerie emerged. They marched through a primeval forest that while the product of REM sleep seemed more concrete than waking life.

Slowly, a second wolf joined them. His fur looked wrong, like strands of black leather; Like a uniform woven into a beast's pelt; disturbing not for what was animal in it, but disturbing for an indescribable stench it carried in its imagery. For in dreams the senses may interweave and cross even with the conceptual; and this stench was a stench of the war of terrible organization that only homo sapiens can make.

The errant wolf gathered others around him and began attacking the other creatures with the aid of his own troops at first, and then he began to attack both the secondary wolves, other animals, and the wolves who had been his own followers.

The main wolf stood on his back haunches and looked at the

moon. He seemed to laugh. His eyes now changed . They seemed to become reptilian, and his front paws became for all the world like squid tentacles. Other features began to enter his physiology that seemed ancient, Cambrian, and deadly. Some of them arthropodian and others not even knowable.

But the most terrifying thing that came was the voice.

"*I will steal all of evolution in my sack, and swat the world with its weight*".

The voice was horrible because it was human. Humanity in this dreamscape was the horror in the heart of beast.

It was the voice of Andre Miacis.

Lindsay knew that there were things in the world like dragons, and gods, and ONLAs and evil Chocolate Victorian Spiritualists. She didn't need much prompting to assume the dream was a warning.

She had already written a text message to Jesse describing the dream in detail, and hit 'send' to transmit it to Jesse as soon as she had landed. The text ended with 'if you send me help... don't send 'D'.

Jesse corresponded with her to inquire how she was, and said he would get back to her as soon as possible, but by the time Lindsay and her co-workers had reached the location of Miacis's retreat area, she had no cellphone signal.

Jesse Perfect walked down the hall to Nellie Gaspereaux's room. Nellie was taking tea at the time he visited her.

He knew the 90 something Haitian widow was sweet on him

and while she did not know everything there was to Jesse Perfect, she knew he was no ordinary man.

Jesse hoped Nellie could enter a trance, and contact the spirits of the Voudun underworld, the Ghede. He hoped they would in turn send a message to Ethan Rhys-Davies. He thought it very likely he might need help for Lindsay and in very short order, and Ethan and Ilitu were his best hope.

"Good evening, Nellie", he said.

"Hello, Jesse", she smiled, "Would you like a cup of tea?".

"Yes", Jesse said.

"You have come to ask me something. Or rather, ask the Lwa Gehde?", she said.

"Yes", Jesse said, "A being... one whom the Lwa call the Immutable One... The Ghede Lwa are never far from him in these days. I need to reach him. I normally can take my time to reach out to him by normal means, the post... the telephone... but that takes weeks... I need the Ghede to tell him to reach me".

Nellie smiled...

"I have just the tool you need", she said as she turned her swivel chair around to fetch something, "Maman Brigitte is speaking to me.. and she says...".

Nellie produced a small notebook computer which she handed to Jesse.

"Ethan and Ilitu are on Skoop right now", said Nellie.

The drive from the airport was nerve-racking. Lindsay managed to drive in the second rental car with Shannon and at least avoid Ruth.

She unpacked in her room nervously, and fiddled with her cellphone, no signal and no word from Jesse.

She returned to the reception area to meet the others as the program brochure, which had been given to them by a crescent faced man on arrival, instructed them that Andre Miacis would have a brief audience with them on their first night.

She found Ruth, Simon, Shannon, Janet, and Dana were already enjoying food and drink. She saw they were mostly eating entrees of some kind of game meats. She sat down.

"What can I get you ma'am?", asked the Crescent Faced Man, "This will be your only opportunity for alcohol, if you want it. Your friends are all having game which Mr. Miacis caught himself... I can get you quail, rabbit, rattlesnake or just about any dish you can ask for, even vegetarian, we can likely prepare".

"I'm being a bad vegan", said Dana, "I smelled what Ruth was eating, and I found myself craving meat for the first time in years".

"I'm not hungry", said Lindsay... "I... I take a medication and can't eat for a few hours".

The Crescent Faced Man grew angry for a moment and then smiled.

"Very well", he said, "Mr. Miacis will be with you shortly", now addressing the entire group.

"Woo", said Ruth as she sidled next to Lindsay, apparently having forgotten their earlier altercation.

"I am getting tipsy, girlfriend", said Ruth, "Linds... Lindsay... I don't want to lose Daddy... the Life Diamond", she said taking it off her fingers, "Will... will you keep it for me?"

"Fine", said Lindsay taking it because she just wanted to shut Ruth up.

Andre Miacis, recognizable from the many magazine covers he graced, entered looking more dressed up when he was dressed down than most people do in their Sunday best.

"Ladies and gentleman", he said, "Welcome to Magical Menagerie. I see many of you here enjoying the game meats. I hunted them myself. There are lots of programs that teach you how to be on the top of the corporate world. Lots of them that teach you how to be a predator. Some teach you to be a shark or a wolf... but only mine teaches you to be the entire animal kingdom... or... the important part at least..."

Miacis smiled.

"I truly apologize but before we begin our weekend, I have one little piece of business to attend to. So I am going to ask you to watch one of my DVD's, just as you eat. This is going to be the last time you get anything but personal hands-on attention from me, I promise".

Miacis exited and somewhere unseen Crescent Face started the video up. Video Miacis took the place of Live Miacis and started speaking.

Lindsay watched the video nervously and began to knead the Life Diamond, made from the ashes of a cancer ridden organ of Ruth's deceased father, as if it was a worry stone.

She dropped it, and the damn thing rolled farther than it should have. It rolled into the hallway.

Lindsay quietly excused herself to retrieve the ring with the Life Diamond. But the Giant Rabbit had taken it in its mouth and was hopping down the hall.

Only a nanosecond later did Lindsay realize there was something very wrong with a Giant Rabbit being there, and much less with it wanting the Life Diamond.

"Damn it, Mr. Bunny", she said and she followed it down the hall. She assumed it was some hormone fed thing Miacis kept around to turn into dinner.

She followed it to a library type of room, where it spit out the Life Diamond and she picked it up.

"Bad, Mr. Bunny, bad!", she said.

She looked up. The walls of this room were coated with prints of photos of ancient walls with glyphs on them and symbols that appeared to have been hand drawn on canvas paper. The glyphs and symbols were ones she had never seen before. It is true Lindsay Barrow was no historian, symbologist, occultist, or linguist, but she did have a nearly eidetic memory and she had read alot of David's books. Those books had alot of symbols, and these symbols were nothing like any of the symbols in any of those books.

Lindsay had a feeling if she had seen the symbols in the books before, that would have been bad. The fact that she hadn't encountered them, she felt was worse.

Her compulsion to do something with her hands when nervous, which caused her to rub the Life Diamond earlier now caused her to subconsciously begin petting Mr. Bunny.

"This Ted Nugent and Tony Robbins hybrid is into some weird shit, Mr. Bunny", she said to the rabbit, "We're talking chocolate level evil here".

She looked down, and she was petting not a giant rabbit, but a naked white-haired girl.

"I am not a Mister", said the girl, "But the petting was nice".

"What the fuck...?", said Lindsay.

A wolf had walked into the room, and in front of her it changed into a tall, skinny, long haired and very handsome man of Mediterranean cast.

"Do not be alarmed", said the man, "My name is Jude... My friend Angela and I are otherkin... we battle the Overkind... This all must seem very strange, but if you will...".

"Otherkin... Shapeshifters... got it", said Lindsay interrupting, "You're the good guys, the Overkind are bad guys, I am guessing Miacis is head of the Overkind, my co-workers are probably dead or in danger... and you want me to come with you".

Angela and Jude were a bit dumbfounded that Lindsay had made these leaps of deduction and faith.

Lindsay picked up on this and offered them an explanation for being up to speed so quickly.

"Ok, one, I have dreams... weird dreams... they tell me

things... two, I dated a guy in the ONLA... and three, before that, I played a lot of RPG video games while I was recovering from knee surgery... Skyrim... Portal... Spider's Frontier, etc... and the way you were talking Little Mister", she said pointing to Jude, "Is the way non-playable allies who offer lots of pre-quest exposition talk".

Lindsay took a few photos with her camera phone of the images strewn on the wall.

"Let's go, boys and girls", she said.

In the other room Crescent Face flipped the lights back on.

Lindsay's co-workers had all passed out from the drugged food.

"Excellent", said Miacis taking two nails and indicating to Crescent Face to lie down on the floor...

"Five live humans... four relics... one more human to lead you to the Sanctuary where the Otherkin have my fifth relic", said Miacis.

"But fine werewolf as you are", he said, "I need more than a werewolf, so although I will skip the step with myself", he said taking a hammer, "With you, I start with a blank canvas... spread your arms please...".

He drove the nails into Crescent Face's palms.

"The cure for lycanthropy", said Miacis, "Eludes so many because it is so damned simple...".

"Normally to start a new therianthropic line", said Miacis, "Requires years of spellcraft. But, this close to the Alignment of I'xswah'korg, a few glyphs", he said anointing the now human Crescent Face with symbols he drew with a simple marker.

"And a sample of the animal one wishes to use as the infusion", said Miacis grabbing a fossil... "It's child's play... Of course my transformation will be... a bit more complex... but, more glorious. Yours will do for the job more immediately at hand"

Lindsay stood in the cavern that Jude and Angela had led her to. She was surprised to find it equipped with electric light powered by gas generators, water purifiers, and rudimentary but modern technology.

Lindsay pointed to the bear who then became a heavy-set shaven headed man.

"Nico... bear", said Lindsay.

"Rowena, snake", she said pointing to the African beauty who was in human form.

"Jude... classic werewolf... Angela, Mr. Bunny and... Daniel... is Biiiirrrd-Maaaaan", Lindsay concluded.

The otherkin did not like her joke.

Rowena spoke.

"Yes", she said, "You know all our names and our other forms".

"And Miacis?", she asked.

"A werewolf", said Daniel, "Thousands of years ago there

were all kinds of otherkin. We lived in harmony with eachother and humans. With the coming of the time of the one God, we hid from humans, but the real problem started when Miacis was inspired by the human world. He admired human leaders like Stalin, Hitler, Mussolini, Bush".

"About 100 years ago he began to preach to werewolves that they were superior to all other otherkin", Jude said, "Most of us were disgusted by him, but some werewolves, as in any group, can be swayed by the ideas of racial superiority and a charismatic leader. Miacis founded the Overkind, a group of werewolves dedicated to wiping out all non-wolf shapeshifters and wiping out any werewolves who don't follow the party line".

"My people and I have been his main opponents", said Rowena, "It's been a ground war in human terms but now I fear Miacis intends to escalate it to the level of the atomic bomb, so to speak, and involve humanity".

"What exactly is he up to?", asked Lindsay.

"We don't know", said Rowena, "We do know he has been collecting fossils of rare creatures, and we do know the alignment of I'xswah'korg is approaching".

"The what?", asked Lindsay.

"Besides being born an otherkin, or bitten, a human can seek to become an otherkin on his or her own through means of shamanic ritual. This is how a new line... Werewolf, Weresnake, Werebear begins... how we came to be. I myself started as human and became a Skin Snake 1500 years ago. I'xswah'korg was a shaman who never had the courage to transform himself, but he would aid others in changing themselves. He lived thousands of years ago in the wilderness. You see, he feared the beast within himself even as a man, and could not allow himself to have a powerful animal body. Despite folklore, only our body changes when we shapeshift. Our mind does not become any more or less primitive, aggressive, saintly, or solemn than it is when we are in our human forms. I'xswah'korg discovered an alignment of stars that occurs only every 3500 years. During this time, the ability to create a new otherkin line can be done in minutes, or seconds by a skilled sorcerer, as opposed to years or decades at times other than the Alignment", Rowena concluded.

"So he is planning a big show for this alignment?", Lindsay asked.

"Yes", said Crescent Face as he entered the compound, "But for that Mr. Miacis will need his property returned".

"One wolf against us all", said Daniel, "Miacis is a fool".

"Wolf?", laughed Crescent Face, "I've gone old school".

The intruder began to change. He grew two, four, six, eight, a dozen more limbs. His body increased in size until he was at least 15 feet long. His skin formed a hard shell which only land dwelling invertebrates possessed and he had now taken the form of a gigantic centipede-like creature.

The front part of his body reared up for an attack.

"How?", asked Daniel, "Otherkin are only vertebrates".

"They don't have to be", said Rowena, "Not if Miacis has drawn the essence of a centipede to make a new line. But he still should only be the size of his human form".

The group backed away slowly. The creature could not move quickly, but it didn't need to. It had plugged the entrance to the cave. The centipede grew closer.

Nico took his bear form.

"How do we kill it?", asked Daniel.

"How about explosives?", asked Lindsay.

"Massive damage to all body systems can kill us, but we have no explosives", said Rowena, "Mammals can also be killed by smaller wounds by silver bullets or daggers, avains by gold, reptilians by iridium... if you can find iridium...", Rowena said.

"So some kind of metal can kill this guy?", asked Lindsay.

Jude grabbed a tuna can from a garbage bag, and pierced a soft spot on the creature.

"Not aluminum", said Jude, "And I don't have time to go through the rest of the periodic table. I say we try massive damage".

Jude assumed his wolf form, and Nico joined him in a full frontal attack.

The creature gripped the wolf and even the bear in its legs, and threw Nico back several feet. It raised Jude in the air, ready to devour him. Suddenly it dropped him.

It went silent. It dropped him to the ground and vibrated for few minutes.

Suddenly its head burst forth in a torrent of organic gore, and when the spray settled, a woman in a long black trenchcoat, a shaven head, and wings came out.

She looked at the assembled group.

"I am looking for Lindsay Barrow", she said, "Jesse Perfect sent me".

"You must be... Ilitu", Lindsay said.

"You have wings but the rest of you is human", Daniel said, "Only master otherkin like Rowena and Miacis can partially shapeshift".

"She's not an otherkin", said Lindsay, "She's... a goddess... succubus... original template of the human race... thingy... right?".

"Succubi are just myths, right?", said Jude to Daniel.

"Seriously?", asked Daniel with a raised eyebrow,

"Close enough", said Ilitu, "I assume Maier applied these words to me."

Lindsay remained silent...

"Is there a way I can shower here and does someone have a mobile phone with a data connection?", asked Ilitu.

"Phones don't work out here", said Lindsay.

"Mine does", said Daniel.

"Is it a magick otherkin phone that gets good reception?", asked Lindsay.

"Even better", said Daniel, "It's an Android".

He tossed the phone to Ilitu who was already beginning to

undress.

"I am going to make a private call. Barrow, come with me. Let me know what's transpired thus far", said Ilitu.

All the information was relayed to Ilitu and using Daniel's phone the jpegs Lindsay had taken of the glyphs were sent somewhere. Ilitu then spent about fifteen minutes talking with someone.

Ilitu explained a friend of hers who knew about these things was going to be on the line on speakerphone.

A British male spoke:

"Miacis is going to use the Alignment tonight to make himself a chimera otherkin. In other words he will absorb the qualities of animals in addition to the wolf and I suspect he collected fossils to draw on the most deadly creatures in the biological record. Five specifically for a total of six, as he already has wolf. Which ones I don't know. This alone will make him incredibly powerful and of course invulnerable to anything but massive destruction. Hybrid otherkin have occurred before, a werewolfhog in Germany. The wolf and hog powers didn't add together... they multiplied... Fortunately, both werehogs and werewolves are killed by silver. In Babylon a weresnakelion occurred. Neither silver, or iridium, or both together could kill it. It seems cross category otherkin when combining animal classes of two different metal vulnerabilities, rather than develop a vulnerability to both, they develop an invulnerability. It had to be put down by massive damage from an entire army... and that was two animals... this will be six animal spirit skins... each raising his power... like adding a zero onto an already large number... and the secondary abilities are even deadlier".

"Secondary abilities?", asked Lindsay.

"All otherkin have secondary abilities... Daniel can hypnotize... Jude can seduce... Nico can heal the mind... Angela can heal the flesh...", said Rowena, "I can read minds".

"*Precisely*", said the man on the telephone, " *We do not know what secondary abilities each new animal energy Miacis absorbs will give him, just that they will be ancient powers, and each will multiply the power of the others. If he succeeds, I doubt there will be anything on a grand enough scale to kill him from sheer damage, and otherkin take millennia to age*".

"But we have the fifth fossil", said Lindsay as she opened the box and saw what looked like a reptile skull of some kind.

"Even four new powers is bad enough", said Rowena, "We stop him now".

"She's right my love", said Ilitu to the man on the phone, "We have to leave now. Our best chance is to stop him before he augments himself. Is there anything else?"

" *Several of the glyphs and symbols do not relate to the Chimera process. They are most likely ancillary precautions he has taken of a magickal nature. And others are Old High Atlantean. He may have surprises of a non-magickal nature for you as well*".

Ilitu hung up on the man unceremoniously after a silent period let her know he was done speaking.

"Let's"... Ilitu started to speak as Rowena's eyes caught her gaze and Ilitu stopped speaking abruptly.

"Let's move", said Rowena.

"Too bad one of you doesn't become a horse", said Lindsay even as Ilitu lifted her in the air. Rowena remained in human form and Daniel grabbed her in his massive talons. The others shape shifted to travel by ground at the best speed they could.

When they arrived, night had fallen. Lindsay's co-workers were each tied to a pillar which held a bowl behind it. The one Ruth sat in front of was empty. The other bowls were all filled with some kind of fossil remains.

"What is he doing with them?", asked Lindsay.

"One does not need another's life force to become an otherkin but legend says for an otherkin to become a hybrid another's life is needed", Rowena answered.

"And to become a chimera", said Miacis walking with complete calm into the circle formed by the pillars, "I need five life forces. Thankfully, the alignment has started, so I do not need to give up my lycanthropy".

Simon began to groan by his pillar and decayed in seconds into a dried husk of skin and bone.

Lindsay ran over to try to help him, and Miacis hit some kind of button.

"Ms. Barrow, I deduce you carry my last fossil. Since you will not be fighting me directly and as such, I cannot take it from you in combat be so kind and drop it in the empty bowl", Miacis said as he assumed his wolf shape.

Jude also became a wolf and charged him. Miacis shifted into a half-man/half-wolf form, and stood over Jude. Nico as a bear also charged, as Miacis grew huge, powerful, muscled tentacles with toothy arms on them. The two smaller werebeasts found themselves restrained by these new appendages.

"How Lovecraftian!", said Miacis as his mass increased, "The Giant Squid beak is kicking in...".

Lindsay was most unnerved by how the beast whose eyes had grown huge still spoke with a human voice, and at that a calm and golden throated one.

Next Shannon withered like Simon had, as Miacis's skin took on Reptillian tones and his mass increased as if Nico and Jude were toys to him. His eyes looked alien now... wolf, squid, and dinosaur all in one...

Rowena shifted into a massive snake and actually managed to coil around the lower third of Miacis.

Ilitu flew in and back out quickly, but not before getting a preternaturally powerful hit in on Miacis's skull. Bone cracked.

"What are you?", said Miacis, "Oh, yes. You stood up to Yahweh, so I must be nothing to you. Yes, Ilitu of Is, I read minds. It seems a dinosaur is even better than an Reptilian, and I am willing to bet better at hypnosis than an Avian... but...".

He swatted Ilitu to the ground with an unidentifiable limb and cast off Rowena. Stone structure grew around Ilitu and Rowena.

"Transmutation of matter", said Miacis, " Not sure how I am getting that from the squid... but... hey... I'll take it".

As the stars moved the pillars and bowls were activating in sequence. Dana decayed next and Miacis now grew to the size of a building as a huge Scorpion tail grew from him, and he became armored and shelled.

Daniel flew over to Lindsay, or tried to. He hit some kind of energy wall. Lindsay tried to remember any incantation she could that might dispel the energy barrier it seemed Miacis had set up. She also noticed the bowls were draining from right to left sequence.

She tried to pull the fossil out of Janet's bowl but a smaller energy wall stopped that.

Daniel got up and fell over in pain, now back in his human form.

"Power of the Werescorpion it seems", said the behemoth that was Miacis, "Is to kill at a distance without contact".

Daniel was the maiden voyage for this new horrible ability Miacis had just discovered.

"Oh bother", said Miacis as something shark-like entered his tooth shape. When the additional properties the Megalodon shark fossil would gift to Miacis's brew had completed their entry to the mix, Miacis was now a collection of biological oddities not even an illustration from a Bestiary could hope do justice to. His former Lovecraft joke made a few moments ago during the onset of his transformation seemed even more appropriate, as his mass reared up to a size that blotted the stars from the sky.

He suddenly shifted into his normal human form and transmuted leaves and other items around him into a suit.

He held Ilitu and the Otherkin down with stone structures he formed around them.

Lindsay finally remembered an incantation about bringing down barriers she read in one of David's books. Her nearly eidetic memory could recall anything almost instantly, but she still needed time to process and correlate her memory's contents. She saw the words in her mind and tried to recite it.

Angela began healing Daniel from the psychic poisoning, as from her current position, even restrained, she was able to reach one hand out to him.

"Don't bother with the incantations Lindsay", said Miacis, "I study history. Anytime a great being is about to become greater, a swarm of interlopers gathers around him and he is undone by something clever. The Cosmos does love the clever, does it not? I knew magick users would be here tonight. The barrier's not magickal. It's a force field. Something reverse engineered from alien-tech or pre-human tech. I own a lot of it and thanks to the efficiency of my new brain structures I can use it now and understand it. Ironically adding animal energy to oneself makes one a better thinker. All the power I have demonsrated tonight is just the gifts of being a chimera. Think what happens when I add all that technology".

"And all that magick..." Miacis continued.

"You are a disease, Miacis", cried Rowena.

"Magick?", asked Lindsay as Rowena's words gave her an idea, "What magick?"

"I don't need two T-Rex fossils", laughed Miacis, "The reptile skull you have is a dragon. It's hard to come by dragon fossils. They shifted off this plane you know and when they were physical their remains would tend to evaporate. But you know, last year when the physical and astral planes crossed, some collection opportunities came up. I assume that weredragon-hood comes with a mastery of magick, but if I am wrong and the secondary power is something else, I'm sure I still won't be disappointed.

Stone now grew around and secured Angela so she could not continue the healing process on Daniel.

Miacis took down the force field.

"You're a null. Has anyone ever told you that?", asked Miacis, "Otherwise, Lindsay, I could have just compelled you to drop the Dragon skull in the bowl. But... why be showy... I can just take down the force field, and rip it from your hands... even in my human form".

Null. David Maier had taught Lindsay Barrow a few vocabulary words of his trade during pillow talk.

"*I am a null*", thought Lindsay as she went over to the bowl by Ruth and dropped in the Life Diamond, "*He can't read my thoughts*".

Ruth desiccated...

The Life Diamond in place of the Dragon fossil... the Life Diamond which had been made from the compressed carbon of the ashes of Ruth's father's cancer ridden prostate...

Miacis went to speak.

"You know Lindsay, I...", he began to grow puffy, then yellow and in seconds liquesced into a mass of organic sludge...

Lindsay had heard stories of beheaded gods, and trapping witches in hamburger, and killing saints with forgotten magic.

She lived her first epic and it ended with her enemy deflating like a marshmallow in the microwave after the buzzing stops.

Angela had healed Daniel from the poison and he stood back up. In bear form, Nico sniffed the puddle of vanquished foe, and finally spoke a single word in Lindsay's presence.

"Disgusting", he said.

Ilitu walked over to the puddle of hazmatic waste that had been Miacis and extended her hand to Lindsay. Ilitu needed to return immediately to whence she had come from. Lindsay thanked her for her Deus Ex Machina arrival and aid, and Ilitu told Lindsay to say hello to David. Ilitu also said she would contact Jesse so Miacis's remains could be somehow collected as well as the non-human technology Miacis had claimed to be the custodian of.

She thought of Ilitu and Angela and hoped she was done meeting supernatural chics who walk around naked.

The otherkin threw a party of sorts, and Rowena said they would hunt down the remaining wolves loyal to Miacis. Nico gave Lindsay the truest bear hug anyone could give. She said goodbye to the others. Jude and Angela suggested they would like to thank Lindsay in a rather intimate group activity, but, she declined.

Daniel, when he was not a giant bird, and in the sometime form of the thirty something Asian-American that bird became, had a car it seemed. He offered to take Lindsay wherever she wanted to go. A year ago she decided her life was no longer normal, then she decided it was. Now she knew not even she herself was normal. Her old life was gone and half of her accounting department was dead and she could not go to David... at least not yet.

"Feel like a road trip?", she asked Daniel.

"Sure", he said, "Where?".

"An old folks home in Pennsylvania", she answered and sent Jesse a text to expect company.

Micio looked in the mirror, obsessively adjusting his tie. Ever since he had become stuck in mid-transformation, the Werecat did his best to make do with the humanoid cat form he saw in his reflection, and dressing to the nines helped him to feel he was making the best of his current situation.

He sat at his fine oak desk, and took in the natural beauty of the lake behind him. He opened the window slightly and breathed in the spring air.

A knock came at the door to his study.

"Come in", said Micio politely.

Charles entered, and sat on the far side of Micio's desk. It was only then that he noticed Micio had set two plates out for them.

"I didn't know we were doing a lunch meeting", said Charles.

"Duck, wild rice, string beans", Micio said, "And you ate on the airplane, didn't you? Oh well, so..."

"So the ONLA got most of the remains, and all of his personal items", said Charles, "I did recover a little of the goo that used to be Miacis", and with that he placed a container on Micio's desk which was both designed to hold biohazardous material and keep magickal energy from leaking.

"We expected the ONLA would get their hands on almost everything", said Micio.

"There's one more thing", said Charles, "Someone else besides the ONLA got about as much of the remains as I did. He has this tattoo".

Charles slid a printed photo over to Micio who regarded it.

"This is bad Charles", said Micio, "This is someone who works for Guy Germaine".

"We're leaving the lake, aren't we?", asked Charles.

"I am afraid so, old friend", said Micio, "I am afraid so".

MAJOR ARCANA

THE TESTAMENT OF DAVID PART II: THE TESTAMENT OF DAVID

The Hero Font is best used for spacing of logos to be released by the Operator for the benefit of the whole meta-tribe. The mere working of its script teaches the Operator what he or she needs to know to master it.

When David Maier and his unlikely entourage finally arrived in Maitland County, Texas it took a bit of doing to find out exactly where the site of Genesis Land was located. With the scandal surrounding it no one wanted to talk about it. Finally a call from Abe to the ONLA yielded GPS coordinates. It was their plan to get a motel as near as they could, but the closest one was still about an hour and a half away. Apparently Pastor Wally had not taken into consideration convenience for out of town visitors to his Creationist amusement park.

The closest place they could find to do their staging was Tessie's. It was a combination diner, rest stop, and gas station, and it was the only place for 50 miles in either direction. On their way in David accidentally bumped into a man on his way out. They exchanged quick apologies, and the man gave David a look as if he recognized him. David was sure he would have remembered him. He couldn't have been more odd looking, his appearance seemed to be almost intentionally gullible and he could not have looked more opposite from the man with him. The other man was dressed in all black save for his tan cowboy boots. David and Abe's instincts told them that this guy was big trouble. If he wasn't on his way out they might think he was going to rob the place.

After they were seated, they ordered. David also ordered for Dug.

"Dug would likes a western eggy thing", Dug said.

"...And can I get a western omelet?", David said.

"We don't have a western omelet", said the waitress.

"Seriously, we're in Texas and you don't have a western omelet?", Abe asked.

"Yup", she said.

"Dug's is needing a new plan", the Goblin griped.

A local cowboy swaggering out of the diner with his fit young wife caught Abe's eye. It was clear he was drinking them both in. Two locals seated to the rear of the diner used the slam of a coffee cup noisily on their table and a stern scowl to communicate an idea to Abe that roughly would translate to, '*You look like a faggot, a Yankee faggot, and maybe we should kick your ass*'.

But Abraham Seiurd was the master of conveying a complicated idea via a single look. As he walked past them to use the restroom, using his intense eyes and toothy smile to respond, they may have only gotten the gist of '*Yeah, I'm bisexual and from the part of the country that won the Civil War, but I'm here to have breakfast with my friends. Now that you see me standing at my full posture, I think it's kind of obvious we'd all rather I don't take the two seconds out of my day that it would take me to kick both your asses, but I can if you guys insist*.

The intimidated dog-with-a-tail-between-its-legs aura they adopted in response required no interpretation, but the belly laugh of the old man at the counter who raised his coffee cup to Abe probably meant, '*Welcome to Texas, son, we ain't all like them boys, and thank you for putting those two in their place. 'Bout time somebody did*.

Abe's participation in local civics was over and it was back to business when he returned to the table.

"They are bound to have scouts and lookouts, so we are only going to be able to get so close with the van", said Abe pounding his third cup of coffee.

"You're right", agreed David ,"I don't suppose there is any way we can get satellite imagery, so we know how close we can get?".

"No, I had them try that when I checked in yesterday. All the imagery comes back distorted for a two mile radius.", Abe replied.

"Ok. That means we will have to get no closer than three miles to be safe", David said.

"I don't know, David, it's in the desert after all. They might still see us even that far out. Either way I don't like the idea of trudging through the desert for that kind of distance", Abe said.

"I know and no matter what direction we approach from it's the same story. No cover at all. I could use the mists to hide us but it would be a bit obvious. I don't think they get a lot of fog in the desert", David said.

"Maybe you could use the mists as a distraction and we could come in from another direction", Na'da suggested.

"Even if that worked it would still let them know we were coming, and they would probably still see us anyway", David said.

"Hmmm, this is a tough one", Abe replied.

"Yup. Na'da and Dug could just waltz right in past the lookouts and guards, but Yaldabaoth and Tipeshiel would still see them. As well as any sensitives they may have", said David.

"Oh, okay, so maybe we should just get captured then. We might get lucky and get the super villain guided tour", Abe said sarcastically.

"Aw, come on Abe. We're smarter than this. We have got to be able to figure out a way to stealthily get to a place that we will be completely and obviously visible no matter how we approach it", David said.

"Davey", started Dug...

"Dug, whatever it is, more 'eggsies' or a 'cloveses' you want , just, not now", David said tersely rubbing his temples, "Abe and I need to think".

Na'da, who was the only one who could see Dug at the moment looked at Dug as if to say, '*Aren't you going to*

continue? , and Dug's shrugging response might be taken as
' *The man wants me to shut up, so, I'll shut up)*.

Across the desert, in a chamber in the lower reaches of a half-
finished temple and fortress located in the center of the failed
amusement park Genesis Land, Yaldabaoth, the being who
once made a defensible claim to call himself God almighty
from the throne of the seventh Heaven, plotted to restore
himself to power and prepared for the possible arrival of
unwanted guests.

His consciousness still resided in the severed head of Pastor
Wally Nagel. It, or he, rested on a pedestal in his as yet
unfinished combination audience chamber and chapel.
Limited though it was in power, this current form allowed
him to communicate directly with humanity. He spoke with
'The voice of God'. All who heard it knew it to be the voice
of 'the Lord' spoken of in the Bible. He had used this to
amass a great number of followers very quickly. None of the
humans around him, save one, had any idea that
Armageddon had already come and gone, and both the Lord
and the Beast were defeated by forces they did not even
suspect existed.

"Tipeshiel!", bellowed Yaldabaoth.

"Yes, Lord Most High?", answered the last angel as he
entered the room with four people in tow.

The foursome with Tipeshiel were the current heads of
Yaldabaoth's fledgling cult.

First was Dean Aberman, the head of the larger of the two
Militia groups subsumed into the cult. He was originally from
West Virginia where he first started his survivalist militia
group, but moved to Ohio for tax reasons. In truth it was for
tax evasion reasons. The original focus of his organization

was about true American freedom... and guns... and beer. All that changed when an Angel of the Lord appeared to him and showed him a severed head that spoke with the voice of God. He was a tall, stocky man in his mid-forties with an impressive beer gut. He sported gray cargo pants, tan work boots, a tan hunting vest, a gray camouflage T-shirt, and Aviator style glasses. His short cropped hair and well-trimmed beard were the only thing military looking about him.

The next two were Rod Houston and Burt Pike, the respective head and second in command of the smaller of the two militia groups. This second group was from Nebraska, but neither of these two men were its founder. They took over after its founder was killed experimenting with new kinds of explosives while drunk. It was soon after that Rod and Burt decided to move the group to Texas. Rod was an average height, well-built, African American with a slightly smaller beer gut than Dean's. He wore jungle camouflage BDU's and cap, and US issue army boots. He claimed to have been in Vietnam, but was in fact a draft dodger.

Burt, the only one of the three with any real military training, was in Vietnam. He was of average height and scrawny but lean build, and his unkempt hair and soup strainer mustache despite his age was a ruddy brown, almost the color of rust. His build combined with his pale yellowish blotchy skin made him look sickly, despite a relative robustness of constitution.

The last of this troupe was Father David Tuchem, the spiritual leader of this new cult and spreader of the word. The fall of Christ from grace, the condemnation of his foolish message of tolerance, the coming of the new crusade to convert all to the service of the true God Yaldabaoth, and the smiting of Yaldabaoth's enemies including the risen Christ were the cornerstones of Tuchem's Dogma.

In truth, Yaldabaoth had the new name forced on himself when he had been converted into Rex Mundi by Hades, but, Tuchem put a spin on it for the congregation that this was a secret name of God only they could know.

Tuchem was a tall slender man in his late thirties. His attractive features and reassuring voice made it easy for people to trust him, even though they shouldn't have. He had light brown hair worn in a tight neat braid that almost reached his waist. His face was accented by an exaggerated widows peak due to a slightly receded hairline and a pair of rectangular wire frame glasses. He didn't need the glasses for vision. He wore them to give himself a more intellectual and trustworthy look. Instead of the more common black suit, he wore long priestly robes at all times. The overall look made him appear like a hybrid of a priest and a character from a kung fu movie. This was almost accurate due to the martial arts training he took in his youth. A native of Manhattan, New York, he relocated to Utah after unproven allegations of inappropriate behavior with young boys and teenage catholic school girls. In Utah he developed an evangelical following, spouting fundamentalist and creationist beliefs.

Though charming, friendly, and pleasant in outward demeanor, Father Tuchem's heart and soul were filled with a cool rage, one in which he cultivated rather than suppressed. He felt that all who could not be converted should be killed, and backed that tenet up with action. Though a devout Yahwist, for he no longer called himself a Christian, he did have a working knowledge of the real goings on of the world of the metaphysical. This knowledge however was all filtered through the lens of his own perception.

Tipeshiel had been sent out to find a spiritual leader for Yaldabaoth's new church, when he saw Father Tuchem preach, he was seduced as easily as all the humans gathered there. So enamored was he by Tuchem's sermon, he declared immediately in front of the entire congregation that Tuchem was to be the bearer of the Word of God.

"We may be having company soon", Yaldabaoth said to the group assembled before him.

"Excellent, shall I have a special dinner prepared?", asked Tipeshiel

"No you fool. These will be unwelcome guests", said the former god.

"Oh, I see" said Tipeshiel, though he didn't understand.

"Someone found us, we were observed", said Yaldabaoth.

"By whom?", asked Father Tuchem in his well-practiced but fake Irish accent.

"I don't know. They managed to hide themselves. But from the method they used, I suspect fey", said the head.

"Those spiritual abominations, surely they are no threat to us", commented Father Tuchem.

"To me no, but to you perhaps they may be", Yaldabaoth said.

Tuchem turned to the others.

"Dean, Rod, tell your men to load their weapons with iron and pull your patrols out of the desert. Let them come, we shall take them here on these hallowed grounds, and send them back to hell!", commanded Yaldabaoth.

"It'll be don' malord", said Dean in his southern drawl.

"And Father, have the faithful stop construction and go into hiding; just in case. I do not want any of my new flock harmed", said Yaldabaoth.

"It shall be done my lord", said Tuchem.

Yaldabaoth's new cult employed the same old rhetoric. Tried and true, it worked perfectly to control the masses.

"Oh ,and Tipeshiel, how is your other project coming?" Yaldabaoth lilted, almost afraid to hear his servant's answer.

"What... oh that," Tipeshiel blushed, "Well my lord, Project Nephilim is ahead of schedule. In four months you should have a new body to inhabit"

Project Nephilim, Yaldabaoth's somewhat dirty little secret. Ruling the world as a severed head was a practical impossibility so some... improvisations had to be made; thus, Project Nephilim was born. Much of the focus of his old religions still rested on his treacherous excuse for a son, Christ; so a new body was required before Yaldabaoth could take back his proper place in the cosmos. Using Tipeshiel, and a young woman obtained from an escort service found in Pastor Wally's rolodex, he intended to breed a human and angel hybrid; a nephilim for his divine spirit to inhabit. He would have preferred one bred from one of his archangels, but since he destroyed all of them he really didn't have much of a choice. Nancy German, the nineteen year old prostitute from Flagstaff was attractive, of low breeding, and would have to do.

Yaldabaoth recognized the Mists of Tyr Afal immediately. The Pagan mongrels knew he was weakened and were most certainly coming for their revenge. Let them come, he thought. He defeated them once and he could do it again. If he could not rule as the one god, he would rule as an immortal tyrant, and eventually, he would find a way to return to Transcendent and Eminent form.

After finishing their breakfast, David, Abe, Na'da, and Dug decided that an approach from the deep desert would be the safest bet. They would pass Genesis Land on the highway by several miles, then loop back to the back of the dilapidated amusement park from the desert.

"Are you sure the Phoenix can handle driving through desert sand?", asked Abe

"Positive, I know she don't look it but she's an all-terrain vehicle", replied David.

"Ok, that should be the least watched area, there are no roads that way and nothing but desert for miles", said Abe.

"Dug has better idea for snekin' on angry fallin' god", said Dug.

"What you got Dug?", asked David

"Dream walk. Hims is only god of solidy things, can't see in other places", said Dug.

"Now that's a good idea", said David, "Why didn't you bring it up before?".

"Davey tell Dug to stop word talk", said Dug smugly.

"Oh that", said David sheepishly, "I... uh".

"You owe Dug an apology, David Maier", said Na'da.

"Dug'll just add to Davey's tab", said Dug.

"You talking to your imaginary friend again?", asked Abe

David shot Abe an annoyed look, "Well my imaginary friend has a way we hadn't considered. A dream walk, and the desert is the perfect place for one"

"Shit, you really think that will work? A god, even a fallen one, should be able to see us coming that way", said Abe.

"Yes. I know you weren't there, but at the end of the battle Yaldabaoth was sentenced by Hades and Christ to be only a god of the earth. Oh man, what did Hades call him? I don't remember. It's not important anyway", said David.

"Wait, wait, you met Jesus Christ?", asked Abe.

"Yeah, briefly, cool guy", said David.

"So that's what you meant at Jesse's. Ok, ok. so you really think this will work?", asked Abe.

"It should. We could leave right from here, and waltz right into Genesis Land unseen", said David.

"Yeah, maybe, but if that will work why could he see you and Na'da, and every seer we sent to look at him?", asked Abe.

"Most likely because they, and we, were looking right at him and got real close. Besides a dream walk is different, you know that", said David.

"I know just wanted to be sure you'd think it would work", said Abe.

They finished up their food quickly then went back to the Phoenix and moved it to secluded spot at the back of the parking lot.

"We better gear up now, we will only have what we have on our persons going in that way, and we can't take the Phoenix with us", said Abe.

Abe went through the equipment he brought with him he changed from his suit into a tactical outfit, black BDU pants, military boots, a black T-shirt, and protective leather gloves. He strapped on two high caliber semiautomatic hand guns and some extra clips. Then his lightly armored tactical vest, replete with surveillance equipment and basic gear.

David strapped his small throwing knives to his wrists, and one of his swords to his waist. Then put on his home made tactical vest that was actually just a black fishing vest with lots of pockets that he added a belt to. It had basic survival equipment as well as a few charms and amulets he had found useful over the years.

"You're not bringing a gun?", Abe asked

"No, you know I can't shoot worth an apple. I'm better up close and personal", David said while putting his trench coat back on.

"Yeah, I remember", Abe said recalling a time David had bested him sparing, and a separate time when David had accidentally shot Martin Belles in the foot.

"You're not actually going to wear that thing in the desert are you", Abe asked David, referring to his trench coat.

"It's not the first time", David replied.

Abe put his designer sunglasses back on and said, "David, if we actually pull this off, promise me one thing".

"Anything Abe, as long as that's not rejoining the ONLA", David said.

"That you will let me help you pick out some decent clothes", Abe joked.

David thought he might actually prefer rejoining the ONLA then getting a makeover from Abe.

"David Maier, I noticed you are only bringing one sword", Na'da commented.

"Yes?", said David.

"May I wield the other?", she asked.

David reached behind the seat, grabbed his other sword, and tossed it to her. She opened her coat, attached the sheath to the belt around her waist, and reclosed her coat.

"Great, I'm with the trench coat mafia", Abe said rolling his eyes, "I bet Dug is wearing one too".

"No", said David and Dug though Abe could only hear David.

"But Dug thinkses maybe he should gets him one", Dug said jokingly.

Dream Walking was part of the advanced field agent training that David and Abe both had. Part of the dream walk ritual involved filling an enclosed area with smoke. David procured a tiny portable BBQ grill from Tessie's and with a hand full of briquettes, some lighter fluid, and a little water the van was quickly filled with smoke. Then they began their meditation and passed onto the dream plane. Na'da and Dug needed no special training or ritual as they could project themselves there just by their nature.

On the dream plane, they appeared in their astral forms.

David was better built and his hair was wild like a lion's mane but longer. His arms body and face were covered in intricate tribal tattoos, and his eyes had a draconian aspect.

Abe looked like a black knight, his armor was shining and reflected color like a beetle's shell. It's design was like a combination of a medieval Knight's and a Roman centurion's. Mostly medieval but the helmet and shoulders were unmistakably Roman.

Na'da looked much the same. Her coat was gone, and the leaves of her outfit were a brilliant spring green. Color rippled through her hair giving it the look of fire. Her eyes were solid blue with white translucent shapes moving across them, making them look like a windy sky.

Dug was about a foot taller and was dressed like a medieval nobleman. Other than that he looked the same.

"Holy crap!", said Abe looking down at Dug, "He is real."

"Yeah, we told you. Ok, look we are all going to be confronted by visions here, but we have to stay focused. We still have a job to do", said David.

They all saw many visions on their long trek through the dream desert, and did a reasonably good job of ignoring them. The oddest part was they could see each other's visions. It was very tempting to use this to get to learn more about the true nature of their comrades, but the task at hand drove them on.

They were close to Genesis Land now. Like in reality it appeared as a dilapidated theme park surrounded by a worn and battered high wooden fence. But unlike reality in the center was a huge temple, undoubtedly it represented what was to be if Yaldabaoth got his way. As they approached David felt something behind him and looked back. He could see a woman in the distance. He couldn't make out her features but he knew who it was, and began walking toward her.

"David", said Abe grabbing him by the shoulder, "That's not her she's not really there. You know that. I know this is a chance for you to work through things, but we have to keep moving".

David knew Abe was right. He had long ago learned to tell the difference between a vision and a presence. But part of him still wanted to go, wanted it to be real. But she was gone and he knew it.

Na'da and Dug could only wonder what affected David so much, but Abe clearly knew what was going on.

They approached front gates.

"You think we should buy tickets", joked Abe.

"Damn, left my wallet in my physical body", countered David

"Oh well, guess we just jump the turnstile", said Abe.

They moved to a spot by the carnival games where the thought they could appear in concealment behind the Knock Down Goliath ball toss, and there moved from the dream plane back to reality.

"Looks like your plan worked, Dug. We're in", said David.

"Yup", agreed Abe, "Now I have a plan".

He produced a small listening device from his vest.

"Ok, if we attach this to Dug, he should be able to sneak around undetected in whatever it is they are building over there and find out the information we need. All he needs to do is confirm that Yaldabaoth and his militia are here and I can radio for the strike team to move in. Of course any intel he can gather is useful but those are the primary objectives. Is he willing?"

"Dug is good at snekin', can get in out no problems", said Dug.

"Yeah, he thinks he should be able to pull it off", said David.

"Great, with this receiver we should be able to pick up whatever he hears, not sure you will be able to hear him over it though", said Abe.

"Good point, we should test that out", said David.

"Good. You do that, and I'll go report in", said Abe.

Abe moved a few feet away behind the Samson decorated strength tester, and contacted the ONLA on his satellite phone.

"It's Agent Sieurd, sir. Right, we're in the compound. Yes, he is Director", Abe glanced over his shoulder at David, "No, I don't think he suspects anything. Don't worry I'll be ready to liquidate".

"Any problems?", David asked crouch-walking up behind Abe.

"Nope, just making sure our asses are covered. We're good. How things on your end?", asked Abe.

"Not too bad. Na'da and I can hear Dug, but it doesn't seem to record his voice".

"That's alright, as long as he can give us verbal confirmation of what he's seeing, and we don't have to depend on interpreting the sounds we hear", said Abe.

"Yea I kinda' figured. Okay, then we're ready", said David.

Abe took out his binoculars.

From where they were he could see the edge of the construction zone some two hundred yards away.

"They've managed to acquire some very heavy construction equipment", Abe informed Dave and Na'da. "And an impressive amount of materials. There seems to be a great deal of deep digging going on. Yaldabaoth must be planning on having the bulk of his temple fortress to be subterranean".

"Malord", said Dean entering along with Rod and Burt.

"What is it?", bellowed Yaldabaoth.

"We have intruders, ma lookout on top uh the coaster spotted 'em", said Dean

"How many?", asked Yaldabaoth.

"Look like jus three uhm'. They appeared outa' nower by them games", said Dean.

"Two males and a female, we don't have positive ID on them yet, but other than the female they don't appear to be fey", added Burt.

"So fer they jus aper to be sittin an watin', they musta be tryin' ta fuger how to get in her' witut been' seen", finished Dean.

"Good work. Keep your eye on them. And let me know what they do. Seems not all my servants are useless", said Yaldabaoth.

"I hope you don't mean me my lord?", asked Father Tuchem who was standing by the right side of his lord.

"No, not you Father, you have learned well my various lessons. You are a greater servant than was Mohammed or Moses, as those fools rebelled against me in their final ends, siding with humanity, though not before serving their purposes. You above all my servants Tuchem know me and my true word. It is that imbecile Tipeshiel I refer to. Of all my angels to survive the treachery of my son it would have to be that pathetic simpleton. Go check on him and the bearer of his seed for me, Father", said Yaldabaoth.

"As you wish my lord", said Tuchem.

"Malord? Yu don' wan us ta kill em'?", Dean interrupted.

"Not yet. We need to learn more about our enemies and their plans", said Yaldabaoth.

"Know thy enemy", Father Tuchem interjected, then went on his appointed task.

Yaldabaoth was a bit annoyed Tuchem would quote Sun-Tzu.

Dug slipped past the militia guards in the outer construction area. They were paying so little attention that Dug may have passed right by them even if he weren't invisible.

He passed the makeshift housing for the militia, and Yaldabaoth's "new flock" and then into the main temple. Just as he was trying to decide what direction to head in he saw a priest walking down the corridor he was in; on a hunch, Dug followed him.

"Just think Tipeshiel, in a few months, I'm gonna' give birth to the lord our savior. We're like Mary and Joseph, 'cept I'm not a virgin and you're an angel ,not a man", rambled Nancy.

Faint hints of beauty remained on Nancy German's face, distorted from long bouts of anorexia. Swollen breasts jutted out from her malnourished frame as she staggered with her beach ball sized belly. She pulled her face into a smile as she stroked her belly, imagining what the rapidly growing nephilim inside her would look like once born.

"Yeah," mumbled Tipeshiel.

This might have interested him if it wasn't the five hundredth time he heard it.

"Don't dare compare yourself to that whore who bore the forsaken son!", shouted Father Tuchem as he entered without knocking, "The nephilim you carry inside you will be the vessel for the True God. He will lead us into a new age, where all will know and worship the True God, and know His True Word. Not the lies spread by his bastard spawn and followers".

"Yeah, that does sound better", Nancy said grinning.

"Tipeshiel, our lord wanted me to...", Father Tuchem was unable to close the door. He looked down and could see nothing holding it open. He leaned on it harder, then kicked the bottom a few times, but to no avail. After a few moments he gave up.

"You should, see about getting that fixed. Anyway our lord wanted me to-"

The door slammed loudly behind him.

"What the devil? Tipeshiel, are you playing a joke on ol' Father Tuchem?", the priest asked.

"Not I, Father", said Tipeshiel.

"Hmm? At any rate, Our Lord wanted me to...", he paused just in case, "To make sure you two were alright, see if you needed anything, and to tell you our guests have arrived".

"Oh goodie, company!", Tipeshiel said clapping.

"Yes. Just stay here and take care of her. I have other matters to attend to", said Tuchem.

Father Tuchem left the room when he realized that trying to explain things to Tipeshiel would be useless. He also realized that his Lord would need better defending than the militia goons or Tipeshiel could provide. He crossed to his room and got his sword. He had a special Tai Chi style sword made. It was black handled with a small white rectangle on each side. The blade was engraved with the phrase *Sino parum liberi venire contra mihi, inquit Dominus*.

Tuchem started back down the hall to be by the side of his Lord. He looked back as he heard Tipeshiel's door slam again.

"Dolt", Tuchem muttered, cursing Tipeshiel.

Dug was certain Tuchem had cracked at least two ribs, and did some organ damage when he caught him in the door. If he were human he would be worried about permanent damage, but, being a Goblin he was already starting to heal.

"Pleas tellses Dug, Davey heard all that", said Dug.

"10-4 Dug we got it. Abe is calling it in now. Get out of there"

"Dug thinkeys' he might just sits here for a wincy bit". Dug said sounding weak.

"Dug are you injured, do you need us to come get you?", asked David.

"Yes, Davey", said Dug.

"Abe, we got a man down. We have to extract Dug", said David.

"Ok, we have to go in anyway there's a change in plans. They want us to extract the woman pregnant with nephilim", said Abe.

"What? What about the strike team?", asked David.

"It's inbound, but they don't want to take any chances. They want a more delicate extraction", Abe said.

David knew what that meant. The ONLA wanted her alive for their own purposes, and didn't want to risk an escape or fatality during the chaos of a raid.

"Great. Dug sit tight we are coming to get you. Okay, let's get this over with", David said.

"I see why you are so brave, David Maier", said Na'da, "When you have one such as Dug to inspire you with his courage".
As soon as they started to move they heard the unfortunately all too familiar crack of rifle fire, and a bullet whizzed past their heads.

"Shit, sniper", said Abe.

"Where is he?", asked David.

"I don't know", said Abe.

"There on top of the Moses out of Egypt coaster", said Abe spotting him.

"I can get...", Na'da began to say.

"Damn it, Na'da keep your head down!", David grabbed the Slyph by the arm and pulled her into the booth.

"But I can...", Na'da said.

 another round zipped past David and Na'da's heads, taking out a stuffed lamb hanging on the wall next to them.

"Na'da shhh stay down!", said David.

Abe drew his pistol.

"What are you do with that. You can't hit him from here with a pistol. He's a hundred and fifty yards away at the top of roller coaster!", said David.

"Wanna bet? I'm going to need a distraction", said Abe.

"Your ass. Fine, don't miss", said David.

David creeped his head around the other side of the game booth and yelled ,"Yahweh SUCKS!"

He heard both guns fire at once. He could feel the wind off the sniper's shot as he ducked back behind the counter. Abe's shot was truer, and ripped through the sniper's hip, and he fell screaming to his death.

"Yahweh sucks?", asked Abe.

"Oh yeah, I forgot he changed his name. I thought you wanted a distraction, not Shakespeare. Nice shot, by the way", David said.

"Not really, I was aiming for his head", Abe admitted, "We better move. That's going to attract attention".

"I could have flown up there invisibly and taken his head off. It would have been much quieter", said Na'da annoyed.

"Oh, yeah. I didn't think of that", said David sheepishly.

"Looks like chivalry got the better of us", added Abe.

"Again", said David.

David and Abe looked at each other and both said: "Australia."

Abe screwed a silencer onto each of his pistols, "Let's move".

Fortunately, most of the guards were busy examining the fallen sniper. One was actually poking him with a stick, giving the threesome a clear path into the temple. Not for a moment did they let their guard down. Abe swept every corner, but there was no one in the construction area. They entered the main temple through a large archway that looked as though it would eventually have large wooden doors. At the moment however, it was blocked only by a white plastic tarp. They made their way toward the spot where they believed Dug to be. Outside they heard the sound of helicopters and crashing as the wooden fence was breached in several places.

"The strike team, damn they're early," said Abe.

Father Tuchem and the militia heads were on their way to get Tipeshiel. From outside they heard gunfire as Yaldabaoth's militia engaged the ONLA strike team.

Tipeshiel opened his door and peeked his head out, "What's going on?"

"The time has com ta defen' ur Lord!", informed Dean.

Father Tuchem pushed the door open the rest of the way and dragged Tipeshiel into the hallway, then turned his attention to Nancy, "Come with me my child, we must get you to safety".

"Where are we goin'? What's happenin'?", asked Nancy.

"The enemies of the True God and his servants are upon us", Tuchem said as he gently took Nancy by the arm and disappeared with her around the corner from which he had just come.

"What about me?", whined Tipeshiel.

"I'll help you," said a familiar voice from the other end of the hall.

Tipeshiel looked over just in time to see David draw his sword. Seeing David Maier wielding what he mistakenly believed to be the sword of Asmodeus, he screamed like a little girl. He panicked and took flight, ripping through the tarp covering over an unfinished section of ceiling.

"I have him!", yelled Na'da as she dropped her coat and flew after him.

"Na'da wait!", David yelled after her.

"David, look out!", Abe shouted and shoved him out of Dean's line of fire. Abe caught the blast of buckshot from Dean's shotgun in the chest at close range sending him flying back at an odd angle. He hit the ground like a discarded rag doll, landing face down. There would be no last words, no final quip for the man David and Martin had traded witty barbs with for the better part of twenty years.

Rage overtook David. The generally rational and compassionate man had but one line an enemy should not cross. Thou shalt not harm the ones he loves, his family.

Abe was like a brother to him and in the end he had proven himself to be the same man David remembered him to be. Without even getting back to his feet David whipped one of his throwing knives into Dean's left eye.

"Ahhhhhhhh pull er ut, pull er ut!", Dean howled.

David then pulled a move he would not have thought himself capable of anymore. He pushed off the wall sliding himself across the floor, dropping Rod with a low scissor leg take down. Rod fell into Burt knocking him down as well. Burt panic fired; and emptied his double barrel shotgun into Rod's head, effectively decapitating him. David spun himself into a kneeling position and struck Burt.

"You heathen son of a...", was all Burt could get out before David's sword pierced his heart.

David heard a distinctive double click. And felt steel against his forehead. Dean had apparently regained his composure and was now pressing his shotgun against David's skull.

"Die inf-i-del", Dean shouted at him, with David's knife still sticking out of his ruined left eye.

David waited for the shot that did not come. Dean began gasping for breath, his neck seized by an unseen hand. His throat opened as if sliced by air and he fell to the ground, spilling his lifeblood on the fresh concrete.

Dug appeared to David, standing on Dean's back holding a nasty looking medieval dagger.

David breathed a sigh of relief, "Thanks Dug. Are you alright?"

"Eys' been better Davey, but goblinses heals up lickety-quick", said Dug.

"Good, Na'da took off after Tipeshiel. If you're up to it, see if she needs help", said David.

"Eys' is all over it Davey", said Dug.

Outside things were calming down. It didn't take long for the militia forces to realize they were out gunned, and they were beginning to surrender. Yaldabaoth's faithful were being more or less peacefully rounded up. However in the sky above a more personal battle was raging.

Na'da and Tipeshiel were making wide circular passes at each other and clashing swords. Finally Na'da decided to match his speed and direction. They locked swords for a moment and Tipeshiel got lucky and managed to use his sword to disarm her.

"Ha!", he mocked leaning close to gloat. That moment was all Na'da needed, his gloat giving her time to counter, and she brought her foot up into the soft tissue of his crotch.

Groaning in pain his eyes opened huge, and he dropped his flaming sword in favor of grabbing his injury. The vines coiled around Nada as she lashed out and bound Tipeshiel. She grabbed him by his toga, driving her knees into his chest, she flipped him over once and drove him the fifty feet down into the ground. On impact Na'da's weight minimal as it may be, shattered Tipeshiel's ribcage. A mortal would have been killed, Tipeshiel was not so lucky. Nada was not done with him, she repeatedly slammed her fist into Tipeshiel's face.

Playing the last card he had, Tipeshiel manifested the hidden eyes which angels of his order had all over their bodies. Na'da removed the vines and recoiled in disgust. She was about to pursue him as he took flight again and finish him off, when something called 'No' to her being. Something far subtler but stronger than Yaldabaoth.

"Yahweh, Yaldabaoth, Lord", Tipeshiel said, "I quit! This job is just not worth the minimal benefits considering the risks".

Na'da felt a sense of satisfaction watching the last angel desert his god. She failed to notice one of the last militia men armed with the iron buckshot get a lucky shot which tore one of her wings. She could eventually heal from this, but it would be some time until she was flying again.

Before the man could fire another shot, a pair of tiny but brawny arms strangled him from behind.

"Dug", said Na'da brightly, "Thank you for your assistance. Let us go find David Maier".

Dug nodded in agreement.

David took a moment to compose himself. The combination of overexerting himself, the loss of Abe and his disgust at himself for taking human life had taken its toll. It wasn't the first time he had to kill, but for him it never got any easier.

He finally worked up to standing. He took a step toward Abe and felt a sharp pain in his side. He turned to find himself nose to nose with Father David Tuchem, who had just driven his sword though David's side. A superficial but painful wound.

"David Maier, I presume?", asked Tuchem.

"And you must be the infamous Father Tuchem", David replied.

"I am", said Tuchem.

"Yeah, I've heard of you. Funny I didn't realize that was your real name. I just thought that's what the papers called you because... ahhg", David said.

Tuchem twisted the sword to silence him.

"You are one to talk of indiscretions, he who consorts with demons and the unclean spirits of the earth. He who stood with Christ and the pagan gods against the true one God", said Tuchem.

Tuchem shoved David back and pulled his sword from him, stepping back into a Tai Chi fighting stance.

"Now servant of Hades, in the name of Yahweh, King of heaven, Yaldabaoth, King of the Earth, I condemn ye to death", said Tuchem.

"If your god is in heaven, I shall go to hell", said David.

"And I shall be happy to send you there", said Tuchem.

David was stalling. The wound he'd been dealt hadn't damaged anything vital, but if he didn't get medical attention he was going to bleed to death. Also the placement of the injury would make it difficult to fight without making it worse. That combined with the fact that Tuchem's stance was near perfect made David think he really knew what he was doing. He was hoping the strike team would intervene, but it didn't look like he was going to get that lucky.

David did the only thing left he could think of and shrouded himself in the Mists of Tyr Afal. David could see clear as day but Tuchem would be be blind.

"Fool, I do not need my eyes to fight", Tuchem thought to himself.

He closed his eyes and listened. After a moment he caught the sound of David's heartbeat and thrust for it. David blocked but couldn't believe how accurate Tuchem's thrust had been. David just barely blocked several more strikes. Each one would have been fatal. He couldn't keep this up. He had to take Tuchem out quickly.

David launched a rapid volley of well-placed strikes, that Father Tuchem blocked so effortlessly it almost made David respect him. With every block Father Tuchem took a step back until finally he side stepped around the corner he had appeared from. When David rounded the corner just after him, he was gone.

Though David was the one shrouded in mists, Father Tuchem is the one who vanished like a ghost.

There was a door at the far end of the corridor. Could he possibly have made it down there that fast David wondered. He hobbled to the room and entered. The room was large and dimly lit. It appeared to be a chapel, but at the far end was a three tiered step platform.

At the back of the platform was an ornate gold and ivory throne. In front of the throne was a four foot tall pillar. On the top of the pillar was the severed head of Pastor Wally Nagel. Inside the severed head of Pastor Wally Nagel was the essence of the fallen god Yahweh, now called Yaldabaoth.

" You have found your way to me. Hear my voice, hear it and know the truth. That I am the Lord God. Come forward and kneel before me, child of God."

David heard the voice, heard it and knew it to be the voice of God. He obeyed, and knelt down before the lord God with his arms slightly spread and palms out.

" Good my child now... "

David slammed his cupped hands onto Yaldabaoth's ears, grabbed the sides of his head and drove his forehead into the bridge of Yaldabaoth's nose.

David knew it to be the voice of God, and he knew that God to be a horrible monster, concerned only with its own advancement in the universe, and that it tried to consume the entire world to meet its ends.

"GAGGGDHS... TUSSHHUM...", Yaldabaoth yelled as his mouth and sinuses filled with blood.

"There is no one left to help you. And I know I can't destroy you, but I can hurt you", said David.

David picked up the severed head by the hair.

To David's right was a doorway covered by a white plastic tarp, the unfinished room that was eventually to serve as Yaldabaoth's personal chambers after he took possession of the nephilim body. David had other plans. The room also had a three foot deep freshly poured, cement floor.

"Any last words?", asked David.

"*GLAGUS FLUGC GLOO MAGGR.*"

"I didn't think so", said David.

David reached out as far into the room as he could and submerged the severed head into the wet cement, and smoothed it back out with a shovel he found nearby. He was about to walk away when a tool box caught his eye. After careful consideration he took a thin center punch out of the tool box and drew the sigil of Asmodeus in the wet cement. If this place where Yaldabaoth was entombed was disturbed than Asmodeus would know. David just needed to remember to tell Asmodeus he had done this. It was almost like putting up a sign reading, "*Dig here for severed head containing essence of former god*", but if someone found it he needed to know about it.

David made a quick bandage out of his shirt sleeve, as he was still bleeding profusely. Calmly he walked back down the corridor toward Abe's body. He rolled his late friend over onto his back.

"SON OF A BITCH!", screamed Abe, "Mother fucker that stings!"

"Abe, you're alive!", said David.

"Yeah, barely. Thank God's stupidity for having them load for fey. Looks like my vest stopped the iron. Hurts like hell though", said Abe.

David punched Abe in the arm.

"You scared the crap out of me, bro, you were out cold for a while there", said David.

"Why, what did I miss?", Abe leaned up and looked down the corridor, and saw the dead militia men, "Looks like you did okay".

"Yeah, well Dug helped. I could have used your help with Father Tuchem though. That guys a monster", said David.

At that moment several ONLA agents in SWAT style gear entered.

"Agent Sieurd, are you all right?", one asked.

"Peachy", Abe said sarcastically. "What's the situation Captain?".

"The area's secure. We're rounding up the last of them, but there's still no sign of the primary objective", the agent replied.

"Hi Mike", said David.

"David? I didn't know you were in on this" said Captain Mike Simmons.

"I'm supposed to be anonymous", said David.

"Oh, so you're the one. I'll keep your name out of my report", said Simmons.

"Thanks Mike. I appreciate it. I also think we would appreciate some medical attention", said David.

"Right. Agents, let's escort Agent Sieurd and Mr. Maier to the triage area".

Two agents helped Abe to his feet and Mike helped David to steady himself.

"Captain we've got some problems," said an agent who had just come running in from outside.

"What is it?", asked Mike.

"We've got fey inside the compound and...", started the agent.

"They're with us, Seargent", interrupted Abe.

"Well, that solves that problem", said the junior officer.

Simmons clicked his radio on, "Fey are friendlies, repeat the fey are friendlies"

"10-4", came the static response from the radio.

"What else, Seargent?", asked Mike.

"Tuchem has escaped with the secondary objective. We had him in that underground parking garage we found. He killed four agents and escaped in a mid 80's black BMW", he said.

"Track him with the choppers", ordered Mike.

"We tried, somehow we lost him. It was as if he just disappeared", said the officer.

"There is only one road out of here, and I don't think he went tooling through the desert in a twenty some odd year old Beamer. How could you lose him?", asked Abe.

"I don't know, Sir."

Father Tuchem was already speeding down the highway. He didn't know where he was going, just that he needed to get Nancy as far from the ONLA as possible. He cursed himself internally. He hadn't expected Maier to be so skilled, even though he should have. Maier had after all bested an archangel. Next time he would be ready. A man like David Maier must have enemies, so Tuchem would seek them out. It was as good a plan as any to start with.

David, Abe, and Dug were resting in the back of an ONLA mobile medical unit. David's sword wound was stapled, and they were all waiting for a psychic healer to become available to help speed there recoveries.

Na'da was being debriefed by a large group of agents.

"You think they have enough agents taking her statement?", David asked jokingly.

"I'm sure there are still a few agents around here who don't think so. But I don't see any of them writing anything down". said Abe.

"Maybe if she put her coat back on it would help", David chuckled.

The three of them laughed, and then winced, when laughing aggravated their injuries.

It was then that David finally noticed that the leaves covering Na'da were green as they had been on their dream walk. He correctly surmised that it must have something to do with the environment. In the autumn of the northeast they were the color of fall leaves, here in a warmer climate they were green.

'So what are you gonna do now?'', asked Abe.

"Back to PA , I guess. I have some old friends I need to track down, and I never did finish my visit with Jesse", said David.

"You really should come back to the agency. You've still got it, and things are changing out there. A lot of things that are secret may become common knowledge. We're going to need agents like you", said Abe.

"I don't think so Abe. I think I'll handle whatever's coming, my way. Heck, maybe I'll start my own organization", said David.

"Really? Hmm interesting, you know I've got some time off coming to me. Maybe I'll tag along and see what happens on your next adventure", added Abe.

Tipeshiel flew until his wings gave out.

"Phew", he said landing on a mountain peak and catching his breath.

"Freelance Angel", he said to himself, "Rogue Angel?. Tipeshiel, Last of His Kind...".

A noise broke him from imagining the opening to the television show he fancied should exist about his life. He peered from the peak he was on into the valley below, to see where it came from.

He squinted and saw a family of humans having a picnic. He was hungry. He waited a moment, and saw a little girl of about two toddle away from her parents, and toward where he was. He lost sight of her in the brush.

"Baah", Tipeshiel said in fear as the little girl appeared in front of him, "Oh, hello...".

"Quiet", she said, "Your strands were originally headed for a very bad day today. I gave you a reprieve. But only to be my penstroke", she said.

"Huh?", he asked.

"Well", she said, "You were always intended to be stupid", even as she covered him in the sticky rope which came from her mouth, which was seemingly now an endless chasm.

PIVOT

*The Empirical is not a card, but a throne, or ruling Operation
Point. It is also a vantage, and in all these things allows the
Operator to sit, or rule, govern, or flow with, and be conveyed
by, primary eruption. The prior sentence can only be
understood when all the verbs in it are understood as a single
concept not present in this text's language.*

Martin Belles unconsciously tapped his foot to the beat of the
song which played over the radio of the rental car. He
thought it might be Nirvana. He was reluctant to admit that a
band which was so influential on his generation was so alien to
him. Only in the months since Kurt Cobain's death earlier
that spring had Martin once again began to pay any attention
to popular music.

He regarded himself in the mirror for the umpteenth time
and wiped the sweat from his brow. Martin had been making
a concerted effort to be a more modern man. The reflection
that stared back at him was an only recently muscular
gentleman with a shaven head. Martin worked very hard to

earn the new look he sported. He still wore the traditional black ONLA suit with a white dress shirt and black tie. But the new physique and lack of hair were his attempt to come slowly and reluctantly into 1994.

"Should I try it again?", Martin said to the second man who still had his head under the hood of the car.

"Just a bleeding minute, Belles. You could always get out here and help me", said Thurston.

"I would but I was just going to try the car phone again and see if we can reach Pratt", said Belles.

"A likely excuse just so you don't have to be out here in the heat", Thurston grumbled, "but if you're going to try Pratt again do it now, I need a few more minutes with this thing".

"Yes, any excuse I can come up with to stay in this metal oven", said Martin sarcastically.

Martin thought this whole business would have been much simpler if he and Waite could have just had a standard ONLA tactical van. Instead they were stuck with this damn rental car. The bitch overheated halfway through route 80.

"Can't you just use magick to fix the damn thing?", asked Belles.

"I only use magick when I absolutely have to", said Waite.

"Isn't this one of those times?", asked Belles.

"No, it isn't, Belles", said Waite, "I thought you were going to try to reach Pratt anyway".

Martin awkwardly uncradled the car phone and began to punch in Pratt's number. Martin heard the strange tones as the call was routed through a ship to shore system. Pratt was somewhere in the middle of the Atlantic.

"Pratt here", said Pratt as he answered the phone, his voice fading in and out from the poor reception on the mobile.

"It's Martin Belles, Sir. Have the ONLA brass unclassified the information we asked for?", Belles inquired.

"There's very little information on anything of interest that ever happened in Bethlehem, Pennsylvania. There was an incident in 1939 when Illuminatus Jesse Perfect stopped Ethan Rhys-Davies and the demon Asmodeus from obtaining the Spark of Artemis. What's of more interest is the fact that I myself was involved in the investigation of a time travel incident".

"Time travel incident?", asked Belles, "Could this have anything to do with the energy signature the ONLA seers saw which we were dispatched to investigate?".

"It was a damned strange incident", said Pratt, "even by ONLA standards. About 20 years ago the body of the man was recovered in Bethlehem. Only a younger version of the man was still alive. It turned out that one was a time traveler from the future, but one who was not affected by changes in the time-line experienced by his younger self".

"How is that possible?", asked Belles, "The laws of causality would dictate what you have just said is impossible".

"You may not believe this Belles, but the man traveled through time outside of relativistic laws. He even traveled backwards through time outside of quantum effects. In fact the best seers and remote viewers could not trace him back to his reality of origin. In short Belles, he traveled backwards through time with the aid of the O factor", said Pratt.

"Then I suppose the Illuminati will be wanting us to see if there's any exploitable use for whatever time loop exists around Bethlehem, Pennsylvania", said Thurston Waite as he jumped in the passenger seat and began listening in on the conversation which played over the speakerphone.

"Waite", said Pratt, "I was thinking you'd left Belles alone on this mission. He would probably have been better off. But just to put your mind at ease, we figured out that because it stemmed from the O Factor whatever time loop there is in Bethlehem, if one can even call it that, is of no use to us. However, I've read the report written by the seers which first sent you two boys to that town. Someone does indeed think that they can exploit the latent energy of that time loop but for a totally different purpose. We need to figure out exactly what that is. Martin, I want you to watch Waite as carefully as you possibly can. And Waite if you didn't have the skills that I thought were absolutely necessary for this mission, you wouldn't even be on it."

"I love you too, Billy boy", said Thurston sarcastically.

"Belles, take me of speaker", said Pratt.

Martin did not but Pratt's next words clearly showed Pratt thought only Martin could hear him.

"Try not to let that towel-headed Mick cloud your mind to our objectives", said Pratt, "He's as bad as Perfect. Belles, best of luck. Pratt out".

"What did you mean by calling a senior officer Billy boy?", asked Martin.

"What did he mean by calling me not one but, two racial epithets? Two for one deal today, I guess", said Thurston with his Irish accent showing more fully now.

Pratt was the liaison to the military and the immediate senior agent who presided over both Belles and Waite, and their respective usual partners, Maier and Sieurd. Pratt was, unfortunately, a fantastic field agent and one of Braxus's favorites. Unfortunately the former military man and ONLA officer had more than a bit of a mountain folk bigot streak in his nature. Waite, Arab by birth but raised in Ireland, and someone who had chosen the eclectic magicks study during his ONLA training days rather than the military or tactical course, was bound to provoke the ire of Pratt.

Belles, on the other hand, showing great promise in both the directorial side of the inner workings of the ONLA and the military structure of the field operations, was proving to be one of Pratt's star apprentices, and his potential has not gone unnoticed by Braxus. Usually Pratt would prefer to have Agent Sieurd on a project he was overseeing, but lately Sieurd had been acting more and more like Maier and Waite, leaving Belles the Golden boy in Pratt's and perhaps also in Braxus's eyes.

While Martin relished the idea of advancing through the ranks of the ONLA this way, he did not necessarily like the praise to come from those two men.

It was an unusual pairing for Martin and Thurston to be partnered, but with both of their usual partners on other assignments they were placed together. The two teams had worked together often enough over the years that Belles and Waite knew each other well. Thurston's partner Abraham Sieurd was receiving advanced tactical training, and Martin's partner David Maier was doing research for a top secret mission as well as conducting his own secret off book investigation into the death of an ONLA cadet.

"So the seers didn't see a damned thing besides the major energy spike which seems to indicate somebody trying to exploit this doubly anomalous time loop", said Martin.

"You're too trusting a fellow", said Thurston, "The ONLA isn't doing follow up. If someone has managed to find a way to use what they weren't able to all those years ago, the mission is to find out how that someone has done that. I'm a bit of a seer myself, Marty, in addition to a mage, and I'm telling you that whoever is planning to do something here has a noble reason for doing so, we shouldn't interfere".

"We have our orders, Thurston. But I agree with you there is more to this than meets the eye", said Belles, "I know this is going to sound a bit odd but I get the feeling of some kind of rogue agency here. An external party that needs to be stopped", Martin said.

"Well I have a feeling that whatever's going on here is something that should be left alone", said Thurston.

"Maybe, I'm sensing something that's going to interfere with whatever you're sensing", said Martin.

"Well if we stay sitting on the side of the road listening to "Weird Al" Nirvana parodies we're not going to get anywhere", said Thurston.

"I'm assuming by the fact that you got back in the car that it's running again?", asked Martin.

"Yes, Marty" said Thurston, "so how far away are we from this town of Bethlehem, is that what it's called?".

"About an hour and a half", said Belles.

"Didn't you say some kind of music festival is going on?", Asked Thurston, "The little arts and crafts and polka and dance like a talking chicken festival?".

"No", said Martin, "this festival actually gets fairly big. It's called Musikfest. In fact all the chain hotel rooms are booked up. The ONLA actually sprang to put us up in some historical inn. Little but some character for once".

"I thought you were the ONLA now Marty", said Thurston.

"You know you can get really far with the sorcery corps", said Martin, "if you drop the damned investigation".

"You mean the investigation Braxus wants me to drop, but Jesse and Nathaniel have no problem with me continuing?", asked Thurston.

"You know what I mean, Thurston. Even David is ready to let it go. Besides she was his girlfriend, not yours. It's like you made some personal damn mission to find out what happened to her."

"She was my friend", said Thurston, "before she even knew any of you".

"I know", said Martin "but you don't go against Braxus".

"Braxus is one scary motherfucker if you ask me", said Thurston, "Still Marty, good to be in the field together one last time. We all seem to be going on to other things. What you did to that cop back on route 80 is not something that I think is in the ONLA handbook", said Thurston.

"We didn't have time for a ticket, Thurston, so I used approved agency methods in my knowledge of hypnosis to politely suggest they let us go", said Martin in an extremely official tone.

"So sending the policeman back to his car saying 'These aren't the droids I'm looking for' is approved ONLA methodology to get out of a speeding ticket and keep the pace of the mission goal?", asked Thurston.

"Well, not in the strictest sense", said Martin with a smile, "but it did get the job done".

"I don't care what anybody says about you, Marty", replied Thurston, "you're an OK guy by me".

"Well, thanks I guess", said Belles and then continuing with a note of concern, "Hey wait, what do they say about me?"

The two agents continued on in the cheap subcompact rental car. Arriving in Pennsylvania after they departed from New Jersey, they first rode through the decaying town of Easton, Pennsylvania. The city was obviously once a hub of industry, trade, and an important link on the route between New York and Philadelphia. Deprived of any economic, philosophical, or spiritual connection to this past this river port city had devolved to a combination of urban sprawl, city crime, and a place generally down on its luck. As the highway ferried them back out of the city and toward the sister city of Bethlehem, they initially saw little difference.

As an extension highway curved off of the main highway and lead into the heart of central Bethlehem, Belles and Waite could both see an immediate difference; throngs of celebrants gathered around small outdoor music venues, booths selling beer from local breweries, street musicians, and stands selling

smoked meats which could satiate the palate of the most
discriminating carnivore. Clearly many of the assembled were
locals either from Bethlehem itself or from Allentown or
Easton, one of the two surrounding sister cities. Others may
have been from a bit farther, either on vacation or in town for
the day to see a particular artist. Waite found the whole thing
wonderfully cheesy and American. The whole site was for
Belles however uncomfortably close to home, as he was
reminded of his family vacations as a boy to the Jersey shore
which he had needed to recount to most high school chums
who by comparison had gone somewhere in the realm of
Disney, either World or Land, due to greater economic
lushness on the part of their fathers.

Indeed for Waite the small town celebration, along with the
unabashedly commercial parading of monikers and signs for
local businesses and sponsors, was one of the things about
America he loved. Other Europeans would balk at this sort
of thing. Though Thurston Waite was not like other
Europeans, in truth if one could even call him that. Thurston
had been raised in Ireland since before he was toilet trained.
His parents, part of the diplomatic attaché from Egypt to the
Emerald Isle, had taken him with them when they were
assigned to the post. Thurston thought of himself as an
Irishman and was proud of his adopted cultural heritage, but
his magical studies had taken him to his Arabic roots, and
then to a more wholly global system. In terms of permanent
culture, he gravitated toward the United Kingdom and
Continental Europe, but in terms of pop culture he had
always had a secret love affair with the type of scene which was
before him now. Thurston Waite was a closet Americana-
phile, and for the past six years now he called the United
States home. He had not yet applied for citizenship, but the
ONLA made certain he was aware that that process could be
accelerated for him upon request. William Pratt on the other
hand had made it known to Waite and others that he could

be sent back to Ireland via one stroke of the senior agent's pen.

As they made their way through the small town, Thurston and Martin began to feel a sense of what the ONLA seers had sent them there to investigate. They did feel the background energy of the time loop which Pratt spoke about. Clearly whatever changes in the time-line, if any, that had resulted from this loop were a negligible and small factor, but, the fact that it involved extracosmic forces meant unusual possibilities were woven into the fabric of this locale. The ONLA had spent time here in the 1970's seeing if they could learn the secrets of the temporal phenomenon here, and failed.

The streets were packed tightly and a place to stow the rental car was unavailable, but fortunately for Belles and Waite the historic hotel in the middle of the Musikfest district provided its own parking deck. They parked the car, and checked into their room. It was surprisingly plush and comfortable. Thurston happily, and Belles reluctantly, changed into plainclothes. They once again had a debate if the energy signature which emanated from the unknown person or persons who hoped to exploit the nascent time loop was positive or negative. Little did they know how close those signatures were. They stopped for a quick drink at the hotel bar, Waite having a beer and Belles a tonic water.

As they made their way down the front steps of the hotel and onto the main street of the town, which was of course actually called Main Street, they bumped into what was presumably another hotel guest on his way up the stairs. More specifically Belles clumsily brushed up against a rather tall, but lanky well-dressed man in a black businesses suit and black turtleneck on his way in. Clearly unlike the garments he had changed out of which were those of a federal agent, Martin realized this young man's choice of clothing spelled out that he came from old money. More specifically, money which was inherited and not earned.

Martin Belles knew people like that all too well growing up.

The man turned around and stared at Belles with a gaze like that of a medieval noble who was angry with a peasant.

"My friend didn't mean any harm", said Thurston in his most charming lilt.

"Tell your friend it's his lucky day", said the well-dressed man, "because I've better things to do than punish townies for their stupidity".

Belles raised an eyebrow and continued walking down the steps. Waite thought to himself that it was actually the man Belles had bumped into who is having a lucky day.

"Townies?", said Belles.

"Let it go, Marty", said Thurston.

"Any idea where we should start looking?", asked Belles.

"Start walking around this Festival in concentric circles" said Thurston, "It would probably also help if we took proper samplings of any smoked meats that we come across".

"Always multitasking, aren't you Thurston?", said Belles.

"What?", asked Thurston, "Multitasking?".

"Never mind", said Martin, "Computer geek slang".

As they stepped out onto Main Street, or as it was affectionately known the Moravian Mile, Thurston noticed something strange. In fact he noticed a lot of strange somethings or rather someones. It seemed that in front of the hotel was a large congregation of members of every popular subculture, some in their own niches, some homogenized. Thurston had to admit he was inspired by this display of alternative cultural diversity.

"Jesus, look at these weirdo's. I hope the whole festival isn't like this.", Martin commented offhandedly. Clearly the significance was lost on him.

The man continued on into the Hotel Bethlehem. He approached the front desk. The girl at the front desk was somewhat attractive and so he feigned a smile.

"Can I help you?", she asked.

"Loren Evans", he said, "I believe I have a room for the next several days".

"Oh yes Mr. Evans. You've got room 214. You know it's supposed to be haunted. We don't usually let it out, but during Musikfest we get filled to total occupancy", she said

Evans stared intently at her name tag and her breasts. The thin strip of black plastic with white lettering said her name was Heather.

"Well, Heather, if something frightens me in the middle of the night, I'll be sure to ring the front desk to send you up," said Evans.

Heather obviously did not take this flirtation kindly. Evans was not a man who handled rejection even in the form of an expression very well. He forced a low-level thrall spell on her, until quite to her own surprise she regarded Evans and licked her lips with arousal. He set the spell to linger for a moment, as he parted with the room key she handed him. In a few moments it would wear off and she would feel disgusted by the sexual thoughts she had about the relatively unattractive man who had just left her presence.

Evans walked into room 214 and indeed could immediately sense the presence of the spirit. An advanced sorcerer such as himself could easily see the dead. The spirit woman who had committed suicide in the room beckoned to him for help. Were he so inclined, he could've easily released her to the next world. He shushed her way with a cold angry energy, and with her silenced moved to his window and regarded the crowds.

Someone was out there in this town, who intended to use the inherent disruptions in time of this area to alter fate. If this was something that could be done, Evans knew it was something he needed to possess. But the area was rife with a plethora of psychic phenomenon and spiritual energy signatures which dampened his ability to pick out anything particular. He unpacked, and took the elevator back to the main lobby leaving the building by a side entrance which spilled him into a parking lot. He found the crowds no less thick there than out on the main street.

A path led him off the street and into a park filled with historic buildings. He crossed over a small wooden bridge into what seemed to be a small empty industrial parking lot. Something of great interest drew him to the trailer of a semitruck, which was parked underneath a highway bridge.

Evans realized that whatever was calling to him, at least in the immediate sense, was to be found under the trailer. He could already tell it was not the thing he was after, but it was something which had knowledge of it and something he could exploit to help him on a search.

Evans picked up a large stick and began to bang loudly on the side of the tractor-trailer. With each bang he cast a broad spectrum intranquility spell that would force anything human or not out of its hiding place.

What appeared to be a man with long stringy and greasy brown hair, glasses, a horrible overbite, Caucasian skin, a dusty and dingy brown cloth trenchcoat, and worn-out motorcycle boots came from beneath the trailer.

"Hey, man, I'm trying to sleep", said the man.

"It's not your fate to sleep well tonight, Djinn", said Evans, "consider yourself recruited".

"My name's not Jan, man, my name is Sean. All the kids around here call me Seany Bear. Because I'm hairy like a bear, you know?", said Seany Bear with a smile.

Evans intoned a strength spell on himself, and reached out his hands and began strangling the man who had called himself Seany Bear.

"Well, Mr. Bear, if you're not a Djinn, then I guess you'll just die, but if you are you'll revert to smoke and fire before you perish in mortal form", Evans said.

"Let go", said Sean pathetically, "You don't get it man. I'm not the kind who grants wishes. There isn't anything you can get by doing this to me. Other than getting yourself hurt really bad. I don't like to do that man, but I will".

"I'll risk it", said Evans doing rather little to hide the arousal he felt from performing physical violence which he was not normally strong enough to do without the aid of spells.

The Djinn could no longer contain itself and reverted to its normal state. Evans had already shielded himself from the effects of the fire. He intoned a rare Bin Martu spell, which caused the Djinn to again take the form of Sean.

"What the hell was that, man?", said Sean.

"Consider yourself conscripted, Sean. Tell me then, what is your real name?", asked Evans.

"D'Irem", answered the Djinn, "Oh, man, why did I tell you that, dude? Oh crap, you really are in control of me, you freak".

"Well, D"irem, I smell something interesting here. Someone challenging the fabric of fate. Now let's go for a little walk, and you tell me what you know", said Evans.

Evans led the Djinn back into the main area of Musikfest via an invisible leash. The Djinn had come here as a do-gooder to play a role in order to aid the person or persons who intended to challenge fate, but it was not he himself who was the central figure in this drama. Evans found himself drawn to a large lawn on which many people were sunbathing, had set up chairs, or were listening to the distant sound of jazz music being played on one of the music stages a bit farther to the south. Somewhere, in this mass of humans actually enjoying themselves, which made Evans sick, was the key to his plan.

"So Mr. Bear tell me, exactly what is it you're here to do?" demanded Evans.

"I can't tell you that man, I...", began Sean.

Evans pulled on the reins of the spell he had placed on Sean and spoke again, "What are you here to do?"

Slightly choked Sean answered, "Ack! I'm here... to help someone transubstantiate into a... a..."

"A what?", Evans demanded hoping to hear the word *fate*.

"An Arda Fravaš ", said Sean.

"A what?", asked Evans becoming more annoyed.

"It's a kind of like a guardian aura kind of thing man. A protective resonance. Only it guards the relations between things and people. It's not conscious. It's also not without consciousness. It's just the purity of his soul and the special conditions in this place. He's not planning it man. It's just happening to him", informed Sean, "I picked up on it and came here to make sure it goes right".

The wheels of Evans machinations began turning. It wasn't quite what he was hoping for but he could use this. In order to change his place in the universe this way, this person would have to shed or alter his existential envelope. If Evans could observe this it would bring him one step closer to his goal.

"Which one is it?" asked Evans, "I can tell if it's one of these people in this area. Point him out to me."

"Why, what do you want with him?", asked Sean.

"Point him out to me", said Evans.

"What are going do?", asked the being D'Irem, known lately as Sean.

Evans dug his ethereal claws into D'Irem, "My intentions are not your business Djinn, just do as I command".

Powerless to flee or fight and bound to the laws of a conscripted Djinn he was compelled to answer.

"Th- that one," conceded D'Irem pointing in the direction of a small group sitting on the grass only about fifty yards away.

As soon as Evans locked on, it was obvious which one of the group it was. Not only because he was the only male of the group but because Evans could see it with his naked eyes. The young man with shoulder length light brown hair, in faded blue jeans and a dark brown flannel shirt, was kneeling down talking to a young girl in cutoff jean shorts, sandals and a thread-bare tie-dyed t-shirt. She was lying on her side with her head resting on one hand, hanging on every word he spoke.

Evans had to focus a bit due to the large amount of ambient energy in the area. When he did he could see the waves of calming energy flowing from the boy's mouth into the little hippie girl he was speaking to. This was his quarry.

As Evans got closer he could hear that the boy was giving her some advice about some boy she liked, or her boyfriend, or some such nonsense. Evans didn't care enough to pay close attention. He regarded his prey curiously, and with a small measure of disgust. The Zen-like calm of this bodhisattva irked him. This child was unworthy of his power, squandering it to help these peons with their petty problems. But he would change all that soon enough. Yet another example of the poor choices the system of balance made in its existential allocations, and further evidence of why it needed a will to direct it.

Belles and Waite had made their way down the same grassy
hill Evans had earlier, and were alternately doing random
scans of the people around them and looking at the various
items at the dozens of small vendor tents that lined one side
of the dirt path they were walking along and the artwork wall
that lined the other.

"Wow, this is like a Renaissance Faire without the costumes",
commented Martin.

"You're not kiddin', Marty" responded Thurston happily
between bites of some sort of meat on a stick.

"You find anything yet?", asked Martin and then added
quickly as Thurston opened his mouth, "Anything interesting
pertaining to our mission?"

"Ha, you know me to well, Marty. Not really but there's a
residual signature nearby I'd like to check on. Might be
nothing, but I got a funny feeling."

The two walked a little further until the dirt path merged with
a paved one then, proceeded over a small wooden bridge and
toward a semi-truck trailer that had been until recently the
temporary home of one 'Seany Bear'.

"You're right, Thurston, there's a lot of residual magickal
energy here. Something happened here. Pretty recently
too.", Martin said.

"Yeah," said Thurston in a tone that suggested he thought the
something that had happened here was seriously wrong, "Give
me a moment here, Marty."

Thurston recited a quick incantation and he and Martin saw
the ghostly vision of what transpired there.

"Shite, Marty, that's that snobby git you bumped into outside the hotel.", said Thurston.

"Yes, and now he's a snobby git with a Djinn. Damn, why didn't I catch that before? He's the malevolent signature I was detecting.", said Martin.

"Probably cause you were busy being insulted. You really need to work on your metaphysical multitasking, Marty", jabbed Thurston.

Martin sneered back at him, "Yeah, yeah... how long do you think we will be able to follow this vision?".

"A few minutes at best. Hopefully long enough to catch up with that smarmy knacker", said Thurston.

The two followed the rapidly fading vision back up the hill and then on for a few blocks. The vision faded completely as they approached a grassy clearing on what was presumably part of the Moravian College campus.

As soon as they were in sight of it they could feel a change. The air seemed to grow heavier, and there was a feeling of pressure. The negative energy was almost tangible.

"Oh, this is not good.", shuddered Martin.

"Yeah," agreed Thurston almost inaudibly, "and it's getting worse."

Like ripples on a pond the negative influence was spreading rapidly from this one spot.

"Thurston, we have to get out of here and find the source of this before...", began Martin but he was cut short by someone shouting a few yards away.

"Fuck you!", shouted the little hippie girl nearly in tears, "You think you can just... just use people up and cast them aside."

"Where the hell did you get that line, a daytime soap?", asked the young collegiate looking man in pre-faded designer jeans and a Penn State T-shirt, "Listen you little dead head, if you thought you were anything but a quick lay you were wrong".

"You jock douchebag, I...," but she was cut short as the young man punched her squarely in the face. She collapsed to the ground and tears mixed with blood as she stumbled trying to lift herself to sitting position.

The surrounding crowd wasted no time responding in kind as the jock was tackled to the ground by two grunge kids. They kicked and stomped him mercilessly. Loud cracking sounds came from the jock as his ribcage was crushed, and blood flowed freely from his mouth.

The violence did not end here as other fights began to break out all over the field, with equally broken and bloody results.

"We need to do something about this!", implored Thurston.

"I agree", said Martin, "By stopping it at its source. If we involve ourselves in this fray things will get worse while we waste time."

Thurston's desire to stop the carnage before him was overridden by his reason and he was forced to agree with Martin's logic.

Thurston sighed heavily "You're right Marty, let's get out of here before we get caught up in this."

As if on cue a small army of uniformed police officers entered the field. These officers that had intended to subdue the brawl before them were quickly overcome by the negative energy wave and only escalated the violence doing more damage with nightsticks and Tasers than the civilians were doing to each other with bare fists.

"You two on the ground now!", shouted a police officer charging Martin and Thurston.

"Officer, we're federal...", Martin began, but was cut short as the officer swung at his head with his nightstick.

Martin dodged easily and grabbed the officer's over extended arm, putting him in a quick wrist lock and bringing him to his knees intending only to restrain him long enough for Martin to identify himself. But this is where Martin's training failed him, and he finally succumbed to the effects of the energy wave.

Martin snapped the officer's wrist and elbow, and with a look of rage and determination on his face grabbed him by the back of his head and under the chin.

Thurston knew what was coming and had to act fast.

"Ne'sahs!", he shouted enacting a magickal stun spell, that sent out a blast that knocked down and stunned everyone in a fifty yard radius.

Thurston grabbed the dazed Martin by the back of his shirt collar and hoisted him to his feet.

"Ack, ya' look desperate. Come on, Marty, move it, before the five-o gets it together", said Thurston.

"The wa huh", Martin stammered trying to clear his head.

"Move you damn header!," Thurston said practically dragging Martin away from the scene of carnage and confusion trying to suppress the effects of the negative energy on himself which was making him feel increasingly and unwarrantedly annoyed toward Martin.

"What's going on?", babbled Martin.

"Get your head on, Marty. We gotta find that guy from the hotel before he can do anymore damage."

Evans paused for a moment to watch down an alley as three police officers mercilessly beat a young man with a Mohawk with their night sticks. He watched with sinister pleasure as sprays of blood flung from the nightsticks onto the graffitied cinder-block walls of the alley
.
"D'Irem, how long is this going to take?", asked Evens without looking away.

"I don't know, you've altered the natural process. All I was here to do was watch over the kid and make sure this went smoothly", answered the Djinn.

"So much for that, ay?", chuckled Evans.

There was a wet cracking sound as the punk's skull finally gave up under the assault.

"No rush", Evans said coldly

"You sick fuck!", shouted D'Irem

"Careful, or I'll have you join in the fun", said Evans.

"You wouldn't?", asked the Djinn.

"Wouldn't I?", Evans asked while glancing over at Andrew who was stumbling around, holding his head and growling in anguish as Evans pumped a steady flow of his own malice into the boy.

"I think even in our short history together you have learned enough of me to know that I am capable of doing just that. And worse."

D'Irem remained silent and looked at the ground.

"We need to move on", said Evans.

"So you can spread this even further", D'Irem thought to himself.

"Yes", said Evans into his mind, "So I can spread this even further. I think a great act of mass violence is what's needed to push our young friend over the edge, don't you?"

"Not even your thoughts are unknown to me now slave, do well to remember that", Evans said out loud, "This way. There's a larger venue ahead I believe".

Thurston and Martin were forced to move through back alleys, gardens, and even a large cemetery to avoid the random acts of violence. They were less looking for their target and more giving Martin a chance to refocus. Coming out from a small wooded area they found themselves in a large outdoor space, featuring a reunion concert of Credible Clean Water Resurrection.

"This is perfect", commented Thurston, "The vibration frequency of this blue grass music should help enhance your calm".

"Cool, I always did like these guys. But aren't they country?", asked Martin.

"No, they're blue grass", said Thurston.

"Good, I hate country", said Martin.

"But you just said... Never mind", said Thurston.

"Yeah, some New Orleans blue grass will fix me right up", Martin said smiling.

"Actually they're from California", said Thurston annoyed that Martin was still unfocused.

"What?!", Martin looked completely dejected.

"Marty, look, across the crowd, it's git-boy and homeless guy", said Thurston.

"So much for relaxation", Martin said through gritted teeth as he used shoulder and elbow to bully his way across the audience. Even the band seemed to notice, and the lead singer yelled out to him ,"Hey! No moshing. This isn't a Slayer concert".

This got a small rumble of laughter from the crowd, but the presence of Evans and Andrew was starting to take its toll and by the time Martin had reached Evans, they had had their fill of him. Just as Martin reached Evans he was pulled back by unknown hands. Evans folded his arms across his chest and looked down at Martin with a smug grin and shook his head. This smugness ended abruptly when Evans realized that Martin had managed a firm grip on his rather expensive belt. The psychically enraged crowd drew back Martin and the attached Evans.

Thurston watched helplessly as both friend and foe alike were consumed by the crowd. Neither were visible amongst the blur of flailing limbs. Thurston's eye fell upon the Djinn disguised as the homeless man standing next to an anguished boy. The Djinn was waving its arms emphatically trying to get his attention. When he saw that he had it, he motioned toward a spot past the far end of the crowd.

D'Irem had managed to get away from Evans and was kneeling on the ground, cradling Andrew's head.

"Help us", said D'Irem.

"Sean", asked Andrew, "Why does my... something hurt... I don't even know what it is?".

"Your soul", said Thurston, "That's what hurts, kiddo".

"He's in final stages", said D'Irem.

.

"Wait... is this boy in an existential chrysalis?", asked Thurston.

"Yes", said D'Irem quietly.

"He'll change in hours", said Thurston.

"Minutes", said D'Irem.

The air grew gray and still. Like a calm sky on the liminal between Autumn and Winter that portended a long struggle's arrival.

Evans began walking up slowly. He had separated from the crowd, and parted them with a hand gesture. He pushed D'Irem aside and kneeled in fascination looking at Andrew.

He was oblivious to any emotional content of the scene, instead bearing the air of an astronomer observing a new kind of star through a radio telescope.

"You are becoming what in plain English would be called a guardian angel", said Evans, "But not an angel... and not of a person. Your job is to preside over a group of souls on the cusp of forming lifelong bonds and success and ensuring they get there", Evans said.

He continued, "I am reversing that. You'll be instead the thing that guarantees little bands of souls don't achieve their great works and they get scattered to the wind. I'm not evil. If you were already heading into rain cloud turf, I would make you a little fucking rainbow... I just have to...".

"Affect him", said Thurston eyeing Evans straight in the face, "Move his transformation from what it's meant to be to something else. Compare what happens to the vision of what should happen from the Djinn's mind, so you can observe the existential envelope".

"Touche", said Evans, surprised to hear these words from this man.

"You want to compare... the vision of what is to happen to what does... like two lab samples... This is all equations to you", said Thurston.

"Oh, no", said Evans, "Equations leading to a distant personal goal. Now, in case you're wondering, I intend to use this".

Evans showed a small crystal.

" *What is it he has?*", Thurston heard a voice in his head, and realized it was the Djinn. Somehow, D'Irem had broken away from the conscription.

"*It's pure disaster, distilled into physical form through meta-alchemy. Tragedy made into matter. Our boy here has studied some serious Ben-Martu*", Thurston replied to the Djinn telepathically.

"I can hear your little telepathic conversation", said Evans, "There's also enough left for this...".

Martin came limping up to the others, but then he fell over in pain. It wasn't clear if it was physical or metaphysical... or perhaps both.

"I can spare enough of the stone to make your friend here die literally of a broken heart. For him every tragedy that could happen, is", said Evans.

Andrew worsened in empathy to Martin.

Thurston walked passed Evans, and hugged Martin.

"What are you doing?, asked Martin.

"Call it a favor", said Thurston as he absorbed tons of energy from Martin.

Thurston stood, and wiped a little blood from his nose.

"*Is fheàrr teine beag a gharas na teine mòr a loisgeas*", said Thurston in Gaelic. He then caused a series of glyphs in Arabic writing to appear on Martin's forehead which read as
"أبادِ اللہ خضراءهم لصديقك دمك وملاك"

"That's not an incantation", said Evans.

"It's a proverb", said Thurston, "Better than all the incantations in the world".

Andrew now started emanating beams of light and shadow, and cried out in pain. D'Irem bent down to minister to him.

Thurston walked toward him, but D'Irem held up a hand.

"He's already been interfered with too much. You can't put him back. Just block any more change!", said D'Irem.

Martin got to his feet, and ran in and took a pot shot at Evans in the face. He then kneed him in the groin. Evans hit back, first with a quick telekinetic blast, then with a magically enhanced strength punch.

"Idiot", said Evans, "You don't have the tools to take me down".

"I have the tools to take your pet rock", said Martin. Martin had managed to get the crystal.

Evans readied an enhanced punch, and found he was held by Thurston's hand.

"All these equations... Tell me? Have ya found one that resolves with you bein' relevant yet? Me... more magick than you... but I'm guessin' your pockets are full of lots of impressive trinkets you could use on me... so let's call the magick even", Thurston said.

Evans knocked him back with a psi-blast.

"I have an edge on you on the physical strength...", said Thurston as he levitated Evans a bit until that familiar headache told him he was over exerting his psionics.

Evans landed with a thud, and managed a fire spell and burned the shirt on Thurston's back.

"You don't have my rage though", said Evans.

"No, I don't", said Thurston as he reached a hand out toward a glittering object, "You got this, I got that. Cancel each other out. But this is going to end like a night in Temple Bar in Dublin when a drunken Brit school boy fucks with a local".

Thurston pulled Evans around and held a broken beer bottle to his throat.

"It ends with a broken bottle", said Thurston.

Martin drew his gun.

Andrew stopped struggling.

"Let him go", said Andrew.

"It's happening", said D'Irem.

Thurston released Evans, but Martin didn't put his gun away.

Evans looked left and right, and stood. He went to run off. Martin tackled him and stabbed Evans with the crystal he had taken from him earlier.

He then turned around to see the homeless man and Thurston looking at Andrew.

A blinding light was showing somewhere, but, more intense was the sound. It was a sound heard by the sensitive in the soul, and not with the ears. And that sound was a painful and glorious hybrid somewhere between digging and unfolding.

This is how Martin Belles processed it.

Then everything went fuzzy.

Martin Belles awoke in his hotel room. Thurston Waite was lying next to him, cold and dead.

"Martin", came Thurston's voice, "Over here... It's a dummy. The Djinn made a corpse with my DNA. I'm tweaking it with energy signatures and what not so it will fool the ONLA".

"What?", Martin asked, "Where's... that guy?".

"Gone", said D'Irem, "Though you put that crystal in his blood. That man already had a chip on his shoulders and a persecution complex the likes of which I have never seen. Now with what you did... I would not like to live in his head".

"So we won?", asked Martin, "I mean... the kid... he was supposed to turn into energy like that?".

"No", said Thurston, "Not like that".

"Andrew was meant to become a force... being... presence... that would keep groups of linked souls together long enough to form lasting bonds and accomplish great works. The cosmos culled him from a human so it would have an element of humanity to it. That man... he... meant to reverse Andrew. Make him something that would block the goals of those soul groups and drive them apart", said D'Irem.

"So, which did he become?", asked Martin.

"Neither", said Thurston, "He can only inspire soul groups... and make them aware of their link to each other and their destinies. For some, that will make them cohesive... others, it may drive them apart... At best he is like a focusing lens now with no ability or desire to push one way or another".

"All that man wanted was to influence Andrew's transformation. So, I suppose he got what he wanted, but, with that crystal in his blood, I doubt he will enjoy his victory. I doubt he will enjoy much of anything", said D'Irem.

"You're leaving the ONLA?", asked Martin, "You know that phony body won't fool them forever".

"I don't want to fool them into thinking I'm dead", said Thurston, "I want to fool them into thinking I fooled you".

"Fair enough", said Martin, "I guess I owe you... a favor. And... I don't mean letting you walk now. I can't remember what you pulled out of me... it was like... nightmares... all at once but... grown-up nightmares... the worst kind".

"The ONLA wanted that boy, Marty", said Thurston, "And that guy I fought there... the last straw... only one man trains pups that way. He's been suckled from Braxus's teet".

"Where will you go?", asked Martin.

"Home", said Thurston, "Home... and I'm taking this guy with me".

The Djinn created a portal.

"Normally I don't have this much magick at once", he said, "but I've been saving it up".

Martin Belles wanted to say more but they were all just emotionally numb.

No one had won today. Absolutely no one.

Martin Belles filed his report.

Deceased: Agent Thurston Waite.

The ONLA sent him on pointless missions with David and Sieurd for weeks until the Seer Corps found that Andrew's transformation had interacted with the time fluctuations around Bethlehem. O-Force data was collected. Some said O-Force stood for Outer or Other or Outré. But it meant something that came from neither magic, or technology, or nature, or another dimension, or even from God. Outside... Other.

Martin was given credit for deciphering the data. He didn't know how. But a month later he found himself having lunch with Abraham Braxus.

Thurston knew the ONLA would find out he was alive. He knew things were coming. He knew things had gone down.

His head was jello.

So he and the Djinn moved into a small house in County Mayo in the west country of Ireland. One that needed a lot of fixing up. One that had a million little things that needed to be done, so he could keep busy while his mind settled down.

A million little trivial things to distract him until the day came when Thurston would need to do big things again; the kind of big things few knew about. Stopping The-End-of-The-World that lives next door to Armageddon. Stopping the invasion no one else can because they're stopping something else.

A million little things... and one luxury.

Thurston Waite had a little time to breathe and a great view of the sea. D'Irem knew Andrew was one of those things that call to you on the wind now. He really, literally was one of those now.

Thurston told him if it troubled his mind, to keep his hands busy.

One day a knock came at the door. It was a dragon.

"Can I help you?", asked Thurston.

"I was studying the energy matrix that governs parahumans... vampires... werewolves... the like... studying why they are governed by the rules they are", the Dragon said sheepishly.

Thurston shook his head that the creature began with no introduction. It was a purple dragon. The purple type of dragons were known for their conversational abruptness.

"And?", said Thurston with a raised eyebrow.

"I scrambled it", said the Dragon.

"Meaning?", said Thurston.

"The energy matrix is chaotic!", said the Dragon, "The rules will vary from manifestation to manifestation".

"That's kinda cool", said Thurston.

"Yeah", said the Dragon, "It is... I don't want you to put it back. I want to have a place to hide out".

"Why would I give you that?", said Thurston.

"I used to role-play as a stock market analyst and also as a corporate attorney. I am good with money. Human money", the Dragon said.

Thurston looked at the solar cell he had rigged himself that powered the home he shared with D'Irem. He looked at D'Irem.

"Okay", said Thurston, "What do you know about Green energy?.

"Nature Magick?", asked the Dragon, "Nothing... the subject bores me to death".

"No... the other kind", said Thurston.

"Ohhhh", said the Dragon, "I know the EU is giving away grants for environmentally sound alternative energy development like they are water".

Thurston opened a good bottle of whiskey. He offered it to the Dragon, and then to D'Irem.

"Thurston Waite... CEO... Yes... I like that", said Thurston.

"Boys", said Thurston, "We're going to incorporate".

DEMONTIA

The Hidden Track of Staves is drawn telling the Operator that full manifestation can be reconstructed from vibrations of lost quanta still manifest in existing quanta. The foamy suds under the world contain not secrets, but echoes of the erased and forerunners of the potential, ready to be thickened up to workable clay.

"Ethereal or incarnated?", asked the sand sprite behind the counter.

"I'm standing here in this stupid android body I had to possess when I got here. If I was incarnated, I would have my own body...", said Presh through the robot's speech synthesizer.

"Ethereal or incarnated?", the sprite asked again, even further monotone than the first time.

Presh realized he was not going to win this battle.

"Ethereal", he acquiesced.

"Race?", asked the sprite.

"Demon", Presh replied.

"Specifically?"

"Luciferian", replied Presh.

"Luciferian demons all perished at the battle of Armageddon when Yahweh absorbed them", the clerk replied.

"I wasn't at Armageddon", Presh said, "I was stuck inside a... host".

A liche with a clipboard walked up to the sprite. It muttered an unintelligible grunt to her but seemed to be scolding the sprite for a faux pas somehow. A look of emotion filled the sprite's eyes.

"You're right", the sprite said to the liche with a sense of shame, "I am being insensitive".

She looked at Presh with some regard of sympathy. And infuriatingly it was sympathy, not empathy, maybe even with a tinge of pity.

"You poor dear", she looked at him, "You're here for survivor's guilt. You're a war deserter".

"No", Presh said angrily, "No one deserted. All demons felt Lucifer's call. We had to go. It wasn't a choice. I was metaphysically unable to disengage myself from my host due to complications. Then Yahweh ate all the demons and angels, and Hades 86'd Yahweh... and suddenly, I'm left solo".

"Poor dear...", the sprite repeated, "Survivor's guilt".

She handed Presh a form stamped in several places with a look of dismissive forced cheer, and Presh wobbled over to a chair in the waiting area.

He sat next to a young female werewolf who was alternating between rearranging the magazines sitting on the table in front of them and licking off large sections of her own fur, never seeming to be satisfied with any level of completeness to either task.

Presh nodded to her as he took his seat. She nodded back, and coughed up a large hairball on the lap of his possessed body.

"I've never met a robot before", she said.

"I'm a demon", he said.

"Oh... no body, huh?", she asked.

"Yeah", he replied, "They insist these therapy sessions occur on the physical plane".

"You have issues with a human body, huh?", the werewolf asked as she started licking her arm again.

"No", he said, "They think I do... so they stuck me in this stupid robot they got from... who knows where...".

"Your arm has an ECE stamp on it. Extra Chronal Event. Means the robot you're in is from another timeline, alternate Earth, or a potential future or something. Like the alien nanotech they pulled out of some closed apocalyptic timeline that almost manifested back east. There's more and more of those popping in and out and leaving little tid-bits behind. Someone should look into why", she replied.

"Ah", Presh said without interest.

"I'm here a lot. That's how I know that. They think I have OCD. I read the magazines here. They have interesting articles", she said.

Presh looked down at the one on the table in front of her. It read *Office of Non-Linear Acquisitions: Abraham Braxus Memorial Charity for Wellness of Hetero Sapiens* on the top. It then had subheadings with that month's entertaining articles with titles such as Sucubbi Celibacy and *Playing Jazz With Soul Even Though You Don't Have One: Crossroads LaRue Tells All.*

"Well", said Presh, "I'm not going to be back here. They pulled me out of my human host after he was caught setting fire to a battered women's shelter. The Seer Corps sent a couple of Junior Onlies to the scene when they tracked my energy signature".

"So they want to rehabilitate you? Burning a battered women's shelter is harsh... even for a demon", the werewolf replied.

"It wasn't me", he replied, "It was the host. He had a psychotic personality disorder".

Presh was going to continue, but the wolf had returned to her magazine shuffling and fur licking.

"Robert Presh", a voice called from one of the rear rooms.

Presh got up and followed the Doctor, who looked like a

rather revolting hybrid of a Plant Elemental and Djinn, probably born during the Pansexual Interplanar Crossing of Late November and a Couple Days of December 1964.

"It's... just Presh", he said.

"Oh, it says robot", the Doctor corrected himself, "I'm doctor Jean E. Leafman".

"*Really*", Presh thought to himself, "*That's his name... a Djinn and Plant Elemental hybrid with that name... You have got to be fucking kidding*".

"Before you ask about my name, yes, I am named after the human musician Jean E. Leafman", said Dr. Leafman, "Everyone asks me that".

Presh took a seat in his borrowed body.

"So", Leafman began, "What seems to be your issue?".

"First off", said Presh, "I'm not a robot, I'm a demon".

"Oh", said Leafman, "The ONLA stuck you in a loaner body. You have Biological Vessel Avoidance Syndrome?".

"No!", Presh said, "I was in a biological vessel until last night. Two ONLA agents grabbed me and pulled me out of my host".

"Did that make you feel powerless?", asked Leafman.

"I was glad to get out. I was stuck. I was so stuck I couldn't get out of that host for the battle of Armageddon... ".

"Ok... A robot demon with BVAS and a war deserter. Interesting", Leafman said scribbling something.

"Not a robot", said Presh, "I told you this is a loaner body".

"You burned down a women's shelter?", asked Leafman, "That's aggressive even for a demon. Are you a misogynist?".

"No", Presh replied, "My human host was".

The demon's ire began to rise.

"We don't treat humans here", said Leafman.

"My human is not here", said Presh, "That's why I am in this robot body".

"You just said you aren't a robot", said Leafman.

"Look", said Presh, "The human I was in was a schizophrenic. I didn't know that three years ago when I possessed him. The possession agent I used lied about everything. Said the guy was a pure Christian and all. But he was so messed up in the head, I may as well have not been there. I would tell him to kill a rabbit... you know, start out small... I was building up to stuff... and Derek... that was the psycho personality... Derek would already have Todd killing the neighbor's dog. Todd was the main personality, the host, however you wanna put it. I tell him to have sexual thoughts about his mother... Derek one ups me and has him molest a nun. I tell him to break into a Synagogue and paint some swastikas... and Derek pulls that Women's Shelter crap... I mean... that was... harsh".

"Did Derek make you feel inadequate?", asked Leafman, "I think we'll need several sessions".

"No", said Presh. Then he calmed down slightly, "Yes, maybe... a little inadequate".

"Hmmm", said Leafman, "Five sessions at least".

"I don't need any sessions", said Presh.

"Are you happy in your robot body?", asked Leafman.

"Well...", stammered Presh, "No".

"Ten sessions", Leafman said further scribbling something.

"Does this count as a session?", asked Presh.

"This is only an evaluation", said Leafman, "And it's over".

"All this for five minutes?", asked Presh.

"Evaluations are important", said Leafman, "It lets me know how many sessions you need. And you need at least ten. Do you like Tuesdays?".

"Do you have any good news for me?", asked Presh.

"Yes", said Leafman as he showed him the door, "We'll keep you in the robot body until your sessions are done".

Defeated, Presh wobbled out of the office and back into the waiting room, only now able to gain control of the Robot. He looked at himself in the mirrored surface of a polished metal piece of decora on the wall. He looked like a curved version of the Tin Man from the wizard of Oz. The whole situation was further worsened by the graffiti that some ONLA member had scrawled all over the front plate of the robot when it had been in storage proclaiming "Papi and Gena 4EVER".

The werewolf was still sitting there and she looked up at him.

"Five sessions?", she asked.

"Ten", he said sitting back down next to her.

"Cheer up, Robot", she said..., "Hey, you wanna go for a coffee?".

"I can't drink coffee", he said.

"So you don't wanna go?", she asked.

"Actually... yeah.. I'd like to go", Presh replied.

As he mechanically wobbled out of the office in his borrowed body, she ran around him excitedly.

"Don't feel bad you can't drink coffee", she said, "My last boyfriend couldn't either. Wasn't his fault. His body could drink it, but, he was just a schizophrenic fragment in someone's head. That's why I come here. For depression I suffer from after the break up. And the OCD".

Presh had a cautious feeling.

"What was his name?", Presh asked.

"Derek", she replied.

DEMONTIA

ARBOR DAY LOVE STORY

The Twelve of Respite is the moment to pause. It purchases for its stated value an interval or moment in which variables are on course even if the will behind them lets go in order to further machine, smith, and maneuver elements of a given reality.

"Excuse me, Director," said Agent Knusch as he poked his head into Director Martin Belles's office, "But your assistant seems to be out."

"Yes, it's Arbor Day. Come in agent... uh...", said Martin.

"Knusch, sir. Is that what it is? I can't seem to find anyone.", Knusch said.

"Yes agent. It's the only holiday we really observe here at the ONLA", said Martin.

"Why is that, sir?", asked Knusch.

"It's... the only one quiet enough", said Martin.

"I see. Well even my partner has taken the day off and procedure requires two agents to sign off to close a case. I'd like to wrap this up, and I would feel more comfortable if I had a second person to sign off on this", said Knusch.

"That's alright, agent. If it was a minor matter Mr. Orin won't care", said Martin.

"As I said, sir, I would feel more comfortable if...", Knusch started.

"Fine, fine. Give it here and I'll...", Martin replied.

"Don't you want to review the file first, sir?", asked Knusch.

Martin took a deep breath and let it out slowly. He may have been in his office on the ONLA's only vacation holiday, but he was rather enjoying having nothing to do today. And this agent who whose name he couldn't remember was ruining his quiet day.

"Fine! Fine, I'll review your findings and sign and file. Happy?", said Martin annoyed.

"Well, not really sir, but it will have to do. Technically two active investigating agents should sign off on it but...", Knusch said.

"You are severely pushing your luck and testing my patience, agent.", said Martin.

Agent Knusch couldn't wrap his head around how following proper procedure was getting him in trouble, but apparently it was.

"Yes, sir", said Knusch.

"OK, file number blah blah, agents blah and blah. Blah blah, blah blah blah blah. Case of the Inverted Love Story? I'm guessing your partner came up with that. Don't answer", the rest was just mumbling and the odd snort or giggle as he read the following.

It would appear that Thomas Rend age 22 of Hoboken, NJ became obsessed with a girl by the name of Sara Engel, age 19 originally from Brooklyn, NY but more recently also a resident of Hoboken, NJ.

Thomas initially pursued her using conventional means, normal human courting rituals which did yield some limited success in the form of sexual intercourse. Sara however was a "party girl" and unwilling to form a permanent bond with any single partner of either gender. After several months of pursuit with varying results, Thomas apparently decided to attempt non-conventional methods i.e. Magick, i.e. (this case specifically Voodoo. He contracted a local Bokor (name withheld) who cast for him a particularly (and unnecessarily) powerful love spell. The spell had instant and satisfactory results at first (according to the Bokor who said "I told the crazy white kid he didn't need a spell that strong, but I agreed just to get him and his blubbering out of my office"). That did not last long however as it is commonly known persons under the influence of a love spells become obsessive and "clingy" and otherwise experience alterations to their personality and orientation toward all aspects of life. As such according to Thomas's friends his relationship with Sara, "Got old quick" and she "Was like totally annoying and shit, dude." At which time Thomas terminated the relationship, or so I surmise from the phrase "He dumped her like yesterday's cellphone". (This particular witness apparently being unaware that mobile communications devices no longer use cellular technology).

It is unclear if at this point Thomas was aware of Sara's involvement with Witchcraft. As is recorded Witchcraft has little to no effect in and of itself, the very reason the general public is allowed to practice it. However presumably fueled by magically induced obsession her spells were augmented (still awaiting lab confirmation). And as the saying goes "Turnabout is fair play." Sara proceeded to cast a love spell on Thomas, at which time Thomas became obsessed with Sara. For the week they were seen in public. They were described as "Totally disgusting and clingy" and "All super lovey dovey and shit.". The relationship ended when the couple was found deceased in Thomas's apartment. They had apparently died of dehydration after three days of ping ponging back and forth the phrase "I don't know, what do you want to do?". The coroner's report also indicated that from the severity of the damage to both larynxes, they must have been "Hoarse to an unimaginable degree."

The conclusion of these agents is that since both parties are deceased and technically no foul play was involved no further action by this department is appropriate. It is however the suggestion of these agents that a study of the interaction of the systems of Voodoo and Wicca be explored by appropriate departments.

"Oh my God, that was the funniest thing I have read all year", Martin said wiping the tears out of his eyes, "Oh goodness, Okay, I'll sign off on this and file it for you".

"Excuse me sir, but how is this incident funny? I fail to see how the magickal deaths of two young people are...", Knusch started.

"Look just... go enjoy the rest of your day off. Have some fun. That's an order Agent... uh..."

"Knusch sir. Yes, sir", said Knusch, still confused, as he walked down the hall trying to think of what he might consider fun.

He heard the muffled voice of Director Belles as he left the building, "Oh, this is too good. I'm gonna have to share this one with Abe when he gets back."

Agent Knusch got into his ONLA issue car still in uniform with the issue of fun still on his mind.

"Hey, got a light hot stuff?", bellowed a rather attractive bohemian looking young woman as she poked her head through his open window.

"Hmm, she looks like she knows how to have fun", he thought.

ARBOR DAY LOVE STORY

UNWRECKED

The Six of Cities sits in the Operator's hands. It is clear how the open places and empty spaces of one cosm or dimension brush the open places of others. How the hearts of cities, for in one form or another such clusters are to be found on all levels, brush against one another across the strands, is less intuitive. This card, when contemplated by the Operator at a frenetic pace, will reveal this knowledge.

Headache.

It's definitely a headache. I remember them well, but, how could I be experiencing pain? I open my eyes, and see I'm strapped to a gurney, still fully dressed, and an IV is in my arm.

Soma. The only thing that will give a vampire a headache is a massive dose of Soma. The last time I was in a place like this was right after I was turned. Fuck... I must've gone berserk.

But how did I?

Now I remember. Andy. He put human blood in my drink.

If you drink human blood it will block the effects of Soma.
And then I remember why he did it. He wanted me to go
crazy, so that I would bite him, and turn him. He thought
being a vampire would be a fate better than the one which was
coming for him.

Did I turn him, or hurt him? Or Hurt Annie? Shit... right
before I lost my rational mind Andy had Annie tied to that
chair. And if I didn't hurt Andy, what if that thing got to him?

I think I remember someone else in the room, tackling Andy
after it threw me out of a window, while Annie was still tied in
that chair.

Supposedly, Succubi and Incubi were even stronger than
vampires. If my half lucid memory of being thrown six stories
down onto East Sixth Street like a rag doll was correct, then
they were definitely stronger than us. A lot stronger.

If that thing had its way with Andy, the first thing he would
have done after he transformed would be to mark the first
female he found. And that would've been Annie. Then he
would've come back for her three days later.

Wait. She must've gotten unmarked by now. I mean, she's
Annie after all. How hard could it be for her to get unmarked
if her life depended on it?

Unless... I remember being thrown back against a wall by that
thing, before it picked me up again and tossed me out the
window. I think it threw me into Annie. If she wasn't up and
around, then she couldn't get unmarked.

I snap back to the present. I tug at the restraints, and clearly whoever put these on me hadn't counted on me waking up so soon. Vampires are usually out for days with a heavy Soma dose. I'm able to break them with ease.

I run through a few corridors, and find a stairwell, and run out the back through the emergency exit. The damn sun is still out, albeit low in the sky. Not enough to kill me, but enough to hurt like a bitch. Twice in one day I get to experience pain.

A rarity for a vampire.

I find an alley to dart into, and some shade.

I realize I need a phone, and some hipster douche happens to be in the wrong place at the wrong time. I hit him with a good sucker punch, which with my enhanced strength easily knocks him out.

I search through the dude's pockets, and find a phones.

"Sorry fella", I say to him. He'll be out cold for a while, but he'll be alright.

The phone tells me it's the 23rd. I've been out for three days.

If Andy is an Incubus now, and marked Annie, he'll becoming for her tonight.

I dial Annie, and a Verizon recording tells me her number is temporarily disconnected. Same thing with Andy. I try Kate next.

She answers.

"Hello?", she says.

"Kate, it's Owen", I say.

"What number are you calling me from?", she asks.

"I stole some guy's phone", I reply.

"You stole someone's phone?", she asks.

"Where's Annie?", I interrupt her emphatically.

"You and Andy have both been missing for three days, and Annie is hospitalized with head trauma after they found her in his apartment, and you think I should just tell you where she is?", Kate says flabbergasted.

"You just told me where she is", I reply, "Just tell me which hospital now".

"I'm calling the cops", she says.

"I didn't hurt either of them. A Succubus came for Andy", I tell her.

"What?", she asks.

"He was marked Katie", I tell her.

"Nolan was marked", she says.

"I know", I say, "And you slept with him to unmark him. But Andy got marked too, the same night as Nolan. He went to Annie to get unmarked, and she wouldn't do it. He had me over to his house to ask me to turn him. He thought being a vampire would be better than that thing coming for him. He put human blood in my drink to try to block my Soma treatment, but it didn't totally berserk me. I think the Succubus got him, and if it got him, after he came to, he would've marked Annie. It's three days. If he's an Incubus, he'll come for her tonight. And the hospital wouldn't have checked if she was marked".

"I'm still calling the cops", she said.

"Kate, the cops don't try to fight those things, they don't have the resources. All they'll do is put Annie out in the street so there's no property damage", I say.

She knows I'm right.

"They say nothing can stop them, not even vampires", she says.

"You have a better idea?", I ask.

"Annie's in Pelham General, room 214", she concedes.

I hang up the phone, not knowing what to say next.
I probably can't stop him, this thing that was Andy, from hurting Annie. If she gets turned, she can't mark me. Vampires are immune. And if I try to get in Andy's way, it's not like he's going to have a stake, or even still retain enough of his rational mind to use it if he does. But they say there is a way to kill vampires besides stakes through the heart or direct sunlight. Supposedly the government did tests and found that incredibly extreme physical trauma all over the whole body can kill a vampire. And a pummeling from an Incubus that a vampire got by being in the way of it and its mark might just do the trick.

If I'm going to get to Pelham in time, I'm going to have to fly. I was never good at flying, and there's still a tinge of daylight in the air. I bump into buildings, and look like a drunken goth Superman, stumbling over the rooftops.

How the hell did I get here?

I started going to that damn bar for one. Back when I was human, I needed a drink or two after work sometimes. I started to know the regulars, and then I made the acquaintance of the Fab Five, as I called them.
Three woman and two men. There was Nolan, a sort of relaxed Alpha male, sophisticated and sarcastic. I had a lot of good conversations with him over the years about pop culture.

Then there was Kate, a spunky little wise ass whose ethnicity you could never place. Everyone thought she and Nolan were an item, but, they insisted they weren't. There was Gina, who seemed to have a new man every week. Rounding it out were Andy, a kind hearted but meek little dude doing his best to fight the middle age spread, and Annie. Annie was an incredibly beautiful woman, but there seemed to almost be nothing sexual about her. Everybody at the bar knew Andy was in love with her. She was oblivious, but, probably would have rejected him if she knew.

I never breeched their inner circle, but, I did become friends with them all. More than any of the other regulars at the bar. After I changed, they were among the few who accepted me as if I was still... well... a human.

That's the other part of how I got here. When monsters that belonged in movies started coming out of the shadows and into the real world. Nobody knows how it started.

Werewolves started showing up in the Midwest. They were the first supernatural creatures the government confirmed the existence of. They never made it to the city.

Vampires did though. I found that out the hard way when I got thrulled by some girl at a club. I thought I was going to get laid. Instead, I got bitten. Luckily for me, I was one of the later victims to be turned vampiric. By then, the government had found Soma.

If you took your Soma injections, your bloodlust would go away, and you would retain your human mind. I missed sex, and food, and the sun. Pleasure was only an intellectual concept to me now. I eventually started going back to the bar. Of course, three shots of whisky in ten minutes would only buy me a fifteen minute buzz. The vampire physiology sobered me up to fast. But I liked going to the bar, and talking to the five almost made me feel... human.

Eventually, the bartenders even got used to me shooting up Soma at the bar. One sort of questioned me once, but I pointed her to the mirror and when she saw I had no reflection, she knew immediately what I was doing.

But the most fearsome creatures were the Succubi and the Incubi. Like the first vampires or werewolves, nobody knew where they came from. They too, had been human once, but no more. They retained no rational intelligence. They were sexual monsters. The Succubus was the female, and the incubus was the male. They were incredibly powerful. The army couldn't stop them. The government didn't bother to do anything about them anymore. They couldn't be hurt by material weapons.

The only thing Uncle Sam did was a public awareness campaign that if someone you knew got marked, you should unmark them. Even if you weren't attracted to the person, or even if you were in a relationship. The government never made it a law mind you.

That was how the Incubus and the Succubus worked. They scratched you and placed a mark on you. Then, like a venomous snake, they left you alone for three days. After that, they would come back for you, and force themselves on you, draining the very humanity from you in the process. You yourself would then become a Succubus or Incubus.

There was a way out though. There was a way to remove the mark. You had to have sex with someone you truly loved. That was the catch though. You couldn't hire a hooker, unless you loved the hooker. Lots of people who got marked were married or in relationships. For them, it was no big deal. Their significant other just did the nasty with them, the mark was gone, and the creature would never come for them.

Other people convinced people they loved who didn't love them back to have sex with them, as a matter of life or death.

But then, there were the unwrecked. I don't know where the word came from. I guess it referred to those who had unrequited love for another, and then got marked. There were some people who wouldn't do it for others, even if it meant the other person would die. It happened more often than you'd think it would. Hell, that's why the Succubi and Incubi could reproduce at all. And the rules were specific, while the person didn't have to love you back, you needed to love them, and you couldn't force yourself on them. It was the only way to remove the mark. So, for those unlucky few who couldn't find anyone to pity fuck them even if it meant their life depended on it, the creature that marked them would get them and 'wreck' them. Only you didn't die. You became one of the creatures.

Unrequited. Wrecked. The unlucky men and women in this category who could only wait three days for their doom became known as Unwrecked.

Nolan got marked by one. But he guilted Kate into sleeping with him, and so he got unmarked. The whole Succubus and Incubus thing wasn't really big on my radar. As a dead creature, the Succubae and Incubi were not interested in vampires. We were already nonhuman. And we couldn't unmark humans even if we wanted to since the dead can't have sex.

There was some gossip at the bar about what happened to Nolan.

One night I got a desperate call from Andy. The sun wasn't quite down, but he insisted I stick to the shade and come to his apartment immediately.

When I arrived there I found him agitated.

"Do you want a drink?", he asked.

"Sure", I said.

He handed me a Powers Rocks. I drank it out of habit, mostly, as its effect on me would be minimal.

It tasted off, but, he continued.

"I was marked", he said.

"Oh my god", I replied.

"The same night as Nolan", he said.

"Andy, that means, that thing will be coming for you tonight!", I said.

He began to tear up.

"I asked Annie to help me, like Kate did for Nolan, but, she wouldn't", he said both sad and angrily, "My life means that little to her that one awkward moment is worse than me dying to her".

"I'm sorry", I said.

"I didn't ask you here for pity. I need your help", he said.

"Andy, I'm not gay and vampires can't have sex. I couldn't unmark you if I wanted to", I replied.

I tried to get up, but, I felt woozy.

"No", he said, "You can put humans in a trance. Put Annie in a trance. Make her help me"

"I won't do that", I said, "Besides, I can't put a human in a trance on Soma, and I wouldn't do that anyway".

"Then turn me!", he said.

"What?", I asked.

"That thing will be back for me tonight!", he said, "But they aren't interested in vampires! I'll go on Soma, like you!".

"Soma doesn't work on everybody, I'm so sorry but... if I changed you... and you killed people... I'd be responsible", I said through a fog.

I knew at this point I knew something was wrong. He opened the door to his bedroom, and there was Annie. He had her duct taped to a chair and her mouth gagged so she couldn't speak.

"I brought her here in case you'd agree to the trance. But I knew you wouldn't", he said.

He now held up his bandaged hand. I knew why I felt wrong. He had put his own blood in my drink. Blood could interfere with Soma. Even as I looked at him and Annie, the desire to feed began to assert itself.

"You idiot", I said, "You have two monsters to contend with now".

But before I could do anything else, through his picture window burst a caricature of a woman. It was grotesque, with slimy skin and no mouth. It had large black eyes, and huge clawed hands. And angry red opening gaped between its legs.

This was a Succubus.

I had heard they were stronger than vampires. I put myself between the thing and Andy, but it threw me hard, and into Annie. I heard something crack as I hit her. It picked me up again, and threw me out the window I had come in.

It wouldn't have been interested in Annie. Or me after it got me out of the way. It had come for Andy. But after it changed him into an Incubus, he would mark Annie and come back for her three days later.

Annie was vivacious, bubbly, and gorgeous. Getting unmarked would normally have not been an issue for her, but, if she was out cold in a hospital bed, that was another story.

I must've wandered around and been taken to a Soma Treatment Facility by the Vampire Control Agents after I was thrown out that window.

UNWRECKED

It's dark when I get to Pelham. I find Annie in her room. I need to pull her covers off and examine her. Her body is gorgeous, but to me only appreciable in an artistic sense now.

On her upper shoulder, I find the mark.

She seems to rouse slightly for a moment, then sinks back into slumber from the pain meds.

I couldn't unmark her of course, being dead. The only thing I can do is try to physically fight the Incubus that had been Andy when it comes.

I don't have to wait long. He is even more hideous than the Succubus that changed him. I remember the rumors I've heard that incredible physical trauma can kill a vampire. I realize I'll probably find this out in a few seconds.

I place myself between the thing and its mark.

"Hello Andy", I say with both sadness and fear.

As it grabs me, all the thing that was Andy can do is roar a scream of inhuman rage.

SPIDER BITE

The Web of Cups has been drawn. The operator is on the cusp of the moment when the primary eruption of the Pleroma itself considers a bypass of the system. Rejoice.

The following text is among the more unusual even we at *Tales of the Unexplained Magazine* have ever received. It is, albeit brief, among the most complicated and onion layered pieces we have ever seen. And, even after multiple readings, nigh impossible to offer interpretation of. In fact, we will offer far more preliminary notes to the text than we usually do. As our readers know, we prefer to let the pieces we print speak for themselves, but this fascinating but convoluted document (or documents) require more preliminary exposition than most of our pieces.

It arrived at our offices by Fed Ex in two parts. A series of handwritten pages within which the handwriting changes, all on long, yellow lined legal paper, and two pages typewritten which are the only part which were addressed to us. The return address turned out to be an ice cream parlor on South Street in Philadelphia. The sender was listed as "No My Names is Dug My Name is not Name".

The following notes will give the reader some understanding

of the text:

"A" This is the typewritten pages, which are written in what seems to be some kind of humorous intentional butchering of the English Language. They outline someone named "Dug" who is angry at someone named "Davey" for not buying him some sort of food product, so, as revenge, "Dug" is sending the yellow-handwritten pages to *Tales of the Unexplained Magazine*, as apparently "Davey" wanted to keep these pages secret for unknown reasons. Presenter's note: We have not made any grammatical or spelling corrections to these texts, merely transcribed them character per character.

A: "Davey says he is gonna get me the Dickyburg meal with the car with the raccoon guy toy ins it, but then he forgets to do it, and he says he gets it for Dug next week, but next week the little one meal comes with the car with the little mouse man in it... Dug wants that one too... but nows is too late to get the raccoon guy... Davey brake promise and I dids all my chores this week and I not tell anybody that he go off his diet and have cheezcake when he lecture Abey about being healthy... so Dug brake promise two and send these writeys to you Davey wanna keep's away.. since Dug sends you this, makes yer cuver a nice puppy instead of an uglie boo... a brown puppies be nice..."

The rest of A is just a description of the puppy "Dug" would like to see on our cover so we omit the remaining narrative.

"B" is a handwritten note to someone named "David" from someone named "Karen". We present B.

B:

"David - As you know, I cannot resist sometimes getting an extra story from a favorite author of mine after I have exhausted his or her entire body of work. I refer here to authors who are excarnate. I recently fell in love with the works of M. R. James, and so, have been channeling through automatic writing, both himself, and Algernon Blackwood.

James, like his writings when he was alive, seems to communicate with me in a tongue and cheek manner, often describing the portion of the astral plane that he occupies since leaving the mortal coil as far more earthly than I would assume it could actually be. What follows here is first his most recent communication with me by automatic writing, then a 'story' he gives me. He claims this story is from a diary written by a living person, but which, for reasons that become apparent by his narrative, is not available to living persons 'of our universe'.

As you know, James was noted for this false verisimilitude inside his stories, quoting non-existent books inside the fiction of his story, but, when asked directly about it, admitting that these were entirely of his invention, and when a location was used as a setting for a story, he was always very clear when asked if the location was of his concoction or borrowed from real life.

I am certain much of his ongoing descriptions to me of his astral world activities are a device of humor, but, the fact that he did not create the 'document' which he 'transcribed' to me I believe... because... well... it seems to describe matters... if you and Ethan are still interested in this subject... well... matters 'de aranea et medicus'...

Hope all is well... Karen...   ”

It should be noted that section "B" comes after the sections we have labelled as "C" and "D", but, we call it "B "because it is labelled with a margin note to read first, and "A" seems to be the wrapping, so to speak, around "B", which 'wraps', "C", and in turn finally contains "D".

"C" would seem, to be nothing less than the words of the long deceased scholar and horror author, M. R. James. communicating, to Karen, whoever she may be, by means of automatic writing.

It is written, nonetheless, in the form of a letter to her.

Here follows, the strangest part thus far, but by far not the strangest we will present.

C:

"Dear Ms. R___,

You will forgive me for the lateness of my reply, but I found myself long upon the locks in a round of golf with Mr. Arthur Machen, a contemporary of mine, whom, though I knew not in life, I have gained a genial camaraderie with in the afterworld. He had been earlier that morning to a shop which specializes in periodicals and books from the world of the living, available to those of us departed, who wish to remain current on our affairs.

This is not only my reason, for I do not offer an excuse, for the lateness for our automatic writing appointment, but, also the origin point for my honoring your request for a new story.

This story is a direct transcription of a portion of a narrative contained in a book which Mr. Machen purchased today. It is not of my authorship, nor his, although it is written in anti-novel, a lost style which was exceedingly unpopular in our day, and even more unpopular in your own. Understandably so, for antinovel defies the conventions of normal writing by being purposely difficult to understand, forcing the reader to try to construct a narrative from disjointed events.

I should correct myself here, for, I should say it would be written in antinovel, were it fiction. It is merely how the author laid her words. As for the reconstruction of events in the below text, I leave that to you, and we can perhaps discuss each of our interpretations at a later date.

I should last add, Mr. Machen purchased this at a store where we ethereal persons may get literature from the world of the living. This implies, as you may have guessed, that the text I am going to transcribe to you here was written by a person living, still living now, as you yourself are. I can only add that you will not find this person, except perhaps as she is in the last portion of the text, and even then I am only speculating, on your globe, nor, will you find the events she describes in the history of your own world. Why this story of a fellow still earthly person must come to you from us in the supernal realms, you will perhaps guess after reading the text.

The period which ends this sentence is the last one which precedes my own words, and, the rest a direct transmission of this curious text I wish to share with you"

This ends, part "C" and now we proceed to "D". We feel "D" needs the least explanation, as what little explanation can be applied to it has already been done in the preamble which we are to believe was written by M.R. James.

Before we proceed to "D", our only comment is that it seems to be in the form of journal of some sort.

D:

"April 3rd

Another dream of offing myself again last night... The dream was somehow worse than life... it was just as bad as this suck ass world except Mom and Dad were dead...   and in the dream I was going to cut my wrists... as I sat in the bathtub, and the blade slid over one hand, found I wasn't strong enough to cut the other... cut the left. I figured I would bleed out slower but still bleed out... so I just let both hands fall... fall in the water... started getting mellow... it was actually nice... then I felt pinpricks on my back... cold... something bites me... and lucid... I picked my hands up again and the wound was gone... the water was full of spider webbing, and... that was what was crawling on me... a spider...   She... it was a girl... she crawled into my ear and talked... she could fucking talk... 'Ellen'... she says... 'I can get you out of here, but it will be piece by piece... let's take care of... you living with this aunt...'

Then she starts kissing the inside of my ear... and I wake up here... Mom and Dad aren't dead... but I am still alone... and in this fat ass body...   I think it will be pills... the dream made me afraid of blades.

May 13th

Woke up from a dream of trying to do myself in with pills... in the dream I was fat... ugly...   I was about to pass out... Ophelia... that was her name... I have seen her before...   bit the inside of my throat... I vomited her up...

She was there on the inside of the toilet... I reached for the handle.   'Gods tremble before me...' she says...'and you're going to flush me down the toilet'... She giggled...

For me... she says she'll weave new flesh... though she would rather weave life.

June 3rd

In the dream I didn't have John with me... he was with

someone else... I was one of those girls who was depressed cause she was alone. I wish it was just that. John is a great guy... oh... yeah... I was a teenager in the dream... I wish these thoughts, this darkness I carry in me was something that was just from loneliness... my life is great... but I am miserable.. it's in the neurons... anyway... in the dream I was going to get in front of a car... and as it hits me... the jaws become giant spider mandibles... only they close around me lightly...

'Silly girl'.. she says... 'fine, for you, the love of another, then the love of self...' and she injects me with venom... sweet venom of mother's milk.

July 18th

The new gallery opened today. It was better than I could have hoped. John kept explaining to people the spider paintings called Ophelia had nothing to do with Shakespeare.

I couldn't have asked for a better night. Wasn't even too hung over even though I drank a little too much wine...

I already had a bidder on one of the paintings... dude with a baby bid on it. Said the little girl's name was Ophelia, ironically... It was the one I am either going to call... I don't know... I was going to call it ... "Self Love Injected"... but I thought people would imply a masturbatory or drug use connotation... I was also going to call it' 'filaments and strands', cause the web image changes into those erupting strands in the back... but I think I am going to call it Final Bite... That's what I pitched to the dude when I told him what it would be entitled.

He asked me if I used different brush strokes on what he called the 'secondary and primary eruptions'.

I guess, he, like everyone, thought the Final Bite was sexual.

Some people are weird. Time to go to bed. So excited for tomorrow. I have a weekend getaway planned with John".

Thus ends Text 'D' and all the material which was contained in the Fed Ex envelope. We leave the reader at this point to draw his or her own conclusions.

MAJOR ARCANA

The triangle is not explained in words...

Father David Tuchem placed his ear to the ground and tried to find a way to rest his head comfortably upon the Earth. He closed his eyes, and tried to listen for a sound.

"Is today the day, Lord?", he said reaching out with all his mind for his God who somewhere was buried in the confines of the North American continent, "Have I been faithful enough with these two lives entrusted to me that you will now reveal your plan to make? I try, I try, oh Lord, but I cannot discern what it is you want for me to do next".

Gog and Magog's laughter reverberated through the garden.

Tuchem pulled his head up from the ground and sighed deeply as no revelation was coming today.

"We must go inside now children," said Tuchem, "I'll fix you some lunch before I get back to my studies".

"Father, may we get fun meals from the Dicky Burger?", asked Gog.

"I would prefer you eat something healthier", said Tuchem, "and aside from that what have I told you about that horrible establishment?"

"They sell idols", said Magog, "and feed us the meat of animals that have not been slaughtered properly".

Tuchem was beginning to realize the girl was swifter in mind than her brother. They now appeared to be about seven years of age, as due to their half angelic parentage, they were growing much faster than normal children. Gog however remained at the exact state of mental development one would expect from a boy his age, or the age he seemed to be to the outside world. The female child however was no longer just regurgitating Tuchem's words. She understood what they meant and said them with conviction.

The children skipped inside playfully and sat on the couch in the living room of the house Tuchem had been living in since he brought the children here from Texas. No sign from the Lord had come, and Tuchem was realizing that God helps those who help themselves.

It was up to him to formulate a plan to move things forward. He needed to put his Lord back on the throne of heaven. But personally, beyond anything, he felt a desire to punish David Maier. True, Maier had played only a bit part in the initial humiliation of his God, and then delivered a sacrilegious blow to Yahweh when he was about to begin his ascent back to the heavens, but most of the others who had brought down the being that Tuchem viewed as God Almighty were unknown to him and for the moment beyond his reach.

But Maier could lead him to the rest, and into the foul world where Tuchem needed to go and extract the power of heathen gods so that it might flow again into his master.

Tuchem looked in on the children one more time, and walked back to the barn behind the small country house he had been renting with what little he had left in the way of funds.

He grabbed one of the small calves, one of the only two remaining alive which he had managed to acquire the from local farmer, and with his clean implements slaughtered it in a manner exactly as prescribed in the law.

He wrapped it in a plastic sheet and carried it into the linoleum floored kitchen and placed it on the ground.

"Children, your meal is prepared," he said as Gog and Magog came in and began to eat their fill of the dead calf.

After he properly washed his hands, Tuchem sat at the table as he watched his children, for that is how he thought of them, and ate his own simple meal of granola, milk, and dates. Despite the priesthood, Tuchem had never been one to deny himself the pleasures of the flesh, but his willingness to indulge the animal part of himself did not extend to the consumption of food. As in his manner of clothing, this was one area where he preferred simple efficiency to the grander ornate aspects he desired in other parts of his life.

He set out the clay from which the children were allowed to play, while he cleaned the carcass out of the kitchen.

He then returned to where he had been with his research on Maier. This organization, the ONLA, which Maier had ties to, was not a way to get to him. They were connected to many levels of government and without the proper backing, were also far beyond anything Tuchem dared to tempt the wrath of. In addition, a faction of that group had it seemed attempted to serve his Lord at one time.

The woman Lindsay Barrow, who would have been simple enough of a target through which to get to Maier, had at about the same time as Tuchem's initial encounter some months ago with Maier and his group, simply vanished after she was in the media for what was reported as a series of violent animal attacks on members of her company while they were on a corporate retreat.

Barrow had survived, but had gone to some undisclosed location to recover her nerves after those events.

As for Maier's other associates, most of them were not of an entirely human order. In addition to being difficult to track, they were at this moment beyond Tuchem's ability to deal with.

The only lead which remained was Maier's involvement the prior year in the public humiliation of the Mother Ava group. This was not known to the general public, but thanks to Gog and Magog, Tuchem was able to see through whatever veil someone had placed over the history of those events so that he knew Maier was involved.

He had uncovered that the Mother Ava Group, though now with a weakened public image, still had great resources and would be no friends of either Maier or Barrow. He was certain he could exploit their weak human frailty and desires for revenge for them to back him in whatever efforts he took to both go after Maier and acquire a source of power to feed his Lord. But he could not go to them without a plan. They would not simply lend him the resources at their disposal without him making a good case. And if he went to them prematurely without solidifying alliance, he risked exposing his whereabouts and those of the children without having his next move planned.

He looked at the newspaper articles and books written by Maier strewn about the desk where his computer sat. He went to the favorites of his web browser and looked at the

websites he had marked for research. He had been over
them a thousand times or more and could see nothing new in
them. He returned to the dead link for an interview Maier
had done the October before last for *Dark Truth with Adam
Goss.* The show continued to be listed as unavailable.

"*Down*", said a voice in in Tuchem's head which he wished
was Yaldabaoth but he knew instead was his own instinct.
Nonetheless, he looked. The show immediately after had
been an interview with the man who had awoken in male
celebutant Loren Evans's apartment after Evan's much
publicized suicide. Many conspiracy theorists said there was
more to Evans's death then was known. In New York, the
Evanses had been one of the families who donated to
Tuchem's church, but he never met Loren Evans directly.

Other than its proximity in broadcast time to Maier's
interview, Tuchem's instinct did not whisper to his intellect a
connection between the events.

Tuchem turned back and saw the children were content to
play in their clay garden. He turned on the speakers of the
computer and began to play the episode where the man Steve
Swiderski was interviewed about the little he remembered
from the night of Evans's death.

Tuchem listened as the words came out of the speakers, most
of them incoherent babble as during the course of the
interview Steve could speak in a continually less linear fashion
as he became more emotional. The words continued to hit
Tuchem's ears without giving a hint of the reason that he had
been drawn to listen to this interview.

Until Steve said a name, which was somehow burned in his
brain during the night he had been in that apartment. It was a
name Tuchem realized was the bridge to the next phase of his
work.

Asmodeus.

It, Tuchem knew, was the name of a demon known in many pagan folklores, but after an afternoon of researching how this name might be connected to David Maier, Tuchem knew for certain that this was his bridge.

He checked his funds carefully and he had just enough cash to get himself and the children to Miami where he could finally make contact with the Mother Ava Organization. He had the children pack their things, and it was not until they got to the door of the small house that they asked where they were going.

"Florida", said Tuchem.

"Are we going to Disney World?", asked Gog.

"No," said Magog giggling and answering for Tuchem, "We're going to continue the Lord's work, brother".

Tuchem mussed the girl's hair playfully and smiled as he led the children of the house.

He looked carefully at the article he printed out from an old online research journal. He regretted having to carry even a snippet of a heathen occult work with him. But he knew enough from the circles he moved in, the name listed on the byline was a pseudonym the author used to mask his true identity: Loren Evans.

Even as they sat on the plane he stared intently at the article heading which simply read, " *Of Asmodeus*".

When they were in midair, and he saw both Gog and Magog were asleep, Tuchem himself nodded off to sleep.

Rain...

The odd thing about rain pouring down on a roof or batting against a window is that it makes a sound which a sleeping person can confuse for something else. Often, this mystery sound awakens a sleeper long enough for them to come back into wakefulness just so they can tell the sound is only rain... then the very same gentle noise lulls them back to sleep.

It wasn't the rain that woke Jesse Perfect. There were storms, somewhere. Maybe they were a linked system of storms, or maybe they were separate but just contemporaneous. Maybe those storms had come for Jesse or they may have been for someone else. But they woke him.

He was too old to fight the storms. He had to count on the fact that the rich legacy he left the world in the form of what he thought of as his family could fight it. Or maybe... maybe he had one more fight in him.

Two years ago, he thought he was too old and the tough old bird still had it in him to help turn back Armageddon. But he was finally aging. He had never opted for the immortality of some Illuminati, just as he now lived in a simple assisted living apartment instead of the mansion full of servants which could be his for the asking.

The dark surrounded Jesse Perfect as he first began dreaming. Quickly, a scene formed and Jesse found himself in a restaurant or tavern which was only vaguely formed and gas lit. While he never visited this place in life, it was familiar. It was a hodgepodge and amalgamation of places he had really been. Wispy dream characters sat at the tables and bar, and other than a background din of conversation with no real words behind it, and the clinking of glasses and silverware,

Jesse's brain had been sparse on providing details for this dream.

He looked up and saw that although it was clearly night for most of the tavern, one of the tables was bathed in bright daylight and at it sat three figures who Jesse could discern perfectly. It was Michael and his wife Ettelia, and the alien Eyah.

For a moment Jesse felt relief at the site of his old friend. He started to make his way over to the table, and reached out a hand so that he could pull out a chair to sit down.

Jesse seated himself at the table and smiled as he regarded Michael.

"I think I'll be seeing you again soon, old friend", said Jesse in Michael's direction and then he turned to the image of the extraterrestrial, "I believe my body is finally slowing down since you're through with me".

"You made the choices you made, Jesse Perfect. My machines have sensed this and no longer preserve your biology the way they once did," said Eyah.

"That's quite all right, Sir. I'm ready to move on to whatever is next. And I'm lucky enough to know that there is a God in heaven, a few actually, and I have somewhere to go", Jesse said.

"I will see you again someday, Dr. Perfect, but not yet I'm afraid," said Michael.

"I may have a few weeks or months left, Mr. Calloway, but it won't be that long until we're reunited", said Jesse.

Michael took a long sip of whiskey and pressed his lips tightly and furrowed his brow the way one does when he has something to say that he does not wish to because he knows it will hurt the receiver of the news.

"I'm sorry Jesse", said Michael, "It will be more time than that. I promise to visit you one more time before...,"

"Before what?", asked Jesse.

Suddenly the window where the sunlight had been coming in shattered and a sandstorm blotted out the sun and began to spill into the tavern. The sand overwhelmed Etellia, Eyah, and Michael and Jesse watched in horror as they were subsumed into shadow and out of his presence.

Jesse's heart began to race and cause him great pain. This was his real heart broadcasting pain into the dream from the waking world. Ever since Eyah's machines had stopped maintaining him by whatever means they had, it was Jesse's heart that began to first show his unnatural age.

Into the tavern walked a figure like a Cubist skeleton made out of Egyptian sandstone. It wore the tailored Edwardian day suit that Abraham Braxus had worn the first time Jesse Perfect had the misfortune of meeting the man after Braxus's restoration to health following Jesse's vanquishing of the sorceress who nearly killed Braxus.

Jesse stood up and turned toward the Braxus image, realizing it was a dream and intending to vanquish it.

"You are either not real or you are not what you seem to be, but you are not Braxus", said Jesse.

"I am not what's interesting here, boy", said Braxus addressing Jesse in the disrespectful manner he had for decades even in the Illuminati council chamber.

The thing reached out its hand and grabbed for Jesse's chest. It pushed him down on the table, and Jesse was certain Pseudo-Braxus intended to tear out his heart. Instead the thing regurgitated a thin wispy fluid with symbols and words strewn inside the nearly gaseous liquid. It congealed it into a sphere with its free hand. Instead of tearing something out of Jesse Perfect it forced the bizarre compound into his chest.

"It's time now for what I have planted so long ago when I first had the misfortune of you darkening my doorstep to grow", said Pseudo-Braxus.

Jesse awoke in a cold sweat, and his poor old heart realizing he was in the waking world immediately began to slow. He got up to a sitting position slowly and was for a moment disoriented as one is when one wakes and a place that is unfamiliar.

His mind was still sharp and only took him a moment to recollect that he'd taken his annual spring trip to Ireland to visit Michael Calloway's grave and that he was in the guest room of Thurston Waite's house in County Mayo.

"Are you all right, sir?", said D'Irem the Djinn floating into the room.

"Just a dream, son, just a dream", said Jesse realizing that this being was centuries if not millennia older than he, but still choosing to address it the way he did anyway.

"It is said dreams are often prophetic", said the Djinn, "but with the astral plane in the state it still is, I wonder if that can be".

"Where's Thurston?", asked Jesse.

"Frustrating himself by trying to repair some kind of impractical contraption", said D'Irem.

"Excuse me while I dress please," said Jesse, "Which one of us will be preparing breakfast today?"

"Thurston's already ready taken care of that, sir, and it's more like lunch. You've slept pretty late", said the Djinn.

"Is it some kind of traditional Irish fare?", asked Jesse with a wry smile knowing that with Thurston the answer was unlikely to be yes.

Jesse marveled at the gray skinned creature with glowing red eyes whose lower body ended in a wispy trail of smoke, at least in the current manner he was choosing to manifest. In a century of dealing with things from the supernatural or the extraterrestrial world, Jesse had never lost his sense of wonder.

The Djinn's face soured slightly and he spoke.

"Actually Thurston has prepared some kind of ghastly version of jambalaya with tuna steak and quail meat. I'll start the oh so pleasurable task of heating it up", said the Djinn.

Jesse looked out the window. It was a beautiful day.

"I think I'll join Thurston out a in the garage and if it's possible could we take our lunch outside today?", asked Jesse.

D'Irem bowed politely and backed out of the room, "Of course, sir".

Jesse strode out into the backyard of Thurston's ultramodern but fairly accessible house. The quaint cottage was lined with rows of solar panels that provided energy not only for Thurston's house but for most of the small village which lay a quarter-mile down the road.

The solar panels continued down the garden path way to the garage. The panels were built by a sort of energy consortium Thurston was the head of composed mostly of the sons and daughters of Irish farmers who owned large tracts of land, but no longer actively produced crops.

Jesse found Thurston in a pair of jeans and sneakers which probably cost the equivalent of what David Maier made in one month on book royalties. Having spent more time even in the somewhat weak Irish sun of his adopted homeland than he usually did, Thurston's Arabic heritage showed through as his skin was bronzing.

"Isn't an Irishman the first person who should put on sunscreen and a hat?," asked Jesse.

Thurston looked up from the large but primitive looking truck he was working on.

"Not when your birth name was Al-Hirwaz", said Thurston.

"You're the, what is it now, eigth most powerful sorcerer in the world, and you're fixing this ridiculous old relic with hand tools?", asked Jesse.

"It's a steam truck" said Thurston, "Steam powered just like a locomotive but meant to go out on the roads. It might've worked if the gas combustion engine hadn't been made so popular by the Americans. Some of these actually saw service. And I'm the seventh most powerful sorcerer now, I think, since what's his name is dead and what's her face is gone".

"I know what this truck is, my boy. These were on the road when I was young man", said Jesse.

Thurston wiped his hands off and moved to sit down at a small outdoor table and Jesse joined him.

"Well, we'll get you a proper pub lunch on the way back from the churchyard today", said Thurston.

"I had another dream", said Jesse.

"Have you talked to Rhys-Davies yet about it?", asked Thurston.

"No. I haven't. I know what he'll say. That I should go with him and Ilitu to Tyr Afal and take the Tuatha de Dannan up on their offer to go to rest there", said Jesse.

"I understand your reluctance, because you don't think of yourself as a hero. But the Professor is right. The ONLA will go after your corpse and whatever secrets it might contain thanks to your little green man friend. And if what Maier told you is true they're moving into outré tech more than supernatural these days. Besides Jesse", Thurston trailed off..., "let your three boys give you a hero's sendoff".

"David and Abraham might be a little upset about your lack of a public appearance for the last decade", said Jesse, "and I have four boys, not just three".

"Okay. If it's just to house my remains, then to Tyr Afal it is. So who should get a message to the Tuatha de Danaan for me? Ethan's been in contact with them, but the last time I saw

David, well, let's just say he has a means of reaching them to", Jesse said.

"Call the Professor first", said Thurston, "I need to get a pint or two in me before I deal with a lecture from Maier".

Lindsay breathed the air of the English summer in deeply, and finished applying the red lacquer to the last of her targets.

Her company had given her a fairly long paid holiday after what happened in Canada, and after hearing another woman answer David's phone she wasn't ready to seek him out yet. Having been a complete emotional wreck after the incident with Andre Miacis and realizing that the supernatural seemed now to be a part of her life, after a brief time spent in the company of Jesse Perfect, she took her new friend Ilitu up on her offer to stay with her and Ethan while he continued research into his own resurrection.

"Are my feet now attractive enough for you, Barrow?", asked Ilitu with some mild annoyance.

Lindsay stared at her handiwork, somewhat oblivious to the fact that she had just gotten the Dark Queen herself to sit through an activity that Lindsay herself had not engaged in since middle school.

"How do I say this without hurting your feelings?", said Lindsay.

"Just say it", said Ilitu.

"I think painting toenails works best on women whose feet don't end in claws", said Lindsay.

Ilitu cocked her head slightly to the ground and strained to hear Ethan's movement.

"He's almost reached the surface", said Ilitu.

"Couldn't you have just dug him out about this time yesterday?", asked Lindsay.

"He gets very annoyed when I do things for him", said Ilitu, "On the other hand being buried in things is something that has happened to him an unbelievable number of times. I'm sure whatever I did or didn't do will still result in a rant of cockney slang from him which, though he is supposedly low in the emotion department, he degenerates into when he is frustrated".

"What happened to him anyway?", asked Lindsay.

"He used a spell from the Codex Shaiodica to open a dimensional rift in hopes of entering other timelines where the laws of reality might be different enough that he could find a means of returning to life. He did it while I was sleeping, because there was a rather good chance he might not have returned. Ever since the Lwa gave him a few hours of an immortal life so we could be together, he has known his curse ways even more heavily on my heart than it did before. Luckily he seems to have found a way back to this version of reality, only apparently 100 feet or so underground", Ilitu explained.

"I thought you said that you thought his best chance of coming back to life was in the two of you going to your city", said Lindsay.

"Ethan seems bound and determined to do it on his own. But I know that when we arrive there he will accept the gift of immortal life that my people can give him", said Ilitu.

"If I understand everything correctly you guys don't know what the hell you're going to find when you go there. He said you don't even know if time flows at the same rate it has for the rest of the world", said Lindsay.

By this time Professor Ethan Rhys-Davies using some kind of black metallic implement had dug a large enough hole to get his upper body out into the daylight.

"Not that this hasn't been a great bit of joy, but, if someone could pull me the rest of the way out I would be most appreciative", said Ethan with great reserve.

Ilitu obliged.

"Rather interesting assortment of versions of history of the worlds that I visited, but I nonetheless remain in the state you would expect me to be in," said Ethan.

"Well, obviously", said Lindsay, "Or you wouldn't have been able to breathe down there".

"I suppose I should be happy that over-tobaccoed know-it-all of a wizard was even able to send me back to this timeline at all, and shouldn't complain too much that he materialized me a bit below the mark, shall we say. Still, he was a more tolerable fellow than that helmeted drama queen sorcerer in the reality I came to immediately before his own", said Ethan.

Ethan threw down the black metal object he had used to help himself dig out of the relatively weak chalky soil of the area they were in into Ilitu's lap. It had two curved blades on the sides, which came out from an aerodynamic center that was decorated with a small protrusion with two forks at the top and a small single pointed protrusion at the bottom.

"What is this?", asked Ilitu.

"I got it from a somewhat intense chap who I helped out of a jam. I thought you might like it", he said.

"It's a little Gothic looking", said Ilitu, "Which means of course I like it".

"Ms. Barrow has been teaching you more modern slang I see", said Ethan.

"Oh, your cellphone rang a couple of times while you were down there", said Lindsay.

Ethan examined the phone and after starting to get upset with what he viewed as its complexity handed it to Ilitu.

"He prefers magick", said Ilitu as she hit buttons on the phone.

"I like technology just fine", said Ethan, "Technology runs on coal and steam and has levers and gears you can see".

"Whoever it was didn't leave a message. It's an American cellphone number though. 570 area code.", said Ilitu.

"Jesse", said Ethan, "would you redial it for me please?".

Ilitu obliged and Ethan began to talk to his nearly century long acquaintance on the other end. Jesse explained the situation, and Ethan said that with mid-summer so close and Asmodeus planning whatever energy work it was the gods had asked him to do on Tyr Afal, he and Ilitu would of course give him and Thurston access to the realm of the Fey when they went there.

"Ms. Barrow", said Ethan after the call, "In about a week Ilitu and I will be headed to a small island off the coast of Wales from which the realm of that which you would call fairies can be accessed. They are in fact the descendants of the de-powered Celtic gods. Jesse has asked that we provide him and Thurston Waite, an old associate of David's and also former ONLA alumni, passage there. And he has asked you to come as well. I understand the two of you have become quite close over the last year or so".

"Why?", asked Lindsay.

"He's dying, Ms. Barrow. Unfortunately even for a situation this grave Ilitu and I cannot miss the opportunity to access to a gateway to her world. We will not be able to remain on Tyr Afal long. He wants you to be there along with a few of his closest friends and associates. David will be there as well. I trust that for the duration of Jesse's, shall we say, going away party, you and David will be able to set aside your differences?", asked Ethan.

"Of course," said Lindsay.

Ilitu despite her occasional coldness toward Lindsay now placed a reassuring hand on the mortal woman's shoulder. She casually picked up the black metal object and hurled it with great force into a tree. It was surprisingly aerodynamic.

"Nice", said Ilitu, "not my style"

Asmodeus missed Earth. Fortunately when he and Hank visited Slim in his eternal reward super awesome kick ass air-conditioned double wide heavenly trailer, it was almost like visiting Earth again. True he would pass briefly in his astral state down to the human world on his way to Tyr Afal, but there were certain rules he had to abide by. Hades expected him to behave like a proper spirit now.

"So did my chaos spell work?", asked Asmodeus.

"Worked like a charm", said Slim as he presented Hank the Dinosaur and the Archdemon Asmodeus with a fine plate of Texas dry rub.

The Domedon Domexodon breathed in deeply. The food smelled fantastic for something which was entirely an energetic construct.

"I don't understand why you would want a chaos spell in heaven, cowboy", said Hank.

"Because the dry rub turned out perfect every time no matter what I did, and that ain't the point a' dry rub", said Slim.

Asmodeus was just about to munch down on the ethereal goodies with his ethereal mouth when a look of seriousness came across his face.

"It's Hades," he's calling me, "It's time for me to report for my upgrade so to speak".

"You know we're doing our part behind-the-scenes for this little experiment", said Hank.

"Don't worry", said Asmodeus, "the Pleroma flow is not going to be divine or even angelic. It's just the flow of energy of human belief into the fey. I can handle it".

Slim got up from the couch and gave Asmodeus a firm and friendly handshake.

Asmodeus nodded to Hank and dematerialized.

"So dumb it down for me. What he is doing again?", asked Slim.

"The flow of the Pleroma to the waking gods and back to mankind ain't flowing quite right. Most of the younger gods of the pantheons receive energy because humans identify them as male or female, or an abstract force which can only be felt by the core of the individual. But ever since Yahweh pulled his little stunt, the nature of what man and woman are not, as well as the heart of the individual is not, the same as what it was the last time the pantheons were awake. Most of the old gods are still being hand fed, for lack of a better term by Thoth and the Lwa, while Hades and Jesus have their hands full, well, running the gull durn ethereal spheres", said Hank.

"So Asmodeus is gonna see if he can get the pipe line flowing right with the energy of belief that goes into fairies?", asked Slim.

"You're getting this Ascended Master thing down pat, cowboy" said Hank, "It's like doing it with a model before you do a full scale. If it works we're gonna adjust the energy flow one pantheon at a time so things can get kicking again".

"Where do I fit into this?", asked Slim.

"Everything ought to be right as rain, especially if the will of the Outer Gods is with us. But Asmodeus ain't the kind of fella who likes backup", said Hank as he extended his raptor claw and made Slim's spiritual widescreen TV come to life.

"I'm going to be completely in dispose doing my part for the energy flow. You just watch Asmodeus on here cowboy, an' if he looks like he's gotten himself into a pickle, I want you to go down there and see if you can help", said Hank.

"Yeah", said Slim with some hesitation about trailing the demon if the demon didn't want help, "I kinda figured".

Martin Belles completed his sixth rep on the weight machine with his arms as he completed his fourth rep on the other weight machine in the gymnasium of the training room which he had managed to move telekinetically. Belles, though no longer a field agent, had begun strengthening both his physical and metaphysical conditioning once again for the first time in years. The heavy bass industrial music he listened to in his youth played through the speakers. He had forgotten how much energy it gave him.

Miriam, a phantom who worked for the ONLA as one of Martin's personal assistants in exchange for transit to the other side by ONLA spell casters after five years of service, materialized in Martin's field of vision.

"Director Belles", the phantasm said, "You have a call. Shall I tell the switchboard to put it through your headset? It's Sieurd".

"Put it through here, Miriam", said Martin as he continued two more of each kind of rep, "And one more thing. Thank you for your service. I hope you'll enjoy seeing your family again".

The ghost was confused. She had three more years of service to the ONLA due.

"I've arranged for you to be sent into the light tomorrow", said Martin.

"Director Belles?", asked Miriam with some confusion.

Belles winked at her.

"Go ahead Abe", said Martin.

"Martin. We need to talk", said Abe.

Despite the fact that they had trained as field agents together Belles had out ranked Sieurd for several years now. He didn't remember the last time Abe had called him by his first name.

"What is it?", said Martin with some alarm.

"It's Jesse Perfect. He's dying", said Abe.

"The Illuminati aren't aware of this, as far as I know", said Martin.

"No. Of course you can report it to them, but that's not why I called", said Abe.

"So David doesn't know how to reach Thurston. Abe, I swear to you as your friend and your commanding officer, I don't know how to find him either. If I did I would put the communication through", said Martin.

"That's not it either, sir. Apparently Illuminatus Perfect is already with Thurston. Jesse wants all of us there. All four of us from the old days", said Abe.

"Your time off is approved. And I will suspend ONLA surveillance on David and his friends for the duration of these events. I can even probably keep the Illuminati in the dark for a while. They aren't what they used to be. In fact most of them, the ones who were left alive at least, are the ones who I know better than they know themselves from Project Archive", said Martin.

"You know why I'm calling, Martin. He wants you there, too", said Abe.

"I can't do that", said Martin.

"Sir, this is Jesse Perfect", said Abe.

"You misunderstand me, Agent Sieurd", said Martin, "It's not that Jesse is not important enough for me to drop everything I'm doing. Instead I'll feel like I'm not worthy of being there anymore. Tell David if he's ever believed anything I've ever said to believe that. And tell Jesse, I'm sorry. Belles out".

"So?," asked David.

"He's not going to come", said Abe, "Excuse me".

Abe then got down on the floor of David's apartment and began to do crunches.

"Why are you doing that?", asked David.

"Thurston", answered Abe.

"He's completely straight. I thought you accepted that years ago", said David.

"No," said Abe annoyed, "It's not anything like that. Every time I see Thurston Waite I get punched in the stomach. He knows nothing compared to me about hand to hand combat, but inevitably, because it's Thurston, I will be hit in the stomach".

"Why is Dug so quiet?", asked David as he regarded the motionless and abnormally sullen looking Goblin, "I thought he would be excited about going back to Tyr Afal... or Avalon... whatever we're supposed to call it".

"I do not know why he is quiet, David Maier", said Na'da as if she was concealing something, "But you had better not refer to my home country as Avalon".

"David can open the gateway there, right?", asked Abe.

"Yes, said Na'da, "But we must first be there so that he may use his gift to bring us into the right vibration".

"So Tyr Afal is part of the physical world?", asked David as he once again curiously eyed Dug who was silent and introspective ever since being told they were returning to the realm of his people.

"Yes," said Na'da, "Many have been there and not even known they were in our realm".

"So how we get there in the first place?", asked Abe, "Some deep cave? Journey beneath a dark lake? Dream walk again?"

Na'da turned around from David's laptop where she had been doing something online.

"British Airways", said Na'da, "I have used your MasterCard to purchase three first class tickets for us, beloved".

Na'da smiled brightly as David felt the trademark stomach upset he got from any kind of stress which was not related to a mission or academic pursuit as he thought of the amount of money she had spent on first class tickets.

"First class?", asked David with a mix of concern and anger.

"Relax, David Maier, I was speaking to Dug", said Na'da.

He had no idea if she was serious.

"Oh, okay", said David, "Wait... Dug has a credit card? Did you just call Dug...",

David's mobile dinged interrupting him from finishing his line of inquiry. He had been texting with Lindsay for the first time in a while. She came clean about the friendship she had struck up with Jesse after David introduced her to him and she talked about her run-in with Andre Miacis. David in turn had told her how he, Abe, and Dug had dealt with the Yahweh or Yaldabaoth cult, but had left Na'da out. The last text she just sent confirmed that she too would be on Tyr Agal for Jesse's goodbye. He realized she and Na'da were going to meet.

David Maier, slayer of archangels and he who defeated an Antichrist wrapped in chocolate, went as quickly as he could for a good strong antacid.

Father Tuchem entered the Art Deco decorated waiting area of Tina Grigg's office, with two children that appeared to be about seven years old in tow; twins, a boy and a girl. They were fair skinned, blond-haired and blue eyed and seemed to glow with their own internal light. They had the most perfect form and features one could imagine. They were dressed like catholic school children, but their clothing bore no insignia to indicate what school they might attend.

"I'm here to see Tina Griggs", Father Tuchem said to the young woman at the reception desk in his fake but well-practiced Irish accent.

"Do you have an appointment?", she asked with a huge vacant smile.

"Yes, my child. I made my appointment several weeks ago via e-mail", Tuchem said leaning in and giving her his award-winning smile that had won the trust of countless adults and children.

"Um... your name?", she asked almost losing her train of thought, and feeling dirty for the thoughts she was having about a priest.

"Father David Tuchem", he said.

"Alright, have a seat and I'll let you know, uh, her know you're here", she said resisting the urge to flirt.

According to the cheap plaque on her desk, and equally cheap name tag her name was Buffy Young. This was confirmed by her coffee mug, the pen she was using, the duffel bag on the floor next to her, her stapler, pencil holder, in box and out box, and tissue dispenser. It was as if she felt compelled to plaster her name on every object she owned, or even that was associated with her.

If Father Tuchem was given one word to describe Buffy Young it would be, round. Not to say she was overweight. Far from it, he wouldn't even call her chubby, but she had Very curvy and full features, a round face and small pot belly.

"Gog, Magog, please sit", Father Tuchem said.

"Yes, Father", they said in unison and sat quietly and politely like two little angels.

Father Tuchem however did not sit.

"So Ms. Young are you Ms. Griggs *personal* assistant?", Father Tuchem asked leaning in and smiling.

"I, uh, yes. Whose children are those?", she asked trying to take his focus off her, and hers off of him.

"Oh, those are my children. I was ordained a Catholic priest, but God found me and showed me the true path. I am now a

Yahwist. It does not require celibacy. I can even be married if I like", he said.

Legally, this was true. They were his children. His name was on their birth certificates as their father. He was in fact not at all genetically related to them. He did however think of them and love them as his own. They were the only creatures in the universe he would put before himself. He might, if it came to it, even put them before his lord Yaldabaoth. This was quite the predicament since it was, in so far as Yaldabaoth was concerned, the boy Gog's fate to be the vessel for his holy spirit.

"Oh?", Buffy said with renewed interest, " So you're not married?"

"No, actually the children's mother...", Tuchem began.

"*Buffy!*", Tina's voice bellowed over the intercom, "*Is my 1:00 here yet?*"

"Yes Ms. Griggs. He's just arrived", Buffy replied, jolted out of her momentary fugue.

"*Good, send him in and hold my calls*", said Tina.

"Yes ma'am, you... can... go...", Buffy stammered.

But Father Tuchem was way ahead of her and had already disappeared into Tina Grigg's office.

"Greetings Ms. Griggs I'm...", Tuchem extended his hand.

"Just hold it right there", she interrupted, "First you can drop that accent. I've heard enough in my time to tell a fake one from real one, even one as good as yours. And I already know who you are and a great deal about you. Your, shall we say, indiscretions in New York, your cult like following in Utah. And most recently something about trying to rekindle a failed creationist theme park in Texas that according to the news recently burned to the ground. Although my sources tell me that was a front for some kind of new cult".

"As you wish Ms. Griggs", Father Tuchem said in his high society Manhattan accent and taking off his fake glasses, "Your information isn't quite accurate, but we'll get to that. You, Madam, are hardly one to pass judgment. Tell me how many people did you turn into unwilling cannibals in your scheme to resurrect poor Mother Ava? Fortunately for you that failed. You hadn't realized she had planned to use you as her new body".

"How did you...?", she asked.

"And let's not forget about your own *indiscretions* in New York during that unfortunate business with...", Tuchem said.

"Alright, alright, so why don't you tell me what you needed to urgently discuss with me, as you put it. Mother Ava merchandise doesn't sell like it used to and I have a lot of work to do", said Tina.

"Well, I have many things to discuss with you, but the most important is our common enemy", Tuchem said,

"And who might that be?", asked Tina.

"David Maier", said Tuchem, "And by proxy, Lindsay Barrow among others".

"I'm listening", said Tina.

"Both of us have had grand plans interrupted by these godless heathens. But a situation may be arising soon that may give us an opportunity to remove this particularly annoying player from the game. I also believe you would like to exact some measure of revenge on Ms. Barrow", he said.

"And what exactly is this opportunity?", she asked.

"The exact details I must keep to myself for now. What I can say is it involves, unfortunately some demonic forces that Maier is also associated with. We will have to amass a great deal more power and perhaps a few more allies before we can confront Maier and his cohorts", he said.

"And just what is it that makes you believe we are allies?", she asked.

"Oh, Ms. Griggs, I can tell just from observing you that this is an opportunity you will not let slip by. That your hatred for these people is as great as mine", he said.

"I think that is the first time I have ever heard a Catholic priest speak of hate, at least his own hate", she said.

"I am no longer a Catholic priest. I serve the True God, once called Yahweh, now known to me by the sacred name Yaldabaoth, directly now. At least I did before Maier interfered. I bear his true word, not the lies of his son", he said.

"What is that supposed to mean?", she asked.

"A long story for another time, perhaps, when there is more trust between us. Tell me, Ms. Griggs is there anyone who can tend to your affairs here? What we are about to do will require careful planning and a great deal of preparation", he said.

"Maybe", she replied.

Tina didn't like how much Father Tuchem was dominating this situation. She was used to being the one in charge. She would have to find a way to usurp him later but for now he knew too much more than her, and she also needed to find out how he was gathering information. He knew things about her and Mother Ava that no one should know.

Tina pressed down the intercom button to talk to her assistant. "Buffy, get me Brent Hapgood on the phone", she said.

No response came.

"Buffy?"

Still no response.

"BUFFY! What is that girl doing?", Tina asked indignantly.

Tina stormed from her office into the reception area followed closely by Tuchem, to find Buffy lying on her desk with her jacket, blouse, skirt, pumps, and tights removed. She had what appeared to be pins jammed into her all about her torso, arms, head, down her legs, and in her hands and feet.

"What the hell?", exclaimed Tina.

"Acupuncture", informed Gog as he perfectly straightened out another of Buffy's paper clips, bringing it to a sharp point with his fingertips. Magog was doing the same standing on Buffy's opposite side.

"Buffy are you alright?", asked Tina.

"Soooooo reeeelaaaxeeed", drooled Buffy, "And I see the brightness..."

"That's nice dear but I need you to get back to work.", Tina said.

"Auuummmm", responded Buffy as if in drunken meditation.

"Ok, Tuchem how do we get her back to normal?", asked Tina.

"I don't know if normal is how I would describe anyone who works for you", said Tuchem slipping back into his Irish accent and removing the pin between Buffy's eyes.

"Cute, Tuchem, real cute", said Tina.

"I'll say" said Buffy coming back to reality.

"Buffy pull out the rest of those paperclips, get dressed, and then get me Brent Hapgood on the phone", Tina said. furiously.

"Right away Ms. Griggs", Buffy responded nervously finally coming all the way back to reality.

"I apologize Ms. Griggs, my children meant well.", said Tuchem.

"I'm sure they did", Tina said sarcastically.

"They are very intelligent, but not very smart", Tuchem whispered into Tina's ear.

"Whose children are they anyway?", asked Tina.

"They are my children Ms. Griggs", he replied.

"Tuchem those are not...", she started.

"Perhaps we should speak in your office", Father Tuchem interrupted, "Children please sit and let Ms. Young do her work".

"Who?", Gog and Magog asked.

"Buffy", replied Tuchem.

"Oh, yes, Father", they said.

Father Tuchem and Tina went back into her office.

"Tuchem those are not your children", stated Tina.

"Legally they are, but you are correct, I am not their father", he said dropping his accent again.

"Then who are they? Those children are not normal", she said.

"Their names, Ms. Griggs, are Gog and Magog, but you are quite correct. They are the last of their kind and I suspect the last there shall ever be. They are Nephilim."

"They're what?", she asked.

"Nephilim, half human and half angel. Their father Tipeshiel was not the smartest of angels. In fact if I understand correctly he is the least intelligent of Yaldabaoth angels. And their mother... well...", Tuchem said.

"I get the idea", Tina said.

"As far as they are concerned however I am their father. I assume that someday they might piece it together, but maybe not. They have great power but seem to also have inherited their father's intellect. They are completely innocent, completely pure. And I intend to keep it that way", Tuchem said.

Tina regarded Father Tuchem curiously. His rant about *his* children seemed somewhat out of place with what she knew of him. He never even bothered to deny the accusations. Yet somehow she believed he was sincere. She decided to tread carefully where Gog and Magog were concerned after some of the other things she had heard about Tuchem. Doing anything negative involving the children might be a good way to get dead.

"Are your children part of your plan?", she asked.

"Not my plan for revenge, if that's what you mean. I plan to keep them as far from Maier and the ONLA as possible", he said, "But... they are one of the few advantages we have beyond human means... so... I fear we will need to utilize them".

"Wait one minute. You're not planning on taking on the ONLA?", she asked.

"*Ms. Griggs, Mr. Hapgood is on line 1 for you*", Buffy interrupted via intercom.

"Hello Brent, Mother Eva smiles on you. I need you to get all the department heads to look after things on their own for a while. You need to meet me at the airport this afternoon. You and I have some business to take care of out of town. And I'll need you to be ready to mobilize resources with very little notice", Tina said.

..."Look, I don't care what you had planned this is important...".

..."I don't know when we'll be back...".

..."Brent, just make it happen. You don't want to challenge me on this... good... Yes. Mother Ava is loving and excepting of you".

"To answer your question yes, I do. But not yet. The ONLA is not as powerful as it once was, and under the right circumstances can be conquered, but first Maier must be dealt with. There are forces he can call on to aid the ONLA. Forces that would not do so without his call. And though Maier no longer works for or even trusts the ONLA there are still individuals within it that could ask for his help and he would give it. And now I have a few questions for you", said Tuchem.

"Alright, ask away", said Tina.

"First, why are you involving this Mr. Hapgood in this?", asked Tuchem.

"Well I have a feeling I am going to need him. He has been with the Mother Ava Organization for quite a while and is aware of certain things. He should be able to be brought up to speed enough to be useful. And I assure you he is not limited by personal scruples as to what actions he will undertake", Tina said.

"Certain things meaning the near resurrection of Mother Ava?", said Tuchem.

"Yes. Next question", asked Tina.

"You know that Mother Ava was using you. And that she was completely destroyed by Maier, yet you still profess to be her devotee. Why?", asked Tuchem.

"It's pure capitalism at this point, Father. A girls got to make a living. By the way we had our people shielded from the ONLA mind wipe spells, but how did you find out about any of this or about Lindsay Barrow?", asked Tina.

"I have my ways", he replied.

"I'm sure you do, Father Cryptic, but if we are going to work together I need to know where you're getting your information. We need to start building some trust", Tina said.

"Nice try, Ms. Griggs, but we are not anywhere near that level of trust yet", said Tuchem.

He wondered if he wasn't picking his ally poorly. Tina's attempt to gain the secret of his information gathering to further her own agenda was transparent. He would need cleverer allies to defeat his enemy. Still Tina had access to the kind of resources he would need, and he could always use her as cannon fodder if things didn't work out.

24 hours later Gog and Magog were digging in the desert sand, seemingly unaffected by the heat and sun. They began to periodically place heavy sounding objects into a small wooden crate next to them.

"And why exactly are we out here in the Texas desert?", asked Tina as she shifted uncomfortably in her high fashion dress and expensive open toed pumps, despite the shade of her parasol and large sunglasses.

"I told you, we shall need more allies before we can confront Maier or the ONLA", said Tuchem.

"But that doesn't...", Tina began.

"I think we have all the pieces, Father", interrupted Gog.

Tina looked down into the crate with a disgusted look on her face.

"We came out here to dig up a corpse?", she asked.

"Oh, he isn't dead Ms. Griggs. Nor shall he ever be. It is his curse", informed Tuchem, "Now children build the puzzle".

Gog laid out a plastic tarp and Magog began to carefully place pieces from the crate onto it. It did not take long for them to assemble it into its former human shape. The only part of its clothing that remained were its tan cowboy boots. They would be out of place with the black clothing Tuchem had bought at Tessie's on the way in, but they would have to do since he had not thought to get shoes. Still, this creature's fashion sense was not his concern.

"There's not much meat on it" ,Tina commented.

"We can fix that, can't we children?", said Tuchem hunching down and scooping up a handful of sand and letting it sift through his fingers.

"Yes, Father", said Gog and Magog as they began to pack and mold the desert sand in place of the missing flesh. What could loosely be described as its face had but one bulging milky white eye. The rest was packed smooth with sand.

It was then dressed in black jeans and a black T-shirt that had an American eagle and a banner that read, "Let's Roll: 9/11/2001". Tuchem's choices had been either that or one with a coyote, which somehow seemed less appropriate.

"Good. Now make it play", said Tuchem.

Magog kissed it on the forehead and it took a gasping breath. As it did the sand fell away from its yellowed teeth.

"Good afternoon, Mr. Devereux", said Father Tuchem grinning , "Can you stand?"

The Devereux Golem thing attempted to stand. Grinding and cracking sounds came from within it, and it screamed a horrible dry and gravelly scream.

"My turn", said Tina hunching down and placing her fingertips on its forehead. A thick dark brown fluid welled up in what could be called its mouth and around its bulging lidless eye. The fluid ran from the sides of its mouth, from the outside of its eye, and down along the side of its head, leaving long dark stains in its sand. It sat up still grinding but no longer in pain.

A touch of some abilities just beyond the pale of mortal had remained within Tina Griggs from the time brief she was mother Ava's avatar.

"What the fuck do you want?", asked the Devereux thing in a voice as dry, gravelly, and otherworldly as it's scream had been.

"Righteous retribution, and you are going to help us get it", said Tuchem.

"Why should I?", it asked.

"Because you don't want to go back into the sand and you don't want to live in unimaginable pain. Well maybe you can imagine", said Tina regarding him and grinning. "You are going to do what we say because you don't want to suffer it's that simple. Now can we get out of this miserable desert?"

"Of course, Ms. Griggs. We have what we came for. Children put your new toy back in its box", said Tuchem.

Gog and Magog each grabbed an end of the tarp and gently placed the Devereux thing in the uncomfortably small wooden crate. Tina dialed her cellphone and called Brent.

"Brent, we're ready. Come pick us up", she said.

The wind picked up and a rhythmic sound was heard as a helicopter crested the steep wall of the strip mine. It set down on the opposite end that was sloped to accommodate trucks from when it was an active mine. Two large men hopped out to load the crate, but Gog and Magog were already effortlessly moving it. The two men just stood with their mouths open looking shocked. Tina was first to approach. She gestured to the man closest to the entrance holding her hand out high and wiggled her fingers at him indicating she wanted to be helped into the helicopter.

Next the children slid the crate in and then hopped in themselves. Tuchem looked at the still shocked gentlemen, shrugged, and climbed up and in. The two men found enough presence of mind to reenter the helicopter and shut the door sealing them away from the noise.

"Ok, Tuchem, I'm almost afraid to ask, but where to now?", asked Tina.

Brent, dressed as inappropriately as Tina in a trendy suit, peeked into the crate at the horror within.

"Oh my God! What is that thing?," he shrieked.

"A tool of retribution Mr. Hapgood. You would do well not to get to close", warned Father Tuchem, "Now to New York, to answer your question Ms. Griggs. There is information there we must acquire".

Tina and Tuchem each settled in their mutual seats in the back of the taxi as they sped away from JFK airport. Gog and Magog sat between them happily watching the small monitor in the back of the cab which played short video clips to keep passengers entertained. The two children for the moment at least seemed as entertained by the idiotic babble as any other children their age might be.

"So why are we in New York?", asked Tina.

"Simple Ms. Griggs", Tuchem answered, "as I told you before, one of the pieces in our puzzle is the demon Asmodeus, and to learn anything further about him we shall need access to the personal effects of the late Great Loren Evans."

"I know a bit about those energies which flow through the hearts of men and women, Tuchem, and you want to resurrect your God. I don't see how a simple demon is going to help us accomplish that", Tina added, "and furthermore how some dead playboy has anything to do with any of this".

"Asmodeus is no normal demon", Tuchem continued, "and prior to his death I doubt there was another man on the planet who knew as much about Asmodeus as Loren Evans. In addition I believe he had the benefit of inheriting the research of a certain benefactor of his whom I have heard whispered about in certain circles".

"Evans has been dead for a few years now", said Tina, "How are we sure the estate hasn't sold everything off?"

"In my days in New York I cannot say that I knew Loren Evans well", continued Tuchem, "but despite his connections

318

Mr. Evans could not avoid having to pay taxes to Uncle Sam. So like many well to do persons, he chose to direct certain funds to charities rather than the government. I was more than happy to receive donations from him and others like him for my good work. In exchange he appeared to be a member of my flock. I don't think I ever met him personally, however his sister Laura Evans did actually attend my services on occasion".

"And that's who we're going to see?", asked Tina.

"Yes", said Tuchem, "and if you just don't contradict me on anything I say, I predict we will do just fine".

After the taxi made its way into Manhattan, they arrived at a high-end luxury building in the mid-50s. Once they disembarked the cab they entered the lobby of the building. A pretty and well-dressed, tall dark-haired young woman rose from a leather chair in the lobby, and went to shake Tuchem's hand. She had the look of a young woman who should have had a carefree life as a socialite, but instead by circumstance and upbringing had been drilled into far too serious of a position.

Tuchem held the young woman's hand a second longer than one might normally, and spoke as he looked into her eyes.

"Laura, my dear, I'm sorry this is the soonest after your brother's passing that I'm able to see you. Other things kept me away New York I fear. You look quite well", said Tuchem.

"I'm getting used to the fact that he took his own life", said Laura, "but still coming back here is a little difficult"

"Laura, I'd like you to meet Tina Griggs. She's with the Mother Ava organization. She's working with me on my new efforts to curb unfortunate timely passings among adults", said Tuchem.

"Suicide", said Laura, "Let's call it what it is, Father. I didn't even know the Mother Ava organization was still around after that bit in the press last year. I've kept his penthouse exactly as it was, of course with the exception of those items the police thought related to the crime scene. Here's the passkey. If anything good can come out of what Loren did then you're free to take anything up there. You had mentioned looking for his journals, but I've already scoured the place for them. You'll forgive me if I don't go with you, it's still a bit painful for me to actually be there".

Laura at this point noticed Gog and Magog.

"Two precious little ones in my care", said Tuchem, "I hope it's not a problem. They will be accompanying Ms. Griggs and myself upstairs, however I feel it's alright for them as they don't really have a true idea what happened here".

"Just leave the passkey with the doorman at the front desk when you're finished", said Laura.

Tina and Tuchem walked the long hallway which led to Evans's penthouse. Tuchem slid the passkey through the reader, and the electric lock mechanism released. They entered and beheld a spacious apartment complete with gorgeous imported furniture. A large kitchen and several bedrooms moved off from the main living space, and around the coffee table and couches were scattered books and papers. Obviously the last days or weeks of his life, Evans had been camping out in the living room.

Tina began to look around. An old worm eaten book in longhand Arabic, several pages of it with diagrams torn out sat on the coffee table. Now empty bottles of vodka accompanied it, along with what appeared to be fetish magazines that Tina had never heard of.

Tina had failed to notice Gog and Magog playfully beating their hands on a section of exposed brick wall next to a bookcase.

"What the hell was this guy into?", asked Tina.

Gog and Magog now laughed as a clicking sound was made from the wall. A few seconds later two sections of the brick parted from one another revealing a doorway to a hidden antechamber. Tuchem manually opened the door the rest of the way.

"It appears the late Mr. Evans was into exactly what we need him to have been into," said Tuchem with the tone of predator was about to eat.

Tuchem once again dropped the false Irish accent he had resumed for Laura's benefit as the sickening grin played on his face. Since they had arrived at the airport, Tina had felt she had almost been in the company of a somewhat normal man. But now no one could doubt that the real Tuchem was present and accounted for.

She followed him and the children into the sealed room.

"I would like to offer you the chance of immortality one more time Jesse Perfect, but I am certain you will turn it down", said Titania, "As you have before so I will not offer it".

"Instead", said Oberon, "We will offer you a hero's resting place for your mortal remains, as we did King Arthur".

"Thank you", said Jesse, "But I will not require a provision as he did that I may be revived".

Puck entered the Hall of the Tuatha de Dannan.

"My King and Queen, the feasting party has arrived", said Puck, the servant of the two regents, who was in a nearly human form in the robe of a monk for this occasion, "Mr. Waite... save Jesse Perfect, the guest of honor, you must exit the hall and re-enter to stand and be counted with the others, as must your servant".

Thurston nodded.

Puck spoke.

"Along with the great King and Queen of the Tuatha de Danaan, stood long the Avatars against the one God. Heroes rose to stand with the Avatars, and today, we honor their leader".

Jesse was a bit uncomfortable with how things were being described.

"Enters now, David Maier, former agent of the ONLA, the watcher of our ward Na'da, he who revealed the location of the weapons that did slay Yahweh, and the destroyer of evil.... um... candy".

"Enters Now Ilitu of Is, last outside of Is to guard that true form of man from the first days, who fought bravely at Megiddo, and who it shall be the pleasure of Queen Titania and King Oberon to open the gate to that city once thought lost, for their great friend".

"Enters now, though he be not seen, the demon Asmodeus. The Scion of Hades, whose deeds and feats be too great for these unworthy lips to recount, but who freed his lord so that this Universe was freed from its would—be usurper, and who shall, with my Lord and Lady's help, restore this very night the Pleroma flow by using Tyr Afal's humble own flow as a template for the larger one".

"Enters now Thurston Waite. Friend of these Isles. Among sorcerers mighty and wise, and his loyal one, D'Irem the Djinn".

"Enters now Abraham Seiurd", Puck said, "Strong and righteous warrior, lover or life, of women and men... and uh".

"That's good enough", said Abe smiling at Puck.

"Enters Lindsay Barrow", said Puck, "The great null of energy. The slayer of Ava and Miacis".

"Oh", said Lindsay, "Yeah, I've got two victories now".

"Na'da, as you are a member of this court, "You need not stand and be counted. The Goblin is... permitted here at the behest of Jesse Perfect".

"And finally", said Puck indicating Ethan.

"I am already invited", said Ethan striding in without waiting.

Puck looked at Oberon and Titania as to how this breach of protocol should be handled, and Oberon waived a hand to say "let it go".

The guests were seated.

Jesse spoke.

"This is my family", he said, "And I have no secrets from you. You know the reason why I am even alive in these moments is because my ancestors had their genes manipulated by the alien Eyah. The Illuminati offered me immortality through magic, but I said no. My immortality is through all of you".

"Jesse", said Lindsay, "You're... not going to go lie next to King Arthur then... you know, and do that... return again one day thing".

"No", said Jesse, "The world will be different after the Pleroma flow comes back. My spirit will continue, and will not be unreachable to you, but the time has come for the man I am here in this life to conclude his final chapter".

"We have been allowed one liberty by Jesse Perfect", said Titania, "He will not pass in these feast days, and this is all of your first night here... please... save goodbyes... This is the moment of hello...".

"As to the food", said Puck, "We have removed any... conditions upon the consumption of food which might normally require mortals to remain among the Tuatha. Feast free of worry".

"Did you remove the restrictions David has on spicy food?", asked Abe jokingly.

"You'd think he could stay away from that stuff", said Lindsay, "He knows what it does to his stomach".

"I'm getting it from two sides", said David with a smile and a bit of protest.

It did not go unnoticed by Na'da, or by David himself, how Lindsay, at least in that moment, seemed to fit in better with David and his friends, even though this was her introduction to them. How Lindsay perhaps even fit in better with his life. Na'da turned to Dug, and saw he was containing whatever emotions he was experiencing deep within.

Jesse was preoccupied with the absence of Martin Belles. Like Bob Cratchet toasting Scrooge, Jesse toasted to Martin among absent friends. No one objected, not even David.

"Why did they address Dug that way?", Abe asked Na'da quietly having noticed that the Goblin's presence seemed barely tolerated.

"I will explain later", said Na'da, "Politics...".

"What does a guy have to do to get a drink here?", asked Jesse.

Everyone looked a little puzzled.

"I'm possessing him at his request", said Asmodeus.

"Shouldn't you be doing something?", asked Ethan.

"I'm here for five minutes", said Asmodeus, "That's it. We have a Pleroma flow to restore".

"Yes", said Ethan with a bit of attitude, "Wouldn't want the gods getting too hungry...".

"You seem skeptical that the choices made here about redirecting the Pleroma flow may not be the best ones, Professor", said Na'da.

"I hope man does not relate to the gods as he did before", said Ethan, "I can say that much. I have little faith in men and less in gods. There are, exceptions in both cases whom have my affection and esteem, but a radical re-establishment of the

Pleroma relationship so quickly may have side effects... both immediate, and those that are not seen for some time".

"Yet, this situation is what will allow you and Queen Ilitu to pass over to Is", said Oberon, "And you seem to have little trouble taking advantage of that".

"The Pleroma flow is being redirected. The portal is being opened. I do not have sway in that. Ilitu and I would be fools to not use the opportunity", said Ethan.

"Relax", said Asmoedus, "We didn't rush into thus. Anyway... Jesse gets the benefit of the buzz I gave him... I'll be back tomorrow to give a more proper greeting".

"Queen Ilitu", said Oberon, "I believe that is our cue, that is, you, Titania and I to begin work on the portal. It must be timed simultaneously to the Scion of Hades's work".

Ilitu rose.

"Coming?", she asked Ethan.

"I think I'll go brood actually. I'll come when the portal is open", Ethan said.

When Oberon and Titania left with Ilitu, and then Ethan made his departure, Lindsay took her chance.

"David... we've been catching up by text... wanna go for a walk?", she asked.

"Sure", said David.

The room, lighter in company now, seemed to grow less festive, but more relaxed.

"I have questions", said Na'da.

"Go ahead", said Jesse.

"Is the professor... Dead... or immortal... or immutable... or?".

"Depends on the day", said Jesse, "No one really understands Ethan's nature... he became what he was during interaction between Yahweh and Lucifer when they were on top but... he was being influenced by far more remote powers. Asmodeus was the messenger of those forces, but, that doesn't mean he understands it. O Factor or O Force elements, the ONLA calls it. No one knows what O means".

"The Spider Incident?", asked Na'da, "Where David was... removed from the ONLA was this... O Force?".

"Yes", said Thurston, "The Spider Incident involves David tracking something he lost. He has no memory of what it was. Nor does the ONLA, or even the Illuminati. The Illuminati just knew they were pissed... and Braxus used it as an excuse... It's called the Spider Incident because a spider carcass washed up on a beach next to David was the only piece of evidence. It was confirmed David was inches from the largest O-Factor event in history and failed to get anything. How it was confirmed, don't ask me, but, it gave Braxus what he needed".

"And all of you?", she asked.

"I knew once I joined the Illuminati I was stuck in it for life", said Jesse, "I became the new torch bearer of the resistance against Braxus... and I recruited these boys... and Martin to be my eyes and ears in the ONLA".

"Jesse had the four of us go on a mission out in Seattle together back in '91 as our first official trek out as ONLA field agents", said Abe, "That is me, David, Thurston and Martin. We ended up.. well... helping a bunch of Bigfoots get back to their home planet. And we met Asmodeus, and helped a local band out there, but, most of all, we defied Braxus who had been looking to bring extraterrestrials in since... forever. That's how we became Jesse's fab four. Yeah, we stole that from the Beatles".

"Mr. Waite, like David though, you were forced to leave the ONLA?", asked Na'da.

"I left the ONLA by choice", said Thurston, "I knew in one form or another, Jesse would always have Abe, and David... and even Marty".

"David never forgave me for that though", Thurston continued, "We lost someone equally special to David and I. He never got that she meant as much to me as she did to him. I kept looking for answers, just like he did, even after I left. I think he thought I gave up".

"Martin is the one who dispatched Braxus", said Abe giving Na'da more history.

"Because Braxus wanted to be dispatched", said Thurston.

"Now you're turn", said Abe to Na'da, "What's with all the hush hush stuff about Dug?".

"While the King and Queen of Tyr Afal were among the avatars, Puck ran the kingdom as steward. We had little interaction with humans, save, a few small matters. But during your Second World War, the Germans used magick to enter Tyr Afal. We... they I mean... as I was not born... easily bested the magicks of the Reich, but as for the human element of the warfare, Dug was called upon. The General proved capable at human style warfare. Too capable... He is a hero, and respected. But to be infatuated with humanity as I am is one thing. General Dug can *think* like a human... and... he is feared as a result. There was a backlash against Goblins after that. Finally, Puck agreed to give Goblins equal rights, as they had not had for several centuries among the Fey and Sidhe even before invasion by the humans, if Dug left our society. He had no interaction with any of us until a few years ago, when Oberon and Titania contacted him to request his help at the Battle of Megiddo... Armageddon as you might say, the exact nature of which still remains secret".

They all took a deep breath realizing some of the festive nature of the evening had left.

"Well...", said Jesse, "I believe I will retire, "Tomorrow I want to play some music.   I trust you all won't be too hung over?".

Jesse quietly excused himself.

Abe looked at a male centaur, a female bon sidhe, and an androgynous water elemental who had been serving drinks...

"I see something I like", he said to Na'da.

"Which of the three?" she asked.

"D", Thurston answered, "He likes all of the above".

Abe nodded in concurrence.

The corpse of Luther Bastian Devereux had been carefully covered with sand and smoothed.   A sort of loose, silt concrete packed over him, hiding the desiccation and making him look smooth, though largely featureless, like a dressmaker's doll, save the bulging eye.

"Dolly is ready again, Father", said Magog.

"Good" said Tuchem, "Leave him for now".

"Tuchem", asked Tina, "I've been your junior partner until now. I followed you to the desert, New York, and now to this bird sanctuary on some god forsaken island".

"We are currently between Ireland and Wales, geographically speaking", said Tuchem.

"And why?", asked Tina.

"Because we are physically where we need to be", he answered, "Just not... vibrationally. We need to open the gateway to Tyr Afal".

"And how do we do that?", asked Tina.

"There are many ways, but... we will do just one", said Tuchem, "It is not tasteful, but... necessary".

"Explain", said Tina.

"Tyr Afal is by its nature, actually a being... a being that cannot ignore the call of aide of an innocent of certain Irish houses if that innocent is being violated".

"Ok", said Tina.

"While you have pointed out my identity is adopted, I am not without certain blood which is genuinely Irish. Blood of the house of Ui Neill. So, I am of that clan".

"You are not innocent, Tuchem", said Tina.

"Children", said Tuchem, "Auntie Tina and I want to play the dress-up game now. I play the girl, and she plays the boy.

Now remember, I don't want to ruin the game, so, while I am playing the girl, help me forget. Then while we are playing, go stay with Dolly and return only when I call you".

"Okay, Father", said Magog.

Tina felt numb, and sat as she felt dizzy. Tuchem seemed too similarly seem dazed, but, in addition, seemed confused. They both had strange sensations in their groins of....something reworking them, a reversal of sorts occurring.

Tuchem was going through something too, but, he seemed to be suffering mental, as well as physical effects.

He flashed on the memory of the day he walked in on his parents. Unlike most children who find themselves in this unfortunate situation he watched the scene before him with an academic interest. His parents' rhythmic motions and strange faces were intermixed with hugs and kisses so it was logical to him assume it was some expression of love and affection.

Tina recovered, and thought she knew what happened. She unfastened her skirt, and, an examination of her body revealed she was correct. She was not altogether unpleased by the temporary change Gog and Magog had worked on her anatomy, even if they did not fully understand what they had done. To them, it was a game.

A strange fog warped Tuchem's understanding of the present moment.

"Mommy?", asked Tuchem, "Do you love me as much as you love Daddy?"

"No", he remembered his mother's words, "I love you more than I love daddy", she said rubbing his inner thy, "But you can never tell him that because it will make him sad". And

then she kissed him the way a mommy kisses a daddy below the waist.

Groggy and confused, Tuchem looked over to see Tina transform into his father.

"Daddy?", asked Tuchem, "Do you love me as much as you love mommy?"

"No Buddy, I love you more than I love mommy", Dad said smirking.

"But I can never tell her because it would hurt her feelings?", Tuchem guessed.

"Ha ha, that's my boy.", Dad said grasping Tuchem's buttocks.

"I think I am the first person who can say", Tina said as she stood over her victim, "That you quite literally asked for this".

The fog further obliterated Tuchem's identity, as shards of it fell away, and whatever being he was now came to the present moment, unsure of his name or age or gender, and sure only of Tina Grigg's menacing face before him.

Perhaps, Tina thought, Tuchem had been reworked into a female as she had become male.   Or was he still male, Tina wondered.

Then Tina realized, as the cruelty deep within the well of her being was given outlet... it didn't really matter which he was right now, did it?

The screams in the distance disturbed Gog slightly.

His sister smiled at him.

"It's just Father and Aunt Tina playing", she said, "Father will stop screaming after the game. When the screams stop and the lights come then we'll take Dolly and go".

Brent Hapgood shuddered and looked to the horizon to see a landscape forming before him, over the fairly non-descript island.

"So?", asked Lindsay as they walked.

"She's just a friend", said David

"Abe is just a friend to you David. She is someone something happened with", Lindsay answered.

"Someone something almost happened with", said David, "But... hey.. Abe is too. Besides, she sees me as a father figure now... as far as I can tell she's more interested in Dug now".

"Dug is brave", said Lindsay, "And has that bad boy thing".

David raised an eyebrow. Lindsay's humor was deadpan and he often had trouble discerning it.

"Jesse said the last time he saw you, you had a friend with you", David said changing the subject.

"Daniel", said Lindsay, "He's nice...he uh... took me to see Jesse, before Jesse made the introduction to Ethan and Ilitu. I invited him to come with me to England but, he said English weather makes him molt".

"Come again?", asked David.

"Long story", answered Lindsay.

"I missed you", said David.

"I missed you to", she said taking his hand, "I don't know what I want, or, better said I don't know that I think I can trust you knowing yourself well enough to know what you want... here and now... but, I know I don't want you not in my life".

"I need time", he said, "You need time, but, agreed, the emailing and texting a few times a month isn't good enough. In some form or another Lindsay, I need you in my life".

"Well", she said putting her head on his shoulder, "That you have, right here, right now".

"So you turned a guy into cancer, huh?", he asked.

"Ruth was involved", she said.

"Ruth", he said, "How is she?".

"Dead", answered Lindsay.

"Wake up, Ms. Griggs", said Brent.

"Where...?", asked Tina.   She put her hand down to her groin, and found her plumbing was now put back to its original configuration.

"I don't know", said Brent, "I was waiting in the chopper, then these lights came... the kids got me out and brought me here".

A scream of something dry and cracked came out of nowhere. Gog and Magog were standing 'Dolly' up.

"Speak", said Tuchem.

"What the hell do you want from me?", asked Devereux.

"You see, when you followed my instruction? In that moment, your pain stopped. And that's when it does, Mr. Devereux. When you obey our orders. I do not torture you when you fail. I am not the one who put you in this torture. But obedience earns you a moment of respite. Do we understand each other?", asked Tuchem.

"Yes", answered Devereux his broken jaw now exposed as some of the sand had fallen off.

"Ahhh.... Ms. Griggs", said Tuchem, "You did well, and nothing more on that need be said".

"Where are we?", she asked.

"Tyr Afal", said Tuchem, "But, more importantly, near the site where the demon Asmodeus is about to link Tyr Afal's Pleroma flow to the rest of the world. What his plan is beyond that, I know not, but, we will take his flow. It will be enough for us to both begin feeding our respective masters".

"And how did you learn this and how do we do that?", asked Tina.

Tuchem looked down and Tina followed his gaze. A small gnome like creature lay dead, showing signs of recent trauma. Iron implements were embedded in its flesh

"The power of my Lord is waned", he said, "But a piece of it may be called up so near my precious little ones. Even before Armageddon, Asmodeus was immune to this but the documents we have obtained from the late Mr. Evans give us quite a bit of useful information on him. I have found a loophole, so to speak. You and I, Ms. Griggs, are still linked from the process we just engaged in. Into that link, I shall invoke the demon Asmodeus, at the moment he connects to the flow of the lower Pleroma, by performing the rite of exorcism in reverse... we have little time..."

Tina was impressed.

"Oh, children", said Tuchem.

Jesse was in a dream eating with the alien Eyah, and his friends Michael and Ettelia again.

"I'm hungry", Jesse said, "What should we eat?".

"We have no time to eat, Jesse Perfect", said Eyah, "I am nearer to you than ever I have been, but, not near enough to help you".

"What is happening here?", asked Jesse.

"Dr. Perfect", said Michael urgently, "All the years I was married to Ettelia, I always had to remind myself to trust her... The girl sees straight. Remember those words".

Suddenly, Jesse was alone. He was in the Illuminati Council Chamber, but, at an earlier state than he had ever seen it in life. The ceiling was gone, and when he looked up, he seemed to see a sky, over which hung an angular black ceiling, taller than infinity.

"Hello, young man", said Pseudo-Braxus.

"You're just a dream", Jesse replied.

"Indeed", said Pseudo-Braxus, "But, I am more as a dream than most men are as kings in flesh".

Jesse wanted to reply.

"Some buried trick you left behind", said Jesse, "You'll kill me a few days before I was to die anyway. Rob me of my final goodbyes with my family... seems beneath you".

"There are no goodbyes, Perfect", said Pseudo-Braxus, "Except perhaps for the real Abraham Braxus... there are...".

The wraith grabbed Jesse's hand, just as the real Braxus had a century before when Jesse joined the Illuminati.

The Braxus stand-in stared Jesse in the eyes.

"...no goodbyes. But I would not expect many hellos from here out, either", it said.

Jesse screamed in pain.

Ethan turned suddenly.

A skeletal woman in a bridal dress approached him.

"Good Evening, Maman Brigitte", he said, "I have been aware of your presence for some time".

"Good evening, Professor", she replied in a dry cracking voice, "I was not trying to hide from you, or I assure you would not have detected me".

"I was unaware the Ghede Lwa had any business on Tyr Afal", Ethan said.

"I am the wife to Baron Samedi, La Croix, Kriminel, and Cimetière", she replied, "Do you not think I need to take a walk every now and then and clear my head?".

Ethan knew her husband well. He also knew Brigitte had been many things. In any form she had ever interacted with him in, she had, somehow consistently been the same being.

She took Ethan's arm.., "Two dead may walk together, may they not?", she asked.

"Yes", he replied, "But how are you even here and why?".

"As to how", Brigitte replied, "I was a saint before I was a Lwa, and a Tuatha de Danann before I was a saint. Or shall we say, those are roles I have played. I know Tyr Afal better than the Fey. I walked these spaces with Bres, Nuada, Lugh, Nodens, Bran, Mabon, and Llud, long before Oberon and Titania"

"As to why", she said, "I came early... You're going to need me soon... and then... you'll really need me"...

"Is this something to do with the Pleroma flow?", he asked.

"Oh, no, she said... you'll get through what goes wrong with that just fine", said Brigitte, "It's after tonight you'll need me. I just felt like seeing you, and giving you a heads up"

"Prophecy is not possible right now", he said and looked at her, "But the Lwa don't require Pleroma like other gods... Can you still see timelines?"

"I can prophesy my hot hoo-hoo off", said Brigitte lifting her skirt, her trademark foul mouth returning, "As you know, I am no ordinary Lwa anyway... And what are timelines? I have more than one origin. As does man, and the world... even you".

"Multiple pasts?", asked Ethan, "Top down cosmology. The theory that a present moment not only gives rise to multiple potential futures, but that the present arises from more than one past. Reality always in dynamic flux as those pasts compete for how much they assert themselves. You... have tapped this web? What is going on?"

She looked off, "They don't want me to spoon feed it to you but... humans... humans are worse than gods sometimes, and gods are bottom feeders if you ask me...".

"Humans can't interfere with any of this", he replied.

"They can if they have a relay", she replied.

"Asmodeus", Ethan replied as he ran toward the shore.

"Professor", said Brigitte calling after him, "Come see us when you're done. We'll cook you something nice if you're blue... oh and for tonight... ignore what is not right... do not mention the square peg to your friends. The square peg is your best chance".

Ethan arrived at the crest of a hill, and saw a flash of light. His mind was filled with images, and words. The same psychokinetic information burst came to Thurston in the same moment, who teleported to Ethan's side.

Ethan grabbed Thurston as he fell over. Magick on the scale of spatial relocation was not something Thurston could do without cost.

"What is going on?", asked Thurston, his living mind unable to process all the data as quickly as Ethan had.

Two figures, formless and enveloped in light walked up to them.

"The perfect templates walk", said the one.

"Anima and Animo. Yin and Yang walk in flesh", said the second.

"What the hell was that light?", asked Lindsay.

A blood curdling scream broke the night from the opposite direction.

"Or that?", asked David.

"It sounded like Jackson", said David.

"Who?", asked Lindsay, "It came from where Jesse is staying".

"What?", asked David, "Who?".

He decided the light in the sky was more pressing, and grabbed Lindsay and ran off in that direction.

They arrived as the glow calmed on the former Tuchem and Tina enough that the hosts of this power were recognizable as the people they had been until a few moments ago.

"Griggs... Tuchem?", asked David.

Tuchem and Tina stood there, as a shambling nightmare of carrion and sand walked toward David's party to attack. They then realized Ethan and Thurston were near them.

David drew his gun and aimed, but before he fired, put it in Lindsay's hands.   She was a better shot than him as they had found out on a date at a shooting range.

She fired at the monster. It had little effect. Not no effect, but little. She emptied the clip, and the thing was still mostly intact.

Tuchem began to move forward but Tina pulled him back.

It was not time.

Ilitu swooped down from the sky. She tackled Tuchem. Two children jumped on her and bit her wings, inflicting pain but doing no damage.

The two adults and children, in unison, began to run away. The corpse thing took a moment to follow them, as if it needed to have its leash tugged.

"Ethan", said Ilitu, "Oberon and Titania opened the bridge. We were trying to clear it up so we could get information on Is and not go in their blind, when the two of them just fell over"

"Ethan and I got a sort of information burst from Asmodeus", said Thurston, "Asmodeus and I have had a bond ever since the hullaballoo with the ape men from space back in the day. But how he got telepathy into your fixed skull, Professor, I don't know. Anyway he basically sent a distress call before he was taken hostage".

"As far as I can tell", Ethan said, "Some sort of bond has formed between Tuchem and Griggs. They have tapped Asmodeus's ability... no... better said they have tapped his quality which allows him to possess other beings and trapped him between them".

"What about the kids with him?", asked Lindsay.

"Two Nephilim", said David, "And some kind of revenant".

"Nephilim?", asked Ilitu.

"Off-spring of a human and an angel. A minor angel and they aren't fully mature", said Thurston, "Not much of a threat, but, watch your back near them. The revenant is Luther Bastian Devereux, a serial killer cursed to eternal torment at the brink of death by the God Coyote. The dragon who serves as my Chief Financial Officer was following his case a little while back. My guess is they found some way to coax the bastard into helping them".

The group gathered with their friends near the portal opening to Is.

"What's their plan?", asked Abe.

"Redirect the Pleroma flow from Tyr Afal to restore Yaldabaoth", said Thurston.

"That's Tuchem's plan... Griggs wants power for herself", said Lindsay.

"No", said Ethan, "Those were the motivations that got them here. Now, they are losing self. Their motivations have changed, and will change".

"And still it's not power yet enough to meet there original goals", said David, "But, if they can pull down the main Pleroma flow, it would be. And Asmodeus was supposed to be doing that anyway".

"One more thing", said Thurston, "This... dinosaur... best as I can call it that flashed in my head right after Asmodeus spoke to me said the... Heavens or whatever you call them... would send us a warrior of light to help. An Aeon".

"Ilitu and I must still go to Is", said Ethan as he glanced to the doorway which Oberon and Titania had opened before they lost consciousness.

"I actually have more at my disposal than Tuchem and Tina do", said David, "I have a fey, a Djinn, a sorcerer, and apparently an aeon. They have two low grade nephilim and a zombie. I can handle things here, Ethan".

"At *your* disposal?", asked Thurston.

"Ours", David said sheepishly.

Na'da and Jackson walked up.

"Our little hottie here isn't feeling so good", said Jackson Prefect, indicating Na'da.

Ethan and Lindsay stared at Jackson.

"Who are you?", asked Lindsay, "And where is Jesse?".

"Who is Jesse?", asked David, "And this is Jackson... you know... Jackson..."

"Something has effected Ms. Barrow's memory", said Ethan, "Lindsay I know your memory seems... off. Perhaps you are recalling an echo of some other reality. But for now, you need to rely on others to help you sort it through".

Lindsay somehow knew that Ethan was lying.

"What's wrong with Na'da?", asked Abe.

"I don't think you understand", said Dug.

They all looked at Dug, shocked that he was able to speak coherently.

"I can speak any language I want, and any variant I want, but now I need you to listen so I'll speak in this painful, unmusical version of English that actually hurts me, like razors on slate, but that you all prefer so muches", Dug said.

"Sorry...", he said referring to the fact that he slipped momentarily into his usual speech pattern "Eventually, Tyr Afal's Pleroma flow will run out. Most of the Fey will be useless, and I won't have magic. We don't know what Tina and Tuchem have become, but when Tyr Afal's flow runs out the higher Pleroma flow comes into them, you'll only have Thurston and the Djinn for magic... and you don't have any human technology to speak of. I think you can also expect quite a bit more pushback from our two friends once they receive the higher flow".

"Oberon and Titania were too tied to the Island itself. Ever since they took exclusive control of the Island from the Sidhe variant of the Fey, they paid a price of their own essences being linked with Tyr Afal. That's why they've fallen into torpor. The rest of the Fey will remain awake, but they will not help you fight without magic. Politics. Culture. Call it what you like. They can wield a weapon as well as a human, but they will let the world burn before deviating from their lifestyle. The Goblins will help. Some. Our strategy should be to separate Griggs and Tuchem before they receive the higher flow", Dug finished eloquently.

"He's right...", said Thurston, "We need to stop them before the localized Pleroma flow runs out. Ethan, if you can help me whip up a little something before you go so I can open that portal to bring the Aeon down... as for tech, are cellphones working?".

"Yes", said Abe.

"You have Belles in your contacts?", asked Thurston as he took Abe's cellphone.

"We're calling the ONLA for back up?", asked David.

David wanted to object, but he knew it was the best option.

"That zombie is cursed by straight divine magick to be indestructible", said Thurston.

"Then the Aeon will be your best bet against it", Ethan said, "But be warned... this being has quite a bit less power than one would normally associate with an Aeon".

Father was not himself. He didn't seem to notice Gog and Magog wander off to the shore. There was some nice mud the children could make toys from, but the mud had something bad in it.

Something bad that kept them from making their mud toys come alive like they could with their special clay.

They got sad.

Then Magog smiled. Whatever the bad stuff in the mud was, it was draining away like water from the bath tub. Soon it would be gone if the children were just a little patient. Then they could make their toys come alive.

Just like the special clay. The mud might make even better toys than the clay, cause it had something nice in it under the bad stuff. It could make toys that would each act on their own.

That would be fun.

Maybe if they made the toys come alive, the toys could go after the bad people. That would make Father happy. Then, he might act like himself.

"Where did you meet him?", asked Lindsay.

"I don't remember where I met Jackson. I remember he's the smartest kid I know. But he doesn't listen", said David.

"Does he live with you?", asked Lindsay.

"I think so. Or... sometimes he does", said David, "Look, my memory seems to be effected too. Wait. He's the youngest member of the Illuminati. I remember that. See, my memory is coming back".

"Are we supposed to know who that overly tan guy in the shiny suit is?", asked Lindsay as Brent came over the hill.

"I was meditating about Tyr Afal, when I woke up here", said Brent feigning confusion, "Then I heard voices, and, when I got up the courage, came over to you guys".

"Calm down", said Abe already turning the charm on, "Everything will be okay".

"Not for you", said Brent as he pulled out a gun and shot Abe.

Lindsay still had David's gun. She pulled it out, the clip now refilled and shot Brent in the head.

"He wasn't a zombie", said Abe in pain as Lindsay knelt by him. Abe was wounded rather badly in the gut.

"Oh", said Lindsay, "Well, apparently whatever he was, a headshot killed him".

David came over to them with great concern.

Ethan and Ilitu had prepared the ritual space for Thurston to summon the Aeon.

"That's it", said Na'da as she handed Abe's cellphone to Thurston, having adjusted its harmonics, "You have a few minutes where your mobile phone can call the human world".

Thurston dialed.

"Fuck me", said Martin Belles as he looked at the long range radio telescope data.

"It's extraterrestrial, sir", said Knusch, "It vaguely matches the signature of the ship that crashed during... Aaaar...".

"The ship that crashed at Megiddo, Knusch, the incident where I was imbued with the Holy Spirit and nearly helped Yahweh destroy the world. You can say it, Knusch".

Martin had decided Knusch had a certain moxie he liked, and with most of his staff otherwise disposed, Martin had personally requested Knusch to be his interim Coordination officer.

"Apparently, there are active extraterrestrials, sir", said Knusch.

"Yeah, well... I've known that since I met Sasquatches with a flying saucer all their own, but we still tell junior officers there are no aliens because... I don't know why. What can you tell me about that ship, Knusch?", asked Martin.

"It's quantum signature is native, so, it comes from another planet in this universe, rather than another dimension. It will be in Earth orbit in less than a week", said Knusch.

"Sir", said another agent coming up, "We've lost all contact with the Facility. Communication from them has been extremely regular since Tipeshiel just walked in there and surrendered himself last week, but now nothing. Full dark from them. Last intel came with something indicating irregularities from... the room with Braxus's body".

"Sir, said another, "You have two calls... Gaga Perry is cancelling your dinner date... and... Thurston Waite is on line 4".

Martin went from stunned, to as stunned as a being could be.

"*Marty*", said Thurston, "*I'm calling in the favor*".

"Thurston?", asked Martin.

"I've got seconds Marty. Tyr Afal. Get your ass here, break the barrier that keeps it out of phase with the rest of the world, and bring on the funk and noise once you do".

"Thurston... I", Martin stammered.

" *Yes, you're doing it or, no, you're not, Marty?*", he asked.

"Yes", said Martin.

At that second, Thurston clicked off.

Martin walked onto the main floor.

He needed to leave someone in charge. Knusch was by the book, but he couldn't assume directorship. Daniels was still dead, and not slated for resurrection until July. Abe was on Tyr Afal.

Operations told him that Orin was unreachable. Even though he was an Illuminatus, in crisis there were certain Illuminati who would take direct agency control. Like Orin and Germaine...

...and Franklin.

"Get me, Ben Franklin", said Martin.

" *Hello Martin*", said Franklin cheerfully over the com.

"How is your new... what is it called... um... Mecha Transformer Robotech sort of body thing working out, sir?", asked Martin.

"*Splendid*", said Franklin, "*Transferring my consciousness into this was a wonderful idea*".

"Sir... I was thinking... uh. To take some time off... even though aliens are coming, and the Facility where we house Braxus's body is offline...   I uh... owe a friend a favor", said Martin.

"*Of course Martin. I'll assume operations. Friendship is very important you know*", said Franklin.

"I... need some resources, sir", said Martin.

"*No one knows the rules better than you.   Events of this magnitude will require all we have at our disposal, which is much less than it used to be. Still, I suppose you could call in some favors from our outside help*", said Franklin.

"Great", said Martin, "Thank you, sir".

"Did you hear that, Knusch?", asked Martin.

"Yes sir, so, until your return I should report to Illuminatus Franklin?", asked Knusch.

"Yes", said Martin, "And who do we have in the way of... Unconventionals who owe me favors? I need a team, but no conventional support is available".

"We have the Egyptian Sorcerer Imhotep... The Flying Dutchman, and a retired agent named Brandon Welks. He was in Financial Manipulations, but he does have training in the field.   4 hours of it. We let him retire early, but, we have the right to call him up", said Knusch.

"Great", said Martin sarcastically, "I'm going to go to the Island of the Fairies with a ghost pirate, a mummy, and an accountant.   Now I know how David feels. Okay Knusch, assemble my team".

Na'da, Ethan, and Ilitu came to the portal site. They saw David and Lindsay kneeling by Abe. Thurston stayed behind to perform the Aeon invocation. Jackson was also summoned by the sound.

"Jackson", scolded David, "Stay back".

"I wanna help", said Jackson.

"As Lindsay has pointed out", said David, "My memory of you is fuzzy. You could be someone other than who I think. But even if the memories I have are accurate then the best help you can give us is to stay back".

"I'm 25", said Jackson Prefect, "And an Illuminatus. You treat me like a kid".

But Jackson was unsure himself. His memory was strange too. There were too many memories. And none that made sense.

And a man was in his head. A man who kept saying that he should take the Pleroma flow for himself. And another man who seemed more inside than the other. This other man kept saying 'resist'.

"You're an Aeon?", asked Thurston.

Before him stood a lanky, middle aged Texan. All in white, like the hero of a western, on a winged white horse. The man himself had wings.

"Aeon... in training", said Slim, "Human until pretty recent... Kevin Gainesport, but... people call me Slim. I was specially put in a bubble of the astral plane near the physical plane so I could be invoked even if the Pleroma thingy went all wrong and the astral traffic was all messed up".

"First of all", said Thurston, "You are fantastic... and, I invoked you. Because, yes, the Pleroma *thingy* went all wrong".

"Yeah", said Slim, "I kinda figured".

Tuchem and Tina stood on a ridge, observing the portal.

"I feel there is better hope for something to raise my Lord on the other side of that portal", said Tuchem.

"No", said Tina, "You are being drawn to the pure essence of what you are, but, if you are convinced that you are still serving Yaldabaoth... so be it... delude yourself".

"Devereux", said Tuchem, "Good, you have replaced the sands you lost. I need you focused so, you are temporarily relieved of your pain because I consider you serving me, if you help me get through that vortex, and then in my absence, kill as many of my enemies as is possible".

"Yes", said Devereux, "I've missed the kill".

Tuchem made for the portal again, floating. Ilitu flew straight on at him, and they fell to the ground together locked in combat.

Devereux lurched forward and down the hill.

Tina threw a blast of what seemed to be fire at Lindsay. Jackson dived on her, and got both himself and Lindsay out of the way without a second to spare.

David realized he needed to use whatever resources he had.

"Na'da, what can we do about Abe?", David asked.

"My magick is already too depleted to heal him, but we can take him to the Cave of the King where Arthur sleeps. His wounds will at least be frozen there, so to speak. It is a different magick than Tyr Afal's that presides there", said Na'da.

"Jackson, do you think you can handle that?", asked David.

"Yes", said Jackson as he and Na'da moved Abe as gingerly as they could.

Ethan gave Ilitu a look as she got up. With a hand motion, he indicated to stay down. For some reason, he wanted to let Tuchem through the portal. Tuchem made his way through.

"Ethan", she said, "It's a time differentiated aperture. He'll have hours on us for every second we waste".

Ilitu and Ethan joined hands and jumped into the blue swirling vortex.

David and Lindsay now found themselves alone with the shambling Devereux coming at them from one side, and Tina throwing fire balls from the other.

"Tyr Afal's magick hasn't run out yet?", asked Lindsay, "And this chic only has access to lower Pleroma, whatever that is, right? So we are supposedly still in the 'easy' phase here, huh?".

"Devereux", said Tina, "Bring me the girl".

"I have my marching orders already", said Devereux.

Just then, a bullet whizzed by in the air.

It hit Devereux in the arm. Chunks of sand and desiccated flesh came out.

"That shouldn't be possible", said Devereux, "From a bullet".

"It's a special bullet", said Slim striding into view.

"I might ask what the hell you are?", asked Devereux looking at the angelic looking cowboy riding what looked like a Pegasus.

"I could ask you the same. But I think what matters most is... I'm the sheriff... and you're the outlaw", said Slim.

Devereux tackled Slim.

Lindsay and David escaped into the brush.

Na'da and Jackson laid Abe carefully down on a stone slab.
A Caucasian man with brown hair, in ermine robes, with a
long beard lay on a similar one, in a deathly repose.

"So that's King Arthur?", asked Jackson.

"Yes", replied Na'da, "His garments have been changed over
the years".

"Doesn't it say in the stories he'll arise one day again in a time
of great crisis?", asked Jackson.

"He wakes up when Britain's in its darkest hour", said Na'da,
"Which is not this".

"There's a joke in there somewhere", said Jackson, "Hey...
wait.   I think I can read this... it says Alfred, King of All the
English".

"Yes, said Na'da, "Artorius Ambrosius Morenus Ferrarius...
'Arthur' as you know him, has ruled Britain twice, and saved
it many more times than that.   Once at the end of the Roman
period he ruled from what is now Wales, and centuries later
he assumed the identity of Alfred the Great when Britain was
threatened with extinction once again.   Your accepted human
history knows more about him from his time as Alfred and
regards his time as Arthur as legendary.   I assure you, most of
what you know about his first reign is incorrect".

Na'da looked at the tall, slender young man called Jackson
Prefect.   He looked like an Egyptian Pharoh.   His skin dark,
but smooth.   Hair shorn close to his head.   He looked like a
statue which had been chiseled under low heat, but now
burned with a fire.

She had seen Jackson before, had she not?

Both their attentions turned to Abe.

"How are you, Abe?", asked Na'da.

"You know how your mouth feels when you're at the dentist. They numb you up... they're doing something in there, but you're not sure what. That's how I feel, except my entire body feels that way", Abe said.

"Pleasant", said Jackson.

"Does one of you have a flask?", asked Abe.

Neither did.

"We have to find a way that I can get out of here", said Abe, "I need to see what's going on out there".

"Perhaps there is a way out for you", said Na'da as she picked up a small object.

"This is a caldra. Its magick is sealed inside it so it is not being depleted by the events outside. When young fey who are not adept at magick first leave Tyr Afal, they take these so they can shapeshift for protection. It must have been left here by younglings who came to have sex at Arthur's grave", said Na'da.

"You do that for thrills?", asked Jackson.

"No", said Na'da, "To pay him respect".

"How does that help me?", asked Abe.

"We can shapeshift you into something unwounded. But, I will only get three tries with it".

"How about a dragon?", suggested Jackson.

"Or a mighty whirlwind... think abstractly", suggested Na'da.

"Or how about we shapeshift me into a non-shot version of myself?", asked Abe.

"Okay", said Na'da, "Here goes".

A flash of light came.

Na'da looked down, Abe's flesh was healed and free of blood. And he was a fish from the waist down.

"It's okay", said Abe, now a merman, "I had already married myself to the fact that attempt number one wasn't going to work".

Digging...

Ethan Rhys-Davies was digging out of something, and he had been for a long time. Nothing new. Something must always put him in this situation.

Back on Earth. Wait. Tyr Afal. Back on Tyr Afal.

" *Back wherever the hell I just was*", he thought.

Back there, Lindsay had killed that man. That was good. And David understood. They were not as black and white as he thought on things.

Maybe they would understand why he and Ilitu had withheld information when they learned it. And not the part about Jesse. The other part.

He only knew it a few hours ago. And he shared it with Ilitu.

Did absolute trust between two beings mitigate that he withheld the full truth from the others?

He had been digging when something started to meet him half way. It was a mechanical digger. When it cleared an opening he crawled out. He was under a blue sky. This was still Earth.

The digger was connected to a sprocket and geared machine that looked like giant watch workings, and that in turn, was connected to a series of up and down manual levers. The operator was a human female. Or, mostly human. There seemed to be a tinge of something dinosaur or birdlike to her. She wore a metallic armor, curved, and form fitting. It was fitted with small pocket doors here and there no doubt containing gadgets. Small, glass baubles that seemed to contain self-perpetrating small flames also bedecked it.

He looked at the machine.

"It shouldn't work", the woman said as she removed her goggles, her dark but almost feathered hair showing now, "I was never one for magick, but... well Is is full of it. You add a little magick to your gear, and steam, and mechanical advantage based technology, just to overcome the hurdle of a few elements of physical laws, and uh. Well, you can build stuff that should only work in a child's imagination. You must be Ethan".

"I assume I have been here some time, and you already have the acquaintance of Ilitu", he said shaking her hand.

"Oh yes", she said, "You've both been here months. Tuchem has been here more like a year. Though Ilitu and I figured out it's probably been hours only on Tyr Afal. You don't seem surprised that I'm...", she said.

"Fully cognizant of everything going on in my world even though you are a stranger to me. It's fairly logical that Ilitu would... over months... fill you in on everything", he said, "I would be the one here who needs to be brought current on information", he said.

"Well", the girl smiled jovially, "Let me take you to her. Today is, well, a good day for her. They aren't all good. I'll try my hand at story telling while we walk. I'm Vayasa by the way".

"So, I am sure Ilitu has told you the history of Is, at least as far as she knows it. You're interested in what happened recently, but we have to back up. I am part of a small group... there are only two of us left now, who thought the key to overthrowing Huwawa and the Ur-Nammic dynasty lay in uncovering the full origins of Is. Is goes back even before Queen Ilitu's time and we thought if there was any loophole in the systems that keep the dynasty in power, it might lie in discovering how Is was really founded", Vayasa said.

"Have you considered it could have more than one beginning?", Ethan asked.

"I'd settle for one. There aren't even really legends about the founders left. Just, legends about how you can find out. My people and I were working on that. Well, as you know, Is was shattered when Ilitu was lost. The many races were all subjugated under humans, and, even then, Ur-Nammu's humans. Most of the non-humans planned to leave, but were returned as slaves. About a decade after Ilitu left, Is shifted into this out of phase existence it has. True, it cut us off from the rest of the world, but, it also cut Ur-Nammu off from getting any more of his people in. Ilitu's rage cry when she was confined took a generation to reverberate. She was adopted as a symbol of freedom by the children and grandchildren of those who had cursed her. Rebellions started", Vayasa continued.

"The time differential seems for the most part specific to your portal, by the way. By our reckoning, even though we've been cut off, for most of the last several thousand years we've been moving in tandem with normal time. A lot of us missed the Black Queen. Ur-Nammu's propaganda became less and less effective. This is all before I was born, by the way. The first generation of rebels went looking for Ilitu, but quickly figured out she was outside the barrier. Ur-Nammu became afraid that Ilitu would return and take the Caduceus, the central source of magick in Is, so, he enchanted it so it could only be taken by Ilitu in combat with the head of the Dynasty, and even then only if she wielded the great Sidearm of the Founder, which is lost by the way. He also put a nasty spell on Is itself so Ilitu would have reduced power and more rage fits if she returned".

"These weren't his ideas. The Mage circle did it for him. They told him it was the only way, but, I've always thought they designed the spell system to satisfy Ur-Nammu on the surface of things but built a slight window of chance into it so Ilitu could be victorious if she returned".

"Anyway", Vayasa continued, "Ur-Nammu lived along time, but, he wasn't immortal. Rather than have a child with Huwawa, he sired off-spring on a concubine, and that son when he came of age, took his place as Huwawa's new king. The rebellion couldn't wait for Ilitu, and couldn't find a way around all the magickal defenses, so, they waited about one thousand years, and attacked the Dynasty in pure force of numbers. The Dynasty took a pounding, and actually after the first rebellion the Ur-Nammic Dynasty and Huwawa herself started answering to the new version Circle of Mages.

Until your friend Tuchem came through the portal, killed Ur-Nammu the XCVI, and took over. Seems he is now tapped into straight lower Pleroma. The operating system of reality. The Caduceus runs on higher Pleroma. His plan was to wait for Ilitu, kill her, then her sister, let the Caduceus drain into him, go kill his girlfriend back on Tyr Afal, then either bring his god back, or, maybe just bypass that step at this point".

"Thank you", said Ethan, "Information helps, and, I understand the condition Ilitu is in. The only information I do not have is you, your compatriots, what resources you have, and if you will help us".

"Of course we will help you", said Vayasa, "If you win, Is gets free and the barrier comes down. As for me, I was a builder, but I came from a noble house. Had natural magickal abilities. Didn't answer my supposed calling, and started building this stuff. I hooked up with a group looking for the Heart of Knowledge and the Sidearm of the Founder. We found the Heart, but, we have no way to get it to reveal anything to us. The rest of my team were all mages. They... were close to opening the heart. There was an accident. A bad one. You could say one survived. Or some survived. You'll see. As for the Sidearm, we know where it is, but, no we have no way to pass the quest to retrieve it. Unless we get the relics up and running, you've got me and my builds. My teammate and Ilitu are not in much shape to help us now. She's either crazy and strong or sane and weak, thanks to the curse on the land. Whatever you don't understand yet, you will, once we go inside".

Ethan Rhys-Davies followed Vayasa into the cave entrance of her inner sanctum.

"Come out and play boyfriend and girlfriend", said Tina.

"She's not using magick or psionics", said David, "I don't know how to stop this".

Suddenly a wall of rock buried Tina.

"That works", said Lindsay.

"I got word to Belles", said Thurston coming around from behind the rock wall he had just levitated on Tina as his latest assault, "So, that's good news. The high Pleroma has just dropped, so, that's bad news, but, apparently with Tuchem in Is, Tina can't link to it, so, her power levels are staying where they are, unless he returns then we're pretty much fucked. But... with the Tyr Afal energy flow drained, D'Irem spotted about a hundred golems ready to be animated, which those two creepy kids ought to be doing right now. The Aeon's on the super zombie. I can actually match Tina's energy levels, but, to be straight with ya' constant magick at that level will kill me pretty fast".

"What about D'Irem?", David asked.

"My ace in the hole", said Thurston, "And my intel source at the moment".

"How can you fight her?", asked David, "You're a psionic, and a sorcerer. She's drawing from the Pleroma... the throbbing of the Cosmos itself".

"Do you even understand that, Pleroma, O-Force, Primary, Secondary Eruption, Primary as Secondary Eruption, Outer Gods, Magick versus Tech versus Psionics stuff?", asked Thurston.

"No one does", said David, "Except maybe Ethan... and Braxus did".

"Others understand it", said Thurston, "And you and I do to a degree, but, do you think Tina Griggs does? Her power and awareness have been notched up, but not the girl's brains. She just knows she can throw fireballs now. She ain't got a care if it comes from a lucky rabbit's foot or an Ironman suit... She just knows she has it".

"So you can match her?", asked Lindsay.

"For a while", said Thurston, "And for longer if I fight to stall her rather than defeat her".

"Right", said David, "So, this is Tyr Afal. Even like this, there has to be something here we can do to change the equation".

"What about all those Pantheons you helped?", asked Lindsay, "Those gods".

"Maybe they are helping us", said David, "Maybe they can't, or won't. Quetzalcoatl would but he's occupied. Christ and Hades are pushing the Pleroma flow on the other side. As for all the others, a lot are still dormant. Some are weak. Some don't care. Ethan is usually the one that gets divine help, and divine isn't what it used to be these days".

"The other avatars... Lwa. Baron Samedi?", asked Thurston.

"I don't understand the Ghede Lwa enough. But maybe... it's worth a shot", said David.

"So all the other gods besides that had no backup plan?", asked Lindsay.

"That was the Aeon", said David.

"Their back up plan to help us was some guy from Texas?", complained Lindsay.

"Tuchem had a guy from Texas as his muscle, and it worked pretty well for him", said Thurston.

Tina had nearly made it out of her rock prison. Thurston stood his ground as David and Lindsay ran.

"General", said a Goblin to Dug, "We have about a dozen goblin lodestones. They have our own tribal magick in them, not based on Tyr Afal's energy. If we can get them into the golems, they should nullify their animation. But there are six times as many golems as stones, and even fewer of us".

"Smashes the stonies to bits", said Dug as he hammered something metallic.

"General, they are not a great asset, but, they are not without use", said the underling.

"I didna says us was not goings to use them... I says... smashes 'em to bits so we can uses 'em", Dug replied.

"Yes, sir", said the Goblin.

"Whats speak from your talk hole was thats soldier?", asked Dug.

"I mean... Yesses, Mr. Bossy. Rights on it", replied the soldier.

"Gooboy", said Dug.

"Three quarters of an hour til we reach the Island", said the skeletal pirate captain.

"Thank you, Captain Fokke", said Martin, "This is faster than the Concorde".

"Captain Hook over there gives me the creeps", said Welks.

"Ok, Welks... my friends are trapped on an island. I have no intel what's going on. I have huge work problems, in the form of possibly an ET invasion, and anything dealing with Braxus wigs me out, even just his body, and those issues are waiting for me after this. You're making fun of our host, and I will have you know, Captain Bernard Fokke has been a huge ally of ours since World War II. If you're going to make fun of him, a Jack Sparrow joke might be better, cause Captain Hook is not a skeleton, okay? Captain Hook is also a stand-up guy, alright. David and I helped him take down Peter and Pan in the 90's. And that ectoplasmic sea dog there is more help than you, an ONLA agent", said Martin as he pointed to the skeletal Fokke.

"Don't you mean Peter Pan?", asked Welks.

"Saint Peter and the God Pan are only referred to as Peter Pan in their merged state, Welks. Don't you read case files? If you did, maybe you would have a decent idea", Martin said rolling his eyes.

"Actually I have an idea sir", said Welks, "Arthur Pendragon".

"You've never read the file on him either, or you wouldn't call him 'Pendragon'. Yeah, Welks, we've been over this", said Martin, "He only would awaken and help our guys out against whatever they're fighting if Britain was in danger".

"Thurston Waite is on the Island though, sir", said Welks.

"Thurston is Irish", said Martin, "Well Arab-Irish. Anyway, he's not British".

"No, sir. Look at this spreadsheet I have prepared. It shows where the collapse of Waite's company in his absence might actually trigger a series of economic dominoes, resulting in some very bad austerity measures for the EU, and particularly the UK. Now, it could be construed as a darkest hour by some. If we were to ask Imhotep to use his sorcery to resonate an email broadcast by wireless against Tyr Afal's barrier, it might interact with the enchantment which awakens Arthur and the information might trigger him to rise. Enchantments with conditions on them are not very complex, sir. Those conditions are easy to manipulate", said Welks.

Martin looked at Imhotep, who was surprisingly golden and brassy rather than linen rapped.

"You're up for this?", said Martin, "If I send an email, like to Abe's mobile from my blackberry, you can bounce it on the barrier wall?".

"You're still on blackberry?", asked Imhotep, "Yes. Yes, Mr. Belles, I believe I can".

"Welks", said Martin, "I owe you an apology".

"I wasn't allowed to retire early cause I was a screw up, sir", said Welks.

"Now, let's see if I can be as clever with a way to get that barrier down when we arrive", Martin said.

"Where are Michael and Ettelia?", asked Jesse.

"This isn't the afterlife", she said.

"But you're dead", said Jesse.

"I am beyond dead", she said, "That's why I am here".

"Braxus is beyond dead. Is he here?", asked Jesse.

"Braxus is nowhere", she said, "I am beyond dead, but no one is beyond dead like Braxus. He's as unique as..."

"As unique as me", the man said, "Trust me, even though I am here, this isn't the afterlife".

"You sir", said Jesse, "Cannot be here. Because I know you're elsewhere".

"I've always been here", he said, "She's only always been here, now, but I have always been here, well, always".

"Have I?", asked Jesse.

"Not at all", she said.

"You're here because that which straddles existence and non-existence comes here. Though in your case it's types of existence you hover between", he said.

"I'd best remedy that", Jesse said, "Thank you. That's clearer".

Abe covered up as best he could.

"There is one more shapeshift left", said Na'da, "I swear this was not humor. I think I envisioned my own body".

"No more shapeshifting", said Abe, "So you gave me tits. Everything else is normal".

It was obvious Abe was feeling better.

"Plastic surgeon can get rid of these later. Better than accidentally being turned into a slug or something. Besides, some would say I've got the best of both worlds", Abe continued.

"Jackson", called Na'da.

"No", said a voice.

"I am Alfred...".

"You're awake?", asked Abe, "And... I thought it was Arthur?".

"You may call me Artorius or Alfred. Arthur was only placed upon me as a name by those of later centuries", he said stroking his thin gray-brown beard.

"Where is Jackson?", asked Na'da.

"Not here", said Abe, "But... your highness... I... do you understand me? I am speaking English, but, perhaps not as you know it".

"Did you not just hear me? I get woken up all the time, sir", said Alfred, as was his preferred alias when speaking English, "I am duped into rising more often than you would think.

Merdwyn's works were mighty but... indiscriminate. I take it evil is afoot".

"When was the last time you woke?", asked Abe.

"Mr. Roosevelt presided over the United States", said Alfred.

"Do you have Excalibur?", Abe asked.

"I had Excalibur's metals melted into something when I was awakened in the days Germany threatened Britain. The American Corps of Engineers gave me a little gift", said Alfred.

"Um, are you going to help us?", asked Na'da.

"I hear what happens on Tyr Afal even in my slumber. Which is why I did not question your bosoms", said Alfred as he looked at Abe, "I fear what I have may buy us time at best".

Abe's jaws dropped as he followed Alfred into an antechamber.

"So... that bad boy has all Excalibur's enchantments?", asked Abe.

"That *is* Excalibur", said Alfred, "In its current fashion".

"That's an antique nowadays", said Abe, "But... I am not going to say no to an M4 Sherman Tank".

"I drive", said Alfred.

Jackson had wanted to help when he left the cave. He decided he would find Puck and get information. Then he would help. And the others would stop questioning him.

But by the time he reached Puck, the voices were gone. The calm voice faded away.

By the time he reached Puck, he couldn't hear the intense voice, because it was inside him now.

By the time he reached Puck, plunging the iron nails into Puck to extract information came all too easily to him. He stopped short of killing the poor creature. He had the information he needed now.

When the time came, Illuminatus Jackson Prefect. *The* Illuminatus would stop Tuchem and Tina easily. Cleanly. He would take the Pleroma flow for himself.

Hadn't it always been his?

"You're not going to toss me around this time?", asked Ethan.

"No", said Ilitu, "Why is it on the days I am sane, I'm weak and on the days I am strong, I'm mad?".

"Curses are like that", said Ethan.

Gorch came up to Ethan. He walked with a limp. He was tall, thin, and scarred. He wore at least two hooded cloaks to hide his body, and most of his face, save his two differently colored eyes.

"You're going today?", asked Ilitu.

"For the Sidearm of the Founder", said Ethan.

"Take both of them with you", said Ilitu.

"No", said Ethan, "Someone should remain with you".

"I'll stay then", said Gorch.

"No", said Ethan, "Vayasa will stay. You'll come with me".

Ethan was met with strange looks but no protestations. Gorch lead him to a deeper section of the same cave system that Vayasa and Gorch called home.

They stood to the entrance to the shrine where the Sidearm was kept.

"Once more", said Ethan, "The terms of the quest please".

"Only a holy one may remove the Sidearm. All others will be consumed by the living solar fire within, a magickal elemental with its own life", said Gorch.

"Surely Is has had a few holy people?", asked Ethan.

"Of course", said Gorch, "But a holy one in our society never touches, or carries, or has anything to do with weapons. We know little about the Sidearm, save that it is a weapon. So in the very act of retrieving it, one becomes unholy and is consumed".

Ethan looked. He walked in. He had not even gotten though the entrance when the Elemental came. It blinded him, but no matter. He walked the room in decreasing circles, until he felt an object. Its configuration was unmistakable, and it was surely the Sidearm.

"You did not fail in your guardianship", Ethan said to the Elemental, "You couldn't have done anything here".

Ethan squinted his eyes. The elemental spirit was a false projection of light. It was not a spirit at all. The fire of intense light was unmistakable though and real enough. It projected directly from the Sidearm.

The chamber was designed to spread the light from the Sidearm everywhere, and no doubt provided it with a continuous stream of energy from somewhere within the pedestal on which the Sidearm rested.

Had any being but Ethan Rhys-Davies entered this chamber, it would have been their end. Design and enchantments made this chamber terminal to any being of the flesh, save the one who had just taken it. But all the forces within the room did was amplify the power of the Sidearm itself.

Ethan exited the cave, and asked Gorch for the satchel, and placed the object he had taken inside.

"Now, you have both relics", said Ethan.

Gorch was silent.

"Vayasa already told me you had the Heart of Knowledge", Ethan said.

"We... we cannot use it", said Gorch.

"Why?", asked Ethan.

"Again", answered Gorch, "We cannot complete the quest".

They finished the journey in silence.

When they arrived at Vayasa's base camp, Ethan walked up to Vayasa.

"Why do you hold him back?", asked Ethan with what passed for anger from him as he pointed to Gorch.

"I don't", said Vayasa, "I am the only one who ever treats him like anything but a freak".

"No", said Ethan, "You treat him with pity. He doesn't need to be pitied. Most beings should be in awe of him. You said there was one survivor of the team of mages studying the Heart of Knowledge. Yet, Gorch doesn't seem to be a mage. I've seen your Sidearm. I have it here. I suspect I know what is going on. Tell me, why have you never produced the Heart for Ilitu or I ever to see?"

Vayasa spoke:

"The mages I met had already had the Heart for centuries. The legend was if you spoke to the Heart the purest word which was not a word, it would open. People tried song, words. Nothing worked. The mages felt the Heart had not always been locked. It had become... wounded with time and so locked itself as a form of protection until it heard the word-that-was-not-a-word. So the mages enchanted a great spell of extropy, the force of things to tend to order, the opposite of natural entropy. They thought in a more ordered state the Heart would no longer be locked. The field... went wrong. There was some kind of horrible accident. When I found them the extropy had kept them from dying. Their remains were fused to eachother and to the Heart. But the Heart was still locked, even though it did seem repaired. I... patched the survivors up you could say, with my mechanomagick... my humble little craft. I think the heart did most of the work really, and the extropic energy. I just made it cohesive. First, the being asked for water. Then food. Eventually, the Gorch persona emerged".

"Why don't you let him speak the word?", asked Ethan.

"Because the word I speak would corrupt the Heart", said Gorch, "I would die. The Heart's knowledge would be lost. And Vayasa would be... alone".

"Your thoughts", asked the weakened Ilitu of Gorch, "or Vayasa's?".

"I...", Vayasa stammered.

"It's alright", said Ilitu as she put a comforting arm on Vayasa.

"Gorch", said Vayasa, "Speak your word".

Gorch removed his cloak to reveal a Frankenstein patchwork body, Vayasa's mechanical editions here and there, and a white metallic cube in his chest. He was far from hideous. His form was like high art, the kind which brought great emotion.

He opened his mouth, like an opera singer about to hit the note which brought the audience to their feet... but uttered the last thing anyone expected.

"Reboot Code, Aten-Omega-Six-112400291".

The Heart lit.

Gorch grabbed his head in pain.

"Gorch!", said Vayasa.

"He's fine", said Ethan, "He's just gotten a lot of knowledge all at once".

"This is... amazing", Gorch smiled.

Ilitu smashed a large rock in twain with her bare hands.

"I am in control of my faculties", she said, "And at full strength".

"Well you have the Sidearm and Gorch by your side, who is the Heart... so the spell is broken", Ethan said, "Now, the next two items on the agenda would be Tuchem and the Caduceus".

Ilitu now beheld the Sidearm Ethan had placed in her hands without her even knowing.

"This is... technological", she said.

"Yes", said Gorch with a knowing look.

Ethan held his hand up to Gorch.

"Not yet", said Ethan, "Reveal all the history you know in the fullness of time. Others cannot absorb as much information as you that quickly".

"How do we get to the High Temple?", asked Ilitu.

Vayasa motioned for the others to follow her. She showed them a contraption which appeared to be a set of back-strapped leathery bird wings, with gears here and there. DaVinci would have been proud of this device. She had even constructed a few spares.

"I've got my own", said Ilitu.

No sooner had David finished drawing the Veve of Baron Samedi than Lindsay felt a hand on her ass.

A tall African man in a top hot and sunglasses, all in dark fine clothes, stood before them.

"Hey", she said.

"I touch what pleases me", he said.

"Lindsay the smoking and the drinking is part of his persona. Don't let it fool you... He's one of the most powerful beings on this world. And if he got to Tyr Afal, it's true then. The Ghede Lwa... maybe all the Lwa... are outside the system", David said.

"You should have a drink boy", said the Baron as he swaggered over to David, "And your bitch too".

"So much for this guy helping us", said Lindsay.

The Baron's demeanor suddenly became deathly serious, and his face morphed into a skull.

"My wife and I have been helping you, fools. Like we helped throw the slave masters out of Haiti. Now, we are helping you to live!", he said.

"Speak plainly then", said David.

The Baron offered the rum bottle again.

"What is less plain than the fucking words... You. Should. Have. A. Drink", the Baron said.

He put his own top hat on David's head, and somehow, the rum bottle was in David's hand now.

The Baron was gone.

David drank, passed it to Lindsay, and she drank.

They looked up to see Thurston literally sliding at them.

Tina was blasting him with energy, and he was blasting back, but faltering.

D'Irem was in his fiery Djinn form, but his magick was ebbing low. He had obviously stung Tina a few times to buy Thurston a minute.

Tina turned her attention to David and Lindsay.

She immolated them with a full fire blast.

The fire rescinded and she saw them... naked, but very much alive.

"What?", she asked.

"We're... indestructible?", asked Lindsay.

"For as long as we're tipsy", said David.

"Like Adam and Eve", said a child's voice.

It was Magog, holding her brother's hand.

"Father will be pleased if we have some of these sinners disposed of when he returns", she said.

At her behest, Devereux shambled out of the underbrush toward the badly weakened Thurston, as well as David and Lindsay.

Slim galloped up, firing a shot and blowing off Devereux's foot.

"Slippery varmint", said Slim, "I was just bein' extra Texan there. I been chasing you all around here".

"I am Luther Bastian...".

Slim fired another shot, and blew off Devereux's jaw.

"Luther Bastian Talks-to-Much", said Slim.

Devereux held up his hands.

"You're surrendering?", asked Slim, "Ah. No. You're unarmed but ya' still wanna tussle. Well, fair is fair".

Slim tossed one of his two holy six shooters to Devereux.

"This isn't the shootout at the O.K. Corral, you dumb bumpkin. This is war", shouted Lindsay.

Devereux and Slim opened fire on each other. The bullets one by one wrecked Devereux further and further, as nothing happened to Slim.

When Devereux was a pile of rubble, Slim retrieved his second gun.

"Holy bullets don't hurt an Aeon , Ma'am. I'm a bumpkin, but I ain't stupid", Slim said.

Gog was sad.

"Don't worry brother, we have more toys", said Magog.

D'Irem had lifted Thurston to cover.

Slim, Lindsay, and David looked up to see an army of small, featureless mud things coming at them.

"We're invulnerable, right?", asked Lindsay.

"To death", said David, "For the moment yes... But that doesn't mean those things can't cause us a lot of pain".

Slim fired a bullet at one, but it had little effect, and then at another, but he couldn't shoot fast enough to make a difference.

"Davey", said Dug as he and several other Goblins crested the hill, "You nakey".

Dug sniffed the air.

"You on cheat codes, Davey?", asked Dug.

"What... ?", asked David.

"Oh, for Christ's sake David, get a modern reference for once. Yes, Dug, we are...", said Lindsay.

"Okeys", said Dug.

Dug stood up. Four other Goblins were behind him. They were holding what could only be described as make-shift Gatling guns. Dug also seemed to have stolen a pack of David's cloves, and apparently was smoking five of them at once.

Dug's weapon opened fire, and obliterated wave after wave of the golems, until they were reduced to dust. The particles of whatever shot the goblins were using did nothing to David and Lindsay.

When the Golems were no more, Dug dropped his weapon and came over to David and hugged him.

"Dug", said David, "How did you?".

David stepped on one of Dug's shot pellets and cut his foot.

"I guess Super Mario time is over", he said.

Tina howled like a banshee, and all the vegetation withered in front of her. Only the vegetation behind her remained.

Then she threw a great orb into the sky, illuminating the whole scene.

Slim drew a gun on her.

"Pleroma against Pleroma", she said, "Things are touchy here. Better not".

It seemed Tina had begun to grow a little wiser about the source of her new abilities.

"I'll take the chance", said Slim.

"No", said Thurston who now in this light could be seen to look like a victim withered by a long bout of disease having used so much high magic, "She could be right".

"I'd say you're out of fluid, lover", Tina said to Thurston.

Thurston fell over, and let out a scream.

The scream grew to a yell, and he fired one last burst at Tina, knocking her from the sky to the ground.

"I've always got a little extra stock put away for the ladies", he said and lost consciousness.

A single shot rang out. Tina looked at her arm and saw a bullet wound heal up.

She saw Abe was the source of the shot.

"When did you get... boobs?", asked David.

"Better question, nature boy, where did I get a tank?", Abe asked.

Tina turned around to see an armored vehicle rolling toward her, but before she could mouth 'What the fu', an enchanted explosive charge blew her into a liquefied mass.

Alfred and Na'da exited the tank.

Tuchem sat on the throne. Bored.

He looked at Huwawa.   She sat motionless, in a state of catatonia.

"Fair haired girl", Tuchem bemused, "All this power... nothing compared to the High Pleroma in the Caduceus. Soon to be mine. Ms. Griggs will then never know hers. Her flow will be mine. I have watched her battle, slowly via the remains of the aperture by which I came to this place, over this past year.

Mere hours for her. God shall need a new Son. But like the lies in the false scripture, which will now be made true, father and son will be one".

Vayasa flew above the high tower with Ilitu in tandem.

"It is a waste", said Ilitu.

"That can be remedied", said Vayasa.

Ilitu swooped low.

Inside the tower, Huwawa spoke from her slumber.

"Sister...", she said sadly.

Vayasa pumped a cannon tied into her pack, and lit the tower ablaze with a sort of make-shift napalm.

Immediately, a gong bell was rung from the tower.

The Five Mages of the Circle teleported to their positions. Ilitu flew down on two of them, easily besting their energy blasts.

One of them cast a spatial warp spell at Vayasa. She began spiraling into a sort of physical vertigo. She tossed a random object into the air as she broke off her attack to maintain flight.

The mage did not even notice she had changed the trajectory of the object she threw, a sort of grenade improvision, to account for the vertigo. He met his death in fire.

Ethan could not control the wings Vayasa had given him. He crashed behind the fourth mage's position on the tower.

He got up from the wreckage as the mage tossed spell after spell at him.

They had no effect. Ethan coldly pushed the man off the tower.

The mage levitated back up. Ethan produced the Sidearm and fired it straight at the man and from there gave his opponent no further thought.

The last mage came up behind Ethan, and Ethan turned to face him.

"Hmmm", said the Mage, "Tuchem warned me of you. You cannot be changed... but the environment can. If the floor beneath your feet is a pit with no end, then that which is forever falls forever. Netus Shantath Ilemini..."

"Pr'asta", said Ethan as he put a hand over the man's mouth thus altering the incantation. The slight change in language was enough to matter. Normally, the operator's will was more important in a spell, but the vibration of words did matter. And Ethan's will was greater than the Mage's as well.

The result was something as to cause the Mage to begin growing multiple digestive organs throughout his entire body, each craving sustenance from his own flesh.

"At least we used some magick", Ethan said as he looked at the man with disgust.

Gorch had caught up by now, and the four entered the throne room.

Tuchem did not rise.

"I will not battle you", said Tuchem, "No... in the beginning... there was the word".

"The Logos", said Ethan, "And Yahweh stole that".

"You think I am fool to pick you off one by one, like Griggs tried with your friends?", asked Tuchem.

"Or like your God did?", asked Ilitu.

"You won't throw me off balance into attacking you in a rage", Tuchem said.

"Why won't he attack?", asked Vayasa, "Why won't Ilitu?".

"Because the Caduceus is Pleroma. As is that which flows through Tuchem. It is best controlled by pure will", said Ethan, "And right now they are battling for that which is royal and elite. They both want to attack each other, but their will must rule over their rage".

Behind the throne the Caduceus stood. It was a simple wooden club with twin snakes carved in it. It seemed so unnoticeable and nondescript for something which was the greatest source of power in Is.

"You are just a glorified demoness", said Tuchem.

"You serve a dead god", said Ilitu.

"Tuchem", said Ethan calling for Tuchem's attention.

Tuchem looked.

The boy Gog stood at Ethan's side. Ethan had his hands on Gog's shoulders. He produced a ceremonial dagger.

Tuchem knew the symbols. Sigilsof Ba'al. Enough to kill a young Nephilim.

"That's not possible", said Tuchem.

"You have all human male Pleroma flow", said Ethan, "Plus the masculine side of the Pleroma of Tyr Afal coursing through you. You would know if this was an illusion created by sorcery. You know Tuchem that this is all too real".

Fear entered Tuchem. Mortal adrenaline surged. He screamed at Ilitu and energy particles began to form from his hands.

He had made the first move, so Ilitu took to the air. She crashed with him against the Caduceus, and even as they brushed it, it knew she was the only true royal, the only true elite there. It filled her, and weakened him.

Tuchem knew he had been bested. Human feeling returned to him. No, he must not have his head ripped off. He felt Ilitu's hands on the sides of his head. He must not mock the memory of his god by dying in the same manner as him. That is God's death, and God's death only.

If he must die, not like...

Too late.

Ilitu tore his head from his body.

The image of Gog faded.

"How did you know that would work?", asked Ethan of Gorch as he stepped into view, the Heart retreating into Gorch's body as it had been projected outward so it could emit a transmission beacon.

"Tuchem was a man of pure faith", said Gorch, "The Founders knew a secret put in man's blood. A scientist who posed as a god once instilled blind faith in humans. It is why humans like Ur-Nammu's and like those of Tuchem's world have blind faith to begin with. It can be... manipulated. He would never have doubted the reality of the false shade of the boy I projected".

Ethan looked at Ilitu.

"What will you do with your sister?", he asked.

"Trial... for her and Ur-Nammu. Tuchem must have him locked up around here somewhere. His remains I mean. In Is we still have ways of putting even the dead on trial".

"We must... part for a time", said Ethan.

Ilitu, who had not been able to resist taking the throne, rose and came up to Ethan.

She spoke to him in a whisper.

"Ethan", she asked, "Stay here. Til we figure out how to tell the others that we had to keep the information we got from Brigitte from them".

"They won't understand our decision not to trust the pantheons or their plans for the Pleroma flow", said Ethan, "And I don't think you understand the revelation I have had. Yahweh's destruction. Hades return. Communication with the Scriptor and the Spider. With the Ghede. That all goes away if I come back to life. My state of being allowed it to be possible. Our quest together was to restore you to Is. We did that. And as far as bringing me back to life, I am walking away from that portion".

"You need to clear your head", she said, "Fine. Take Tuchem's remains back to Tyr Afal".

She saw him and the cart they placed Tuchem's still living remains in back to the portal opening.

"I love you", she said as he entered the vortex.

Love for Ilitu was the one emotion in Ethan that was not dulled.

"I love you too", he said. And she was frightened by his sincerity.

Ethan emerged. He found his friends assembled back at the feasting hall, but only in hollow victory. Abe was altered. David and Lindsay were dressed in ill-fitting borrowed clothes and were freezing cold. Thurston was drained. Na'da had grown fatigued without magic and lost consciousness like Oberon and Titania.

It was not like battles before it.

Dug grew melancholy. As soon as the threat was over, most of the other goblins had turned their backs on him. Without crisis, he was pariah. Though a few of his loyal troops, who remembered that part of the condition of Dug's exile was that Oberon and Titania finally granted Goblins equal rights, remained by his side waiting for their commander to give them the okay to depart.

Slim, despite his power, was perplexed by everything he had seen.

Only Jackson Prefect seemed strong and confident. Their confused memories about him, especially Lindsay's... only made things worse for the others.

"Where have you been?", David asked Jackson.

"Getting info", said Jackson, "To get Asmodeus out, and, let the high Pleroma flow out".

"Ethan?", David now noticed his friend had returned.

The liquefied mass that had been Tina Griggs began to coalesce around Tuchem as soon as Ethan dumped the remains out of the cart.

It did not go unnoticed by the group.

"Let it happen", said Jackson, "It needs to".

Above the earthly island which corresponded to Tyr Afal, Martin stared from the ghostly pirate ship.

"How do we get in?", asked the Captain.

"I can bring you in phase magickally", said Imhotep to Martin, "And you alone. But mixed magicks may leave you in a limbo between planes. Whether you get in phase with Tyr Afal or return here, or remain in that limbo... depends on your will. And with raw Pleroma flow so close who knows what dimensions may cross this one".

"I'll try it", said Martin, "My friends are in there".

"Be warned", said Imhotep, "Magick is a less exact thing then it once was in these times. It's precision is greatly reduced".

Martin nodded.

The mass assembled itself into a formless, organic goo. The faces of Tina, Tuchem, and a tortured Asmodues bubbled on its skin. It took human shape, and then collapsed.

"WE WERE THE ANIMA AND ANIMO. THE YIN AND YANG, BUT NOW WITH THE HIGH PLEROMA WE ARE THE ONLY ONE. WE ARE THE SEULEMENT".

"You sound like the Absencded", said Jackson as he punched into the center of it.

"Jackson", said David in alarm.

"Illuminatus Prefect", Jackson corrected.

"FOOLISH BOY...", said the Seulement, but Jackson seemed to have the upper hand.

"What are you doing?", asked Thurston.

"Pulling Asmodeus out", said Jackson.

"He's ethereal. You can't physically pull out...", Thurston trailed off.

There had only ever been one man alive who could do that. Abraham Braxus could cross planes with the ease of a breath.

"The High Pleroma... is mine", said Jackson.

The Seulement writhed in pain.

"Ethan", cried Asmodeus in torment.

"You sound like fucking Braxus", said Thurston to Jackson.

"You would be better to sound like Jesse Perfect", said Lindsay.

Lindsay concentrated as she never had before. She was a null. Could she nullify whatever made the others forget Jesse? Could she will energies as she had seen others do? If she combined will with love.

Jackson was real now. He had a history, but somehow... Could she bring his memory back?

"Jesse", she thought.

David remembered... flashes... and Thurston... Abe... they remembered.

"But... there's no Jesse... it's Jackson", said David.

"It's Jesse Perfect. Jackson Prefect. Both real. Both one. Jackson has been in Jesse for a hundred years, put in by Braxus. Jesse is in there somewhere", said Thurston as he began to understand.

"Mr. Belles", said Braxus, "How... nice to see you".

"You're obviously not real", said Martin.

"No, I am a dream. You know dream versions of Abraham Braxus well", said Pseudo-Braxus.

"I see them in my nightmares", said Martin.

"But you aren't afraid of me, when normally, even as just an image, I would be enough?", asked Pseudo-Braxus.

"You're a thought parasite. Tied to a spell. A powerful spell, but, really just you're a fancy form of fear", said Martin, "Besides, I was never afraid even of the real Braxus... when he was around...".

Martin indicated Jesse Perfect with his hand.

"Martin", said Jesse pleased, "You came. I was feeling very alone. Even with all the others. I think you made the difference Martin".

"I never could resist a Braxus existence removal", said Martin, "Whether... real to unreal, or unreal back to unreal".

"Turn me into your heir?", asked Jesse angrily of Braxus, "A version of you... just one who wanted to exist. I think not. I love too much, Braxus. You are not, nor was the real precursor to you, either, a match for love".

Pseudo-Braxus begin to fade.

"The spell is already executed", it said.

"I know", said Jesse, "And I am still here".

Jesse looked at Martin.

"Is this goodbye?", asked Martin.

"Not at all", said Jesse as he hugged him.

Jackson let out a primal howl. He did not want this power. This was not him. He did not know who he was but he knew who he was not.

And he was not this.

He pulled Asmodeus out, and the Seulement reduced into a shapeless mass of mortal flesh.

Martin found himself standing among his beleaguered friends, dazed as to how he got there.

The Pleroma flew out, not up to the gods. Not forming a link between them, but just out. Permeating all things. Available equally to man and god, living and dead, so long as they had will... and love.

Asmodeus wasted no time taking a human host, and Martin Belles would do.

"You... this is what you wanted for the Pleroma", said Asmodeus, "You knew this was going to happen".

"Yes", said Ethan.

Like all of them, like Jackson Prefect, confused by the power he had just held, like the world itself, despite his condition, Ethan Rhys-Davies... was tired.

Ethan turned his back on the scene and walked to the shore.

"Ethan", said David, "Where are you going?".

"For a walk", Ethan said.

He left the victors and fell into the sea from a cliff, plunging deep to the ocean floor and just began... to walk.

Asmodeus remained in Martin until a link to the astral plane came from Hades. His instructions were simple.

"Cohabitate the body", Hades said, "Stand by. Remain on Earth. What has happened to the Pleroma may be good or may be bad".

Gag and Magog collected the remains of the Seulement and took them to the place they knew as home. They started separating Tina and Tuchem slowly.

Above the world, in a spacecraft Eyah admitted his mistake to his companion.

"Your home world does have magick. It is real", he said to the other traveler.

"Yes", said the second. He tracked the energy signatures on his monitor.

"Magick can do what technology cannot", said the second.

He watched the thing that had escaped from the Facility and what it carried as it walked toward the site where Tina and Tuchem lay.

"Magick seems to require a world though", said the second, "It does not work in empty space... but I believe, it can be melded with technology at the level you have given me to get around that issue... the precision of one and the unlimited nature of the other".

"Think of the good we can do for many worlds", said Eyah at this thought.

"We?", asked the second.

The second pulled a weapon out and fired it at Eyah...

Tuchem opened his eyes, as his own eyes, for the first time in ages.

A figure burst through the wall in front of him, headless, but carrying something. It was that thing in its hands that called to Tuchem.

"Lord?", he asked weakly.

The now loan pilot high above looked down on Earth.

Nath Vagnos thought after sixty five million years, it was good to be home.

Beaten heroes rested, while broken monsters came together.

Perhaps only in Is was there joy.

And somewhere, Ethan Rhys-Davies was on a long walk.

ABOUT THE AUTHORS

Chris Ebert is the creator of the Ophelia Mythos and current CEO of Ophelia Myth Media. He lives in New York City.

Adam Nebel is the continuity editor of the series.   A native of Long Island, New York, he lives in the Pocono Mountains.

'Nuff said.

MAJOR ARCANA

MAJOR ARCANA

MAJOR ARCANA